QUINLIN'S
ESTATE

Books by

David Ryan Long

QUINLIN'S ESTATE

David Ryan Long

BETHANYHOUSE

MINNEAPOLIS, MINNESOTA

Published by Bethany House Publishers
A Ministry of Bethany Fellowship International
11400 Hampshire Avenue South
Bloomington, Minnesota 55438
www.bethanyhouse.com

Printed in the United States of America by
Bethany Press International, Bloomington, Minnesota 55438

Library of Congress Cataloging-in-Publication Data

Long, David Ryan.
   Quinlin's estate / by David Ryan Long.
      p. cm.
   ISBN 0-7642-2662-2
   1. Historic buildings—Conservation and restoration—Fiction. I. Title.
   PS3562.O4926 Q56   2002
   813'.6—dc21   2002002471

For Sarah and Greta

From a house on a hill a sacred light shines
I walk through these rooms but none of them are mine
Down empty hallways I went from door to door
Searching for my beautiful reward.

—Bruce Springsteen,
"My Beautiful Reward"

"What haunts are not the dead
but the gaps left within us by the secrets of others."

—Nicholas Abraham

Prologue

The thought creeps in.

During lunch at my desk or in the quiet moments before sleep comes, I find myself thinking back on it all—the last twelve months—wondering where I, Eve Lawson, would be if I hadn't taken that first step last January and resolved to try to keep Quinlin's Estate from falling. Would I still be in Lowerton, or even Pennsylvania? Would I have met Ben and Philip and Embeth Graveston and the others who helped me along the way? Would I still be searching for the secrets buried among stone and stair? Or would my greatest fear have driven me away, fleeing from the one sight I couldn't bear to see?

These thoughts come to me with their poisons of doubt and worry, yet they don't linger. This journal—if that's the right word for these writings; mostly it's a collection of scenes and memories—has seen to that. It's my testament of what happened last year, my proof that kneeling means something. I've read how Pascal sewed a scrawled statement of conversion into the

lining of his coat so he could keep it close to himself at all times.
I can't carry this memoir with me everywhere I go, stored as it
is on my laptop. Just remembering it's there is enough, though,
to see me through the moments when again I harbor the doubts
of a skeptic.

I never expected the journal to become anything more than
a means to vent my frustrations or linger for a while over the
small successes. Typically I would come home and type away
and create both a record of my efforts on behalf of the Estate
and a place to save the miscellaneous items I'd accumulated in
my research—bits of Lowerton history, descriptions of the
Estate, even my own memories of it. If everything went well,
the information could be used as a source for the doctoral dissertation I hoped might lie down the road. Instead it became
something else; it became a map.

I realize it's not original to describe one's journey—be it of
faith or simply through life—in the language of mazes or paths.
People have been drawing labyrinthine images for centuries that
hint at the same thing. But no other terms seemed suitable, and
I suppose that is because of what Philip and I saw, looking down
over the great maze within Quinlin's Estate from the hidden
room we uncovered. There I could finally see the entire twisting, turning web all at once and could trace path after path from
start to finish.

This journal offered me the same sort of perspective so that
before me lay a clear look at my own life. It allowed me to hold
a year's worth of writings in my hand and then take in the
emerging pattern winding all the way through. The shape of my
journey isn't the cross of the old French mystics who built
Chartres or the chilling simplicity of those who caged the

Minotaur on Crete. No, my path traces the outline of Quinlin's Estate itself, and to speak of one is to tell the tale of the other.

This is the story of Quinlin's Estate—the decades it has seen, the secrets it holds. It is also my story, the story of Eve Lawson.

Walk with me.

Eve
January 22, 2000

Part One

==============================

FRIDAY, JANUARY 8, 1999

This is what I know.

Ten days ago a sign, plastic and yellow, went up at the south entrance to Quinlin's Estate. On it was printed, CLOSING DECEMBER 1999.

Four days ago—the first workday after the new year and the first day of the new semester—Brighton Entertainment held a press conference at their downtown Pittsburgh headquarters clarifying the decision behind the yellow sign. Office hours and an early morning class kept me from hearing the announcement firsthand, but Brighton's publicity department was eager enough to fax me a press release that repeated the information, which I handed to Dr. Wilkins this morning along with my written request for a leave of absence from the university's Ph.D. program. He looked at both for a few seconds, read each in silence, gave them back, and told me to see him in a week.

I asked him why.

"Because in seven days," he replied, "this will be a decision, not an impulse."

It was a fair response, and I could tell there'd be no changing his mind, so I left his office and fled campus for my apartment. The freshmen planning to fawn on their history graduate assistant today would have to wait—I needed to get away to figure out if this was really what I wanted to do. And so now I sit facing the computer screen, trying to piece together a paragraph or two that explains, even to me, what's going on. At the moment it starts and ends with this:

Quinlin's Estate is going to come down. I want to save it.

Why?

I know that's the question Dr. Wilkins will ask of me when I return in a week. It's the question others will ask as well, those whom I tell about my decision.

Why the Estate? Why spend the time and effort to save a building everyone else has given up on?

My answer: I stayed at this school through my undergraduate and graduate years for one reason, and it isn't the central Pennsylvania winters. I stayed because of the Estate. Nobody's ever written a detailed history on it, and I wanted to be the first. I wanted to spend long hours roaming the halls and studying the rooms, to piece together all the stories from its past. I wanted to explore its grounds again like I used to when my father, Glen, who worked there, took me with him summer mornings. I wanted to find out the truth behind the legends and uncover why the Estate captured not only my imagination but the interests of others too. For not everyone has given up on the Estate. I know that and I'll prove it. Give me a year and some help and the Estate will still be standing.

That is what I'll tell Dr. Wilkins and anyone else who asks. Whether they buy it or not isn't so much my concern, because I doubt if this answer is something I believe myself. I can't voice the real reasons, though, for right now they don't make much sense to me. I'm a 27-year-old woman still dealing with the fears of the 12-year-old girl I guess I never outgrew. I stayed here, at the place I know best in the world, and now my single driving worry is the idea of being lost. Not along the roads or alleyways or woods like when I was a kid, but something much worse. Lost to who I am and who I will become.

It's a lot, I suppose, to put on a building, yet the Estate has looked down upon me my entire life, longer by far than any one thing or person. Glen gave up on fatherhood when I was ten, Mom's but a ghost, and I won't pretend to think Meryl cared. So what else am I left with? The building saved this town once, and although that was long before my time, it seems only right that somebody return the favor. After all, salvation should never come cheap, otherwise it's something smiling and tacky and plastic that fails just when it's needed most. I've fallen under that spell once in my life. But I know the Estate is something larger; it's broader and higher and *permanent.* If I could get people here to see what I see, they'd work to save it in a minute. To them it's just a house on a hill, and they're tired of looking up. Myself, looking skyward's the only thing I know.

WHERE IT ALL BEGAN—SUMMER 1977

I was the first to notice him when, stepping out of my trailer, I caught sight of a shadow I'd never seen before. We knew all about shadows in Little Pines Trailer Park; even those of us

outsiders not old enough to go to school heard the whispers.
Which is why this one fascinated me and I stood staring at it
for a long while before finally hearing the voices of the other
kids as they came running from all over.

"It's him," said one of them, and I finally looked up. Sure
enough, there was Santa. Snowy beard and dappled cheeks, red
coat with thick black belt. He stood watch from the top of our
neighbor Mr. Mulligan's flagpole and didn't move.

I was only five at the time yet still remember everything
with that cut-glass precision of moments that change a person.
I must not have been wearing socks or shoes, for I remember
feeling the morning dew between my toes as I crossed our patch
of grass to join the others gazing up from the base of the pole.
And I stood next to Wanda Maxwell—Wander, we called her. I
know because I was the one who heard her speak when she
whispered, "What's he doing here?" in that tiny sparrow voice
of hers. I had no answer for her and so stood there waiting till
one of the older boys, Cal, took a stab at climbing the pole. He
got three feet up before his hands slipped and he slid back down.
Twin brothers Matt and Evan tittered, prompting Cal to wheel
around and point his finger at them. They shut up immediately.

"How's Mr. Mulligan going to put up his POW flag?" Wander chirped, this time loud enough to be heard.

"Who cares about his dumb black flag. Anyhow, that ain't
the real Santa." Cal had muttered it and then bent down and
gathered a few stones. The first missed, but the second bounced
off Santa's fur-trimmed hat with the same hollow *plink* we all
knew from knocking empty two-liter pop bottles off the fence at
the back of the commons, or swatting pebbles with Wiffle-ball
bats. Santa, looking down on us with that kind little smile, his

hand raised in a papal half wave, was plastic.

"Figures," Cal said and stalked away. He spoke for all of us. Little Pines got so little, and this had lasted only a few minutes.

Mystery solved, our group began breaking up into twos and threes. Parents would soon be awake, which meant we would either return home for breakfast or clear as far out of sight as possible. Blue sky hinted at endless possibilities for the day. Within hours we'd be caught up in playing tag, racing dirt bikes, fishing down at Overland Creek, tossing bottles in the vacant lot across the highway, building the fort in the back grove, hunting groundhogs, and whatever else could fill our hours. Soon I was the only one left.

The *plink* hadn't disappointed me the way it had the others. I knew right away this Santa wasn't real. Of course the real Santa couldn't be *just* here. How would he look over the rest of the girls and boys everywhere? But maybe, I realized, this Santa had been placed here with the specific purpose of watching only us.

Right then a door creaked open and sad Mr. Mulligan appeared from behind his screen. He nodded to me, walked in silence to his pole, untied the rope, attached his black flag with the equally sad face on it, and pulled the rope until the morning breeze caught the fabric and snapped it straight. He never once looked up but stepped back inside without realizing what stood just a few inches from his unhappy flag.

That convinced me. Santa had been sent here for us kids. Adults would go about their days, not bothering to take the time to look up. But we would. We knew he was there and that he was keeping watch. In that moment I understood what it must've been like for everyone else in town who fell under the shadow of Quinlin's Tower, what it meant to have something high up looking over everything, seeing it all. And I liked it. The other kids could ignore it if they chose to, but not me. I knew he'd come for a reason, and a terrified part of me wished it was to help me escape.

Even then I was thinking about it.

TUESDAY, JANUARY 12, 1999

Four days have gone by and I see already this project's going to be more than just a simple campaign waged to save a building some folks see as historic and others as an eyesore.

First, there's the cost. Brighton's selling price is $5 million, which includes the building and seventy-plus acres of grounds. That's double what they paid for it when the Lowerton budget hit a rough patch of years following Reagan's departure from the White House. Their improvements and maintenance of the place after they'd converted it into a "Realm of Living History"—a colossally bad idea that I'm surprised survived as long as it did—kept it from falling down but never caught up with the deterioration that'd come before. An engineer I spoke with at Brighton said that the renovations needed to bring it within shouting distance of the building code would push $2 million, bringing the cost to $7 million total.

Second, I've found myself drowning in memories. Thinking on the Estate as much as I have these past days has been like stumbling across an old picture album. I spent so much time there as a child under Glen's eye and later as a summer employee, hired to wander around the halls or punch tickets or roam the maze, that each room and wing has the potential to send me back through the years until I see myself as a child: flat red hair tucked behind my ears, eyes the color of moss as Glen always said, legs bowed in at the knees, and back held bolt upright in place with leather and straps. How much different I am these days, I'm not sure, though at least the scoliosis no longer requires a brace. Even the memory of spotting Santa came back to me because of the Estate. And all I can do is play witness, recording the memories that seem to open as much of my story as possible.

The third thing I've learned is that my journal isn't going to be just about Quinlin's Estate. It's going to be my story as well. And Glen's, also. The townspeople—those with whom I talk about the Estate—won't let that pass. After all, what's more pathetic than a man obsessed with a legend never proven true if not the man's estranged daughter following in his footsteps? More than Glen and me, it's got to be about others too. Perhaps there are people for whom the Estate means something more than just our annual autumn fair, a silly middle-school play, and the building itself, which stands high on the ridge overlooking the town.

I need someone who remembers why stone after stone went up, who can share why the dream of Gabriel Quinlin shouldn't be given over to the dust merely because of others' forgetfulness.

AN INTRODUCTION TO GABRIEL QUINLIN

Gabriel Quinlin was born in 1892 and died in 1937. Gabriel grew up lonely. His mother passed away from pleurisy two years after his delivery, and his father—too busy running the empire of mines and forges he'd constructed in the rich hills of central

Pennsylvania—chose to employ a series of nurses, nannies, and private tutors to attend to his son's upbringing. As heir to the Quinlin fortune, expectations were high that Gabriel would step into his father's shoes at the appropriate moment, and all pains were taken to ensure that would happen. And it did, just decades sooner than anyone expected.

Gabriel's father died in 1915 when a prototype mortar shell being produced by Quinlin's Metal Works for the Great War failed its demonstration in a field outside Lowerton, killing eighteen, including the Quinlin chauffeur. At age twenty-three, Gabriel, recently graduated from Yale, received a military exemption from combat in order to remain in Lowerton and head one of the country's primary munitions factories.

Following the end of the struggle, Gabriel Quinlin accepted further government contracts for the continued production of armaments and slowly portioned off offshoots of the empire his father had created to concentrate on a centralized unit focusing solely on large-scale metalwork.

This is what Quinlins do well. The rest of it is rubbish, he wrote one of the DuPont sons.

The business now honed and efficient, Quinlin found the time to engage his two great interests: reading travel narratives from cities and locales across the globe, and writing long letters couched in economic theory to the few compatriots he'd kept from New Haven. Most remained on the coast, working in the exploding investment world, and they would often send short replies back to Quinlin about how the view from the ridges of Lowerton must be clearer than Wall Street because he seemed to be dead-on with his predictions and nearly every time.

Over the next decade Quinlin's investments would, accord-

ing to remaining documents, quadruple his own personal fortune even as the factory managed slow but steady growth.
Quinlin distrusted the boomtowns of places like Pithole, Pennsylvania, those built on the lure of a quick strike. To him these
towns were inherently irrational and unpredictable. Lowerton
suited him perfectly, and by controlling the growth of his factory—the area's main employer—he controlled the town's population, allowing it to climb from 895 people to only 1,900
during the first thirty-eight years of the new century. The workers benefited from this sensible management and rode union
instigators out of town naked, save for their hats, when they
tried to stir up dissension among the laborers. Quinlin treated
his employees fairly, and he in turn became the next closest
thing to royalty. The fact that he was at least a decade younger
than most meant little. He *was* Lowerton.

And so it came to pass, according to a secondhand account,
that in the fall of 1926, Gabriel Quinlin announced to his man-
agers that his hated enemies of irrationality and unpredictability
had taken control of the stock market and that an economic
maelstrom would soon be coming unlike anything seen before.
He closed by saying, "Towns and townships will be cut loose to
fend for themselves. Young men will leap from high windows.
Sustenance will not be found, and soon dogs will sup better than
men and women. I want to assure you now, gentlemen, that this
factory will not close and this town will not die. The two are of
mutual importance, and disaster for one spells doom for the
other. I am working on a plan even now, a contingency to get
us through even the darkest that might befall. Fair warning,
sirs: Beware Wall Street."

Friday, January 15, 1999

The voice I hear speaking the words above is not one I have invented for Quinlin. Instead, it's the voice of Glen Lawson, my father, as a sixth-grader performing at the fall fair in the annual production of *He Saved Lowerton*, a tribute written the year after Quinlin's death by a woman named Embeth Graveston. Every year since, the middle school stages the one-act drama, and a lucky sixth-grade boy is chosen to play Quinlin. Glen was given that honor. Years ago he had me sit down with him to play for me a cassette recording of his performance. Going by the expression on his face as he listened to his wobbly, cracking voice without blinking, I could tell how important the moment must have been for him. And now, because he can't speak any-more, it's only the memory of his voice that I have when visiting him at Truant Gulch.

The nurses and caretakers there know me by name. They wave or smile when I enter for my weekly visit, and almost always one takes the time to praise me for being such a good daughter to Glen. They don't know how wrong they are—but I have never corrected them. I don't go to Glen's bedside and suf-fer through hours of silence and stifling heat because I am his daughter; I go because he backed out of being my father and instead allowed himself to become *Glen*.

To some this will make no sense. *Why not return the favor? He deserves it after all.* And I suppose he does. What bothers me most about our lives together isn't his withdrawal from me; it's that he never apologized or seemed to feel bad about the deci-sion. So if and when he rouses from his strokes, I want him to see my name listed again and again in his visitors book. I want him to talk to the nurses and hear about how his daughter didn't neglect him. And then I want his heart to break.

But there are two hitches in my plan. First, Glen isn't getting better. Not even a little. Second, there's another name that always follows mine in the visitors book—Meryl Lakewood.

Eve

Meryl

Eve

Meryl

And on and on.

I guess it doesn't surprise me. The woman stole everything else from me when she moved into our trailer; why not this as well?

I wonder what the nurses say when Meryl flounces in there, her hair a tangle of blond curls, her tired sandals scuffing over the linoleum. Do they smile and wave and commend her for being such a good friend? Or do they see her bored eyes and understand there are other reasons for visiting the dying man?

Enough about Meryl and enough about Glen, for what he is most to me is *nothing*, a *tabula rasa* to which I speak my ideas and hear them in the air. That's what I used him for tonight when I visited. I sat down, held his fevered hand as I always do, and spoke of meeting with Dr. Wilkins and formally requesting a leave from the program.

"You'll lose the grants you've secured, you know," Dr. Wilkins warned me. "And the scholarships."

"I realize that. But if I don't do this, I'll be throwing away a once-in-a-lifetime opportunity. Instead of just studying history, I have the chance to be a part of it. There's nothing keeping us from being in the textbooks rather than writing them."

Dr. Wilkins gave me a half smile and said I'd rehearsed my speech well. I admitted I'd thought of it the night before but that I still believed every word. He nodded, and we got down to making plans.

"For seven million dollars you're going to need either a huge private investor or the government, at least at some level."

"I think the state is my best option. Lowerton's dropped its last dime on the Estate."

"Well, then I only have two other suggestions. First, don't go it alone. Nobody's going to listen to one person, especially when she comes begging for seven million. Form a team. Find some students here and also a few Lowerton citizens and work together toward your goal."

"Okay. What else?"

"The Estate isn't enough. You need a face, a voice to put with it. People don't relate to mortar and granite; they relate to people and the stories that can be told. Find someone."

"Someone who remembers." I'd thought the same thing.

"More than that, someone who can make the place come alive in the minds of others."

I couldn't have agreed more, and so my search is on.

Glen, of course, had no suggestions at all.

BRINGING THE ESTATE TO LIFE—MY ATTEMPT

The main thing to understand about the Estate is that the layout and design emerged directly from Gabriel Quinlin's obsession with far-off lands. Thwarted in his desire to wander throughout the world, he sorted through bits and pieces of what he'd read and melded them into what would become his tribute to the design and vision and beauty of the entire globe.

The three outer walls stand twelve feet high and are thirty inches thick, coming together to form a perfect equilateral triangle. In the middle of one length is an arched entranceway, fit with a drawbridge that spans a small stream. Built at each corner of the triangle are lighthouse towers, complete with rotating searchlights. With Quinlin having gone to Yale, the towers were the only feature of the Estate's inspiration that he'd seen with his own eyes, and so they mimic their coastal counterparts to the minutest detail.

Stepping across the drawbridge to the inner court or bailey, one can't help but look up. Quinlin was awed by height, and the Estate seems to burst heavenward in a mad rush. This is no sprawling mansion. It is bunched and compact and focuses every ounce of energy on extending up toward the sky. The closest comparison would be a confined grove of tall trees, each straining to catch the sun's light.

Four imposing Doric columns guard the entrance, flanked on either side by turrets and flying buttresses that are capped with snarling stone lions. Behind this facade and more easily seen from the rear of the building are the odd pairing of an Asian-influenced gambrel roof, upswept eaves and all, with a set of domes, one onion shaped, which appears to have been plucked off some Muscovite cathedral, and a second, broader one of Turkish heritage. The rest of the roof is heavily gabled with no peak appearing to be at the same height. Finally, in the middle of this crush rises a single, magnificent tower, its tetrahedral spire reaching upward to eighty-five feet, which catches even the most hardened visitors by surprise. Not surprisingly, the Tower has generated different legends through the years, two that have been around almost since the final stone was set into place.

The first is that the Tower is haunted by the ghost of a small girl. Like most legends, there are variations but they are slight. In each, a girl undertakes to climb the Tower's spiraling staircase in the vain hope of either escaping her evil stepmother or finding Quinlin's gold, depending on the version. Up and up she winds until nearly reaching the little wooden door, when she trips on the fourth-to-last stair, hits her head on the stone, and falls backward the entire length of the staircase. The most interesting part of the story is the shining nugget of fact at its heart: the fourth step, because of a miscalculation, happens to be only three inches high rather than the standard six. Many have stumbled on the step while ascending the Tower. And one did fall.

The second legend involves the shadow of the Tower. No citizen of Lowerton living outside the Tower's shadow will experience blessing or favor. Every day, like a massive sundial, the shadow sweeps across the town as evening draws to a close, stretching farther and farther until the sun sinks so low, the shadow dissolves into night. It has never reached far enough north to touch Truant Gulch Retirement Community, nor has it ever made it across Marker Road and into Little Pines Trailer Park to the south. I know this and so does every other person in town. Somebody doesn't grow up on the wrong side of the tracks in Lowerton; she or he grows up outside the shadow. In the end, though, it's saying the same thing.

There's lore tied to Quinlin's Estate as well.

One tradition holds that the building will stand until the well within it runs dry. I called this morning and found out that 85 feet of water remain. This is down from 87 feet in 1956 and 91 feet when the building was erected. Demolition is slated for late December. I don't want to think about what kind of terrible thing would have to happen to dry up the Estate's well.

The final legend is the one I'm most familiar with, and that's because of Glen. Glen took this legend to heart, and like one of those bloodhounds that can't do anything but chase the scent it's been given, he tracked this one every chance he got.

Simply put, some believe what was left of Quinlin's fortune still lies hidden in the Estate. It's true that Gabriel converted his investments to gold before the Depression. It's also true that public records of spending on the Estate, which he funded, fell well short of his fortune, leaving a large amount unaccounted for. For years many felt it was only a matter of time before the gold bars were found in a hidden room within the Estate's walls. However, more than sixty years have gone by and no gold has surfaced. Eventually believers in the gold legend dropped their search, except, that is, for one—Glen Lawson. Glen never turned away from the scent.

GROWING UP WITH THE SEARCH—SUMMER 1976

With the other kids called inside for dinner or still engrossed in a game of kick the can, I'd spend the late afternoon writing words like *love* and *hate* on the asphalt road in purple chalk. Purple was the color I liked best. The pavement had cooled enough so I could practice spelling without burning my hands and knees, and I'd continue writing until Meryl remembered me or my chalk crumbled or I ran out of words. I was only four years old—this was the year before Santa appeared on top of Mr. Mulligan's flagpole—and often didn't understand the meaning of what I wrote, just that Glen promised me words had the power to get me out of here someday.

I'd scrawled out ten or twelve words that day when I was interrupted by the unmistakable growl of Glen's Chevy Nova as it pulled up behind me. The yelling, I knew, would begin soon between Glen and Meryl. He hated catching me in the road. All I wanted to do was finish this last word, and I couldn't puzzle out the final few letters. Glen used the word a lot, most times under his breath, and I still remember the odd sideways look he gave me when I asked how to spell it. So far I had *somewh.*

Before I could finish, the Nova choked to a stop, the door opened, and Glen stepped around the car and said, "Where's Meryl?"

I shrugged. He knew the answer; there was no reason to ask me. Then he scooped me up and headed for our trailer. His stride was long, his arms thick and hard from long days spent working at the Estate, where he managed the maintenance crew and tended the landscaped acreage surrounding the building. He smelled of grass, and his neck was tanned a dark brown that nearly matched the color of his hair. Taking the stairs with a jump, he shoved open the door to our trailer, and I heard a gasp from our couch to the left. Meryl, as usual, hadn't been ready.

"Glen, you're home!"

"She was out in the road again, Meryl."

Glen set me down and pushed me into the kitchen. I peeked around his leg and saw Meryl, all curves and blond hair, trying to untangle herself from the beach towel she'd been using as a blanket. Her hair, which Mrs. Kelvin called a mop, looked even wilder than usual. There was nothing about her mouth or groggy eyes that struck me as pretty, but then the older boys around Little Pines hardly ever mentioned her face. Meryl finally got herself settled. I could see she was wearing her black T-shirt with the letters *KISS* carved across it as sharp and silver as knives. Before she could say a word, Glen spoke on.

"I said she was out in the road again, Meryl. I don't ask much in return for letting you stay here, but watching out for her is one of them."

"But . . . I'm sorry, Glen. I thought she was off playing with the rest of the pack. How was work, sweetie?"

He didn't answer, just looked at his wristwatch and glared. A twist of anger flashed on Meryl's face before she turned, muttering and stripping off her shorts and shirt. Glen stalked into the kitchen without saying anything more.

In the living room, Meryl had stepped into her Perkins uniform, an emerald frock that's still the greenest piece of clothing I've ever seen. Some nights, when Glen didn't find me out in the road or when he'd come home from being out with Dwight and the others, he'd zip up her back or caress the swell of her hip. This particular night he clattered around in the bedroom until she gathered up her purse and left the trailer.

After her footsteps died off, Glen came out and set to making dinner. A flash of blue meant it was macaroni and cheese night. I helped by clearing my construction paper and sticker books from the table, then sat and waited for Glen to speak to me.

"Switch on the set."

I did. *Family Feud* was on, and soon Glen set a bowl of orange noodles in front of me, along with a fork. Except for the occasional blow to the television to keep Richard Dawson's head from turning green, dinner was quiet. And when the last person had been kissed and the winnings tallied, the TV was turned off and our empty dishes washed. Sometimes I could head outside after dinner; however, on nights like this one I knew better and so joined my father at the kitchen table.

From Glen's briefcase came two squat rolls of paper, secured by rubber bands, and the morning's news. He gave me the newspaper, and before long I had it spread out wide and began coloring in the faces of prime ministers and CEOs and sports heroes with my purple marker, all the while seeking out new words to learn. Glen, meantime, unrolled the other papers, weighted them with a set of matching McDonald's glassware, and took out his magnifying glass. These weren't the same papers he looked through every night, although I'd seen enough of them to know they were similar. Thin blue lines traced squares and circles in perfect patterns, and Glen would study every inch, always muttering the same thing under his breath. That special word I wanted to learn but had forgotten earlier out on the road.

"Somewhere. It's got to be here somewhere."

WEDNESDAY, JANUARY 20, 1999

We all have our searches, I guess. For Glen, his search seemed to be all there was, so when he wasn't scanning blueprints he would return to the Estate itself to tap on walls, shine a flashlight into dark corners, or just stare at the walls and ceiling. A man gets a reputation for such behavior and people start to talking. Yet this never appeared to bother him. Sometimes I wonder if he even knew there was a world around him.

My search, or part of it at least, looks to have been answered by a visit to the Lowerton Historical Society on the far side of town. The place is cramped, poorly lit, and entirely unsuited to holding most of the things they transferred there when Brighton Entertainment undertook the Estate's going from historical landmark to historical theme park. Still, I know one of the curators, and she's always been a big help to me. Today was no different. She knew right away whom I should use as the voice for Quinlin's Estate—Embeth Graveston.

"The woman who wrote the play?" I asked. "She's still alive?"

She nodded. "Doing well too. She stops by on occasion and loves to talk about all the time she spent at the Estate. Wonderful woman. I'll track down her number for you."

Twenty minutes later my call was picked up by a steady voice that sounded full of sunshine. I introduced myself, explained why I called, and got a yes before I was halfway through.

"Of course you can talk to me, dear, it's the one thing I'm still good at." Embeth followed this with a chuckle.

"I won't be intruding?"

"Nobody's ever intruded who wanted to hear me go on about the Estate. I worked there, you know, back when it was an orphanage. And my husband spent his service time at the radio installation there during the war. I've plenty of stories for you."

Since she was headed out of town for the weekend, we made an appointment to meet next Tuesday for my first interview. When I asked for directions to her home, I wasn't surprised to hear she lives in one of the apartments at Truant Gulch, not more than a couple hundred yards from the extended-care wing where Glen lies in stasis. His search emptied me from his life;

mine brings me practically to the foot of his bed.

I doubt the other facets of my search will be saturated with as much irony. The money, I'm already certain, will take me to Harrisburg, while the gathering of others to join the cause will take me to an empty classroom next Thursday evening. I've hung flyers around campus announcing the meeting and encouraging students to join the fight to save Quinlin's Estate. An undergraduate communications student called this morning to set up a short radio interview for the school station and, given the shape of my finances, I'm not in a position to turn down free publicity. Thankfully I know the editor in chief at the weekly Lowerton paper—she used to teach English and coach the drama team when I was in high school—and she was willing to squeeze in a classified ad for me at a quarter the regular price. Now I just wait for Thursday and hope others will show, that a group of four or six will tell me this isn't a waste of time after all.

The problem is perspective. Most people, students especially but even townies now, view the Estate as simply an attraction— like Busch Gardens and Sea World—because of what Brighton Entertainment has done with it. They go in packs of eight or ten during discounted fall weekends to toss pennies in the wishing well or race each other up the tower steps or pair off in couples and make out in the dark corners of the basement. Most of all, they show up for the Maze, pay their three dollars, and spend a few hours playing Theseus, conqueror of the Minotaur.

The Maze fills the entire third floor of the Estate, over eighty-five-hundred square feet. There are two doors at opposite ends, and the rest consists of so many convoluted passageways that the average newcomer spends ninety minutes inside before finding the end.

It's a different, disconcerting world inside the twisting walls. Those people entering as a pair often find themselves separated from each other in the space of minutes. Children who'd otherwise love a place to run and explore become hesitant and end up clinging to their parents. The anxious sometimes have difficulty breathing, the nervous unable to keep their pulse from racing. Two have experienced seizures within the Maze, and there've been countless cases of men and women simply freezing up and refusing to move another step, many without ever exhibiting any signs of claustrophobia before. To that end, roamers—trained employees of Brighton Entertainment—scour the Maze at all times and offer hints to the frustrated, help to the overwhelmed. Twelve roamers walk different routes simultaneously, thereby covering every nook and dead end and spiral. I roamed for three summers when I was in high school and college, and nine years later I still find myself dreaming of that wild and tangled route through the heart of the labyrinth.

But taking the Maze, unique as it is, and ignoring the rest reduces the Estate to the level of a carnival fun house. There's much more to it than that. I've written just one question for my meeting next Thursday, and it has nothing to do with people's favorite rooms or warm childhood memories of visiting with their favorite aunts. I want others to tell me why they think the Estate should be saved. If they can articulate that, and if we have enough voices speaking enough good reasons, then we'll at least have a chance.

The Reasons I Think the Estate Should Be Saved

1. It was there, whenever needed and in whatever capacity, and there are few things in life as constant or dependable. Built to save Lowerton, it never gave up the role.

2. Humility. A ridiculous quality perhaps to assign to a building, but if the Estate mirrors its creator in any way, it is this. The one architectural style absent from its design is the self-aggrandizing of the ancient Egyptians. And through the years the Estate has always given back, no matter its various owners and their agendas. That's to be honored.

3. To tear the place down before it has been thoroughly researched and explored is a risk. Yes, someone should have made the effort years ago. Regardless of this, the value and history of the place shouldn't be lost just for reasons of expedience.

4. Because, with it standing, it's near impossible to become lost in Lowerton. The tower reaches so high above everything else that it's visible from almost anyplace around town. More than once I've made it home from a long walk through orienting myself to the tower.

5. Finally, because at the same time the Estate makes it known where you are, it also points to where you want to be. It offers a dream of someplace better. To sit on one's trailer steps, trying to ignore the heat and the flies, and stare up at the tip-top of its tower cresting far above the trees and power lines—well, it made you believe in some place just for you.

Neither of these last two will be heard in Harrisburg if I'm called upon to speak my mind. Nevertheless, they're what convinced me that staying around here to attend college was the right thing to do. I stayed to find out how true was its promise.

I remember thinking there are not too many things that can offer the safety of home as well as a taste of paradise.

That's why losing the Estate would be so very hard. Not only would I feel lost, but those years would have been a waste too. And any escape would come to nothing. It would just be me—alone and wandering.

TUESDAY, JANUARY 26, 1999

Already, only a few days into this project, my view of Quinlin's Estate has been turned on its head. I didn't expect or plan it, yet somehow Mrs. Embeth Graveston uprooted me within a short time after my arrival at her apartment, before we'd even gotten to our discussion of the Estate. She welcomed me, took my coat, and pointed me to a spindly armchair situated in the tiny space I guessed to be her living room. Like most homes for the elderly, her apartment was terrifically hot. I noticed she put the uncomfortable conditions to use by keeping a good number of flowering plants. The place was mostly sage and cream with only a small television cart and a china hutch against the walls.

Embeth herself appeared from the kitchen carrying a plate of cookies in one hand and a cup of coffee in the other. She favored her left leg as she crossed the room; her arms trembled a bit as she lowered the tray to the coffee table. But her back was straight, and while she turned and settled into the divan across from me, I realized how beautiful Embeth was. Eighty-three and regal—despite having buried a husband and a daughter.

"Your father is Glen Lawson, yes?" she asked. After I nodded, she narrowed her eyes as if expecting as much and said,

"My husband taught him. And he was a classmate of my daughter, Evangeline, God rest her soul."

I waited for her to continue, perhaps mention the stories
she'd heard about Glen. She instead gave a sad sort of smile and
said, "Your father paid visits to her, even during her troubles,
and Charles and I were always grateful for that. No one else
would've done such a thing. You have his eyes."

I didn't know what to say. Of all the things I'd expected from
this meeting, hearing about my father, young and helpful, wasn't
one of them. I'd expected Gabriel Quinlin, in full vest and trousers. Or Embeth's husband, Charles, whom I knew had worked
many years at the Estate. Anybody but my father. That's when
it hit me that the history of Quinlin's Estate was going to
overlap the story of Lowerton itself and all who lived here.
Separating the two would be all but impossible, as damaging as
separating the Maze from the rest of the house. So I smiled,
pulled out my mini-tape recorder, spoke the date and time into
it, and set it on the table near Embeth so that it would catch
every word. Then I asked her to share with me her first memory
of Quinlin's Estate and waited for the words to come. The rest
would come as well, including Charles and Embeth's troubled
daughter, of whom I knew nothing.

For nearly two hours Embeth talked, and without needing
much prompting. The stories didn't come out tidy or concise,
but no matter because I'll edit it all later. I'll put together the
scenes and moments from her life and the life of the building in
order to reconstruct the early years of Lowerton. The interview
had turned out exactly the way I'd hoped. Before leaving I
thanked her and said I could return a couple times a week if
she'd be willing to continue to tell me her stories.

"That's fine," she responded, except there was a bit of hesitation in her voice, so I asked if there was a problem.

"No problem ... as long as you let me tell the story exactly the way it happened. Some people refuse to hear anything bad in the slightest, but life isn't just sunshine and daisies. It's not that easy."

"I wouldn't want anything else."

"Then, when can you come back?"

A First Memory of Gabriel Quinlin, 1927—Adapted From Embeth

Embeth Herr turned eleven years old two weeks before the configured furnaces in Quinlin's Iron Works fired hard the first load of Pennsylvania clay. Cokers and scarfers who'd once danced amid the heat of molten metal now toiled at new jobs, managing kilns that would bring forth the bricks with which the dream of Gabriel Quinlin would spring up from the Allegheny foothills. Elsewhere, hard men whose work some considered as tending the very portal of hell now found themselves hewing trees for lumber or chiseling stone, to gather together the basic construction materials necessary for building. This was the promised period of "laying in," as Quinlin had described it during his Easter address to the town at the First Presbyterian Church of Lowerton.

Embeth, a pale sliver of a girl, sat cowering next to her mother in the balcony as they listened to the speech, Quinlin's promises of food and shelter and work no matter how deep the country plunged into depression, and the subsequent applause. Easter Sunday was the one day a year her mother forced her into a house of worship, and as usual the heavy silence and vacant stares intimidated her into anything but listening to the service. Men prayed and then a choir sang as wooden plates were passed among the congregation to be filled with the jingling coins and worn dollars of people hoping a little more might buy a good planting season, relief from a rheumatic knee, or quick end to the hard times ahead. Embeth never knew what her mother requested when dumping in a trio of coins, but she herself added a little wish to the silver as the plate went by— that this would be the year Mr. Quinlin would sweep her far away from the whispers of a mean-hearted town.

Service ended with more plates being passed, these containing bread and small tastes of wine. And for the first time that Embeth could remember her mother wasn't skipped by ushers deciding that an unmarried woman with child could add to the church's coffers but not partake in the sacraments. The man who served them this time wore a dark gray suit like all the rest, and when Embeth looked up, she saw the earnest, pleasant face of Mr. Quinlin and felt as though her small prayer had been answered in a way. Nothing was said, though the simple act had to mean something, and for the remainder of the morning all Embeth could think about was the day she'd march through the gates of Quinlin's great house and smile as he told her to pick her room. Any room. Any room at all. Then what would all the frocked girls at the schoolhouse say? What sharp little poems would the boys rhyme about her?

The bells pealed high in the belfry, celebrating the mystery of Christ returned from hell, and as the congregation let out, Embeth's heart felt as light as it had ever been on Easter morning. She had her own dream of a new life offered.

THURSDAY, JANUARY 28, 1999

I read a short portion of Embeth's story to open the informational meeting I arranged for those interested in saving Quinlin's Estate. It explained who Embeth was and what her role would be in our efforts. Afterward I asked my single question to the three women and two men who'd shown up and took notes on their replies. This is what I wrote:

Sandra Guerrero. Junior, History major, Latin American Studies minor. Composed, very articulate and attractive. Possible spokesperson for group. Her reasons for saving the Estate are similar to mine. She mentioned how it "played a part in history rather than just standing outside of it, pristine and inviolate, like most of our monuments." Liked how it is rough at the edges, called it "amazingly blue collar" given that it was built by an industrialist. SHE'S PERFECT!

Taryn Siming. Sophomore, Journalism. Appeared bored and didn't have all that much to say about the Estate except that she thought our efforts would make a good story. Maybe helpful for writing. Doubtful she'll return.

Ben Sterling. Architecture graduate student. Quiet. Great thoughts on the building but could barely get them out. A bit heavy, especially in the face, and flushes crimson when he speaks. Good alternative perspective. Loved the building's unconventional design. Said it was all energy coiled up inside. Also noted that it was a palace for the people. Valuable to team—just no public speaking. Great university contact.

Kim Felsch. Freshman, Secondary Education major. Young in all the worst ways. Said she'd been to the Estate last semester with some girls on her floor and that she couldn't believe they'd tear such a neat place down. Don't know what help she'll be.

Philip von Maarsten. Out of school, works at airport.

Couldn't guess his age if you paid me. Could be twenty-four,
could be thirty-four. Wants to honor Quinlin's vision, also
thinks Estate gives Lowerton something worth looking up to.
Vague, but it'd be good to have another "townie" other than me.
Getting ready to leave, he donned an old-style fedora that
would've made most men look silly. He looked like he just
stepped off a movie screen.

When they'd finished I handed out packets filled with pro-
motional and press information from the Estate, a copy of
Brighton's press release announcing the closing, and a single
sheet of paper on which I'd written the number 7,000,000.
Nobody needed to ask what the figure represented. We closed
by scheduling our next meeting for the following Wednesday.
Only Taryn had a conflict that night, and she didn't suggest we
reschedule, so I'm betting we're minus at least one next week if
not more.

Otherwise the group appears to be set. On leaving, Kim
asked if she should go to the library and study up on the early
years of the Estate. I told her she'd be hard pressed to find anything and that if she truly wanted to read something I could E-
mail her the research I'd already put together. She nodded, and
both Sandra and Ben, passing by, said they'd also take a look. I
was glad for their eagerness. Overall it was an encouraging
night, and I think we took a great first step. It's good to be
surrounded by people again. The last few weeks putting this
together has been hard, but the work's beginning to pay off. I'm
now ready to begin sifting through fragments and paragraphs
I'd written last fall, to piece together a few stories that'll spark
the group's interest, make them want to fight all the harder.

This is what I was called here to do.

AN ABBREVIATED HISTORY OF QUINLIN'S ESTATE

June 1927–May 1937—The Estate is built

Life in Lowerton during the years of construction followed a different path from the rest of the nation. Want and worry were not part of the everyday thoughts of the workaday citizen, nor were issues of hunger or poverty. The unemployed didn't overrun the streets, because everyone in town had a job: teacher, tailor, apothecary, farmer, deputy, and of course, Quinlin worker. The 1930 census showed 1,934 residents of Lowerton. Quinlin's employee roster listed 1,474 workers. The youngest employee— Gunther Maston, age ten—worked half days running messages along with other boys around his age between the Estate and the factory, for extra pennies or rations. At eighty-seven, Horatio Piedmont was the oldest worker. He assisted in the inventorying of everything from cattle feed to iron tacks to schoolroom chalk.

With the exception of water and wood, both in abundant supply, the services and goods in town were all regulated through strict rationing and monitoring. What kept the entire system from collapsing was that the majority of families received more food, more coal, more of everything than they ever had before. Funded privately through Gabriel Quinlin's enormous wealth, the town of Lowerton closed itself off to the greater stricken country and held together for eleven years. Just barely. For the seams were beginning to pop in their sealed world by the end of those years. By then, however, the Estate was completed, and America had taken enough steps in recovering from its precipitous economic decline that the town could again open its doors, rejoining county, state, and country.

October 12, 1937—Gabriel Quinlin dies

Five months after the Estate's completion and without ever spending a single night under its roof, Gabriel Quinlin passed away. Legend, of course, hints that he died of a broken heart, but there's no evidence of any love in Quinlin's life, and the death certificate on record simply reads "failed heart" instead. Either way he was gone, and Lowerton, led by his guiding hand for so long, didn't know what to do.

And so time stopped in town. Work ceased in the factory; schools and businesses closed; even the local pub plugged up its taps. The only person working, apparently, was Embeth Graveston, who used the time to write *He Saved Lowerton.*

For three days the town waited, holding its collective breath. If the number seems cumbersome with symbolism, blame the townsfolk of Lowerton. For three days they waited as if expecting some Messianic return. When nothing significant occurred—ignoring the birth of Glen Lawson, my father—Pastor Thomason led the people to the cemetery where they buried Gabriel Quinlin, and then everyone returned home to start the wheels of Lowerton to turning once more.

More or less, things went back to normal. The factory's board of directors met for five nights and appointed a new president, and operations continued on smoothly as though nothing major had happened. Lawyers doled out Quinlin's holdings—those they could find—to the recipients he'd named, and soon his belongings were auctioned off or donated to the local museum. Ridiculous as it sounds, only the Estate was left unaccounted for. Finished so soon before his death, Quinlin never got the chance to include the building in his will. And so it sat.

Walter Mulligan—father of the man who lived one trailer

away from me, the man who flew his black flag every morning—received a modest salary to tend the grounds of the Estate.
But nobody entered, made use of, or visited the great mansion
on the hill. A quote from a letter written at that time says it
best: "It's as if that monstrous thing were nothing less than
Gabriel Quinlin himself, watching over us from the very heights
of heaven."

Sixteen months later, the changes began.

February 1939

Faced with a shortage of space at the factory warehouse, the
officials at Quinlin Metal Works open the doors to the Estate
and begin using the property for storage.

March 1942

The U.S. Army, entangled now in World War II, notices the
Estate's strategic and unimpeded location atop the Allegheny
ridge, strikes a compromise with both Lowerton and factory
owners, and purchases the building for use as a radio installation.

September 1947–June 1958

In the wake of the great spring fire that burned down the
elementary school and high school, the town buys back the
Estate from the Army, which was eager to rid itself of the now
outdated facility. For the next decade the building plays school
to every Lowerton child, first grade through senior high. Education reformers eventually send the kids back down the hill,
though for another two years the boys' basketball team continues to play their games in the grand ballroom that school officials chose to turn into a gymnasium.

August 1958–November 1972

A few months later the state of Pennsylvania purchases the Estate from Lowerton, renames the place Maple Ridge, and modifies the space for use as an orphanage and sanitarium to serve the otherwise ignored portions of central and western Pennsylvania.

November 1972–October 1975

Eventually children's advocates trumpeting social reform join those fighting for the rights of the disabled in the effort to shut down Maple Ridge, thus forcing the state to sell the building. In the quickest turnaround ever for the Estate, the building is sold to a commune called Road to Damascus, led by a young millionaire by the name of Martin Peterson. This period ended in a disaster that resulted in the only death ever on Estate grounds (it just so happens that I share the same name with the woman who died; her name was Eve), and the group left in a rush, giving up the building for whatever Lowerton would offer.

March 1976–June 1988

After a vote in the November election, Lowerton officials follow public opinion and convert the building from its latest abomination to a museum commemorating Quinlin and the town.

October 1988–present

Facing a budget crisis and a strained economy, Lowerton bites at the offer Brighton Entertainment presents them and sells the Estate once more. It then becomes the Realm of Living History.

The Estate's future?

Either it stands or it falls. Ashes to ashes, dust to dust, brick to crumbling brick.

Monday, February 1, 1999

Today I thought I was to have another chance at interviewing Embeth. Instead, I found myself preoccupied with faces I'd forgotten, ghosts I'd given up on, all because of stopping by Glen's bedside for a brief visit. For who would I run into but Meryl Lakewood. When I arrived she was sitting in his room and reading an article to him from *People* magazine about two married country singers.

I knew she'd been a regular visitor since the stroke and yet it never occurred to me that Mondays were *her* day. The way she looked up at me from her chair today, I thought she was going to come after me with those claws she has done at the salon downtown twice a week. She didn't budge, though, and we stared at each other for a few moments before saying anything.

This was the first time I'd seen Meryl up close in almost ten years. Her mouth, which used to be like a model's, full and pouty, has sagged into a scowl. That and a few wrinkles here and there were the only noticeable changes. Her chest is as aggressive as always, and she's still got that wild blond hair. It was when she looked up at me that I saw the similarities. Her eyes became slits and it was as though the flame of rage instantly rekindled itself, and I knew she hadn't stopped hating me. Perhaps even more than the last time we'd spoken. That terrible night ten years ago when things had gone so very wrong.

"Didn't know you visited on Mondays," Meryl said, her

index finger marking the place in the article she'd been reading.

"He's my father. I can visit anytime I like."

It sounds mean to me now that I write it and I suppose it was then too, but that's the only way I knew how to talk to Meryl. Everything was a matter of possession with her, and so that which I didn't claim, didn't hold on to with all my strength, she would take away from me with a bat of her eyelashes.

Today a small tremor passed through her hand but she said nothing to indicate anything was wrong. She closed her magazine, scooped up her jacket from the foot of Glen's bed, then took a moment to lean over my father and whisper something into his unhearing ear.

Standing back up, she looked at me and said, "I'll come back later." Then she stalked out without another word.

I stayed with my father for another twenty minutes, and when I got ready to leave to interview Embeth, the scent of Meryl's perfume still spoiled the air. Ten years hadn't been long enough. On my way out I left a message at the nurses' station that they should let Ms. Lakewood know that from now on I would do my best to avoid visiting my father on Mondays. That day was hers to own.

As I already said, even listening to Embeth tell her stories couldn't rescue me from the stirring Meryl had boiled up inside me. I tried to pay attention as Mrs. Graveston spoke but soon found myself gritting my teeth over the exchange I'd just had with Meryl or in reliving moments from the deep past. Embeth must have sensed my distraction and so kept her memories short, concentrating on the years during the Estate's construction. I have them on tape, thankfully, and in listening to them again, I'm wondering when Mrs. Graveston is going to get to

the part she thinks of as less than sunshine and daisies. Everything so far has been wholesome and according to town legend.
Even the photos I saw tonight back me up. Embeth pulled out
some pictures when she was eighteen, and in each one she looks
stunning, graceful and poised, with long legs and a schoolgirl's
smile, what Wander and I used to call "pretty-pretty" during
our hours together playing make-believe in the back arbor or in
my bedroom. Even then, we knew there was a difference
between someone like Meryl and someone like Embeth, the
same kind of difference that separated those who lived in the
shadow from those of us who didn't. We doubted either of us
would grow up to be pretty-pretty. Left with trying to figure
out how to escape the stigma of existing outside the shadow, we
were eight-year-olds planning our way out of Lowerton,
whether by bus or magic carpet or in the embrace of a woman
who'd love us to call her Mom. Every hour of play brought a
new solution until one evening Wander chose the easiest of
them all, the one we'd never even talked about, and simply
walked away.

So tonight I've been thinking of Wander's odd disappearance, seen the aged face of Meryl Lakewood, and been granted
a vision of Embeth Graveston in her youth. In the midst of all
this am I, with my father's green eyes and broad Gaelic nose,
my poor mother's coarse red hair and slender hips, and a bent
spine I still don't trust even after all these years, despite what
the doctors say. I stand among them all as I mine the past for a
hint at the unknown future and hope that, in the end, this path
has been the right one to walk.

A GLIMPSE OF LIFE FOR EMBETH DURING
CONSTRUCTION—1931–1937

Through the years of the town's restraint and withdrawal,
Embeth Herr matured—hips thickening, skin clearing, and legs
stretching long and lithe. Daily rationing of milk, eggs, butter,
meat, and bread kept the icebox and pantry better stocked than
what they'd been previously on her mother's income. And
Embeth's after-school job of mixing mortar for the Estate, along
with the rest of the girls in her class, had toned her arms and
pared off any remaining baby fat. She was fifteen and already
boys and men began to stare.

Circumstances continued in her favor. Private wealth having
been obliterated in the name of saving Lowerton, she found herself dressed the same and with similar hairstyle as every other
girl in school, yet few wore either quite so well. Boys stopped
whispering behind her back. Girls whispered even more.
Embeth soon learned to ignore the greedy eyes of men.

At seventeen she finished high school and afterward turned
down an opportunity to leave Lowerton for nurse's training.
Her truest desire had never changed: she wanted to be part of
Gabriel Quinlin's world; she wanted him to invite her into the
mansion rising from the hill above town and announce before all
the town that Embeth Herr could choose any room she liked for
herself. The second glances of other men, their endless soft
whistles meant nothing to her. Gabriel's nod alone would be her
justification. Two weeks after graduation, Embeth interviewed
for and then was offered the position of assistant secretary at
the factory. It was 1935 and by now all the bricks necessary for
building the Estate had been made. Quinlin, looking this time to

Europe rather than Wall Street, saw the signs of another storm approaching and understood it was time to begin the slow restoration of the factory as an armaments manufacturer.

At a board meeting called to announce his intentions, Quinlin supposedly said: "Once more young men will line up to be trampled beneath the inexorable urging of the machine of history rolling forward. In this cause, I do not doubt that it will again fall to us to rain death from the sky."

He never saw the slaughter, but his vision came true. Two years later, and just one month after Quinlin's death, Adolf Hitler issued his Hossbach Memorandum at a secret conference in the Reich Chancellery, where he declared his aim in gaining *Lebensraum* or living space for the German people at the expense of other European nations.

Embeth was now twenty-one and about to get married to Charles Graveston, one of the two greatest men she'd ever met. For her there was no war, no rumors of war, only the bright future opening wide before her.

Tuesday, February 2, 1999

This evening I spent a number of hours in the Lowerton Public Library preparing for tomorrow's meeting with the SQE (Save Quinlin's Estate) group. I prefer the library to the university because they've got the past thirty-plus years of the *Lowerton Express*—the town's weekly newspaper—on microfilm, and while the reporting is generally poor, it's the only paper to cover the lesser known happenings around the Estate.

Up for a stretch at one point, I decided to satisfy a curiosity of mine and see the face of Embeth's daughter, Evangeline

Graveston. The library keeps copies of high-school yearbooks in their reference section. Since I knew she was a classmate of my father's, I simply pulled out the volume that included Glen's senior class, 1955–56, and scanned the listings—Gonnig, Gowl, Grabbel, Grant . . . Graveston.

Above the name, instead of a woman's face, there was a photo of my father, his hair cropped close and an unexpected smile across his face.

I stared, unsure of what I was looking at before realizing what had happened. I lifted the page and, as my father's face remained still, I saw the hole from where someone had cut Embeth Graveston's portrait from the book. Glen's portrait took the same spot as hers, only among the Ls on the next page. The open window now framed his face.

Because this kept me from seeing what Evangeline looked like, I went back a grade to the 1954–55 book. Again she was missing, only this time, instead of Glen's face in the cutout, it was Wendy Laplander.

Her sophomore and freshman photos had been removed as well. By the time I closed the last yearbook, I began to wonder if Embeth Graveston hadn't been forthright with me in speaking of her daughter's so-called troubles. I made a note of this as a possible question to ask but wasn't sure how I'd go about pursuing it. The woman hadn't volunteered to be harassed after all.

Before leaving the shelf, I found the yearbook from my freshman year, '86–'87, and paged through faces I hadn't seen for a dozen years. Some I remembered in an instant due to some small kindness or cruelty, while others registered only as somebody I'd once sat near in class or passed regularly in the halls. I found my friends Trudi and Karen and me—those hideous glasses and that ruffled collar, what was I thinking? I then came upon Wanda Maxwell.

I suppose it was too late to remove her from the yearbook, but Wander never finished her freshman year. She'd disappeared several weeks before school ended that year. In fact, this photo was the only evidence of her ever setting foot in Lowerton High School. She stared out from beneath greasy black bangs with a look of quiet desperation. Maybe it's only because I know what happened to her, although I doubt it'd take a genius to pick her as most likely to vanish. And vanish she did. From everything but this page.

What a strange night it turned out to be. Having come to the library to research and gather more information to pass along to my group, I'm instead confronted with a girl's image where there should be none and a void where a different girl's face should be. Perhaps that's what this whole search, this whole quest, will be—solutions where I expect none and silence when I need an answer most.

Until I find out, I cannot help but write the stories that come to me.

THE NIGHT WANDER DISAPPEARED

Two nights after Easter 1987, Wanda Maxwell left Little Pines. I can't be sure, even now, but I believe I'm the last person to have seen Wander in the trailer park. In some ways I feel this made me an accomplice to what she did, a fact I have mixed feelings about.

I remember it had been an unusually warm stretch of days for early April. With everything closed for the holiday, both

Glen and Meryl hung around the trailer all weekend and were getting on each other's nerves. I was trying to work through my algebra homework at the kitchen table when their latest argument broke out, this time over what to watch on TV. Somehow the quarrel twisted to the topic of Meryl bringing in more income, and that brought them both to screaming. At this point I closed my books and slipped out the front door.

Walking by Mr. Mulligan's trailer, I heard the electric wailing of a rock album pounding through his aluminum walls and moved on. In three months' time he'd die howling at a full moon, rubber tubing knotted about his arm. Music played that night too, a song by the Velvet Underground caught in a skip until a paramedic shut it off—*Ooh, white light. Ooh, white light. Ooh, white light.*

Despite the fine weather, everyone remained inside, taking in the Sunday night movie or an early season baseball game. The same flicker shone out from every front window in the park, so I could crisscross the dark trailer court without a care, paying no mind to Glen's constant warnings to stay out of the night. The grove, the back lot of trees and shrubs into which I walked, had always been owned by the kids of Little Pines, and while I wasn't a kid anymore, I still fled on occasion to the fort we'd built the year Santa arrived on top of Mr. Mulligan's flagpole.

Squares of wood nailed to the tree trunk served as footholds. After I'd pulled myself up onto the rough planking, I could stand and see over all of Little Pines. Two cars idled, their brake lights glowing like the red eyes of jackals, in the empty lot across Marker Road. Money and vials were probably changing hands, perhaps a gunshot if things went badly. Tonight the cars stayed for just a minute and soon all was crickets and a hush of wind. Up in the fort a person could see how it was possible to get out of Lowerton, and that was by getting above it. Quinlin's Estate was above. So was Santa. I lay on my back and watched the night sky for fizzlers, our word for falling stars, when I heard a screen door open. Propping up on one arm, I looked to see who it was. Just seconds later Wander appeared, pausing in a pool of light cast down by a nearby lamppost.

Her hair was long in the back, her bangs cut straight across at her eyebrows, and it gleamed black and shiny as oil. In the right light her hair looked almost blue. I can't remember her voice ever making it above a whisper, even when we played together in the privacy of my room with Glen away and Meryl sleeping. I've made my own guesses as to why she whispered all the time and they all ended up right at Wander's front step. I couldn't take them any farther because of never having gone inside Wander's trailer. Nor did she ever speak a word to me about what went on inside. I just know she didn't like being there. The reason she'd gotten the nickname Wander was because of her constant walking. Regardless of the weather, she could be seen around the paths and along the perimeter of Little Pines.

So seeing her this night was no surprise. What she did, however, was.

Without hesitating she walked directly for the grove, her steps confident and steady. I could see that she had on pink sweat pants, white sneakers, and her favorite denim jacket, the one with a rainbow patch sewn on one shoulder and a crescent moon on the other. Darting forward suddenly, she found the trail that led to the stand of trees, passed right below the fort where I was crouched down, and disappeared into the darkness.

Just that quick.

Enough time to shout, perhaps, but I didn't.

She was gone, never once looking back.

WEDNESDAY, FEBRUARY 3, 1999

Tonight brought our second SQE meeting, and just as I expected there was a thinning in our ranks. Neither Kim nor Taryn showed up, but Philip, Ben, and Sandra all arrived anxious to move forward. In a remarkably short time we decided both on an overall plan and our individual tasks within that framework.

Sandra will lead research on other tourist homes and their economic viability in small rural areas. She will also be our primary spokesperson.

Ben, obviously, is going to serve as our architectural expert. In addition, he'll search out ways to reduce the costs of an eventual restoration. Since as a grad student he has the most contacts on campus, he'll act as our university liaison.

Philip will be our community representative, beginning with soliciting individual and business support for the Estate. The money we receive will never be enough to cover the costs, but if we can prove to Harrisburg that the community is willing to lend financial support, they might be more inclined to send funds our way.

The same is true for grants. If we could secure a few endowments, that small amount of money might make a large impact in the minds of the state legislature.

I'll be in charge of grant writing as well as putting together the SQE proposal to be presented at Harrisburg.

All this took only an hour. The rest of the time we chatted, getting better acquainted with one another and talking more about our interest in the Estate.

Sandra is from Towson, Maryland. Her mother's a music professor at the university there, her father an editor in Baltimore. Both are Dominican. She's an only child and credits a grandmother outside Santo Domingo for her love of history. The Estate, in fact, reminds her of a church in her grandmother's town and how it towers over everything else around it.

Ben Sterling did his undergraduate work at Buffalo, and his family still lives up near Niagara Falls. He loves the references in the Estate's construction and mentioned a few of his favorites.

"You know the dungeon rooms downstairs, how they have curved, braced ceilings? They're supposed to mimic the inside of Jonah's whale. And the wishing well just down the hall is modeled after the pool of Bethesda in the Bible, where if the water stirred, prayers for healing were answered. There are a lot of biblical and classical allusions. Most aren't very subtle, but who cares? At least they're interesting."

Philip asked Ben how he knew all of this.

"Journals," replied Ben and went on to explain how one of Quinlin's journals from before construction began gave clear notes on why certain features were included. "The tower, for instance, reminded Quinlin of Adam's outstretched finger as he reaches out to God, from Michelangelo's painting on the Sistine Chapel ceiling."

"What about the Maze?"

Ben smiled, the first I'd seen from him, and said, "Wasn't even mentioned."

"Really?" said Sandra.

Ben shook his head. He had everyone's attention now. "The most distinctive thing in the whole place and he never says a word about it. The obvious connection would be the Labyrinth in Greece, or some of the mazes in the cathedrals of Europe. But this one's very different. A labyrinth has one path, no dead ends or cutbacks. You walk it to get to a specific point. Christians used it to symbolize their journey to God. The Cretans put a Minotaur at its center. The one at the Estate is just wildness. I think it's great."

Philip, the only one of us who hadn't shared, suddenly grinned as if he couldn't help himself and gave a couple of quick nods, saying that for a number of years after moving here from outside Pittsburgh he and some friends visited the Maze every week.

"At first we just tried to race through it, but after a couple of weeks that changed. We did sort of the same thing they do in cathedrals," he said to Ben. "We used the Maze to help us pray or meditate or think through things. It could be pretty focusing and relaxing if you let it. Most people just get frustrated in there."

We all nodded, and I expected Philip to say more but he stayed quiet, and the silence seemed to mean the evening had come to an end. Sandra and Ben gathered their things and said they would see everybody next week. I was about to leave also when Philip's voice stopped me.

"Do you think we'll win?"

I turned. "Win? You mean keep the Estate from falling?"

He nodded, crossing to me. He had a flecked wool overcoat that swept down to his heels. No fedora tonight, instead a thick black scarf he'd looped casually about his neck in a way that was too effective not to have been deliberate. His eyes would normally be pale blue, I think, but because of his coat and the dim light in the room they looked almost silver. Pewter maybe. He was shorter than I remembered, five-eight or so. With different shoes I would've been taller than him.

"Honestly, I don't know. I don't think it's hopeless, though."

He took a deep breath at this, like he was going to say something, but then contented himself with another nod and motioned for me to leave first from the classroom. I did and in the hall we said good-bye and headed different directions. Again, just before I was about to leave, his voice stopped me.

"I'll call you sometime this week," he shouted, then turned and disappeared outside, that trailing scarf the last thing I saw.

It was a fine exit.

Thursday, February 4, 1999

Philip didn't call today, but Dwight Carter did, asking me to lunch on campus at the graduate commons. After more than a decade tending the grounds of the Estate together, a rift between him and Glen over religion had forced him to move on. Now he's the foreman of a grounds crew with the university's Office of Physical Plant.

If there is such a thing, Dwight would be my physical opposite. He's bald and stout, with a round face that almost always has a smile on it. He's got that deep black skin that's not seen too often here in central Pennsylvania. I've walked through Lowerton with him more than once when people coming the other way have stopped what they're doing to watch us go by.

That is Lowerton in all its glory.

Anyway, I'm surprised more people don't recognize him by now. The church he goes to is always helping with community service, whether refinishing storm-damaged homes, plowing driveways for the elderly, or coming alongside a Jewish congregation when vandals routed their synagogue. Given his expertise, Dwight always seems to be at the center of these outreaches, and on more than a few occasions I've opened the weekly paper and found a photo of him swinging a hammer or directing others where to go.

It's a far cry from what and who he used to be. He and Glen were once drinking buddies until Dwight's conversion in the early '90s drove a pretty nasty wedge between them. I was at the university at the time, and since I never came home or even called, Glen thought it'd be funny to send me some letters. In them he called Dwight a traitor, a sap, and worse. I could tell my father felt abandoned, a little afraid even. Dwight had been one of the few who'd stood by Glen when the rest of the town called him nuts. Without him, Glen was left with me, a daughter who, though only a few miles away at the university, might as well have been a thousand miles away, and Meryl Lakewood, who might have been worth even less if that's possible.

Dwight's turning to religion was no simple phase. His life changed. Lots of outward things disappeared—the disturbing-the-peace charges, the dime bags, the occasional brawl—but his personality seemed altered as well. Gone was the idleness, the indifference to others. He resurrected a marriage long thought dead and, at forty-six, even became a father for the first time. The passing of time eventually narrowed the divide between Dwight and Glen, and during my infrequent trips off campus,

Dwight became my one confidant in town when it came to the subject of my father. Like me, he was worried about Glen's growing obsession with Quinlin's gold. But today he wanted to talk to me about something else. When I met him at the entrance to the cafeteria, he swept me into a long bear hug that lifted me clear off the ground.

"How've you been, Eve Marie?" he asked, still the only one to use my full name.

As we got our meals, a turkey sub for me and Caesar salad with grilled chicken for Dwight and his cholesterol, I caught him up on what I'd been doing since withdrawing from the university, including my meetings with the SQE group and my interviews with Embeth Graveston.

Once we'd taken our seats in the small dining commons area, I said, "Embeth is the woman who wrote *He Saved Lowerton*. Did you know her daughter was in Glen's high-school class? She gave Glen a pretty glowing report."

Dwight paused with unfolding his napkin and flicked me a look with his eyes.

"What?" I said.

"You know who her daughter is, don't you?"

I shook my head.

"Think about it while I pray, Miss History."

He bowed his head for a moment, and when he looked back up I still hadn't figured it out. "Who is she?"

"Evangeline Graveston."

I shrugged.

"The woman killed at Quinlin's Estate when it was run by that commune. She fell down the tower stairs."

"I thought her name was—" I started, but Dwight waved me off.

"Everybody called her Eve. She's the one." He took a great bite of his salad, and though he said nothing more, his face grew sadder by the second.

"So you know something about Glen and her?" I asked.

Dwight sighed and appeared to consider his words with care. Finally he lifted a hand and said, "This isn't the time or place, Eve Marie. You caught me a little off guard here and I need some time to think this over. Why don't you stop by the house on Sunday for lunch. Monique would love to see you, and we can talk it through then."

I nodded in agreement, and we ate in silence for a few moments before Dwight gave another big sigh and stretched his arm out to look at his watch. I knew he didn't have long to spend with me and he still hadn't brought up what was on his mind. Typical Dwight, letting his own wants fall by the wayside.

"I had a whole lecture prepared for you, but I don't seem to have the strength for it anymore," he said after a while.

That's when I realized what this had to be about—the only thing it could be. Meryl.

"You keep in touch with her?" I asked.

"She goes to our church. We saw her Sunday; she told me about seeing you."

I knew what was coming next: the call to forgiveness. Since converting, Dwight was big on the need for a body to forgive. He'd apologized to Glen and forgiven him for things so long forgotten my father had hardly known what Dwight was talking about. And my father never said a word in return. Just nodded

and looked confused. This was going to be my call to forgive
Meryl of all the things she'd done to try to drive me away.

"Eve, I think you're wrong to act the way you did to Meryl.
I don't mean to make a big fuss over it, and I promise I won't
mention it again. It's just that you two have been blaming each
other for a long time. It just might be that you're both blaming
the wrong person." He folded his napkin in front of him and
tapped it once. "That's my piece."

The tears came instantly. They didn't fall, but they pooled in
my eyes and for a second everything went blurry. Getting
rebuked by Dwight is the closest I've ever come to disappoint-
ing a father. Each time he chastises me I feel as if I've disappointed the world. The words I spoke to Meryl came back to
me with all their venom so that I heard how mean I'd been,
which made me want to apologize to Dwight, except I knew
such a thing would only frustrate him. He wanted me to go to
her, and that was something I couldn't do. So we sat, neither of
us saying anything, him picking at his salad, me sniffling and
feeling no older than ten.

"Well, this was a bust," he said with a gray laugh after a
long couple of minutes. And I joined him in it. His time about
up, he started gathering his tray together. I didn't want to part
on such depressing terms so I quickly went back to the thing
he'd intrigued me with earlier and begged him to give me at
least a hint about how Glen knew Evangeline Graveston.

"Stupid Glen," he said, almost under his breath, and then
looked at me hard. "She's your namesake, Eve Marie. Evangeline
Graveston is who Glen named you after."

That shocked my eyes dry and left me without any way to
reply.

GLEN LAWSON: MY FATHER

This is the Glen I know. Not the one who named me after a dead woman who fell the length of Quinlin's tower, but a different Glen. I expect these memories will change greatly in the upcoming weeks and figure I should get them down now.

Glen Lawson was born to Matthew and Rose Lawson on October 13, 1937, on the second day of Lowerton's mourning of the death of Gabriel Quinlin. For a town prone to pettiness, superstition, and bouts of illogic, it wasn't surprising then that this became a black mark against him from birth. Glen certainly has his faults, but even I can't believe the number of times we'd walk through town when I was growing up and I'd overhear an old-timer whispering to an elderly friend about how that fella over there was Glen Lawson, born during "the waiting." It must have been a sad thing to be a boy of five and hate your birthday.

Otherwise, Glen's childhood—what I know of it—was typical for Lowerton. After the school burned down in 1947, he and the rest of the children headed up the ridge to the Estate to attend classes. Glen excelled in natural sciences and athletics. School photos show him with a sly smile and an untamable cowlick. On his one remaining report card is written a teacher's comment that praises Glen as "the most outgoing and pleasant of students."

This must have been the case, because in sixth grade, teachers selected Glen, despite his obvious difficulty with reading, to play that part of Gabriel Quinlin in what had become the annual production of *He Saved Lowerton*. It remains the single memory he always looked back on fondly, though it didn't start out that way.

At first the choice appeared to have been a disaster. Glen couldn't remember his lines and began breaking out in fierce hives at the thought of going blank onstage. Two weeks before the production, there was a discussion among the teachers about replacing him. All were in favor except for the math teacher, who thought he understood the problem and worked with Glen after school every day, reading lines aloud which Glen would then repeat back. More and more lines and scenes would be added, and Glen would soon memorize these as well. Slowly Embeth's long soliloquies settled into the right order in Glen's brain and on the night of the play he gave a rousing performance as Gabriel Quinlin, and the photo of him with shovel in hand became a lasting reminder of his triumph.

I heard these stories and thought only that my father must have some undiagnosed learning disability. Like most everything else with Glen, it's just speculation. There's very little I actually know as cold hard fact. As a lover of history this has been just another wall between us.

Life didn't find a great many more triumphs for Glen after that performance. He completed school in 1956, and the years following are a blur. Traveling with friends, they spent seven years in the industrial cities of Erie, Akron, Cleveland, and Cincinnati, finding work where they could and pretending they were seeing the world rather than just Ohio.

It was a construction accident that had forced him to return to Lowerton. Again, the facts are hazy. I know a beam fell and I know it killed one of the friends with whom he was traveling, but I'm less clear where Glen was during the accident. I seem to remember him saying the falling steel actually grazed him in its plummet, yet I'm not sure about this and I know he never showed me a scar or any such physical proof.

Anyway, Glen returned in 1963 to Lowerton, apparently broken and saddened. He found a third-shift job at Quinlin Metal Works and a second position working weekends tending the grounds of the Estate, now in its orphanage stage. At some point he met a recently graduated Dwight Carter.

Seven years passed.

In 1971, he met Roxanne Wren at a factory event, and after a short courtship he married her. He was thirty-four, she nine years his junior. One year later I was born. Two years after that Roxanne died of a savage cancer that had whittled her to the bone. The commune sold the Estate back to Lowerton, and Glen quit his factory job to join the grounds crew as the town turned the Estate into a museum. Working there full time, he began in earnest his search to find Quinlin's gold.

In 1997 he suffered his first stroke, a mild one with no overwhelming side effects.

Late 1998 brought a second, this one devastating. It's been downhill since.

Broad descriptions and an indistinct picture, but this is the life of Glen Lawson.

Or it was.

Now I know that at some point during this timeline, Glen met a woman named Evangeline Graveston and that she meant enough to him that he would christen me in her honor. It waits to be seen exactly where this piece of the puzzle fits.

SATURDAY, FEBRUARY 6, 1999

My day had three very distinct parts today.

This morning was all frustration and dead ends. I spent most of the time scouring the databases at the university library, looking for leads on grants the Estate might qualify for. The problem isn't locating them—there are more than enough groups and societies out there devoted to saving historical treasures—it's the deadlines that are proving to be the roadblock. Too many of these nonprofits have fiscal years that end in June, so the submission deadlines are set for early fall with the announcement of the "winners," as Philip might say, later that winter. The Estate won't last that long for us.

I located five grants that might work. If somehow we found ourselves awarded each of them, our bank account still wouldn't top a measly $150,000. It's almost not worth the effort, except I know they would look good on the proposal we're putting together for Harrisburg. So I'll draw something up over the next few days. Just not today.

Today I needed an escape—if not from the Estate, then at least from its bleak future for the moment. Without even calling ahead, I drove straight to Truant Gulch and found myself in the middle of lunch.

Embeth Graveston was just locking her door when I arrived. Together we headed downstairs for a meal in the retirement community dining room. During the week, she explained after she invited me to join her, she just fixed herself something small in her kitchenette. But on the weekends she liked to take something more substantial early, in case the evening activities forced her to skip dinner.

Today's entrée was smothered chicken. While taking our trays into the sitting area, Embeth leaned over and whispered for me not to say anything about why I was visiting. I had no time to argue because we'd come to a half-filled table and took our seats. Embeth introduced the other four women and gave them my name, saying only that I was a friend. The women at the table, hunched over bowls of aspic or small glasses of cranberry juice, said nothing to this, and soon conversation lapsed into an unfortunate recitation of last evening's TV news magazine and the unsettling exposé on cleanliness at fast food restaurants, something that had scared them all. Both Embeth and I stayed quiet throughout lunch. Only when we had returned to her room a half hour later did she explain why she'd asked me not to talk too much.

"There are people in here, and in town too, who wouldn't be too thrilled about my telling you my story."

I must have looked surprised or confused as to what anybody could object to, because she then patted my hand and gave a small smile. "The hard parts are still to come, dear."

"Your daughter?" I asked, thinking back to what I'd learned from Dwight.

She gave a nod, motioned for me to sit, then settled into the beige love seat opposite me. She sat straight and prim, and her hands were folded restlessly in her lap as though she wanted to occupy them with knitting or something. I pulled out my tape recorder and waited.

"None of this," she began, "was Charles's fault."

What followed showed me mostly how much things have changed in our times. That she still feels the least bit embarrassed or uncomfortable is hard to believe, considering some of the things people confess these days. Still, I don't want to make light of what she told me. Playing the tape of our talk tonight, I can hear the regret in her voice, and these moments must find their way into my retelling of her story.

But before I do that, I need to replay the other recording I heard this evening—Philip's voice on my answering machine, waiting for me when I got home: *Eve, this is Philip. I promised to call and so this is it. The Estate's the only thing I can think about right now. Well, that and the pierogies at Kowalski's in Lock Haven. Have you been? I'm thinking about taking an early dinner there tomorrow. I've got some ideas I'd like to run by you. Give me a ring if you're interested.* Then he gave me his phone number and said good-bye.

I memorized the number, went straight to my laptop, and entered it as a contact. The name sat alone in the *V*s of my computer's address book.

von Maarsten, Philip

Pulling up a blank task, I wrote *Call Philip* and set the reminder for noon the next day. I then opened this page and began writing these very words of what happened tonight. It's 10:43 P.M. and I'm now caught up, able to live in the present. But only for a minute or two. Another deep breath and I must dive back into the past, into the story of Embeth Graveston and Charles and the daughter who came early.

EMBETH, CHARLES, AND EVANGELINE

None of this was Charles Graveston's fault.

Charles accounted. Numbers danced for him the way colors might for an artist. And he was scrupulous and unerring with his pen, rarely tallying a wrong figure. Hired in 1934 at the age of twenty-eight, he was the youngest of the three-person team assigned to keep track of Gabriel Quinlin's increasingly complex books.

With the town closed off and each penny spent, every dollar earned warranted magnified inspection. Goods and services had become interchangeable with dollars and were all figured together by use of a symbolic shorthand that resembled hiero-glyphics the first time Charles saw it. For seven years the grand, closed society stood on the ability to regulate both population and exchange. Now that ability was beginning to weaken, and the pennies became more and more important.

Charles Graveston walked home each night with his fingers stained black with the ink of his labors.

At the factory he occupied half of an enormous metal desk. A single lamp with a green glass shade was placed in the mid-dle, and even when sunlight spilled into the room, that single bulb shone. It was on when most of the workers, including Embeth and the rest of the secretarial assistants, arrived, and it was on when they left as they filed by the big desk.

One night Embeth whispered, "Don't stay too long!" as she passed and was surprised when Charles looked up, smiled, and replied, "Thank you, Miss Herr. I won't."

She would've never guessed that he knew her name.

After that, it was a traded sentence or two every night. Before long, conversations at the factory gate if Embeth hap-pened to arrive early enough. And then the announcement.

Embeth Herr was to become Mrs. Embeth Graveston on November 30, 1937.

The townsfolk of Lowerton couldn't have been more

shocked. Some knew they spoke together at the factory but few surmised the interaction could lead to a bond strong enough to hold marriage. Most in the quiet of their homes voiced dire predictions for the couple. Others, Charles's sister Lydia included, renounced the marriage publicly, making vague suppositions about the character of a woman whose mother lived the life of a slattern. Such protestations did nothing to deter the couple; a small service finalized the vows and the two became husband and wife.

Whispers began three months later when the first swell appeared under the dress of the new Mrs. Graveston. Seemed all too early for a wife to show herself to be with child. When Evangeline Graveston came into the world in June of the next year, it didn't take a mathematician of Charles's proficiency to realize the numbers didn't quite add up. Odd glances were cast at the couple, and women around town wondered whether Embeth hadn't trapped herself a husband with a swing of the hip or a bat of the eyelashes, directed at the poor Mr. Graveston. Men refused to answer their wives, although when talking amongst themselves they agreed that Charles was perhaps the cleverest man alive to allow himself to be trapped by such a woman.

Idle chatter meant nothing to the new parents. They lived quiet lives. Embeth remained at home with her daughter; Charles walked the same tired streets to his factory office where he now tallied the accounts of our government stocking for a conflict it wasn't sure would happen. All who saw the family agreed that, at least on the surface, they appeared to be functioning quite well. A few months later, at the first ever fall-fair production of *He Saved Lowerton*, the town forgave the trespasses of two people in love. Or most of them did at least. Some continued to murmur at every turn, and that, Embeth and Charles came to find out, would never stop. It would go on as long and delve as deep as needed to make sure Embeth never forgot she'd walked in sin.

SUNDAY, FEBRUARY 7, 1999

Now that I'm no longer in classes, the proximity of my apartment to campus makes less sense and has become an annoyance, especially during times like this morning when my neighbors below me brought in the dawn with a bootlegged Grateful Dead concert. By the third stanza of "Saint Stephen" I gave up on sleep, got dressed, and headed into town for a bite at one of the few places I was sure was open so early on a Sunday morning.

Clyde and Dale's is a dark little spot a half mile up the road from the trailer park. I know it best from my childhood and the occasional visit with Glen when our fridge was empty or a bad spell of humidity made turning on the oven in our trailer a foolish idea. Their coffee's strong, they sell the Sunday paper, and since Clyde went under the knife for heart problems, they serve a surprisingly good egg-white omelet. I covered my table with the Metro section and nursed a pot of coffee until it seemed a reasonable hour to make a phone call on a Sunday morning. Only nobody answered at Dwight's house, and I realized they must have gone to early church this morning.

I asked Dale, who knows everything about Lowerton, when the first service at First Baptist ended. She looked at her watch and guessed ten minutes. So I paid my bill, and because the weather wasn't too chilly, I drove over to the church to surprise them outside on the sidewalk as they exited. Except I was the one who got the surprise.

Dwight and Monique appeared, but only after Meryl Lakewood, who I startled so bad she nearly lost her gum, and Philip too. He just about walked past me, and when I said his name I know he didn't recognize me at first glance.

"Eve?" he said finally. "You go to church here?"

I shook my head, told him I was waiting for some friends, and complimented him on his suit. Like everything else he seemed to own, it looked to be vintage, an eight-button jacket that reminded me of something worn in a Cary Grant film.

He took my praise with a nod, then snapped his fingers. "Pierogies. Did you get my message about meeting me for dinner?"

I told him that sounded great and that I'd never been to Kowalski's before.

He grinned. "I came about an hour away from moving back to Pittsburgh when I found that place. It'll be fun." He stared over my shoulder with a puzzled look on his face before saying, "I think those might be your friends."

I turned. Dwight and Monique were walking toward us, only neither seemed all that happy to see me. Dwight's face softened a little as he approached but Monique managed only a quick smile and stopped a few feet short.

"I was wondering why you weren't home this morning," Dwight said, not giving me a chance to respond. "We got some bad news this morning and are on our way to Nique's parents once Vanessa finishes talking to her friends." He gave a worried little glance over his enormous shoulder to his wife.

"Did somebody die?"

He shook his head and leaned in a little. "Her sister . . . she struggles with things," he murmured, "and I guess hasn't been doing too well the last few days. We'll reschedule when I get back, all right?"

"Of course," I said and out of the corner of my eye saw a flash of green. Dwight's daughter, Vanessa, came jogging up, shouted my name, and hugged me tight. I hadn't seen the girl in at least a year, during which time she'd passed through that weird stage between girl and woman. Her skin was lighter, like her mother's, yet I could see Dwight's sculpted jaw and broad nose. The combination was almost Egyptian royalty, and only when she spoke did she sound like a kid again.

"Who's this?" she asked, pointing past me. I realized I'd forgotten Philip entirely. Introductions were made, hands were shook, and Vanessa even gave me a wink before Dwight reeled her in and directed her toward the car. I waved good-bye and turned back to Philip.

"They're sort of a second family to me," I explained.

"Neat," he said, and I couldn't read what this meant. We parted ways then with the promise to meet up at five-thirty for dinner at Kowalski's.

I thought my afternoon hours might be wasted by too much worrying over dinner, but when I sat down to work on a draft of my grant proposal, I found the words came easily and soon had seven pages of reasons why the Central Pennsylvania History Group should divert their Lordson Grant in the direction of Quinlin's Estate. While the draft printed, I tried to coax my hair into something a little more exotic than a ponytail, gave up, and searched through my closet until I'd chosen a thick forest green sweater that complements the red in my hair nicely, and the only jeans I could find that fit right. That's when I admitted to myself that Philip had gotten more of my attention than any guy had in quite a long time. I looked at my watch, saw I'd already taken far too long, and left my apartment in a rush. Thankfully the ride to Kowalski's was clear. I arrived just in time to see Philip step inside the front door.

He greeted me by shaking his head and saying, "How stupid was it for me to not offer to drive the both of us?" I said no bother, and he waved for me to join him in line.

At one point in its life Kowalski's had to have been a fast food restaurant, a KFC maybe, for they haven't done much to the interior, though the food's definitely an improvement. The pierogies I'd had the misfortune to eat before had been slick with butter and jellied onions. These, however, were soft pillows of dough resting in broth. I'd ordered mine stuffed with just potato and cheese, while Philip's came crammed with sauerkraut, potato, and even broccoli. He said grace before he ate, a quick bowing of the head, and then we set to enjoying our dinner.

Overall the evening turned out to be as much a surprise as Philip. I'd expected him to come dressed in his vintage clothes, but this time he'd gone casual and normal—khakis and a denim shirt. Which is exactly how the conversation and everything else went. We talked about everything, from Philip's ideas for the Estate ("Nothing much," he said. "Just some possibilities for fund-raisers. And maybe a way we could get some press through a friend of mine in New York who works at *Dateline*. He told me they love 'dying Americana' stories.") to how he came to Lowerton from Pittsburgh, to where he got his unique clothes ("My great-uncle died and left me his wardrobe. He'd been a pretty successful lawyer and dressed the part."), to our favorite books and movies. Most of the questions he asked were about my studies and how I'd come to love history so much. I realize now that I offered little about Glen or Meryl or living in Little Pines Trailer Park.

The conversation moved like breathing, gathering a simple rhythm all its own and slipping along without us hardly thinking about it. The only hitch at all came when I followed a mention of his sister, Karen, by asking about her. His eyes fell a little when he explained that in 1993, as a thirteen-year-old, Karen had disappeared. He was a freshman at Bucknell University at the time. It'd been the hardest time of his life.

"They never found her," he finished, and the silence that followed was the longest we'd shared all night. I wanted to say something to comfort him, but the only thing that came to mind was my friend Wanda Maxwell, the girl who'd walked away from Little Pines as a fifteen-year-old. I kept quiet, the reason being I'd never found out what had happened to Wanda, and that said more about me than I cared for Philip to know at the moment.

The silence lasted just another second or two before Philip changed the topic, mentioning that he'd worked once with Dwight Carter on a Habitat for Humanity house out toward Snow Shoe. We chatted about the Carters for a while and the evening drew to a close soon after. I can't say we accomplished anything wonderful for the Estate tonight, though I do feel excited about pushing forward on it. Having another come alongside me is a powerful thing, and tonight I felt that Philip and I really have a common goal. Something good may come of this yet.

But before that, there remains one lingering image from the evening and that is of Wander. Wanda Maxwell never left my mind after I conjured her during our discussion tonight. A part of me feels I need to find out what happened to her, not just so I have her full story to tell Philip should the memory of his sister come up again, but because she was a friend with a common goal as well. We both wanted out of Lowerton. Only she made the decision to leave; I was the one who stayed behind. I don't want that to happen again. I don't want to abandon my goal this time. The Estate needs me to be its Wander, to live and to act with purpose.

A Memory of Wanda Maxwell

Wander and I were such different people growing up. One story comes to mind that explains it all. It's the thought that came to me that night in the arbor when I watched her walk away forever. It's the memory that resurfaces every once in a while in my dreams, where nobody comes to find us and we stay lost forever.

It was the summer following third grade, and in a moment of inspiration, the Kleine family, a newly arrived addition to our trailer court, invited Wander and me to join their daughter, Susannah, for an afternoon of family fun out at Bald Eagle State Park. Actually, our families were invited as well but the Maxwells rarely left their trailer, and Glen, unlike me, was such a bad swimmer he hated being anywhere near water. So it was just the five of us. The plan was to grill hamburgers and hot dogs, go swimming, and throw the Frisbee around. Only the whole thing fell apart twenty minutes after arriving at the park.

While Mr. and Mrs. Kleine got the food ready, we decided to play a quick game of hide-and-seek. Susannah was *it*, and as she began her count to twenty, Wander and I bolted into the woods nearby, just off the lakeshore. We could hide anywhere within five feet of where we entered the woods and never be found. But Wander continued to walk deeper in, so I followed her, assuming she knew a better spot. She was better in the woods than I, though, and soon it was all I could do to keep her denim jacket in sight. She weaved in and out of tree trunks as if she was headed somewhere—someplace she was needed badly.

We walked and walked until finally, for no reason I could see, Wander stopped. And then sat. I caught up with her and I still remember the look on her face, angry almost, with eyes that had seen too much. They reminded me of Meryl's more than any of the other kids. Or maybe Betty Francis, a high schooler a few trailers down from me, whom the police came to get one day after her boyfriend stumbled out into the street with a steak knife buried in the meat of his thigh.

"She won't find us here," Wander said through a smile.

I looked around. We'd stopped in a small clearing ringed by large firs. Wander was now sitting on a moss-covered boulder. It didn't seem like that great of a hiding place. "Where are we?"

Wander looked at me from her rock and shrugged, that same little grin on her face. Suddenly the whole forest seemed cold. I remember wrapping my arms around myself and turning about in slow little circles. We were lost.

"How do we get back?" I asked after a moment.

"Back? But she's looking for us. We'll lose if we go back."

I tried persuading Wander to stand up, to start finding our way back to the lake.

"She'll find us," she kept saying for ten minutes or more before I finally came up with an argument even Wander couldn't refuse.

"The food will be done by now, Wander. The game will be over, because lunch will be ready. I bet they're calling us right now. Susannah won't win because her parents will make us come in."

She blinked a few times at this, stood, and without a word began walking a straight line back through the woods from which we'd emerged.

Last time I play with her, I said to myself. I was glad to get moving again. The bugs had found us now, and my shorts and T-shirt offered little in the way of protection.

We walked on and on in a straight line. Until we came to a hill.

"Did we climb a hill . . . or come down one?" I called to Wander.

Again she shrugged.

This time the tears came. It was one thing to not know where we were going, but it was quite another to not know how to get back to where we started out, back to the familiar.

Wander began tromping up the hill, her little feet pointed straight ahead, her legs as efficient as the relentless second hand of the watch I'd taken off back at the picnic site. She would walk till the earth fell out from under her, and I knew following her would do no good.

"Wander!" I called and called, but she wouldn't stop. In another few seconds she'd crested the hill and disappeared.

I moved to the closest tree and leaned against it, trying to think things through. The only thought that came was a random piece of advice Meryl had spouted off some years before on a special trip to a nearby orchard to pick apples. She was talking about her home in Richmond again, of the peach trees that grow there, when suddenly she veered into a story about getting lost on the back acres of her uncle's farm and how all the other kids wanted to try to find their way back but Meryl alone knew what to do—stay put. When lost, just stay put. That way the one lost won't be moving away from those people out searching.

So I sat.

Twenty minutes passed. The air started swirling with gnats and mosquitoes. Above me, blackbirds called to one another and flitted from limb to limb. I tried singing to myself but the only line I could think of was "Somewhere over the rainbow, way up high" and soon I grew tired of repeating it. My tears had stopped for the moment, replaced by a sudden thirst. And everything seemed very bright. I closed my eyes and rested my head on my hands for a minute until the bugs forced me to my feet.

Another five minutes or so went by. Staying put began to seem like a stupid idea.

What if . . .

I never finished the thought. I heard voices.

They were somewhere off in the distance yet still very much voices. I screamed the only word one screams at such a time: "Help!"

Instantly the voices drew a little closer. I yelled again, waving my hands as if that might help. There was a crash of underbrush, and Mr. Kleine stumbled into the clearing where I sat. His face was a vivid red and shimmered with both sweat and anger. But he didn't shout at me. He just beckoned with a finger, and I went immediately to him.

"What in the world were you two—" He looked around. "Where's the other one? Wander, or whatever you call her?"

I couldn't say the words. I just pointed to the hill over which Wander had disappeared.

Mr. Kleine looked confused. "She kept walking?" he said to himself. Then he looked at me. "Didn't you try to stop her? Why'd she keep walking?"

I shrugged and then said the thing I'd been thinking the moment Wander took that first step up the hill, her small feet breaking twigs with every step. "I think she wanted to get lost, sir."

I realize now I was wrong in saying that. Wander never wanted to get lost; she just wanted very badly to go someplace, anyplace, else. She was only nine years old, so getting herself lost was the only road available to take her there. It's what separated us all these years. We both wanted out, but she's the only one who risked the journey, who put foot in front of foot and crossed over. I've just stayed put, unwilling to hazard a directionless step. Only no one's come crashing through these woods, nobody's stepped down from the high hill.

But to finish the story, Wander didn't get lost that day. She came upon a road, and a patrol car that happened to be passing by picked her up and took her back to Little Pines. I didn't see her until a week later. The Kleines never again invited either of us to do anything with their daughter, fearing, I suppose, that Susannah would follow us into the woods one day and never be heard from again.

We hated her for having parents who cared so much.

Friday, February 12, 1999

The week has been busy, leaving me few opportunities to think more about Wander, thank goodness, but also taking away any time I would've used to sit down and write. This evening, in fact, is the first real chance I've had without feeling exhausted, and the list of things to catch up on is large.

On Monday three things happened. First, I got a return call from our state senator's office that said they might have time to meet our Save Quinlin's Estate group and that I should pencil in a meeting at the capitol in Harrisburg. Later that day I went into Lowerton and rented a post-office box for the Save Quinlin's Estate Foundation, and after two evenings spent plastering posters with Ben, Philip, and Sandra all over campus and around Lowerton and the nearby towns of Bellefonte and Clearfield, we got our first donation yesterday. The check was for one hundred dollars from Flower Me With Love florists. I took the check directly to the bank and deposited the money into a savings account we'd opened up for the Estate's rescue. So our balance, including the fifty dollars it took to open the account, is now $150. I don't want to do the math necessary to figure out how many more checks of this size we'd need to reach our goal.

Finally, I took the same opportunity at the bank to check my personal finances, and the situation, though not yet dire, needed supplementing. It was a problem solved before I could even begin to worry. Walking across town to my car, I passed the small storefront office of the *Lowerton Express*, the local weekly paper. A sign taped to the window announced they were looking for part-time reporters/editors. When I poked my nose into her office and told her I was interested in the position, editor-in-chief Flora Howardson agreed to interview me on the spot. The interview lasted ten minutes; my first assignment is to cover the upcoming school board meeting on Monday. The pay is pitiful, but the hours are slim enough not to interfere with my work on behalf of the Estate. And the chance to be given press access to the more important men and women in town certainly can't hurt. Who knows, maybe I'll meet someone willing to lead our cause at city hall.

What remains of the week: a stack of photocopied grant applications, the originals sent out yesterday, and a mass of contradictions between two stories I can't seem to find my way around. The first I heard from Embeth Graveston during my visit with her on Wednesday afternoon. The second story came from Dwight.

He and Monique were back in town following that unexpected visit to see her sister. I was glad to hear that things, for the moment at least, had settled some. We ate dinner in their living room, after which Monique hugged me, expressed her thanks for my coming over, and said she and Vanessa were going out to see a movie. Dwight sat down on the couch with a mug of coffee, and while he still seemed reluctant, he offered me everything he knew about how my father, Glen Lawson, knew Evangeline Graveston, Embeth's daughter.

I don't know what to do other than to write both next to each other and let them stand. If research into the past has taught me anything, it's that sometimes such a thing is necessary. One would never think such wildly divergent stories could exist at the same time, but they do, and often the truth rests somewhere in between. In this case that's between madness and sunshine. All the while the Estate towers high above it all in its solid, immovable way, the only thing that doesn't appear to change from story to story.

THE GRAVESTONS: CHARLES, EMBETH, AND EVANGELINE

"Looking back over one's life, there are years that can be boiled down to a single memory or two, and then there are the years that can be remembered for each individual day. The year 1942 was one of those." This was how Embeth started.

The nation had changed. Americans had gotten out from under their weariness and pulled together, readying for the fight to come in Europe and the Pacific. These were some of Lowerton's finest days, the factory at full steam and everyone in town full of conversation about what might lie ahead. Yet not a single person predicted what would happen next.

The Army arrived, just three Jeeps parked at city hall, and finalized the sale of Quinlin's Estate. Less than two days after the transaction was announced, twenty-two men showed up along with a half dozen engineers to turn the Estate into a radio installation. The town wouldn't have been more proud had Roosevelt himself decided to set up the war room in the Estate's ballroom. Not only were they manufacturing artillery shells, but now they'd become a communications crossroads as well. Young women strolled through town awaiting the next wave of fresh soldiers, and men bragged that Lowerton had become strategic enough that Hitler could find worse places to send his Luftwaffe. Charles didn't enter the conversation but as always let his actions speak for him by enrolling in the U.S. armed forces at the age of thirty-six. He'd heard a rumor that they could use a part-timer, one good with calculations and figuring.

"It's mostly just a formality," he explained to Embeth at home that evening. "You can't be a civilian to get in the place." He tried to stifle a smile yet was unable when he added sheepishly, "But I am going to get a uniform."

Embeth cocked an eyebrow and told him she was all in favor of that, then together they put almost-four-year-old Evangeline to bed early that night.

The days rolled by. With spring, the flags bloomed like crocuses on storefronts and housefronts. Any day of sunshine could find Embeth, Evangeline, and Charles walking together to the Estate or the factory or sometimes just around town. They ate picnics in the shadow of the thick outer wall and left Evangeline with friends from church or with Charles's sister when invited to the occasional officers' dance, Charles surprising everyone with his smooth lindy hop and Charleston steps. These good days continued for almost two years, until the day after Evangeline's sixth birthday when, for no reason she ever explained, Evangeline screamed through her bedroom door that she never wanted to walk to the Estate or the factory with Embeth and Charles again.

After that, the years began to merge and topple over one another, and it seemed that Evangeline was both young girl and blossoming woman at the same time; Charles both sturdy and afflicted with palsy; Lowerton both proud and grim. Embeth, however, changed little. Some gray hair, perhaps a bit of waggle beneath her arms. Even so, her back stayed true, her eyes bright, and her smile constant. But soon enough even she faltered.

Charles, who'd gone directly from the Army into teaching mathematics at the Estate, began to tremble to the point that writing out the equations on the chalkboard for Lowerton

High's students became near impossible for him. Evangeline grew worried at her father's condition and spent nights and weekends at home with him, rather than out with friends or other students from the university. It was 1959 and she was preparing to become a teacher. Lowerton would hire her a year later when she graduated, and she'd walk the short distance from their home downtown to the new high school where she'd teach mathematics just like her father had.

"Soon, anyone who can add in this town," Charles toasted one evening after the start of school, "will have learned from a Graveston." Evangeline had just given a small smile and then the moment ended, and before long Charles was making the trip to the hospital three times a week for medication, and the days and months couldn't be remembered because they were almost all the same. But the pills worked, or at least seemed to, and the trembling lessened. For the next few years father and daughter taught side by side, until the day Evangeline packed her suitcase and said it was time for something new. She wanted to join the commune that had moved in.

It was impulsive, yet Embeth and Charles focused on her need finally to get out of the house. At the time, this felt right and good, like the first moment in another stretch of years for which Embeth would remember each day. But then the call came and she and her husband found themselves hurrying down to the hospital to find out their daughter had fallen, tumbled down Quinlin's winding stairs, and that there wouldn't be days or hours or anything else worth remembering. Only a sense that just as things seemed to be going right, it'd all gone horribly wrong.

On the tape, Embeth took a deep breath. *"How's that for forty years in a nutshell? And there's not much else to add since then. Charles died seven years ago, only months after we moved in here. Strange how that is. The only two people worth anything in my life died almost as soon as they moved from our home downtown. I never know what to make of that. I never know why I'm still living here either. Maybe there's one more move I have to make."*

WHAT DWIGHT KNEW OF EVANGELINE AND GLEN

Glen Lawson knew Evangeline Graveston—"Eve" he always called her—in two different periods of his life, claiming he knew two Eve Gravestons. "The two faces of Eve," he'd say over drinks. It was one of his few jokes and he repeated it often.

He met her as classmate. Born just months apart, they attended the Estate together in the years after the fire. They took math with her father, acted together in *He Saved Lowerton*, she the ministering angel who whispers a vision of the Estate into Quinlin's ear, went to the same dances, separately, and walked across the same ballroom floor to receive their diplomas.

"Prettiest thing in Lowerton," Glen often said, usually while on his fourth or fifth beer. "Would have made Meryl look like the worse half of a donkey."

Sometimes Meryl was present, sitting in the booth even, but he'd say it anyway. She'd stare right through him or just get up and stalk out. But whether she was there or not, the first half of the story always ended the same way. Glen would shake his head as if disappointed by the very passing of life and say, "Eve's only problem was her being nuttier than a Baby Ruth." Another round would be finished and then part two, "the daffy part," would commence.

The second time Glen knew Evangeline began seven years later in 1963, after he'd returned from seeing the world of industrial Ohio, with cold sweats interrupting his nights from seeing visions of a friend getting crushed under a steel beam that had let loose and fallen. He admitted to barely recognizing himself, and Eve had changed as well. A different Glen, a different Evangeline.

She'd earned her degree and accepted a position teaching geometry and algebra at Lowerton High. Otherwise she stayed entirely in her own world in the Gravestons' house downtown. Townsfolk couldn't understand why such a pretty girl—"She was like Grace Kelly, only she filled a sweater," Glen claimed—sheltered herself inside so much. A fellow couldn't start a conversation with her, let alone request a date, and she never lingered outside on the porch like most everyone else. To talk with her a man would have to get invited into the parlor, which for many seemed too much work, especially when teams of two or three attractive aides retreated from the orphanage on their nights off and headed into town looking for somebody to ask them to a drive-in or a dance at Walt's, the club outside of town. Despite the obstacles with courting Evangeline, Glen had two things other men did not: perseverance and good timing.

His third-shift job at the factory over at seven, Glen hoofed it back to his room at the boardinghouse to get some sleep. From this he'd wake up hungry and have a bottle of lemonade and half a sandwich on the porch, leaning against one of the posts by the steps.

The town clock would soon chime at half past two, and

within minutes kids would come running down the lane, thrilled at the end of another school day. He'd call out a greeting to the friend of a co-worker or laugh at a bully chasing a classmate. Mostly, though, he'd just stand there biding his time, waiting another half hour for when Evangeline Graveston hurried by.

"Afternoon, Miss Graveston," he'd yell. Or "Keep warm, Miss Graveston," during the bitter January days. Every time, without fail, she walked past without even turning her head. For months he watched her go by and never got frustrated or bored. After all, there was nothing else to do at three o'clock on a weekday afternoon. Evangeline walking past him was as good as it would get.

Finally, on an April day in 1964, Evangeline stopped when he called to her, turned, and took two steps toward the porch. She sized him up with eyes that narrowed to slits, and Glen felt his breath catch in his throat. It was as close as he'd seen her; she looked chiseled from marble, one of those Greek sculptures come to life.

Eve took one more step toward him and said in a voice like arsenic, "Mr. Lawson, I am *not* Evangeline Graveston and would appreciate if you stopped referring to me as such! Good day." She then turned and stormed off.

Glen couldn't even take pleasure in the sway of her departure. He just swirled his bottle of lemonade and wondered. Wondered what in the world she meant. Wondered if the rumors around town were true and something had happened to the girl. Wondered who, if not Evangeline Graveston, she thought she was.

He'd find out a few months later.

After their odd conversation Glen gave up yelling out to

Eve, but he didn't stop standing on the porch to watch her as she walked by. He'd just wait, sip a bottle of root beer or RC Cola, breathe a long sigh when she appeared, and think to himself that it was all just a crying shame. Then came summer and school let out, and Glen thought he'd forget the whole mess.

One Saturday, though, while replenishing the gravel in the circular drive outside the outer wall of the Estate, Glen backed out of the way of an approaching new Buick and was surprised when the driver said his name.

"Glen Lawson? I heard through the wind that you were back in town."

An older silver-haired gentleman stepped out of the car, and Glen couldn't believe that Mr. Graveston recognized him. It'd been years since the man had sat with him and taught him to remember lines for the Quinlin play. Before he could say hello, another voice called out from behind them. It was Mrs. Embeth Graveston, her hours helping to care for the children finished. She approached, kissed her husband on the cheek, and turned when he introduced her to Glen.

"Yes, you were in Eve's class at school, weren't you? So nice to see you."

"How is your daughter?" Glen asked, wanting to know if they'd admit to her having slipped round the bend.

"Wonderful!" Mrs. Graveston answered, and it sounded as though she believed it. "In fact, I think she'd be thrilled to see an old friend. Would you care to join us for dinner?"

Glen declined once but both Charles and Embeth insisted and soon he was agreeing to meet them that very evening. As the couple drove off with a wave, Glen wondered what he was stepping into. Was the whole family batty?

His answer came that night and was unexpected. The family seemed perfectly normal, even Evangeline, who gave no hint as to what had happened before. She chatted, smiled, laughed at Glen's weak attempts at humor, and dazzled him before dessert even hit the table. Perhaps he'd misunderstood her. Probably she didn't like being yelled at in public. No good woman would. He finished his lemon chiffon and couldn't believe his luck when Mr. and Mrs. Graveston offered to step out of the room so he and Evangeline could catch up on things.

The minute they left, Eve transformed. Her round, pleasant eyes narrowed. The smile vanished and she cocked her head in a way that made Glen think of a snake. The worst of it was that she looked even more beautiful than she had before, and he couldn't stop staring.

"I swear if she'd pulled out a gun, I couldn't have made myself get out of the way," he'd recall numerous times later.

Eve asked him why he was here.

"Your folks invited me," he quickly replied, then decided to try a little sugar. "And I wanted to see you again."

She smiled. Wickedly. "I'm not my mother. That won't work on me."

Glen didn't know what that meant and, gorgeous or not, he was now becoming a little fed up with her. She didn't have to like him, but there was no reason to glare at him like he was dirt.

"What's the matter with you?" he asked. "The whole town's talking about you." Her eyes widened. "Saying you're not all the way right, and I'm inclined to believe them."

"I'm just fine," she said, regaining her chilling stare. "I know who I am."

"We all do. You're Evangeline Graveston."

She didn't answer right away, just stared. At first Glen thought she was continuing to glare but then realized she focused on something just past his shoulder. It was like she'd gone into a trance. He was about to get up when her eyes focused on his. They were a cold blue, the color ice will take on sometimes.

"I need a friend," she said. It sounded like a threat. "Can I trust you?"

"Sure," said Glen, though he didn't much mean it.

"Okay."

She leaned forward.

Glen leaned too.

"I'm Evangeline Quinlin," she said. "That house on the hill is mine."

Part Two

I've read both stories back to back three times since writing them and don't see how they match up without someone lying, or someone being lied to. A quick call to Dwight convinced me it wasn't my father. Glen may have been a lot of things, but never a good liar, especially when he'd been drinking.

"And the story went exactly the same every time, Eve. It's hard to tell a lie the same way twice; trust me, I've done my share."

Which left Embeth. My call to her still has me confused.

A woman, not Embeth, answered after the third ring. She had a sweet voice and asked how she could help me. I introduced myself, explained why I was calling, and asked to speak with Embeth. There was some whispering and then the voice said, "I'm sorry, but Mrs. Graveston no longer wishes to continue her communication with you. Good day."

A click followed and that was it, silence.

After a stunned minute I called back. No answer. I checked

the number, dialed again, and still got no response. Now, ten hours and twelve tries later, I've given up. I'll drive in Monday since I have to deliver my first article to the *Express*, or tomorrow after church, and try to see Embeth in person.

It feels strange to write that sentence, because I've only been to church, counting Christmas and Easter, maybe two dozen times in my life. Glen had little use for church while I was growing up, and even though it was true Meryl had grown up in a charismatic home down South, she hadn't bothered to stick with it while living with us. I'm not sure when her recent bout of religiosity began.

The last time I attended church was my junior year of college. A sophomore girl on my floor, Amanda Owens, invited me after we'd gotten to know each other while trying to counsel my roommate, Tara, through a miserable stretch of months that included her parents splitting up, a high-school friend breaking her back, and a few bombed exams. Amanda always seemed to calm Tara. When I asked her how she got so good at listening to people, she explained how her faith made it possible. Dwight's conversion had taken place around this time, so I thought there might be something to this religion thing, but a half-dozen visits to a Christian and Missionary Alliance church off campus didn't reveal it to me. Eventually the semester ended, and I only saw Amanda the next year by chance, when we happened to run into each other in the student union or on our way to class. She asked me once to join her for church, and I turned her down saying I would be too busy studying that weekend. It never came up again.

Until this afternoon, that is. Philip called to invite me to tomorrow's earlier service.

"It's totally not a Valentine's thing," he said. I gave a surprised glance to my wall calendar to check the day. Tomorrow was Valentine's Day.

"Do you typically go to the early service?" I asked.

"Usually I go to both. I sing in the choir. So you can come to either one, if you're interested. And maybe we can get a cup of coffee afterward?"

"Why not?" I said. He told me the easiest place for me to sit in the sanctuary so he could join me when the choir finished.

I thought that'd be it for the conversation, but he didn't seem eager to hang up and so we ended up chatting for almost an hour. I told him about the odd phone calls to Embeth's apartment, and he agreed something must have happened to cause Embeth suddenly to want to avoid me. He asked how she'd seemed when we'd last spoken. I couldn't remember anything out of the ordinary to tell him. Maybe her delving into the past and resurrecting her dead daughter and husband was harder than she made it look. But I still can't imagine she wouldn't just tell me herself that she was unable to tell me any more stories. What I couldn't understand was the other voice. Who was that? I concluded that, until I heard Embeth's voice myself, I wouldn't believe she no longer wished to talk to me.

We also talked about the upcoming trip to Harrisburg, which had finally gotten final approval for Thursday. Philip was sorry he couldn't switch his shift at the airport to come along, but I assured him that Sandra and I could handle it. I was nearly finished with my portion of the proposal, and we were scheduled to meet on Wednesday to go over our presentation and work out any kinks. After a few more minutes we hung up and I found myself staring at the calendar again, at the empty little square for February 14, and thinking that whether he'd intended to or not, Philip had filled it all the same.

I turned my attention back to the Embeth situation, turning over explanations in my head that might explain what could possibly be going on. I then recalled a conversation I had with Dwight right after his conversion. It was the most serious talk we'd ever had about his faith, and it mostly centered on Glen and how poorly he'd reacted to the whole thing. Dwight blamed it on Glen hating change and worrying how their friendship would become different. I remember shrugging and saying that might be true.

"And anyway," I added, "Glen's never trafficked much with God. I'm sure this baffles him as much as if you'd announced you wanted to become a woman."

Dwight gave me an odd look, and I remember worrying that I'd offended him. He rubbed his bewhiskered chin. (This was when he had a beard, one that itched constantly. Soon after he shaved it off, along with the rest of his hair, Glen muttered to me one day in the trailer, "If that's what religion does to you, I want no part of it.") Dwight motioned for me to be seated on his couch. He said, "Your father's got a bit more theology in him than you might realize." He then told me a story that frustrates me to this very day because of all it explains and all it leaves unspoken.

CHRISTMAS, JULY 1977

Glen and Dwight had returned to Little Pines from the Estate at a quarter past midnight after responding to an urgent call from the night watchman about someone lingering at the top of the tower. The perpetrator—three feet tall and plastic— sat between them now on the vinyl seat of Glen's Nova, a rosy grin on his face. In spite of the stagnant nighttime heat, Dwight hummed "Here Comes Santa Claus" the entire ride home.

"How do you think he got up there?" he asked as they pulled into Glen's drive.

"Blitzen," Glen replied, irritated. "How should I know."

Dwight grabbed Santa, and he and Glen got out of the Nova, careful not to slam the doors and risk waking the neighbors. They were walking to the trailer when a voice spoke out from the darkness.

"Merry Christmas."

They turned. The orange tip of a cigarette glowed from the steps of the trailer next door. There was a squeak, a few shuffling steps, and then Vic Mulligan appeared. He had on a bathing suit that looked wet, and nothing else.

"Evening, Vic," said Glen. "Heat keeping you up?" It was a polite question. Everyone knew Victor Mulligan didn't sleep at night, not since receiving the news of his brother's disappearance outside Da Nang.

"Sure is," Vic said. He pointed his cigarette at the plastic man tucked under Dwight's arm. "What's with Saint Nick?"

"Rescue operation. He was about to take a high dive from four stories up."

Vic nodded as if the answer made sense. The three stood in a tight circle and before either could move, Glen motioned with his head to the trailer. "How about some beers?"

Dwight checked his watch, obviously pretending to be worried about the time. It was now half past midnight. The beer was why he'd come in the first place. "Sounds good," he said. Vic agreed too.

"Stay here," Glen said. "I'll go get 'em." He disappeared inside, the aluminum door squeaking just a little, and soon returned with three Rolling Rock longnecks. Once the bottles were open, the three sat, clinked necks quietly, and toasted the night.

"To Christmas in July," Dwight said.

"To Christmas every day," Glen added and they all drank.

There was the chirp of crickets, the buzz of the nearby streetlamp, the occasional car growling down Marker Road, but for the most part the night was quiet. Vic was the first to break the silence.

"You ever believe in him?" he asked, pointing over his shoulder to the plastic Santa standing on the trailer steps as though waiting to be let in.

Both Dwight and Glen nodded.

"Did you teach your little girl about him?" Vic continued, looking at Glen now.

"I don't *teach* her. She's seen the Christmas specials on TV so knows all about it. Makes a list out to him every year. I wouldn't doubt if Meryl still makes a list for him." He laughed, sadlike.

Vic shook his head. "It's a scam. Raising kids' hopes to believe in something that ain't gonna come true."

There was silence after that, and Dwight thought Glen might be chewing over some choice things to say to this part-time junkie who sat and drank Glen's beer while criticizing how he raised his kid. Instead, when Glen spoke there was more sadness in his voice.

"What else they got? It's something at least, a little hope. I'm bringing up Eve to get as far away from here as possible. But she's got to be able to look forward to something in the meantime."

More silence. Dwight finished his beer, rolled the bottle across the grass toward Glen's trash can, and stretched out in the lawn chair. Above, a lazy half-moon slipped behind a bank of clouds. Dwight didn't bother checking his watch.

"Eve's going away from here?" said Vic.

Glen nodded.

"How do you know?"

"She just will. She's smart. I can just feel it."

Dwight perked up at this. Glen talked a lot about his feeling things. Dwight couldn't count how many times he heard Glen say how he *felt* he would find the gold at the Estate, and Dwight never knew what he was talking about. Now seemed a good time to ask. "How do you mean by that?"

"I don't know," Glen answered and shifted in his chair. He seemed uncomfortable, as though he didn't like talking about it. "That's just what it is—a feeling. Like something's watching over her."

Dwight and Vic traded glances.

"Like a guardian angel you mean?" Dwight asked. He hadn't been kidding, but Glen glared at him anyway.

"No," he growled.

"Then what?"

"I don't know!" Glen said, his voice low but angry. "I just feel that way. Like I'm looking out for her, but somebody else is too."

Vic smiled to himself. "Like Santy Claus."

"Shut up."

"The girl's not going to know which way to turn. Especially if you fill her head with thoughts like that."

Glen stood up and reached into his front pocket. Before Vic or Dwight could move, a knife came out, its blade gleaming in the moonlight. Dwight struggled to his feet. Vic stayed seated but set his beer on the ground to prepare himself for what might come next.

But Glen didn't advance. Instead, he walked over to the trailer steps, picked up Santa, flipped him over, and buried the knife into the base. He hacked at the plastic until a disk the size of a pancake fell to the ground. With Santa tucked under his arm, without a word Glen walked to Mulligan's flagpole and started climbing. He got six feet up using just one arm when Santa slipped from his grasp. He cursed and slid back down. Dwight and Vic stood transfixed. Glen stripped off his belt, lashed it around the plastic figure, and grabbed the strap with his teeth. Two hands now free, he scaled the twenty-foot pole in seconds, hoisted the Santa high and slammed it onto the flagpole.

"Better?" he yelled down to Dwight and Vic, then slid back to the ground.

"You crazy?" Vic shouted.

"There," Glen said, pointing to Santa. "That's who's watching over my kid, since you both were so bent on having an answer. Now get out of here."

With that, he stormed inside. The aluminum door shook on its hinges, and somewhere in the trailer park a dog started barking. Dwight could hear Meryl's voice coming from inside the trailer, but soon all was quiet. He looked at his watch—it was after one o'clock.

Vic Mulligan stood staring up at the Santa that seemed to hover high in the air over the trailer park. With one hand he lit himself another cigarette, stared for another few seconds, and turned to Dwight. "You believe that?"

Dwight shook his head. He wasn't sure what he believed anymore.

"How you getting home?" Vic asked.

Dwight looked at the Nova and cursed. Glen had promised him a beer and then a ride back to his place. Vic didn't have a car. He thumbed his way all over town. It was too late for hitching tonight, though, especially for a black man.

"Sleep in my bed," said Vic. "He'll have cooled off by tomorrow. I'll wake you so he'll give you a ride to work."

"You don't need it?" Dwight said, although he knew the answer.

"Naw, I like seeing the day in."

Dwight couldn't describe the pain he saw in Victor Mulligan's eyes when he said this, as though the last thing Vic wanted was to spend another sleepless night sucking pack after pack of coffin nails on the steps of his trailer, staring at the blackness of space and trying not to think of his brother, half a world away, dead or dying in a heat that never quit.

SUNDAY, FEBRUARY 14, 1999

That story stayed with me throughout church today, I'm ashamed to say. Every time the pastor mentioned God or Jesus, all I could picture was a little apple-cheeked man with a pipe,

red fur clothing, and a herd of reindeer following him like dis-
ciples. When I tried to explain this to Philip over coffee he
didn't appear to understand. Now that I think back on it, I don't
blame him. I'm impressed he wasn't offended. My turning the
Son of God into an overweight gift wrangler would cause most
Christians to cry blasphemy. Or some at least. The two I know
best, Dwight and now Philip, would just look at me weird and
change the subject.

That said, I didn't get much from the service. To be honest
I was too busy feeling like everybody was looking at me. The
church is small, seats maybe 150, so a newcomer's easy to spot.
And they do the drill where everybody stands up and shakes
their neighbors' hands, which is when I got asked four times if
this was my first visit and how wasn't that great when I said
yes. Philip coming down from the choir to sit beside me only
made things worse. I heard at least two couples murmuring to
each other as if everything made sense now. My only consolation was that Philip was uninterested in sticking around afterward to chat, and so within minutes of the service letting out
we were across town at the Dunkin' Donuts and sharing a box
of Munchkins.

"Glad you could come," he said after taking a bite. "How did
you like it?"

I nodded and he seemed content with that, which pleased me
more than anything else that'd happened. I'd expected him to
make his spiel at some point, his pitch for First Baptist Church,
but so far he hadn't. I was impressed.

A minute later he said, "You know what I like most about
that church?" and I couldn't help smiling. He'd earned a
response, though, so I asked, "What?"

"They have a good perspective. People can disagree with each other. They all know there are only a few really important things that matter, so they learn to live with their differences. I just bring it up because I got some more questions from choir members today about my maze walking. Other places, my church in Pittsburgh, get too freaked out about stuff like that."

I had no idea what he was talking about. I asked him to explain his maze walking.

He slapped his forehead, realizing he'd jumped ahead of me, and began explaining how he visited the Maze at Quinlin's Estate once or twice a week to walk and meditate and pray.

I remembered now him mentioning this before, at one of our meetings, and asked how the idea had come to him. Most people find the Maze so flustering that meditation is the last thing on their minds. The story that came next was the spiel I'd expected earlier, except I didn't mind because it answered the question I'd asked and gave me a bit deeper glimpse at Philip and his life. We all have our stories to tell, I guess, our spiels to give. This was his. As we left, he promised me that next time I'd give mine. All I could think was, *Next time. He said, "Next time."*

How Philip Came to Walk the Maze

They kicked Philip out of Bucknell during his junior year, after his third run-in with the law left him with a shattered leg. The first two times—drunk and disorderly once, and part of a dorm brawl another time—were forgiven since he was suffering so much due to the disappearance of his sister. But resisting arrest and a high-speed chase across the twisting roads of Pennsylvania that ended in a car so mangled it took four hours to pry him out couldn't be overlooked. The dean discharged him with a phone call. He managed to avoid prison because a lenient judge sentenced him to counseling and community service as soon as he healed. But that was the rub; he wasn't healing, and soon the painkillers they prescribed weren't enough either. His parents felt something else was needed and so they sent him to recover at Astonbury.

Ten days after checking in, Philip felt the first indications that his life might come back under control. Scared and hobbled by constant pain in his leg since they'd begun weaning him off of Percodan, Philip woke just after midnight on his tenth day to the tremors of a vicious thunderstorm. For nearly a half hour he watched out his window at the swirls of wind and shattering fingers of lightning seizing the area. One bolt even struck a tree in the orchard below his room before the storm blew past and he was able to return to sleep. Waking a few hours later, Philip remembered not the storm but the fact that he'd remained transfixed for almost thirty minutes without feeling any pain and had fallen back to sleep with hardly a second thought. His leg still ached that morning, but he swore the discomfort was less. His nurses were thrilled by the news, and his counselor, Anne Bowers, nodded as if she'd been expecting the change all along.

"You're on the way," she said.

In the week that followed, the discussion stopped focusing on Philip's pain, which lessened with each passing day, and began addressing his future. Without a college degree, without financial resources, what would he do with his life once he left Astonbury? It was recommended he see Pastor Louis Hopper, a specialist in corralling the lost.

"You got a world-view?" the pastor asked in their first meeting. He was a giant of a man, with a thick beard and friendly eyes. His voice filled the small meeting room as though he were speaking to an entire congregation rather than an audience of one.

"World-view?"

"Answers to the big questions. You know—'Does life have meaning?' That sort of thing."

"I haven't had an answer to anything in a long time," Philip admitted and Pastor Hopper commended him for being honest.

"There's wisdom in realizing what you don't know, as much as there is in understanding what you do know."

"I'm a real wise man then, because I don't get that either," Philip said with a smile.

Each day, for that last week in Astonbury, Pastor Hopper and Philip examined where Philip should be aiming his life. At first the discussions were difficult for Philip, but soon he began to understand something. The pastor's suggestions were not to look to college or career or even marriage and family. Instead, he took out a small cross dangling from a chain and said this was the better answer, better than anything else.

"Careers end, relationships fail, education fades. But God never changes; He's always there. Life is just the long walk following Him. And if anybody calls you crazy along the way, you can just say, 'You don't know what I know' and then tell them about it."

A day before his discharge, in the small chapel at Astonbury, Philip's request for baptism was fulfilled. It hadn't been a hard choice—the memory of barely being able to steady his hands was still fresh, as were the darker recollections of nights filled with inescapable chills. He'd cried out many times for some kind

of help, some kind of escape, and now the answer seemed so
obvious, so astonishing. Before a group of five witnesses that
included his parents, nurses, and his counselor, Philip confessed
that all the steps he'd taken in his life had been in the wrong
direction. He wanted to stop. With God's help, with God's urging, his eyes might never fall again, and his journey might be
straight ahead to the Cross on which his life had been rescued.

Three weeks later Philip realized how hard that task would
be when shreds of his sister's shirt were discovered tangled in
some briars along the Allegheny River. The night of Jack and
Cokes that came after was nothing that could ever be considered
a straight path to God, but the sorrow he felt, both for his sister
and for losing control hinted that if he'd strayed, at least it
hadn't been too far off. Another session of counseling had him
confronting the fury he'd buried inside since Karen's abduction.
The next six months were not without their side steps—the
warm staggering of a boilermaker wasn't easy for him to forget—although he'd come to see that even his sidestepping had
somehow served a certain purpose. He couldn't explain it until
moving to Lowerton at the suggestion of a friend and visiting
the Maze for the first time. There he saw the puzzling contra-
diction of having every step be both in the right and wrong
directions. What mattered, he decided, was the walking, and
when he passed a man pressed trembling and sweating against
the wall, unwilling to move one more step, he felt it even more
clearly. Two hours later Philip emerged determined to return to
the Maze every chance he got, to remind himself of the greater
maze he walked every day, from morning to night.

THURSDAY, FEBRUARY 18, 1999

After all our preparation, after two nights of researching other historic homes—Carnegie's old estate outside Pittsburgh, Hearst's castle in San Simeon, the Boettcher mansion in Colorado, the David Davis mansion in Illinois, even Pena Palace in Portugal—after praising her for knowing her facts cold, Sandra abandoned us, abandoned the Estate. Just this morning and without explanation. She never showed up for our trip to Harrisburg, not even leaving a message.

What keeps me writing still, instead of calling this whole thing off, is that we persevered and the day turned out better than expected. Ben found a way to switch his class schedule so he could go with me to Harrisburg, and we were both floored by the enthusiasm we received. Eventually anyway. At first all we got was lukewarm coffee and wary glances from Senator Worley and her staff.

In fact, the meeting couldn't have gone worse. Ben broke into a coughing fit, I dropped my notes midway through the presentation and never regained my place, and the esteemed senator appeared about as receptive as a stone wall. She didn't yawn but she might as well have.

"I'll have my aides do some further investigating. Good day," she said when we'd finished. She then got up and left without even shaking our hands. It was the second time in recent days that somebody wished me a good day and then cut out on me. Thankfully our next visit with Representative Greg Evans salvaged the day.

We met in his office, and both Ben and I were amazed at how it resembled the cramped graduate-student offices back on

campus. Local representative is obviously designed as a way-
station career on the road to a position higher up the legislative
ladder. Greg Evans appears to at least make an effort to care.
For I couldn't help but notice the brochures, articles, and other
paraphernalia related to the Estate that littered his desk. He'd
done his research. I thanked him for that.

"I love that old place," he said. "Visited it a couple of times
a year when I was in college."

Dressed in slacks, shirt, and tie, sporting a square jaw and a
Kappa Phi's neat haircut, it didn't look like college could've been
too far in the past. Ben and I must have been staring at each
other wide-eyed, because Greg asked why we looked so surprised. Ben recounted the pathetic meeting we'd just had
minutes before a few floors up in the well-lit, spacious office of
Madame Senator.

"Ah, Senator Worley," he replied, a hint of knowing in his
voice. "Word around here is that she's going to try to make the
jump to a national race. Her energies, you'll find, are likely to be
divided."

"And yours?" Ben asked. His directness sort of shocked me,
yet didn't seem to faze Greg one bit.

"My energies are to do what's best for the families and
workers in my district. Saving the Estate may well be a step in
that direction. Now let's have a listen."

He took a seat, leaving Ben and me to go through our presentation once more. The difference couldn't be quantified. No
coughing, no dropping of placards, no bored look in our lis-
tener's eyes. Greg made a few informed inquiries about the
extent of the repairs needed to the Estate, asked about the number of jobs a functioning historical landmark might create, and

wondered about the feasibility of a partnership with the university.

In all, after I'd finished presenting two successful case his-
tories of other state-funded historical renovations, the meeting
lasted twenty-five minutes. Greg requested a copy of all the
information we'd carried with us and assured us he'd be contacting us with more questions in the near future. He also hinted
that he'd be back in the area around the middle of March, and
that it'd be great to set up a second meeting, perhaps even a tour
of the Estate at that time. He shook hands with both of us,
walked us to the nearest exit, and left us with the charge to
"keep fighting." Ben and I were speechless our entire walk back
to his hatchback.

"That went really well," he said finally, once we'd gotten in
and started worming our way from the capitol building to the
westbound highway. His thick fingers danced on the steering
wheel, and he looked like he was about to burst into a smile. As
we sped across the river onto 322W, it dawned on me how
instrumental he'd been in the day happening at all. The morning
was a blur and I'd called him out of panic. Now we were driving
home with a charge to keep moving forward and the feeling that
we might win this thing after all. I thanked Ben for five minutes
straight. Never once did he even glance over at me.

"Sure thing," he said after I finished and then grinned like
I'd never seen before. "I feel like singing."

The rest of the ride home we shared a few horrible duets to
whatever songs the radio offered for which we knew the lyrics—
the Beatles, U2. Ben surprised me by going solo with an awful
hair-band ballad, and we laughed ourselves silly through Celine
Dion's tribute to a love that not even the Titanic disaster could

kill. Both our voices hurt after that so we gave up the radio for conversation. We talked about future plans for the Estate, threw out reasons why Sandra might have bailed on us, and I even got him to talk about his plans once he graduated with his master's degree in architecture. He said he was considering a firm in Buffalo back home where he'd interned during his undergraduate years. They'd already offered him a spot in the company. Even with his Master of Architecture degree, he needed to apprentice somewhere for a while before earning his stripes as an architect.

"It's a commercial firm, though, that specializes in shopping mall design. I'm not sure if I want to get into that full time."

"What would you like to work on?"

He stayed silent for a moment, his eyes fixed on the road. I was about to repeat the question when he said, "Community."

I thought he might explain so I waited. But finally I had to ask, "Like houses and parks and schools?"

"No . . . I mean the anti-shopping mall. A place where people gather just to be around other people rather than to buy a pair of culottes."

The word struck me funny and I laughed. Ben turned, embarrassed.

"I know it sounds stupid and touchy-feely—"

"No, no," I said, trying to stifle a smile, "it was just the word *culottes*. I wasn't expecting it. I like your idea. We've become lots of little isolated lives being lived in close proximity."

He nodded. "Not too much of a market for that kind of design, though. So we'll see."

We drove another twenty minutes without touching on too much else of consequence and got home just after six o'clock. When he dropped me off I thanked him again for his help, and he said it was great it worked out so well. After he pulled away I hiked upstairs to my apartment and found two messages waiting for me. I expected one to be from Sandra explaining where she'd been. Instead, the first was from Philip to wish us luck and to say he'd be home that evening if I wanted to call and tell him how things had gone. The second was from Embeth Graveston.

"I'm calling from a neighbor's phone," she whispered. "I still want to talk with you. Lydia is the one not letting me. How can we meet. . . ?"

I've listened to the message four times since getting home, and in looking back through my notes, I found only one mention of a Lydia. Lydia Furrow—Charles's sister, Embeth's sister-in-law—the woman who never wanted her brother to marry the illegitimate daughter of the town jade.

SUNDAY, FEBRUARY 21, 1999

Another few appearances at church with Philip and I'm going to start feeling guilty for not putting anything in the little wooden tray when it goes by. Not that I wouldn't ever, it's just that money is tight, even with my most recent check from the *Express*. I noticed Philip doesn't put anything in either, but I didn't ask him about it at coffee today. A man, his money, and his God are a triangle with which I don't want to interfere. And it wouldn't have come up anyway, because today was a day of lost girls: Karen, Wander, and, in a sad way all its own, me.

It started with me telling him about Embeth's cryptic phone message and how I still hadn't been able to get in touch with her at Truant Gulch. I mentioned how it was almost as if she'd been kidnapped, and soon enough Karen's name came up.

"Did you ever find out what happened to her?"

"Only circumstantial evidence—clothes fibers, some bone fragments, an unreliable witness saying he saw a girl who matched her description get into a rusted-out Camry. The case is still open, but she's one of thousands."

"I never found out what happened to my friend who disappeared," I said, and his look reminded me that I'd chosen not to tell him about Wander before. "She was different from Karen. She was a runaway."

I gave a quick rundown of Wander, our pact to leave Lowerton, and how, as a freshman, she'd stepped from her trailer, slipped into the darkness, and was never seen again.

Philip seemed to think this over as if puzzled by something. "She was never seen again, by anyone?" he asked.

It was like he thought I'd been keeping something from him. And I was.

"Well, nobody reliable. The woman who lived in my trailer, Meryl Lakewood, swore she saw her a few years later, but I never believed her." After what I'd learned that day about how everything went so terribly wrong, why would I believe her? She had every reason to come up with anything that might take the spotlight off her.

Philip gave a shrug. Seeing as how he didn't exactly agree with me, I asked why he'd brought it up.

"It's just that runaways almost always get spotted by somebody, even long after they take off. I did a lot of reading when Karen vanished because the police kept trying to pin her as a delinquent. I think it makes their job easier if they can hang it on something other than a snatching. Your friend might've been telling the truth."

"She's not my friend."

And that was all the talk of Meryl Lakewood for the evening. After that, Philip shifted the conversation to me, saying it was my turn to talk today. He'd filibustered through our last coffee meeting and now he wanted to hear a story about me growing up. The one I told him was not about Wander or life in the trailer park, or about how I always feared being lost, or even how I came to know the Estate inside and out. The story I told was the one that seemed closest to his tale of Astonbury. It was about me growing up crooked and finding not a single person willing to help me straighten out.

STRAIGHTENING OUT

My fifth-grade teacher, Ms. Wesson, was the one who discovered it. She called me out of the relay race line, had me follow her inside to an empty classroom, and told me to stand straight for a moment. I thought I was being punished for pushing Margie Houser, but Ms. Wesson just looked at me, her mouth working as though solving a hard math problem in her head.

"Your stripes are crooked," she said finally.

I looked down instinctively but of course could see nothing. The outfit I had on, a long-sleeved navy dress with orange stripes cutting across the width of the dress, always made me think I looked like some sort of exotic tiger. Now Ms. Wesson seemed to be criticizing it.

"My stripes?"

"Come with me," she said and once again we were out in the hall, marching this time toward the main entrance. Principal Wright's office was near there. For a second I worried I might be in trouble for wearing crooked clothes, but then Ms. Wesson veered into the nurse's office and I followed. For three minutes I did toe-touches while the nurse and Ms. Wesson circled me. That night Glen explained the note I'd been asked to deliver to him.

"Scoliosis," he said. "We'll see what the doctor says."

Two weeks later, the doctor said "wait and see." I did have a curve in my back, although it wasn't dangerous as yet—not like any of the pictures he showed me of kids with an S for a spine—and might very well straighten out on its own.

"Stand up straight and tall. And make sure you sit that way too. Can you do that?"

I said I'd try and we left with an appointment to return six months later. During the car ride home I sat like a statue, fearing that one slouch too many might twist me into a question mark.

School ended, summer passed, and I entered sixth grade at Lowerton Middle School at the opposite end of town. Greasy boys with their eyes too close together imitated me, called me "Queenie" because I walked with my chin stuck out, my nose in the air. But I didn't care. I just wanted to get better.

"I'm not boring you, am I?" I asked Philip at this point. He seemed to have gone into a bit of a trance.

"No, it's just that Karen also had scoliosis. Too many things remind me of her."

"I can stop."

"No, no. Keep going, please."

Before I knew it, my six-month appointment neared. It was

winter, two weeks before Christmas, and Glen had started fishing for ideas of things to get me. The night before my visit to
the doctor, he was out driving Meryl to work through the falling snow, and I was making a list of a few things I wouldn't
mind finding under the tree. I couldn't remember anything I
wrote down, just that when I finished I pulled open the window
blinds and watched the snow cover the courtyard.

From our trailer's window I could see Santa Claus standing
on his perch, high above everything. Mr. Mulligan was gone,
dead now a couple of years, his flagpole just as it was the day he
died. Snow dusted Santa that night, and staring at him I
thought of the one thing I wanted more than anything else that
Christmas, the one thing Glen couldn't give me. I wanted to be
healthy. I wanted to go to the doctor tomorrow and find out that
my back had set itself straight again.

"That's what I want," I whispered at Santa, with a small,
silly hope in my heart that the words might mean something.
All they did, though, was fog the window, and the next day in
the doctor's office I found out once and for all that Santa was
just plastic, a stupid doll. There was nobody available for wishes
that big.

It was the doctor's expression that tipped me off. His mouth
was set and eyes narrow, not the expression of a man looking at
good news. He made no immediate comment, just kept moving
forward with his tests. I was asked to walk, bend, twist, lie down
flat while the doctor examined me. Just like six months ago, X-
rays were shot and then the doctor disappeared for ten minutes
to study the shadowy images of my spine. When he returned he
requested that I get dressed and asked the nurse to call in my
father.

"It's a tricky situation," the doctor said when Glen had stepped in. "The curve has progressed since our last visit, but not too much. There's no predicting what could happen next. It could stop, it could continue, or it could even speed up."

The room went silent. I remember not knowing what to think. I'd been hoping for the best, expecting the worst, and had gotten neither. I felt I'd been handed nothing at all.

"What now, then?" I asked.

The doctor pulled a small, rolling desk chair to himself and sat down, hands on knees, leaning toward me. "I think that's going to depend on you," he said.

I felt my feet go numb when he said it. He was the doctor and yet he was making this come down on my shoulders. And Glen still hadn't said a word.

The doctor continued. "I always recommend precaution. But in this case that would mean wearing a brace that might not even be necessary. It's a lot to ask of you."

For the first time Glen looked at me. Both he and the doctor waited for my answer. I'd been listening, partly, but was still trying to figure out how, in the end, I'd been left alone with this choice.

"Is it big?" I asked finally.

The doctor nodded. "It'll go under your clothes, but others will be able to tell you have it on."

I knew what he meant by that. Kids would know I had it on and would make fun of me for it. They called me Queenie now and no doubt would come up with something else even worse, those slow boys with their rattails. Meryl herself might snicker at it. At the moment, however, I didn't care about any of that. Mostly I felt angry that Glen had begun staring at his shoes again, unwilling to meet my eye. More than ever I wanted to leave this place and I knew that when I did, I wanted to walk out tall and proud.

"It's up to you," Glen murmured now.

I understood that more than he ever realized. It was totally up to me; it was my decision. I looked at the doctor and said, "I'll wear the brace." Glen didn't make a sound.

MONDAY, FEBRUARY 22, 1999

Late last night, after shutting down my computer, the phone rang. Part of me hoped it was Embeth, calling again in secret, and a small part of me hoped it was Philip, having found some reason to talk some more. I've enjoyed our Sunday coffees and get the feeling he has as well. The phone call wasn't from either of them. It was Sandra Guerrero, almost in tears as she apologized for missing our meeting. She'd just returned from her grandmother's funeral in the Dominican Republic and was so very, very sorry for not calling before. She'd found out just after our rehearsal, and in her rush to make plans, the meeting had slipped her mind.

"My grandmother and I were very close," she said and began to cry. I guessed she wasn't just calling to apologize but to step back from the whole project. Our team would be down to just three.

Wanting to make it easier for her, I suggested she take some time off. It would be hard enough for her to focus on her studies without something else hanging over her.

"Maybe ... if some small things come up, I can help with those?" she said.

"Sure, I'll let you know," I promised, then gave my condolences and said good-bye. I didn't sleep well after that; I'm not sure why. The meeting in Harrisburg had been the most optimistic shot in the arm we could have hoped for. Yet everything else surrounding our attempt to save the Estate appeared to be crumbling. Sandra was out. I hadn't found a way to contact Embeth. Two rejection letters had arrived in response to my grant requests. Everyone seemed to be waiting for me to take the next step, but I didn't know what that was. I've always hated setting out when unsure about where I'm going. A dream I had of wandering through Quinlin's Maze didn't help things, so I awoke today determined to make at least one step forward. It took only breakfast and another unanswered call to Embeth Graveston for me to decide to go to Truant Gulch to find out what was going on. This big leap forward ended up being just another closed door. Worse yet, I almost ran into Meryl Lakewood in the process.

I just missed her as I was leaving my meeting with Jonathan Groat, administrator for the assisted care wing. Her Monday visit to Glen had concluded, and rather than heading straight home, I decided to sneak in a sit with my father. Minutes after she'd left I could still smell the lingering presence of her perfume.

Glen moaned this afternoon when I spoke. It didn't surprise me. If he could understand me at all, I think it must've been a slight shock for him to hear me repeat the stories Dwight told me. Every minute or so he'd let out a soft groan, like I'd just hit on a sore spot. I don't know if it felt bad or good. Hearing about Glen has helped me cement a few thoughts about him that I always suspected but never knew for certain.

The first thing is that when he thought about my future, he envisioned me leaving Lowerton. The second thing is that he didn't feel wholly responsible for helping me get out. It's the second thing that I've never understood. Knowing he was the one who put that Santa Claus on top of Mr. Mulligan's flagpole doesn't help me in the least. Like I've mentioned, the small hope and faith I put in that little plastic man failed me as much as Glen did.

What's hard is that, right now, things can't be made better. I can talk to Glen all I want—yell, argue, whatever—but he can't answer back. At times a moan would fill the silence, but what good is that? Unless he improves, our relationship can't change from this point on. It's frustrating.

Then there's the other broken conversation dominating my life. Embeth Graveston has all but holed up in her room at Truant Gulch, and I can't reach her. Jonathan Groat listened to my request with a deadpan expression this afternoon and did nothing but check a dining room report to make sure Embeth continued to take all her meals.

"You're not family?" he asked about five times during our talk. The last two, it came out as more of a statement, his explanation for why I wasn't allowed upstairs.

"I'm a friend," I answered each time. "I was interviewing Mrs. Graveston."

"I'm sure she has her reasons for not taking your calls," he said, shrugging. "The privacy of our residents is quite important to them. We will never contradict their requests unless it is a matter of life and death. I'm sure you'd like us to uphold the same policy with your father, correct?" He raised his eyebrows when he said this, and I heard the vague threat hidden in the question.

Out of patience and arguments, I thanked him for meeting me and stormed out of the office. The whole thing still knots my stomach, causing me to put aside the article I was editing for the *Express* on a fire that burned down an abandoned warehouse out on Watershed Street. Just another building outside the shadow that fell first to shambles and then to flame. I didn't write that, but I'd like to—I'm sure most of the readers would nod their heads at it. I wonder if people in town ever look at me and wonder when I'll eventually come to ruin too. Things started off crooked and now it's been twenty-seven years outside the shadow. They must be thinking, *any minute now.*

SUNDAY, FEBRUARY 28, 1999

I didn't meet Philip at church today because he was scheduled to be at the airport for an early shift and didn't get off work till after the services had ended. He did call to meet me for lunch at a bagel shop midway between his work and my apartment. This is week three now of Sunday afternoons together. He told me today how much he enjoys talking with me.

"The people at work . . ." he said and seemed to be trying to find the right word. "Well, let's just say they don't care whether the sun rises and falls, let alone about something like Quinlin's Estate."

He was wearing his ticketing agent's uniform, a navy blazer with white oxford shirt and crosshatched tie, and had on glasses for the first time since I'd known him. His hair looked tousled, as though he'd barely made it to work on time. And there was a pencil behind his ear. The whole getup made him look more an Eton prep school student than anything; I guessed he was one of those people who could make even sweatpants look good. We both ordered chicken salad sandwiches, and he put his pickle spear on my plate on our way back to the table.

"It was the first thing you ate at Kowalski's," he explained, "and I don't like them."

I thanked him, he said grace, and we set to our meals and conversation.

I thought it would be his turn to share something this time, but instead he threw it back on me, saying there was something he didn't quite understand from our last conversation.

"Wanda Maxwell ... why didn't you ever try to find out what happened to her?"

I know I blushed. I know I stopped chewing and sat there without saying anything for what seemed like minutes but was probably only ten seconds. And then I know I gave the most useless answer of all: "I was fifteen."

I wasn't sure if he'd push the issue and this time he did. "But she was your friend."

Finally I admitted to having the same thought about Wander just two weeks ago over dinner at Kowalski's. It hadn't gone much further than that. It only surfaced, made me feel guilty, and disappeared. "At least you brought the guilt back."

He smiled, understanding I was kidding. He said, "We should be able to find something. Why don't we see what we can track down?"

It was all we's. I didn't know what to say but then I didn't have to—he just kept talking.

"My suspicion is that she wasn't trying to hide herself. She just wanted out, somehow found a way, and tried to have a normal life. Even though it's been a number of years, we should be able to find something."

Things became clearer now. I wondered if some part of him felt angry with me for letting a little girl disappear into the night. Had he been the one up in the fort, he'd have sprung from his watch and wrestled Wander back into Little Pines because he knew sometimes you don't just get out. Sometimes you get lost too.

"Philip, that's really okay. I mean, we're busy with the Estate. I don't want to impose."

He nodded like he heard me, but thinking back on it now, I'm not so sure. Finding Wander seemed to have been his only focus. Soon he was explaining how this could take the place for Embeth being AWOL, how it'd be great to interview Wander about the Estate. Maybe she misses it. Maybe she's snuck back to visit the place. And on. And on. Finally I just agreed.

"Great," he said.

My homework is to write down everything I can remember about Wanda, her family, her friends, her relatives, and her life that might be able to point us in a direction.

Then E-mail it to him. He'd start tomorrow.

I sincerely hope we don't find out she's dead. Or worse, find only dead ends, like with his sister. I worry about what the ghost of another missing girl could do to him.

WHAT I KNOW OF WANDER

Name: Wanda Millicent Maxwell

Birthday: 3/4/72

Father: Powers Maxwell. Wanda lived in the trailer with him. Also living with them were her grandmother, Millicent, her unwed aunt, Donna, and Wanda's sister, Jessie, who was eight years older than her.

Mother: Brenda. She left Little Pines and Lowerton when Wander was five or six. I can't remember too much about her except that she'd been the family member with long shiny black hair and that some of the other kids thought she looked like Morticia Addams from the TV show. I'm fairly sure there was no legal divorce, just a long white sedan that pulled into the trailer park one summer day, picked her up, and sped away. After that day Wanda only mentioned her mother twice that I can recall.

The first time was when Wanda showed up for the first day of seventh grade wearing a Bruce Springsteen concert T-shirt for his *Born in the U.S.A.* tour. Walking with her in the halls, I couldn't believe how many kids stopped to ask her if she'd been to the show. "My mom," she said every time. "She saw him in Philadelphia and sent this to me." Her listeners frowned, disappointed. But I saw that for Wander, a bit of her mother was the real prize, not a few hours of rock 'n' roll.

We were standing on the auditorium risers for our eighth-grade graduation the second time. With Glen working and Powers doing whatever he did night after night, we were without family in the audience. The whole thing felt pointless. Then, just before we stepped down, Wander gave a little wave to someone I couldn't see. When I asked her later who it was she'd waved to, she said, "My mom, I think. But she's gone now."

The rest of the time I was with Wander, her mom, Brenda Maxwell, or whatever her name is now, didn't come up. A few times Wander explained that she didn't want to make me feel bad about not having a mom; other times she said she hated Brenda. Rarely was the answer the same, so I never knew what to believe.

As far as friends, Wander had few: Me, and a sickly girl named Betsy who missed most of eighth grade due to mono. Betsy didn't move on to high school with us, so she wasn't part of our lives when Wander walked out of Little Pines. Wander never had friends over to her place, and I can't remember her going anywhere else except my trailer, especially after the hide-and-seek incident with the Kleines.

As for her home life, I have no idea what went on in their trailer. But whatever it was, home offered nothing that made Wander want to stick around. Just the opposite; she always wanted out. She never spoke bad of Powers or showed up on the bus with bruises. Still, she walked away from food and shelter and risked being lost, and that has to mean something. I know how bad it was in our house, but I could never imagine leaving it all for the thrill of walking into the dark.

A NOTE ABOUT MY MOTHER, WHOM I BARELY KNEW

Writing about Wanda and her missing mother caused me to think back on my own mother. She comes to me, sometimes, in moments like these, which is as close as I've ever been to her. Most of the time she's nothing more than a list of facts that

Glen shared with me, a face remembered secondhand through snapshots in old photo albums, and her name: Roxanne.

She grew up in Scranton, Pennsylvania, the only daughter of Phyllis and Oliver Wren. Her father passed away when she was twelve, her mother the year after she graduated from the university here. Nothing remained for her back East, so she took a job at the orphanage in Lowerton. This was during the waning years when children ran wild through the halls and state officials were taking the first steps to close the place.

With little else but a degree in social work, when the orphanage closed, Roxanne turned to the major employer in town and got a job capping on the floor. Slowly the factory started shifting from brute and molten metalwork to more intricate projects that required dexterous fingers rather than strong forearms. She met another girl on the line who needed a roommate and a week later shared a room with her in a cramped apartment on the opposite side of town from the factory. Every morning—even during winter—the two would trundle across twelve blocks, slipping in just before the whistle blew. There's an old Instamatic photo in one of my father's albums of Roxanne pulling a navy wool overcoat up to her chin, large flakes of snow dotting her hair and shoulders. The coat now hangs in my closet; it was probably the most expensive thing she owned.

In 1971 she got teamed up with Glen for a water balloon toss during the annual factory picnic and ended up with a soaking T-shirt. Glen, playing the gallant, loaned her a windbreaker for the rest of the festivities and offered her a ride home from the picnic at nightfall. At her apartment she ran in quickly to change out of her soaking shirt so she could give back his jacket, and when she returned to the car he asked her on a date the next Friday. She accepted.

Three months later they were married. Ten months after that, I was born.

The cancer first appeared when I was thirteen months old. It moved with ferocious speed so that just six weeks after my second birthday—a party spent at the Centre County Hospital—Roxanne died.

I have no solid memories of my mother, only vague impressions from faded shots in family scrapbooks and the occasional story from Glen. I will say this: he always spoke well of her, and nearly everything I remember him saying was tinged with an enormous sadness. Meryl Lakewood never liked it when Glen brought up Roxanne and soon he stopped altogether.

My mother, to me, is a navy overcoat, a slender woman sitting propped up in her bed watching me with tired eyes as I blew out a candle on a cupcake, a wisp of a memory is all.

I don't miss her.

I do miss having the chance to miss her.

FRIDAY, MARCH 5, 1999

Good news today, some of the best in a while, and all of it arriving in the SQE post office box. First, the Save Quinlin's Estate Foundation received its first grant money. The Centre County Historical Heritage Group has awarded us their full budget for this year—fifteen thousand dollars. I haven't held that much money in my hand in years and didn't keep it there long. Our savings account finally appears respectable.

Perhaps the most encouraging sign from this award is that

the CCHHG is a respected organization that has successfully lobbied Harrisburg for the purpose of funding projects. With their support, we'll have even more to present to Representative Evans if it works out for him to visit the area and tour the Estate in mid-March as he'd talked about. I'm hoping for an answer real soon.

Both Philip and Ben agreed with me on the magnitude of the grant. The money could never be the important thing—it's the prestige. They both congratulated me over the phone, and when I spoke with Philip, I found myself wishing we were together at a coffee shop instead. Someplace where I could see him smile.

Philip would definitely smile at the second piece of mail we received today too. Which was a handwritten note and a check for twenty dollars. Again, it's not the amount but the donor that's important here. Mrs. Embeth Graveston tracked us down and even managed to sneak in a few words.

Eve,

When I saw the Save Quinlin's Estate ad in the Lowerton Express *I remembered that you were heading up this group and felt this might be my best chance to contact you. Lydia has seized control of so much else, but she is allowing me to donate to the fund not knowing this note will reach you.*

I never knew the force she'd expend to keep the story of the Estate hidden, however, there's a chance you and I might still be able to meet. Lydia has approved my attendance at the Truant Gulch trip to the Carnegie Museums in Pittsburgh on Tuesday the ninth. She will not be accompanying me. The group will be leaving Lowerton at eight A.M. *I will wait for you in the west wing of the second floor of the Museum of Art until noon. If my memory holds from last year's visit, this area contains their permanent collection.*

Must go.

Embeth

P.S. I feel a bit like a secret agent or spy. Life doesn't get this exciting for an old woman very often.

Despite everything else, her postscript made me laugh, but Embeth's note left me wondering how Lydia is managing to control as much as she seems to be. Looking through archives at the *Express* might uncover something on her and why she holds such sway over others' lives the way she does. While I'm at it, I might as well look up Evangeline Graveston and my father's name as well. *Something* happened in those years after Glen returned to Lowerton. The thought has even crossed my mind that if the story is dark and twisted enough, it could very well be the kind of book a publisher might be interested in. An advance of any kind would be money I could put toward the SQE Foundation. I don't know what kind of daughter it makes me to hope my father's sordid past might earn some money for my cause, but perhaps there are some things for which a person should never wish.

SUNDAY, MARCH 7, 1999

My apartment building woke up with a hangover this morning, stinking of stale smoke and spilled beer from a neighbor's party last night that told me again why I need to consider a new place when this lease runs out in August. Not wanting to linger in the stench any more than necessary, I got myself dressed and on the road before I'd even had much of a chance to consider where to go. Breakfast was an option but I'd been spending too much money recently, and since I wasn't due to meet Philip today, I wanted to try to keep my pocketbook closed. Sunday mornings don't offer much for entertainment, though, and less that's free, so the only thing that came quickly to mind was church. I went hoping to see Dwight or Philip.

Instead, I saw Ben Sterling dressed in a suit and tie a few rows over and heard a sermon that reminded me so much of my father that I took some notes on the bulletin they handed out. On it are written: *wind chaser, Paul Racine*, and *This is Glen!*

The whole message centered on one's passion and focus, and the futility that results when those things get pointed in the wrong direction. The pastor repeatedly referenced Ecclesiastes, showing how this wise king had devoted himself to learning and wealth and having fun and yet how none of it had given him anything more than a few moments of pleasure. *Chasing the wind*, the writer said over and over again.

I liked the subtlety of the phrase. The two people the image seemed to fit most were my father and a professor who had sent me searching the library at Indiana University one summer for a ghost of a man named Paul Racine.

My junior year as an undergraduate I applied for a summer research position at history departments across the country. The only one that responded with both credits and room and board was Indiana. A Dr. Henry Stillman, adjunct professor of nineteenth-century American history, called and said he was looking for some help on a side project while he continued work on a book about the Reconstruction. I accepted and not long afterward was trapped in the library searching the annals of late-nineteenth-century Americana for someone even Dr.

Stillman wasn't sure existed—Paul Racine.

A collector as well as a researcher, Dr. Stillman owned an authentic letter from Henry Ford, written to an unknown friend in which Ford describes Paul Racine as perhaps the brightest and most inspired thinker Ford had ever heard. Unfortunately no other record confirmed Racine's genius, or even his existence. School records proved as fruitless as the censuses. The name Racine appeared, but none with whom Ford might have crossed paths. Eighteen weeks of my life were lost to this phantom.

What I realized for the first time during the sermon was how much Dr. Stillman reminds me of my own father. His spirit and faith never waned during those difficult days, just as Glen's never dissipated in the years he searched for Quinlin's gold. Like Solomon of Ecclesiastes, Dr. Stillman and Glen were swatches cut from the same cloth, idealists focused on an illusion of fame and prosperity. My only hope is that such misguided dedication doesn't run in the family. I don't want this fight to save the Estate to become my own private Paul Racine, my own buried treasure.

So that was my big discovery during church. After the service ended, I caught up with Ben in the lobby. His white shirt and royal blue tie made him look trimmer somehow, and I wondered if maybe I'd overlooked him during my previous visits.

"No, I don't normally come here," he explained when I asked. "Philip invited me earlier this week, but I guess he isn't here." He glanced around to make sure he hadn't missed Philip and then looked back at me. "Did he invite you too?"

I told him about my previous visits and the smell at my apartment building, and he seemed to understand. We stood in silence for another moment, and I was getting ready to say good-bye and leave when Ben leaned in closer and asked under his breath, "Do you know that woman over there?" He darted his eyes to his left. "She's been staring this direction like she knows one of us, and I've never seen her before."

I'm not real good with situations like that. Another person would pretend to look someplace else, a clock maybe, but I couldn't help myself. I turned and saw Meryl Lakewood watching me from the far wall. Her hair made tame, her dress a muted blue, and her arms folded primly in front of her, she didn't look at all like the Meryl Lakewood I was used to seeing. Our stare held for a few seconds and then she did something that still baffles me: She held up her hand to her ear like an imaginary phone and mouthed the words, *I need to talk to you.*

My face must have bunched itself into confusion, because she began mouthing something else. For once that vibrant lipstick came in handy. I could read almost every movement of her gawking mouth. Almost. *It's. About. Water.*

Water? I mouthed back. It made no sense.

She nodded, sent it back to me. *Water.* Only this time there was something different to her mouth. It wasn't *water.* It was something softer sounding. It was—

I turned back to Ben, apologized, and said I had to go.

"No problem," I heard him say as I rushed through the front doors, trying to get out of there before Meryl could say the word again.

It was *Wander.* She had something to tell me about Wander, and I didn't want to hear what it was. She'd done enough to the poor girl years ago.

Meryl and Wander

The bitterness between Meryl and I didn't always exist. It was only during the last years in the trailer that we came to despise each other. Before that, we managed to get on by ignoring each other's existence as best we could. She forgot that I was out playing, and I didn't ask her to drive me anywhere or request her help with my hair. Our schedules helped in this by keeping me in school during the day and sending her to work at various restaurants on the dinner and night-owl shifts. With Wanda Maxwell, though, Meryl was openly mean and, to my never-ending surprise, Wander, normally meek as a whisper, sniped back.

"Little weasel," Meryl would say, often to Wander's face. She hated the girl's slick black hair, and probably her slender frame too. Meryl never lacked for hips.

"Hag," Wander sneered, so much so that she'd taken to referring to Meryl this way all the time. "The hag served my sister and her friends at Ponderosa the other night," she once said. We were nine then. "Jessie said her blouse was unbuttoned so low that every time she reached across the table you could practically feel the stretch marks forming." We laughed at this like it was the funniest thing we'd ever heard, though I remember I had no idea what it meant.

And so it went. They glared when they saw each other, traded nasty remarks if any came to mind, and generally grumbled about the other's presence. Nothing had sparked the mutual disgust that I could finger; it seemed to have always existed as though the two had come to an understanding without my knowing about it. The thing was, sometimes I couldn't blame either of them.

TUESDAY, MARCH 9, 1999

I followed Embeth's instructions and got in my car early to make the two-hour drive to Pittsburgh. Having wound my way out of the endless spines of the Allegheny Mountains this morning, I made it to the museum at half past ten. A few miles from the city center, the museum stands as a great example of Pittsburgh's commitment to updating its coal-choked past. Sparkling buildings, shiny new restaurants, riverfront renovation, and a battery of world-class museums have helped revitalize the area, and present plans to build a new baseball stadium are sure to keep the progress moving. I've enjoyed my last few visits to the city, and today I was sorry I didn't have more time to look around. My purpose was to meet with Embeth Graveston and get to the bottom of this cloak-and-dagger story.

Embeth sat waiting for me in front of an appropriate painting, given our topic of conversation. It was a Degas portrait and the painter's impressive rendering of the concept of industry, perhaps the least impressionistic topic imaginable. A fierce and bearded factory owner—decked out in top hat and coat—stood staring off canvas while behind him smokestacks belched forth great plumes. Though it was titled *Henri Rouart in Front of His Factory*, circa 1875, it could very well have been a portrait of Gabriel Quinlin himself. We didn't sit for long under the man's gaze.

"You made it!" Embeth said, standing when she saw me. "We'll need to get out of here. Lydia has friends on this trip. I'll meet you on the front steps in a couple of minutes."

With that she disappeared around a corner and left me wondering if I was involved in something more substantial than just a small town's history. But then I remembered that in small towns, history is often the *only* thing that matters, especially when the future begins to look bleak.

A few minutes later I rejoined Embeth and together we headed down the stairs, past the columns of the neighboring Natural History Museum, and down the street. One block later, I finally asked where we were going.

"Schwartz's Bagels," Embeth replied.

Six blocks later we stepped under Schwartz's green awning and found ourselves inside the comfortable, clean bagel shop. Forbes Avenue marked a boundary for the University of Pittsburgh, and the place looked to be clearing out from the morning student rush. After we ordered—I tried the asiago and sage on sourdough—we took a seat in the back corner.

"Is everything okay?" I asked her.

She shook her head. "No, dear. But I'll make it through." She broke off a piece of her egg bagel and chewed for a moment before continuing. "Lydia's been a terror these past few weeks. According to Truant Gulch she's just my guardian, but her husband, Lorne, sits on the board, and she's got the administration on a short leash. If she says I've been spending money recklessly, they'll cut the phone and watch my mail. If she says I've been taken in by people trying to con money out of me, they'll lock you out and put a staff person outside my door." Her voice started to waver now, and the piece of bagel she held was trembling a little. She didn't cry; she fought through the moment and kept talking.

"I don't want to make trouble, Eve, but she's not going to stop me from getting this story out. Somebody's got to hear it."

I waited. There had to be more to this than what I'd been

told, that was obvious. Nobody would go to such extremes to keep hidden the things Embeth had told me so far. What I wanted to hear was the truth behind Evangeline's claim that she was a Quinlin and that the house on the hill was hers.

Embeth glanced at her watch and said she had only a half hour before she had to return to her group so they could continue on with their tour.

"I won't finish," she said while staring over my shoulder out into the street, "but at least it'll be a start. And this time it'll be everything. I've been nervous about sharing some things, only we don't have time right now. Lydia's too intent on stopping it. The rest I can tell you in your father's room. They can't keep you out of there. I can sneak down during the all-staff meetings." She took a deep breath and closed her eyes for a second. "I'm tired, Eve."

"You don't have to do this," I said and meant it.

She shook her head and shuffled herself upright in her chair. Her blue eyes found mine, and she said that was her least complaint. There wasn't time.

"This is the story of Gabriel and my time with him before his death."

The name, the way her eyes softened when she said the name, got my attention. Before it had always been Gabriel Quinlin or Mr. Quinlin. Just the soft flutter of her voice as it rounded from her lips changed the story in an instant.

"I've mentioned before," she said, "that, especially as a girl, I had the hope that Gabriel Quinlin might one day rescue me. Open the doors of the Estate and tell me to choose any room." She paused. "In a way, that desire never faded. I made the same wish for years on end until finally, after I got my position at the factory, I began to realize that wishing might not be enough."

An image came to my mind. The photo Embeth showed me of herself as a younger woman, perhaps when in her early twenties. In it she had her head cocked to the side and her mouth puckered for a kiss. Her hips were turned but she had lifted her skirt to reveal a slender calf, her knee, a slight burst of thigh. "I was imitating Rita Hayworth," Embeth had said at the time, and I remember thinking that Rita Hayworth would have had herself some competition.

Now the image dissolved and I was left with what Embeth had just implied. I didn't know if she wanted me to ask questions or if she would just start talking about it. I'd never had a mother with whom to discuss such things. Meryl Lakewood had laughed the one time I asked her about sex, telling me that with my lack of figure I wasn't going to have to worry about it for a long time.

Embeth met my stare and sighed. "I'm not proud of this story," she said. "Let me make that clear. A lot of bad things have happened because of it. But some good things as well, including my marriage to the most dedicated, magnificent man I've ever known."

I nodded and clicked on my tape recorder, prepared myself to be shocked.

Tonight, listening to her story for the third time, I find I'm both puzzled and amazed. Her story has put yet another twist to this tale. I can't guess where it will end.

EMBETH'S STORY

The difficulty, Embeth learned, was not in getting a man's attention but in attracting the *right* man's attention. Gabriel Quinlin nodded to the gaggle of secretaries every morning upon arriving, yet never appeared to be looking at any of them individually. They were as much a part of the factory landscape as the smokestacks, the tile floor, or the twelve maple steps Quinlin climbed every morning to get to his office. Still, Embeth didn't lose hope and took every opportunity she could to deliver important messages to him personally or stay after hours so that when Quinlin appeared, hat in hand, he nodded only to her on his way out.

This continued for three years. Thirty-six months of *Here's an urgent message for you, Mr. Quinlin* and *Good night, Mr. Quinlin.*

After fourteen months Quinlin began saying, "Good night, Miss Herr." After twenty-two he added her to the short list of women to whom he would give dictation. After thirty he offered her a raise and promotion to assistant executive secretary, and finally, after thirty-six months they worked together for a full week when the senior secretary, Mrs. Florence Truman, had to be in Harrisburg for her mother's funeral.

Though the country was still buried by the Depression, Quinlin swore he saw the dawn that would end this long night. His main objective was to begin renewing contact with both public and private sector companies that had also weathered the storm, hoping to forge alliances that might position the factory favorably when industry began its slow recovery. To her delight, Embeth soon became his first choice for any dictated correspondence, since Mrs. Truman's hearing had been touched of late.

Embeth's real hope began, however, with her assignment to a three-person team appointed to predict the consequences of Quinlin's four options for restarting his town. Embeth would attend all meetings and record the minutes to present nightly to Mr. Quinlin himself. This would last about twenty weeks. The group—accountant Charles Graveston, economics professor Jay Miller, and town foreman Lester Barnes—had five months to prepare their recommendation to Gabriel Quinlin. The Estate was nearing completion. He couldn't keep Lowerton closed forever.

Embeth saw this as her chance. Each night she would walk into Quinlin's office, notes in hand, performing a service as vital and important as any a woman had in the company. She would stand before his desk and hand him the transcript, and he would have to notice her.

Her opportunity came on a warm evening in early August. As the group began to work later and later, Gabriel Quinlin was staying just as late, for he refused to leave until Embeth showed up with the notes and suggestions of his transition team. That particular night when she arrived, Gabriel was caught standing in front of his lead-glass window, staring down on the factory courtyard.

"Miss Herr," he said, lifting his eyes to look at her in the reflection of the window.

She could see his unknotted crimson bow tie dangling over one shoulder, and his sleeves were rolled up. Mother-of-pearl cuff links glittered on the table next to an empty glass; a cut-glass decanter with only a thin splash of amber liquid sat nearby.

"Miss Herr, your diligence is an inspiration." It was the first compliment he'd ever given her. She nodded and placed the group's notes on his desk. She thought he'd then dismiss her but instead Quinlin continued to gaze at her reflection, not turning around. His mood, the disarray of his desk, the empty glass— Embeth hadn't seen such things from Mr. Quinlin before. She asked him if he was feeling poorly.

"Never better," he murmured. He then spun around and took a seat in his chair behind the desk. As always, his eyes were sharp, focused. There was no physical sign he'd touched any alcohol. Even when he spoke, his words came out clear, not slurred in the least. "May I do something for you, Miss Herr?"

What surprised Embeth was not what she heard in his voice, but that she'd never recognized it before. His words were choked with loneliness, as though each one were unfamiliar, a sound being spoken to another for the first time. She wanted so bad just to soothe him. Stroke his hand. Rest his head close to her heart.

"Mr. Quinlin, you've been so good to me," she stammered. "I should be asking if there's anything I can do for you." She took a step forward and touched the edge of his desk with one outstretched finger.

"Child," he sighed and she flinched at the word. "My dear, there is nothing you can offer to calm this rattled disposition you see before you. You'll forgive me, please. I am ashamed you had to see me this way. I assumed God would allow me a few hours of self-pity, but I see He's to hold me to the flame a little longer after all."

Embeth couldn't respond. She was still thrown by the way he'd spoken to her—almost as a father. Or at least how she imagined a father would speak.

"May I advise you, Miss Herr," Quinlin said, getting up and

turning back to the window again. She saw him staring at her in the reflection and nodded.

"Don't wait on others. Move ahead with your life and if others join you, so much the better. It's better to forge ahead than be left behind."

"But where shall I go?"

Quinlin paused as if to consider this, perhaps realizing to whom he was talking. "God will lead," he said finally. "I know that if nothing else."

"What," said Embeth, putting to words the thoughts she'd had for so long, "if God led me here. Tonight. To be with you." They were said with the voice of that six-year-old girl who'd squeezed her eyes shut and wished over her mother's coin during Easter service. This was the only aspiration for which she'd ever wished, and if it wasn't from God, then He'd provided her with exactly as much as her earthly father—nothing.

"No," said Quinlin without turning. "He wouldn't call you to such a thing. You're worth more than that in His eyes." He held out his hand to stop her protest. "Whether you believe it or not, you are worth far more. He'll show that to you if you ask."

Embeth took one step back, then a second. Quinlin nodded to her and she lowered her head in return, hoping he wouldn't see her eyes fill. All she'd wanted was for him to feel she was worth more, and what he offered her was God, as though that were an equal trade. Slipping from the room, she shook a moment's worth of tears from her eyes and tried to slow her thoughts. The one thing she returned to again and again, however, was the crumbled ruin of her hope for a home in Quinlin's Estate. Those doors were locked forever, and she felt as alone as Quinlin had looked when she first entered his office.

"You're staying late this evening, Miss Herr," a voice said from behind her. She turned to find John Driver tipping his hat to her. He was a copywriter one floor down, whom Embeth knew mostly through the titters of the other secretaries.

"As are you, Mr. Driver," she answered, trying to keep her voice smooth. It didn't work and Driver moved to her side immediately,

"Are you okay?" He placed a hand on her elbow. She nodded but then swayed too much with her next step, so he wasn't persuaded. "You won't make it twenty steps out the gate," he said. She felt the warmth and strength of his arm, offered to her to lean on.

"I suppose not," she said and without another thought let him guide her through the maze of desks, outside, and through the courtyard to the factory gate. She never thought to turn around and see if Mr. Quinlin still stood watching. His loneliness meant nothing to her so long as she could forget her own. Even for only a slip of hours, a few days at the most.

THURSDAY, MARCH 11, 1999

The weekly edition of the *Lowerton Express* arrived at my door and inside I found two articles I'd written, our second Save Quinlin's Estate ad, a short editorial on mining contracts being argued one county over, some out-of-date coverage of the local high-school basketball season, and a photo of Lydia Furrow. If Evangeline looked like Grace Kelly with curves and her mother Rita Hayworth, then Lydia Furrow placed someplace closer to the Hepburns, especially Audrey. Cool and elegant.

The snapshot in the paper was supposed to be a candid of

Lydia and her husband, Lorne, at a fund-raiser for the local children's hospital, but there was nothing candid or spontaneous
about it. She'd tilted her head at the camera in a way that
showed off the strong sweep of her neck, arched her back the
way models learn so they look lean and long, and offered a prac-
ticed smile.

The photo, of course, looked perfect. Lydia, probably sixty-
something, had long hair that looked lustrous and silver. She
had her arm crooked through her husband's, and he had none of
the doughiness wealthy men sometimes fall to when they
become lazy in their money. Both of them were sleek, and I
could tell the two had energy to spare for things like keeping a
sister-in-law from sharing family secrets. It made me worried,
to be honest. Who knew what this woman was capable of doing?

After finishing the paper, I went running, as the sun had
finally broken through the low ceiling of clouds that always
seem to clog the sky from December till March. Returning to
my apartment to get cleaned up, I found my answering machine
blinking at me. The message was from Philip. He'd called for no
reason at all, or no real reason. He was making slow progress
on Wander's whereabouts, work was fine, and he was sorry to
hear he missed me at church. He said Ben was taken aback when
he saw me there. Philip finished by saying I could give him a
ring back if I wanted, but it wasn't urgent. And he hoped my
days were going swell.

I reset the machine and showered, and when I came back out
was surprised to see yet another message blinking. I sort of
hoped it was Philip, calling back with more thoughts from his
day, but the notion was absurd. How would he have known I'd
heard his first message? Rather, it was a voice I'd been avoiding

all week, that of Meryl Lakewood.

This is the third time I've called, Eve, and I won't stop. I don't have that much going on in my life to be bothered with you ignoring me for a little while, so you'd be better off just getting this over with. It's about Wanda. And that boyfriend of yours. He's looking for her, says you put him up to it, and I just want to check some things with you before I talk to him. You know my number.

Sometimes the body just can't help doing clichéd things, and this time I know my mouth dropped open. I'm not sure why people are wired to show surprise this way, but Meryl's words were enough to trip my instinct and I stared at the answering machine without moving for a few seconds before deciding I needed to listen to it again.

It's about Wanda, she said. *And that boyfriend of yours.*

Boyfriend.

It was such a middle-school word and so very like Meryl to use it. Even when she'd been in our trailer eight years, Glen was still her "boyfriend." I wonder if she refers to him this way to the nurses at Truant Gulch. Was it her boyfriend lying there, comatose and moaning? Or had he become just Glen Lawson for her too? I know he'd become that for me long ago.

But *boyfriend*? She had to have meant Philip, only who told her we were dating? Was it an assumption on her part, having seen us together at church? Was it something she picked up from talking with Dwight? Did Philip introduce himself that way to her? I sat down, rifled through all the possibilities, and decided it was ridiculous. Regardless of how she'd come up with the idea, the most important thing was that it hadn't come through me. There were a few things I still needed to find out about Mr. Philip von Maarsten. The fedora and the scarf and the sweet thing he does with his mouth every time he tries to hold back a laugh are all nice, yet they are not enough. Besides, there are too many other important things happening right now to think about it.

I will, however, spend a moment thinking about love.

ON LOVE AND QUINLIN'S ESTATE

I learned a lot about people working at Quinlin's Estate. I worked there all summer long during my last two high-school years and also the summer after my freshman year of college. Part of my time was spent roaming the Maze, helping the frustrated and lost to find their way. Other times, I welcomed people at the front gate or wandered the grounds, walkie-talkie on my belt, looking for trouble. I saw it all during those years, including the small stories of love and hate that people brought with them across the drawbridge, people who found themselves unable to hide within a building that seemed to see straight through them.

A countless number of people have fallen in love under the eaves of the Estate, from ardent teens passing notes back and forth when the Estate served as a school to modern lovers gazing at each other in the secluded bower. On average, fifteen couples a year are married either inside the Estate—in the ballroom or solarium—or outside on its sprawling grounds. Dozens more arrive in lengthy caravans to arrange for photos to be taken on the main steps with the imposing columns at their back or else along the landscaped path of the Estate garden. In the springtime, armies of crocuses, daisies, marigolds, tulips, forsythia bushes, lilacs, and flowering dogwoods supply a rich palette of colors to complement any bridal color scheme.

For those anticipating marriage, the large Atlas fountain—a copper sculpture of a man bent beneath the weight of the world—is rumored to be the finest place for proposals of wedlock. Following close behind are the soaring tower room, the solitary library, and the wooden bridge that spans the wishing well. One surprised fiancée was so excited she dropped her shiny carat into the eighty-five feet of water beneath her and had to wait until closing time when workers lifted the grate at the bottom to retrieve the day's gathering of spent wishes.

Besides witnessing declarations of intent and ceremonies of lifelong commitment, the Estate has seen the lustier quality of love as well. Passion and hunger have played themselves out within its many rooms, and every year a few couples are caught and expelled after some unsuspecting tourist stumbles into some corner the trysters believed would go ignored.

On the flip side, the Estate has served as the setting for numerous arguments, breakups, abandonments, even assaults. One fellow had his ex-wife halfway out the tower window before other visitors came to her rescue. An infant was found forsaken at the very heart of the Maze.

In all, the very best and very worst of human nature have been revealed at Quinlin's Estate. It's not a stolid monument or towering memorial. It is a vibrant, living piece of history that has reflected society for over sixty years now. I still can't believe this thing may be coming down. But it seems people these days have no stomach for anything complicated enough to reflect back both the Dr. Jekyll and Mr. Hyde all at once.

What a listless town. What a dull-witted way to live.

Sunday, March 14, 1999

Perhaps I wasn't being quite honest before when I said the fedora, scarf, and all the rest meant little to me. This morning before church, I saw Philip for the first time in over a week, and just sharing coffee with him made me realize he had more going for him than I gave him credit for the other night. He also apologized when I scolded him for calling Meryl without telling me.

"I was wondering why she didn't call me back," he said after I told him about her message. "Have you called her?"

I shook my head.

"She told me she saw Wanda that night just before your senior year, Eve, and I believe her whether you do or not. There's no reason to lie about it now."

I didn't answer and soon we were on our way to service.

First Baptist Church, Church of the Open Door, and the Lowerton Church of God combined services today at the community center for an ecumenical service, to promote unity among the different Christian denominations. I suppose it did that, but also it somehow united the disparate parts of my life at the same time. I sat with Philip, of course, and also Ben. Dwight and Monique Carter were sitting one section over from us, and I recognized another one or two classmates from high school and a graduate student who'd been part of the history program before I left. I could even see Meryl Lakewood's hair in the front corner of the auditorium. Missing were Glen and Embeth.

The sermon, given by Dwight's pastor from First Baptist, was all wedding stories. Funny, modern stories, portions of wedding parables from Judaic culture, and several references to everyone in the auditorium and their being the bride of Christ, who anxiously await His return. Much of it made little sense.

Afterward, Dwight stopped me in the commons area to kid me a little about getting a reputation if I kept showing up in church. He slapped Philip on the back, shook Ben's hand, and chatted some about the Estate before moving on to others he knew. Ben, Philip, and I had moved to the door to head to lunch when a thin woman with silver hair stepped in front of us. I didn't recognize her at first, but then her voice gave her away.

"Eve Lawson," she said, all sweetness. "My name is Lydia Furrow." She didn't even so much as hold out her hand, and over her shoulder I could see her husband, Lorne, waiting, keys in hand. They were about to leave. Her eyes narrowed as she looked me over with a sweep of them. "I wanted to meet the young woman who's been stirring up so much trouble."

To my left I could hear Ben clear his throat.

"I think you've mistaken me for somebody else," I suggested. I admit, I wanted to see how she'd react. She didn't, just continued on as if we were discussing the spring planting ahead or the best shade of lipstick.

"Friends of mine at Truant Gulch, knowing of my concern as Embeth's guardian, said my sister-in-law barely made it back to their tour the other week. Apparently she'd been whisked away by a thin redheaded woman and was so traumatized she would hardly speak of what happened when questioned."

"She's a free woman," I replied and was instantly annoyed at myself. I might as well have said, *It's a free country.*

She reached out a hand and patted mine. "You'll do well to leave Mrs. Graveston to the peace and rest she desperately requires."

"Or?" I asked, a little too loud. A few others around us turned their heads.

"My dear," Lydia said, taking her hand back as if I'd offended her, "the doctors at Truant Gulch and I only want what's best for Embeth. We hoped you'd feel the same way." At that she took a step back to leave, glanced at Philip and Ben, then back to me. "Go with the stout one," she said as she nodded her head in Ben's direction. "His eyes flash. This one here"—nodding now to Philip—"is prettier, but dull."

She turned on her heels then and left, her long dress pooling around her ankles. It was as if she glided away. The three of us were left silent for a few seconds until Ben spoke. "At least she didn't call me fat."

I gave an embarrassed laugh, and Philip gave a weak smile. I couldn't help but notice as we exited the community center that Meryl Lakewood stood watching us from against the wall with those closely set eyes of hers and what could've been a self-satisfied little smile or just the usual inexpressive slackness of her jaw. Who knew with her? She seemed content to go another day without hearing from me or maybe had decided to give the whole thing up. Either way, it was a small blessing after the firebombing Lydia had just dropped on us.

Lunch would've been okay, except Philip kept bringing up Lydia's insults so that by the end I was almost in agreement about him being dull. Ben tried to steer the conversation away from it, but tired, I suppose, and after an hour we had little to say.

Driving home was even worse, because now *I* couldn't get her words out of my head. Not only her rudeness to Philip, but her words about me. They repeated themselves, and soon it was all I could do to not punch the empty seat next to me in anger.

I found a few distractions at home—a quick phone call confirming our meeting with Greg Evans next Wednesday, an edit of an article due tomorrow about the closing of the old feed and tack store across from city hall—but when finished with these, I became rattled again. It was seven-thirty now, and I knew I had to do something or I'd be thinking about Lydia Furrow all night.

My first thought surprised me—I almost prayed. I think it was because Philip talked about how he used prayer as a way of stilling his mind when it raced. Talking to the air, even if there is a God and He can hear, seems a bit sketchy to me still and so I filled in the space the best way I knew how. I went to visit Glen.

I've done this before, gone and spoken at him just for the pretense of having a living, breathing person in the room. It's as useless as talking to a plastic Santa. I talk to the cataleptic form that is my father, for he's the only one who won't confuse me with words and suggestions. He'll moan and I can let that mean whatever I want. Tonight I heard, *Keep going.*

Keep going.

Only, that's the hardest thing for me.

I'm the person who learned early in life that the best thing to do to avoid being lost is to sit still. I'm the girl who convinced herself that doing my undergrad here was a smart choice and not just an easy one. I'm the one who thought all the time about leaving and yet did nothing but watch and talk. And now, I have an unknown path in front of me and for the first time I see how important those first steps really are.

I know that's why Wander never looked back—so she

couldn't see Santa or Quinlin's Tower.

I guess that's why Philip refuses to do anything but keep moving when he's in the Maze.

Because for the first few steps into Quinlin's Maze, one walks between lost and found, between safety and the unknown. And I need to just keep going. Step forward and move into the dark.

WEDNESDAY, MARCH 17, 1999

Embeth phoned me at six forty-five. She'd taken an early morning walk and found a pay phone a couple of blocks from Truant Gulch. Last week had failed because Lydia turned up unexpectedly that morning and there'd been no way to notify me. Today, Lydia was in Harrisburg—it was perfect.

And so, just like last week, I arrived at Glen's room and waited. All the words I'd spoken to him last night came back to me, and I felt that dull embarrassment that comes when the bright light of morning shines on things spoken in the night. I'm not sure where all that talk of paths and disappearing came from, but it seems foolish now. I did my best not to think on it too much. When Embeth arrived, the remainder of her story made that the simplest thing ever. This is what she said.

EMBETH'S STORY: THE REST

For nearly two weeks, John Driver offered her the comfort that she thought she needed. The type of comfort that can complicate a person's life. But soon he grew weary of her and began avoiding her glances at work. Feeling more alone than before,

Embeth latched onto Charles Graveston, the first person who showed her any kindness

At first it was just small talk between them: *Isn't this weather fine? Have you heard the latest about Germany? What'll you buy when the town is finally open again?* Yet Embeth found herself craving these brief conversations with Charles as though they were food or drink. Perhaps it would be just a few sentences shared as they took their lunch or a question or two when walking the halls. Even so, Embeth coveted the moments; she felt safe in Charles's presence because he looked at her not with hunger but with eyes bright and caring.

It was these same eyes that saw right through her five weeks later when she tried to pretend everything hadn't started to collapse in her life.

"Are you feeling well, Miss Herr?"

"Yes," she said with a nod and turned so he couldn't see the evidence—swollen lids, red nose—of her long night of weeping.

He said nothing else for the moment. During lunch, however, when he found her sitting alone on a low wall outside the factory rather than at the usual table where they'd dined for the past weeks, he couldn't hold his tongue.

"I have a sister and a mother, Miss Herr, so there's no need to pretend you haven't shed tears. You won't spoil"—he glanced down to the lunch pail he'd brought with him—"my hard-boiled egg or beef sandwich if you'd care to tell what's wrong." With that he nodded and began unloading his lunch onto the wall next to him.

Embeth said nothing at first and Charles didn't seem to mind. He peeled his egg and popped the thing in his mouth whole, then unwrapped wax paper from around the beef

sandwich and took a bite. September painted Lowerton in gold
and crimson, and the midday breeze was warm. From the corner
of her eye Embeth watched Charles move through his lunch, and
when he had one final bite of sandwich left, she decided she had
to speak now or risk him walking away.

"Have you ever been lonely?" she asked.

Charles nodded immediately.

"And what do you do when you feel that way?" She smiled a
bit. "In case you haven't guessed, I weep."

"Yes," said Charles with a short laugh. Then his eyes nar-
rowed in thought. "To be honest, Miss Herr, after some years of
allowing myself to feel miserable, I now pray when I feel alone.
For a long time I'd convinced myself that if I felt alone it meant
God had abandoned me. What I learned was that I was ignoring
Him on purpose."

Embeth was puzzled. "Why?"

"Well, I'd come to Him in anguish about not having more
friends or a wife and I'd end up getting a lesson on my selfish-
ness or lack of discipline. He'd comfort me, but there'd always
be that instruction too."

"You sound like Mr. Quinlin."

Charles nodded, then said, "Is that good or bad?"

"Neither," said Embeth. "Just not very helpful." Even as she
said it, she realized it was a lie. Just talking with him had been
an immense help. And if what he said only made a glimmer of
sense, how could she totally deny that glimmer? He, along with
Mr. Quinlin, was the only person, after all, treating her with any
kindness and decency.

After that lunch Charles and Embeth hardly ever mentioned
the weather anymore. He asked how she was doing and she

replied honestly, if not completely. As the days passed, her assurance grew that her weeks with John Driver had left her with more than just weariness and loneliness. She was her mother's daughter—pregnant to a man who refused to look her way, a secret she kept from the world. How could she admit this to someone like Charles who spoke so strongly of faith? And yet she felt their time together meant more to her than ever.

Before long she began to hear in Charles's words something very unexpected. She thought she knew the judgment of God on those who'd done what she did. It was something her mother had to face every time she entered a church. But Charles talked about a peace and hope offered to all, no matter what they'd done, so long as they'd ask and accept forgiveness.

Two more weeks convinced Embeth that she needed to find out if Charles's promises were true, though she still couldn't admit what she'd done to him. And there was only one other person who'd spoken to her with such sympathy and care, one other person who seemed to understand the workings of God.

Stepping into Mr. Quinlin's room that early October evening, she wasn't sure how she'd ever get the words out, but when he smiled at her and asked how he could help, she couldn't contain herself.

"I've come for advice, Mr. Quinlin. A few weeks ago you offered me kind words that I ignored. I want to ask your forgiveness for that and to ask if you really meant them."

Quinlin's eyes widened. "I'm not sure I remember exactly—"

"You said I was of great worth to God. Is that true, even if I've lived very badly?"

"Well, certainly. We're all prodigals at one time or another. He knows everything that's happened anyway. All He wants is for you to own up to it and thank Him for forgiving you."

"I see," said Embeth.

Quinlin must have seen the lingering doubt because he said, "It's also right to share your burden with another believer, child. He'll forgive it all, but He's put others down here to help you out. You won't be alone."

Those words gave more hope to Embeth than anything else she'd heard, and she buried her head in her hands, speaking through sobs. "Mr. Quinlin, I've made a wreck of it all."

Quinlin waited. Embeth knew he wouldn't force anything from her. She had to tell him herself. Finally she said it as plain and true as she knew. If Quinlin had flinched or altered the expression on his face in the slightest, Embeth would have fled the factory forever. Instead, he took in a slow breath and held it, thinking.

"You've told no one? Not even the father?"

Embeth shook her head.

"And you're not thinking of ways to escape the problem, are you, because I can't give that advice."

"I'll live with my choice, Mr. Quinlin. My mother did with me. I can offer that much at least."

"So now you want forgiveness?"

Embeth nodded.

"Then we'll go back to what you said when you explained what happened. You've made a wreck of it. Do you know why?"

A thousand answers came to Embeth but she said nothing.

"Because you tried to go it alone, my dear. A month ago I advised you to forge ahead, and I fear that I failed you because I wasn't clear enough. I wanted you to not wait for any man. But for God—we must move when He does."

"How do I then go back?"

"No, Miss Herr. Not back. Forward once more. But not alone this time. Our Lord is ready to walk at any time."

Embeth nodded.

"Then kneel, child. Kneel and speak your sorrow for not following sooner. Pledge your heart to walk in His steps."

Embeth bent to a knee, emptied herself of all that had failed her, and swore herself to the pursuit of something invisible and undeniable. Her words were apology and thanks. When she opened her eyes Gabriel Quinlin was holding out his hand, a slip of paper in it. On the paper Embeth saw *First National Bank of Lowerton*, her name, and a sum of one thousand dollars.

"Don't protest," he said. "I can't very well lead you to the decisions and then leave you to fend for yourself. This is from my personal account, which I draw from to meet needs that I come across. And really, this isn't for you. It's for the little one."

Embeth stood silent. Was this just the first sign of the Lord's leading? With a quiet *thank-you* she accepted the check, wished Mr. Quinlin a good day, and slipped out of his office, her heart overflowing.

Lunch with Charles Graveston at the wall became an opportunity to ask questions about the direction of her new life. She asked about the words she should use while praying, about which church she should attend, about what her new faith should look like to other people. Graveston answered each question simply and usually included a Scripture passage for support. He never asked what it was that had changed her mind, just seemed pleased it had happened. He was now her closest confidant in the world, the shoulder to which she turned when news of Mr. Quinlin's death stunned the factory a week later.

On October 12, 1937, Gabriel Quinlin's maid stepped into her employer's library to ask if she might have next Wednesday afternoon off to visit her mother in Bellefonte and found Gabriel dead in his sitting chair. A doctor was called as a formality, but as soon as he touched the man's stiffening hand, he nodded and the bells of churches throughout the town rang their mournful song. School and factory alike were released. Farmers came in from their plows. Shop boys abandoned their shelves. Children gave up their hoops and dolls. Lowerton retreated indoors and cloistered together to talk over the sad news.

For once, Charles had no answers for her questions. She wanted to know how such a thing could happen, out of the blue, to such a godly man. Graveston only called on her to remember both the goodness of God and the faith of Gabriel Quinlin and celebrate that the two combined meant eternal blessing far greater than Quinlin's earthly wealth and a home far more beautiful than his house on the hill. Embeth took the three days of mourning to thank him the only way she knew how: by transcribing the deeds of his life into what would eventually become *He Saved Lowerton*.

Following their return to work, Charles asked Embeth if she would consent to his courting her. For a moment Embeth was left without answer. Every part of her wanted to be the object of his pursuit, yet she couldn't say yes without having told him about the secret she carried. It came out in a sob.

Graveston reacted with measured words.

"In light of this news, Miss Herr," Charles began and must've realized how formal he'd become because he stopped and took a deep breath. When he started once more, his voice was soft, thoughtful. "Embeth, I don't know how this is going to change things. I will need a few days to think things through, if you can grant me them."

She nodded and he pulled her to his chest.

Four days later, in the small prayer room of Quinlin's Estate, he gave his answer. If she'd accept, there'd be no courtship at all, just a proposal and marriage soon after. The town could think whatever it liked, but they would live as though the child were his. He took from his pocket a ring and offered a pledge to serve both as father and husband in the months and years to come if she would have him.

"Thank you," she answered, and he took her head in his hands and kissed her on the forehead. She let herself be held and prayed thanks to God as well. She'd never met another person willing to sacrifice so much. He'd saved her life.

Part Three

Despite my preoccupation with the things Embeth told me on Wednesday, we were, I believe, at our best today during our meeting with Representative Evans. Ben and Philip both dressed for the occasion, and I even managed to convince Sandra Guerrero to join us—partially because she's an eloquent young woman who loves the Estate and partially because of the diversity she provides for our little group. I wasn't sure she'd come, but when I told her this was a second chance to bring our plans before one of the few people who could really help save the Estate, she accepted right away.

We didn't plan or strategize for this meeting, just met up at the Estate and awaited Representative Evans. When he arrived I introduced Sandra and Philip and then we started our tour.

This was where the meeting really went well.

Inspired by different rooms or designs or stories, we each spent time talking both about the Estate itself and what it meant to us. Without even trying we covered its history, architecture, aesthetic value, social symbolism, religious characteristics, and position in the mythology of central Pennsylvania. It can easily be guessed which of us talked about which topic, and that's what was so great. The four of us come to the Estate from such different perspectives that it shows the magnitude, the sprawling breadth of influence, of the place. The wonderful thing was when Evans joined our discussion with impressions of his own.

"This has always been my favorite room," he said as we stepped into a small parlor off a back bedroom at the extreme corner of the Estate. It was a room I'd gone through without a thought many times before and had simply stopped visiting because of it being so far away. Evans must have seen the surprise on my face.

"I know, I know," he said. "But let me show you why." He walked to the window, lowered himself to a crouch, and pointed. The rest of us squatted behind him and tried to see what he saw.

It came in a flash.

Standing on the low roof of the solarium was a small sculpture of a robed man, arms outstretched. The alignment of the sculpture, however, was so perfect that he blocked out Atlas's stooped form from the fountain in the garden below. No longer was the weight of the world on a man's back; this new figure held the world as though it were a balloon. I didn't need those last three weeks of church to tell me who the figure was.

"Wow," Ben said behind me.

"I'm not religious, but it still blows me away. That sort of detail just doesn't happen by accident," said Representative Evans, standing up. Philip and Sandra stood too, while Ben continued to stare out the window. Evans continued. "That's why it irks me a little when people call the design of this place juvenile or amateur. I don't think Quinlin was an architect, but I'm pretty sure he planned every angle in this place."

Ben stood and said, "Me too."

Evans nodded for a second or two. When he stopped, he looked at us, took a short breath, and said, "This place is important, I realize that. Gabriel Quinlin was a man whose example and accomplishments I respect very much. He's also a man whose life will be lost to the years if we don't do something about it. Saving the Estate is one way to go about that."

Our faces glowed like those of children at Christmastime. He then raised a finger in warning.

"But," he went on, voice changed now, "I don't think it's the only way, and I'm not sure if it's the best thing for the community. In the end, that's where my decision rests—in what's best for Lowerton and the other towns around here."

"What can we do?" Philip asked.

Evans tapped a finger on his leg for just a second before answering. "You don't need to convince me anymore. I agree that the Estate is special. What I need convincing about is that *Lowerton* believes the Estate is special. You guys are great and enthusiastic, but you need more voices behind you. And I'm not talking petitions; I'm looking for something that says the town is willing to sacrifice for this place."

"Money?"

"Could be. Or it could be people giving their time and effort toward restoring the Estate. Could be a decision by the high school to send volunteer crews up here. Anything that tells me the town's concerned." After waiting a beat he looked down at his watch and said, "I've got another meeting at five. What say we go take a look at that maze before it gets too late?"

With that he turned and walked out of the parlor. Evans knew his way around the Estate and didn't need our guiding. Following on his heels, Sandra and Ben murmured to each other while Philip waited for me to catch up. I hadn't been able to make my legs move.

"Good news, huh?" he said. "What, you don't think it's good news?"

I started to shake my head but couldn't bring myself to do it. I had no idea whether what Evans had said was good or bad or something in between. It just wasn't what I expected.

"He gave us a focus, at least," said Philip. "Now we just take it to the town. It isn't on our shoulders as much anymore."

I nodded. He was right about that.

Philip gave me a nudge, and I followed him out the door, down the tiled hall, and up the sweeping marble staircase to the Maze's entrance. Evans, Sandra, and Ben were all waiting for us there. The door attendant, a rail-thin woman, took three dollars from each of the others, nodded at my all-access pass I'd earned as Glen's daughter, and opened the two iron doors to let us in. A cool dampness felt even at the ankles instantly spilled from the complex space.

"See you at the other side," Evans said, took a sharp right, and disappeared.

Sandra asked Ben if he knew his way through and when he said no, she said neither did she and suggested they team up. He nodded and together they headed straight in. The entrance to my usual route.

"Have a good walk," Philip said. "I guess you'll finish first." He then took the path Evans had chosen.

The Maze waited for me. I could follow Ben and Sandra straight ahead and walk the path I knew in my sleep or I could try something different. After a moment's pause, the choice felt obvious. Going left, I stepped forward and was immediately surrounded by gray granite walls that towered nine feet high on each side. I knew that stopping only made it feel as if they might topple over on me, so I kept moving. Lefts and rights came and went. Soon it seemed the ceiling, twenty feet above, had somehow lowered itself to the top of the walls. The room was closing in, and for the first time I felt that dread claustrophobia so many others have experienced in their wanderings through the Maze. Another left, another right, and still the same gunmetal gray on all sides, until finally after a half hour I saw a flash of denim and began hearing a faint voice up ahead. Words were being spoken, yet I could never round the corners quick enough to catch what was said. There was a quick instant when I wasn't sure if I was in a dream or actually walking the Maze.

Eventually I found my way. It took me just over an hour and would have taken longer if I hadn't recognized the little marks past roamers had left to help them remember the route, things like scrapes on the floor that point in the proper direction. Philip and Evans showed up fifteen minutes after me, having met up right before they finished. Sandra appeared five minutes later. She'd lost Ben and couldn't explain how it'd happened. Ben finished shortly after and said he didn't know how they'd split apart either.

"It's the Maze," I said, and everybody nodded as if they understood completely.

RELIGION AND QUINLIN'S ESTATE

Both the view from the parlor window that Greg Evans pointed out, along with the door Embeth opened into Quinlin's past, has made it impossible to ignore the role religion played in the building of the house as well as in Gabriel Quinlin's own life. Embeth mentioned that he attended the First Presbyterian Church of Lowerton, although his journals and writings profess no strong allegiance to the teachings of that denomination. What I've discovered is that rather than being tangled up in the whole of theology, Gabriel was primarily concerned with just two biblical principles: mercy and provision.

How these two came to be so important to him would be hard to pin down, but references to each one in his correspondence increased greatly after his return from Yale. The easy conclusion is that while at university he came across either the touching displays of both mercy and provision or the willful disregard of them. Something happened to him in New Haven, that's almost certain, which infused his life with qualities rarely seen in industry leaders, particularly at that time.

During the few months his father lived following Gabriel's return home, the two quarreled often about the role of ethics in commerce. Perhaps years of hard tutelage under Lucas Quinlin might have crushed Gabriel's generous spirit, but with his father's unhappy accident, young Quinlin set about defining the standards of conduct for himself and his company. Excellence, honesty, quality, and accountability all ranked high on the list. Right up there with these were mercy and provision. And in the Depression's coming woe, it was these two standards that saved Lowerton.

The one thing that wasn't as thoroughly influenced by Quinlin's faith was the Estate itself. There are the chambers in the
dungeon reminiscent of the story of Jonah, with the whalebone
ribbing on the ceilings. There's the statue of Jesus that can be
made to hold up the world. But only in one area can be found
the cross-shaped floor plan so typical of cathedrals and other
buildings Quinlin had to have researched when planning the
Estate's construction.

The small cruciform chamber is where Charles Graveston
asked Embeth for her hand in marriage. It's tucked at the rear
of the second floor and is one of the darkest rooms in the house.
Cramped and for the most part undecorated, tradition holds that
Quinlin designed it as a place of prayer and contemplation.
Small benches sit at the foot, head, and end of each arm as if
waiting for the penitent. Were such a room built by a Catholic,
one might expect rows of candles, fonts of holy water, confes-
sionals. Here, though, there's only darkness and the hope that a
person's prayers will be heeded, sins forgiven, the life altered.

I've been there many times and have always left feeling only
the silence. Now, with all that's happened, I feel I should maybe
go back and speak one more time into the dark, then wait for an
answer. Or would my words not reach that high? Would I come
away with even a greater sense of the darkness and silence,
more than before?

WEDNESDAY, MARCH 24, 1999

Finally, my job with the *Express* paid off today. Not in
money—I'm barely keeping my head above water—but in information. I'd finished my edit of another article about the latest

school board meeting and was poking around in the archives when a name caught my attention: Lydia Furrow. Her confronting me at church last week still knotted my stomach whenever I thought about it, and because I hadn't heard a thing from Embeth since Monday, I was hungry for anything I could find on Lydia. This article was about a charity golf tournament. I found other articles too. It turns out the Furrows are an active family in the Lowerton community who have been making headlines regularly since the paper's inception thirty-four years ago.

The earliest mention of Lydia was an engagement announcement in the society column, which wouldn't be worth mentioning except the photo was just a simple headshot of Lydia alone. Her beau, Lorne, was missing. And since both her parents were dead, I can only surmise that Lydia herself placed the message. That, in a nutshell, captures the personality that emerged from all the other articles over the years. Whether chairing a committee to raise funds for a new pediatric wing at the hospital, hosting a Fourth of July celebration, or leading a demonstration against the orphanage, the message always came off secondary to Lydia herself. She demanded that credit be given where it was due—namely to her.

The two most interesting articles I found were both about funerals. One was a quarter-page article covering Charles Graveston's funeral in which Lydia Furrow was mentioned seven times. For such a short space, the number seemed so excessive that I counted three times just to make sure. But there they were—everything from her impassioned eulogy to what she wore, to her fainting as the casket was borne away, to the wake the Furrows hosted. For comparison's sake, Embeth, the widow, was mentioned twice.

The other article was more unusual. It was written in the aftermath of Evangeline Graveston's death at Quinlin's Estate and stood out not because of Lydia's presence but her noticeable absence. She wasn't at the funeral, and her refusal to attend took up two paragraphs of copy. Though she loved her niece, she wouldn't appear at the ceremony so long as a single member of Martin Peterson's commune attended. In her mind they were the ones responsible for her death. Lydia had protested the commune's coming to Lowerton, and although not stated, it was obvious that Evangeline's death was some sort of vindication for her. Again, Embeth and Charles, who was still alive at the time of his daughter's death, warranted only a single mention.

"Spotlight grabber," Philip said when I'd finished rereading him the article over the phone. He'd called to invite me to church, and we'd quickly gotten on the topic of what needed to be done to raise awareness of the Estate in Lowerton, then we shifted to Embeth and then Lydia. I guess he was most interested in the article on Evangeline, which is why he made me read it to him a second time.

"One thing's always confused me about this whole mess," he said after a pause. "Why did Evangeline think she was Quinlin's daughter? Where did that come from when she was really the daughter of this John Driver guy?"

I suggested that it might have just been the town rumor and heard him murmur something that didn't sound like agreement.

"I think it could've been more than that. I mean, for her to join this commune and move into the place she thought she was going to inherit—she must've been obsessed."

"Dwight said the whole town thought she was crazy."

"But obsession is different. People don't just create things to be obsessed with. Normally they're based on something real, something true."

I couldn't help giving a scoff.

"You disagree?"

"Haven't I told you about Glen? He dedicated his life to searching for something that wasn't true." When Philip didn't reply, I said, "You're asking questions I don't know the answers to. If I could get in touch with Embeth, maybe we'd find out. This is taking way too long."

Philip sighed. "I just think there's something unusual behind all of it. It's frustrating."

Sitting here a few hours later, recording the conversation, I see his point a little clearer. There are holes in the story and most of them surround Evangeline Graveston. For the moment I'm at a loss as far as how to fill them. Even the library year-books have had the woman's picture removed from them. I can't think of any other sources of information. But maybe the best way to move forward from here is to try to uncover the world she lived in at the time of her death. There must be connections to the commune that had bought the Estate. They must have some sort of story to tell. At this point, the mere possibility of a story is better than the silence facing us everywhere else. I don't know what I'll do if I find this road blocked too.

Road to Damascus

A couple of days of research has uncovered the information that follows. Most of it came from a feature article published in the university's student paper that profiled the commune and its leader, Martin Peterson. The rest came from *Express* articles, conversations with townspeople who remembered the commune's arrival, and one commune member herself who still lives in the area. She'd left the Estate before Evangeline moved in and so could provide no clarification on that story.

Named after the setting of Saul's blinding meeting with God, the Road to Damascus began in 1967 in a two-story A-frame in Boulder, Colorado, a few blocks outside the University of Colorado campus. It was just the latest home for Martin Peterson, a 24-year-old seminary dropout and recent multi-millionaire.

The heir to a San Diego investor's fortune, Peterson had begun trekking east after his parents died in a boating accident off the Baja coast. His search for a home became a hunt for a church. In small towns across Nevada, Arizona, and Utah, Peterson would settle for a few months until word of his wealth had spread and the invariable change in attitude toward him became too stifling. Whether offering him an immediate position on the board of elders, making special requests for lavish changes to the church building, or matching him with the most beautiful of parishioner daughters, the churches always managed to focus in on Peterson's fortune.

In Boulder, among the foothills of the Rockies, Martin gave up searching and decided to start his own church based on the lives and examples of early Christians. He purchased a home for its proximity to the University of Colorado campus, knowing those most likely to be interested in his church would be the young, the seeking.

The name Road to Damascus was chosen because the story held such personal weight in his own life, having temporarily lost his eyesight at age seventeen following a car accident.

During his months of darkness, while doctors and family tried to persuade him to get used to the idea of never seeing again, a member from his parents' church visited daily at the hospital and later at his home to pray with Martin for the return of his vision. Three weeks later, shadows began to creep back into Martin's sight, and within two months his eyes had been completely restored. Only one word existed for that kind of healing, and Martin Peterson dedicated himself to finding out *Who* had allowed such a miracle.

By the time he'd moved to Boulder, Peterson's days were consumed by three things: mornings of prayer and Bible reading, afternoons of sidewalk ministry on campus, and evenings of personal interaction with students and community members who stopped by his house to talk.

"I originally wanted a place where people could discuss rather than just listen," Peterson said in one interview. "Eventually it became much more."

The transition came as more and more people visited the A-frame in Boulder and fewer left. Students seeking a place to study or chat sometimes wouldn't leave for days. Some started growing their own food so as not to burden Peterson, and within two years the vegetables at Road to Damascus were featured in a Denver home-and-garden magazine. Bedrooms remained filled not only on weekends but throughout the week, and soon students weren't even returning home during summer vacations. They'd found a new home, a safe place away from the economic, social, and political storms of the late '60s and early '70s.

For five years this went on with hardly a hitch, but then small intrusions by campus administrators, concerned parents,

city officials, and even the police began making life more difficult. And with thirteen full-time residents, the A-frame had
become cramped rather than cozy. After two weeks of discussion
with the others who called Road to Damascus home, Martin
Peterson decided once more to head east on a search. Where it
ended was Quinlin's Estate.

A friend of Peterson's, attending university just outside
Lowerton, is credited with alerting him to the failing orphanage
and suggesting he move Road to Damascus from the shadow of
the Rockies to the peak of an Allegheny ridge.

In November of 1972 the Central Pennsylvania Children's
Orphanage closed forever and Quinlin's Estate was sold for $9.2
million to Martin Peterson. Nearly all of the orphans disappeared in the days following the sale without a single mention
of their destination, as though some mad piper had opened a
hole in the Allegheny mountainside and charmed the children
away from their hilltop Hamelin. Those that remained were not
the lame this time, but those old enough to sign on with Road
to Damascus remained as converts. Three boys and one young
woman welcomed Martin Peterson and the other twelve residents when they arrived from Boulder.

The town of Lowerton did not offer quite so warm a reception. Local churches, headed by Lydia Furrow, organized a demonstration demanding that the "hippie hedonists," as a photo of
a protest sign can be seen to read, take their lives of sin elsewhere. Cultural revolution was on a time delay in a place like
Lowerton, and the town had never faced the fallout of the '60s
counterculture movement. They'd heard secondhand accounts of
protests and rallies at the university but that was simply a different world. Plus, the lessons of Quinlin's closed town had

never been forgotten. Now this quasi-religious sect had purchased their only landmark and was moving in with siren calls
of free love, thick blue plumes of marijuana smoke, and insurrec-
tionist notions that the boys dying over in Vietnam were something less than heroes. Lowerton knew what they were in for;
they'd seen the news reports.

This was a rift that would never heal and was the primary
reason Road to Damascus became a commune. Refused service
at most Lowerton shops and castigated if seen in public, the
members grew self-sufficient and preferred to stay inside the
Estate walls, finding that the great building offered a world all
its own.

Unfortunately, little remains as to the daily existence of
Road to Damascus members. It is known that the Estate's two
solariums were turned into greenhouses to grow vegetables
throughout the winter, and that a portion of the grounds was
converted to animal pens for some chickens and a pair of Hol-
steins. Local streams provided a source of trout, while some
members of the Estate enjoyed hunting the abundant whitetail
of the area—that or the occasional wild turkey.

In understanding how the Road to Damascus survived on its
own for eight years, it's best to remember that they started with
only a few people and never climbed higher than twenty-seven.
Peterson's inheritance had certainly dwindled after his purchase
of the building, although the interest he earned on the remaining amount was more than enough to keep his family—as he
now called them—well stocked and fed. And when group members earned extra income selling trinkets, woolen knittings,
baked goods, and even stitched kick sacks on campus, they found
they had more than they needed.

The townspeople of Lowerton, their short memories on dis-play, did not accept that this closed community could thrive despite being ignored by the populace below. Whispers began.

You know what they're growing in the greenhouses, don't you?

Did you hear that the seven basement chambers have been turned into caves to raise hallucinogenic mushrooms?

And those were among the kindest rumors.

Town enmity had reached such a pitch in the weeks leading up to the first Halloween of the commune's existence that the local police chief ordered his men to search the place. They found nothing, but that just cemented in the town's mind how clever these deviants were, so that on October 31, 1973, Lydia Furrow gathered over a hundred citizens to make a march on the Estate. They would not allow the Road to Damascus to unleash whatever it'd planned on this devil's day.

In what one observer called a pitch-perfect reenactment of *Frankenstein*'s mob scene, a horde of schoolteachers and butchers and factory workers armed themselves with hammers, crowbars, and even a shotgun or two for their march to the Estate's entrance. There they were met by Keith Wilcox, chief of police, and Anthony Servais, foreman at Quinlin Metal Works.

Servais closed his eyes, stepped forward, and said, "In fifteen seconds I'm going to open my eyes. If I recognize any of my employees, they'll find themselves jobless in the morning. Fif-teen, fourteen . . ."

The crowd withered from a hundred to about sixty during his counting. Wilcox was next to speak.

"Those of you that remain are now in jeopardy of being arrested for trespassing. The Estate is now private property. Those kids inside don't want to prosecute, but they will if need be. They're tired of the witch-hunt, and I don't blame them. They're smart kids, though, and have offered to allow five of you to go inside and look around but under my supervision. Mr. Peterson said you can search any nook, enter any room. You can walk through the Maze if you'd like. You can even smoke their cigarettes to make sure the leaves are right. Lydia, you seem to be at the center of all this. Pick your four and let's get going."

The next week's *Express* editorial page made its offer of contrition. Motivated by a proper sense of protection, they had overstepped their bounds. The rumors turned out to be unfounded and unfair, and though the town still didn't understand the life-style choice of their neighbors high on the hill, they would, nevertheless, respect and tolerate them. The Road to Damascus could stay.

Only two years later, in October 1975, when the moan of an ambulance siren wound its way down the mountainside and the attendants wheeled the broken body of Evangeline Graveston into the local hospital, Lydia Furrow shook her head on the local news and said, "I knew we were right about them. What a tragedy that something like this had to happen to clear the scales from our eyes." Her scaleless eyes, it should be noted, were noticeably free of any sign of tears or sorrow for her niece.

Four days later Peterson hosted the mayor for a quiet breakfast and sold the Estate for just under a million dollars. The next day the Road to Damascus—now twenty-six in number after Evangeline's death—vanished as quickly as the orphans had before them. Even with their rushed departure, they left the Estate in remarkably good shape. The only real damage found by the city council during their tour of the Estate later that week was an inscription chiseled into the wall of one of the dungeon chambers: *The engulfing waters threatened me, the deep sur-rounded me.*

In a room ribbed like the inside of a whale, someone had felt a similar desolation and carved a fragment of Jonah's lonely lament.

TUESDAY, MARCH 30, 1999

This morning, with the *Express* nearly ready to print, Flora gave me a look at the UFO-sighting April Fools' Day article they'd be putting on the cover, apparently a tradition since she took over as editor in chief. The article made me smile and reminded me again I am not working for the *New York Times*.

What's been most interesting in reading through old issues is how no other place in the world seems to exist except for Lowerton. There's this peculiar kind of willful ignorance that radiates from the paper, particularly during times of crucial national or international news.

The week of the *Challenger* crash, the paper's lead story was the purchase of a snowplow that could be fitted to one of Lowerton's fire engines. When the wall came down in Berlin, Lowertonians learned of the high school's plan to overhaul the school's lunch menu after winter break. The San Francisco earthquake was ignored for a profile of Gavin O'Connell, a thirteen-year-old Irish exchange student starting for the high-school varsity soccer team.

What I've realized in reading back through so many issues is that it's *my* view of history that's unusual in this town. Folks here remember Desert Storm, they remember John Lennon's murder, the eruption of Mount St. Helens, but what they really remember—what they talk about in barbershops, at Little League games, at factory spring picnics—are the things that made the *Lowerton Express*, the stories that have somehow rolled over into town legend.

They remember the mandatory locker checks in the fall of 1987 that broke a fairly major cocaine ring run by three Lowerton High juniors. The freak autumn blizzard in '90 that forced *He Saved Lowerton* to be performed a week later than normal, the only time in its history. The weeklong buzz in '97 after a first-grade teacher spotted a mountain lion, thought to have disappeared in this region of the state, prowling outside the elementary school playground. The fire that gutted Howard's five-and-dime on Main Street and the subsequent arrest of its owners for arson and insurance fraud.

Everybody reminisces fondly about Howard's now that it is gone. They miss walking from the factory during lunch for a quick hot dog or dropping by after church for a newspaper. They fail to mention their ignoring the place for anything other than a place to dump loose change. For *real* shopping people drove out of town to shop at Wal-Mart—cheaper prices and a clean new lunch counter that served both Pizza Hut and Taco Bell.

But, they do miss Howard's. That loss is for real. And I don't want them to make the mistake and end up feeling the same way about the Estate should it fall. Somehow we've got to make the town recognize its feelings for the house before it's too late and Quinlin's Estate becomes another legend, another ghost. In many ways, it already has. What we've got to work on is making sure that it's *saving* the Estate that people remember rather than its destruction.

To do that, I've come to see we need to switch our tactics. Just reading through the *Express* is enough to convince me. Representative Evans is right in that my love for the Estate's history, Philip's love of its spiritual resonance, Ben's love of its design mean little to these people. I could talk all day about how every time the Estate changed hands it reflected our country's shifting cultural focus—from the stolid patriotism of its military installation days to the socialistic reform of its orphanage stage, from the dashed Utopian dreams of Road to Damascus to present day—but few here in Lowerton would care. That's outside news—the daily paper and CNN. What stays in their mind is *Express* news.

I'm now convinced that Embeth Graveston's confession, Evangeline Graveston's sad death, Lydia Furrow's secrets, what happened with Wanda Maxwell, and my father's obsession are the keys to capturing the support of this town. These are people they know, faces they recognize, names they've heard. They are front-page headlines of the *Lowerton Express*.

FRONT-PAGE NEWS

From its first issue in March 1965 until today, the *Express* has featured Quinlin's Estate as its front-page story seven times. Six are unsurprising.

The closing of the orphanage.

Evangeline's death, October 1975.

The subsequent sale of the Estate and midnight evacuation of Road to Damascus a week later.

President Carter's visit in 1978.

Brighton Entertainment's purchase of the Estate and

planned renovation as an amusement park.

Brighton Entertainment's announcement regarding the scheduled destruction of the home.

And it is nearly the sixth anniversary since the day the most unexpected headline, in 36-point type across the top, landed on the doorsteps of Lowerton.

Quinlin's Gold Discovered!

According to the story, the years of searching finally paid off for groundskeeper Glen Lawson on March 30, 1993. For while making his evening rounds along the outside of the Maze after the building had been shut down for the night, Lawson stumbled over the uneven ground and lurched forward and at the same time lifted his nightstick to shield himself. The heavy baton slammed into the Maze wall, opening a two-inch-deep hole in the surface of the brick face. When he had regained his bearings, Lawson noticed something glittering beneath the newly created hole, something smooth and yellow. Chipping away at loose bits, Lawson made his monumental discovery— Quinlin's gold! The legends were true after all. And didn't this make sense, to use the gold bricks in the actual construction of the building? Hiding them, effectively, in plain sight? So Lawson's perseverance had paid off and with quite a windfall. Brighton Entertainment's lawyers were meeting to determine the legal split of the treasure, but it is rumored that Lawson could stand to take home more than a million dollars in a finder's fee. Quite an ending to an epic quest.

The story, of course, was an April Fools' Day hoax.

There was no happy ending.

No gold.

No reward for Lawson's quest.

Just another illusion of answered prayer.

SUNDAY, APRIL 4, 1999

The Carters caught up with Philip and me outside church this morning and invited us both over to lunch. It had been a while since I'd seen them and so I was grateful for the invite, especially because I knew it would delay my conversation with Philip about why I hadn't bothered to call Meryl back and give her permission to talk with him.

It was the first time Dwight and Philip had spoken at any length, and they immediately bonded over their shared disgust by the downfall of the Pittsburgh Steelers and their respect for Charles Monroe, the pastor at First Baptist. I joined Monique in the kitchen. As the two of us prepared the brunch, we chatted about Vanessa, about how the high school had changed, and a dozen other small things. It all felt very domestic. Soon we were sitting around the table, bowing our heads and holding hands while Dwight said grace. The meal of grilled London broil, tossed greens, and Monique's homemade pickles, along with iced tea, was perfect for ushering in the promise of spring. Conversation went here and there, and only after Dwight recalled how his crew filled his helmet with shaving cream on April Fools' Day did I think to ask him about the joke article in the *Express*.

"Did Glen ever see it?" I asked. If he had, he certainly hadn't shown it to me.

"Yep, he saw it," said Dwight. "Did a good job of laughing it off in public too. You'd have thought it would've bugged him, but I'm pretty sure he really didn't care."

"Why?"

"Well, about three days after it came out, we had him over for dinner—you remember this, Monique?—and when the topic of gold came up he asked me if I thought he was crazy. I told him I loved him like a brother but that it'd been a number of years he'd been searching and with nothing to show, maybe it was time to forget it, give up. You know what he said to that?"

Philip and I waited.

"He said, 'You don't know what I know.' "

Philip, who'd been spooning more greens onto his plate, quickly asked, "What did he know?"

"No idea," said Dwight. "I guess it's the thing that kept him going for so long, though. And the reason he could ignore people making fun of him. He was sure about Quinlin's gold."

"So, do you think he actually knew something the rest of us don't?" Philip hadn't even blinked this entire time. He wore the same expression when talking about his sister, or now when he mentioned Wander.

Dwight shook his head. Slowly. Three times. "No, son. I think Glen Lawson—sorry, Eve—was a deluded man."

What could be said after that? I didn't want the subject to continue any further so I began telling Dwight and Monique what I'd realized about Lowerton residents and their obsession with local news. Both agreed that the stories of Embeth, Evangeline, and Wander would grab the town's interest.

"Here's my problem." I said. "Lydia has thwarted me from contacting Embeth, so the story's going nowhere. Glen's not coming out of the coma, and Evangeline is dead. I'm blocked."

Monique shook her head with sympathy. Dwight sat in

thought—my adoptive father trying to solve the problems of the world for his skinny white daughter. His response caused more problems than it answered.

"You're missing somebody, Eve," he said. "I think you know who it is."

"You think I didn't uncover every stone? Who am I missing?"

"Think."

"Dwight—"

"Meryl."

"No," I said without even thinking.

Dwight lifted his hands. It was off his shoulders and onto mine.

"Why her?" I demanded.

"Because she knows your father, maybe better than any of us. She definitely knows this town and its gossip better than us."

"She knows about Wanda Maxwell too," said Philip, getting in his little dig.

Dwight nodded, then added, "She also knows Lydia Furrow."

"*Bleh*," I said, and that pretty much summed up my feelings. "Those two know each other?"

Dwight nodded. "Meryl works for Lydia. Cleans her house and does some cooking for her, has for five or six years now." Then he shrugged and said, "People hear things, Eve."

I let it go at that, not saying anything more. The unfortunate thing is that he's got more of a point than I'd like to grant him. Perhaps unsurprisingly, Meryl has become a central figure in all of these stories whether I want her to be there or not. She always managed to weasel her way into everything else, and now I have to decide if I'm strong enough to bridge a ten-year gap between us and ask for her help.

Philip, of course, can't stand that I'm hesitating at all. Driving away from the Carters', he said, "It's been ten years! What happened between you two, anyway?"

I think I hurt him a little when I told him I didn't want to tell him that. He didn't look my way the rest of the ride back to my apartment and then dropped me off rather than coming upstairs. I've seen the look he had on his face before. Glen got that look after a long empty night of searching. The Trevor twins from Little Pines got it when we told them they weren't allowed into the tree fort with us. I know I got it when Lydia Furrow answered Embeth's phone and told me to mind my own business. It's the countenance of a person who's just had a door closed in his face. I suppose it's the face we'll all bear if Greg Evans contacts us and says there's nothing he can do, the Estate must fall. I wonder if I should tell Philip to get used to disappointment.

Monday, April 5, 1999

After reading and rereading my accounts of the Road to Damascus, I decided to focus my search on just Martin Peterson. He would, after all, be the most interesting person to talk to about Evangeline Graveston, since he was the one who allowed her to join the commune. He was there at the time of her death, and he faced the greatest portion of the blame in the aftermath. I thought finding him after so long might be difficult, but it took just some careful reading of the interviews and articles to decide on an individual still in Lowerton who might help me—Chief of

Police Keith Wilcox. He's always seemed far more understanding of Road to Damascus than anyone else in town and facili-
tated them staying as long as they did. A quick call to the
station found him about to leave for lunch, but he said that could
wait when I told him whom I was seeking.

"Martin Peterson," he said almost to himself, "I haven't
heard that name in years."

"Oh?"

"Yeah, he kept in touch for a while. At first it was because I
requested it in case any new evidence appeared tied to that girl's
death. After a few years, we got to trading letters about every
other month or so. He'd send postcards from different countries.
I kept him up-to-date with things happening here. He was still
fascinated by Lowerton, which I thought was a pretty charitable
attitude seeing as how bad the folks here treated him."

"Why don't you keep in touch anymore?"

"That's just the way things go. It's not like we were best
friends or something. He ended up getting married, and I guess
the gossip of a small town halfway around the world stopped
mattering so much."

"Do you remember where he was the last time he wrote
you?"

I heard Wilcox *hmm* to himself, thinking, then he said, "New
Zealand. The capital city—I can't remember its name right now
and I didn't keep the letter. He was teaching English to Japanese
and Taiwanese students at a language school there. Met a girl
and settled down."

I thanked him for his help, he told me to say hello if I ever
found Martin, and then I turned to the Internet. Five minutes
later an on-line phone directory in Wellington, New Zealand,

offered me a potential phone number. I called but got no answer so left a message explaining who I was and how I'd tracked him down. I left both my telephone number and E-mail address. This evening, when I logged on, I found that he'd sent a brief note.

From: Martin Peterson
Sent: Tuesday, April 6, 1999 1:42 PM
To: Lawson, Eve
Subject: RE: Inquiry about Road to Damascus

Ms. Lawson,

If you'd mentioned anybody other than Keith Wilcox,
I probably wouldn't be writing this. But Keith was a
friend to me in Lowerton and so I'm willing to help
you out. I'm sorry to hear that the Estate's going to
be torn down. I hope in answering your questions I
might help to save it somehow. Just realize that
it's been over twenty years. Memories, even terrible
ones, do fade.

Martin Peterson

The pieces are beginning to fall into place. I have a door reopened to the closed life of Evangeline Graveston. And, if (big if) I convince myself to talk with her, Meryl Lakewood could possibly provide more information on Glen, Wander, and even Lydia. All that remains is to somehow regain contact with Embeth (she didn't come down to Glen's room today) and finish her tale. Oh, and raise a few more million dollars to finish off the plan that started this whole process in the first place!

Sometimes it feels like I've gone astray from my original purpose and that all these detours are merely dead ends. Other times, like when I talked to Dwight and Monique about Lowerton's preoccupation with small-town history, it seems this is exactly where I'm supposed to be headed. The uncertainty is the hardest part. In spite of what Philip says about the Maze, not every step is one taken in the right direction. There's right and wrong, forward and backward. I've walked the Maze many times; I know there are quicker ways through. Philip says it's the journey that's the important thing, but in the case of saving the Estate I don't have that luxury. The journey might teach me more about history than could my years studying at the university, yet if the Estate is destroyed, it'll all come to nothing. A chasing after the wind, as the pastor might say. And wind chasing is something I have no time for right now.

THURSDAY, APRIL 8, 1999

Another thing I haven't the time for is bureaucratic insanity, and yet that's what we have. Mayor Wes Hundley's city council meetings are a study in organized chaos. He's broken up the management of Lowerton into sixteen "action committees" that meet four at a time for thirty-minute intervals in different corners of the VFW great room out on Jackson Avenue. Every half hour a bell chimes and the council members and citizen volunteers jump up and scatter across the room to their next meeting.

Ben, Philip, and I addressed the Town Planning Committee at eight o'clock and then the Parks and Recreation group an hour later. Two men overlapped on both teams and so about fourteen people in all heard our pitch.

There were three main components to our plan.

First, we sought the formal designation of September 15 as Gabriel Quinlin Day.

Second, we proposed a special partnership between the town of Lowerton, the state of Pennsylvania, and the university to use Quinlin's Estate as a research and work-study setting for history, architecture, engineering, horticulture, and other degree programs. Such "QE classes" would be in charge of maintaining some portion of the Estate, and even students in criminal justice programs could be trained in security techniques at the Estate.

Third, we requested that the heretofore free production of *He Saved Lowerton* be changed to an annual fund-raiser for the Estate. More than three thousand people attend the three weekend shows so even a four-dollar cover charge could raise a decent sum of money.

The bell Wes Hundley rings to signal the end of a session rang just as we ended both our presentations, and so there wasn't a single question or even a comment put forth. I've never seen Philip more annoyed.

"How do they accomplish anything?" he said afterward. "It's like we're in Freedonia and Groucho's running the show."

He and I had said good-night to Ben, who was the most optimistic of our group ("Maybe," he suggested, "they'll get confused and just pass the whole thing without debate.") and started walking to our cars a few blocks over on Chestnut Street. Two blocks west and we'd cross the outer limit of the shadow's sweep and enter into Little Pines Trailer Park. I knew the area well.

"From what I've picked up from the stories I've written, the groups meet individually during the week to discuss the items presented at council. That's where the real work is done."

"And we're not invited there."

I nodded.

Philip kicked a stone across the street and it clanged off a metal garbage can. His hands were shoved deep in his pockets, and he looked far more upset than he had just moments ago when shaking hands with the small group of people who wished us good-night. I asked him if he was okay.

"Frustrated," he said, lifting his face to stare at the moon. In its silver light, his face appeared strangely old. "I hate not being able to do more about this. It always seems to be that way with everything."

I knew what he meant. Karen. Maybe Wanda. I'd cut him off from the one person he wanted to speak to most. "We have to be patient, Philip. It's hard for me too, but what else can we do?"

"Buy it," he said.

For a moment I couldn't tell if he was kidding or not, because his face was half hidden by shadow. Then he leaned into the lamplight and I saw he was serious. Or at least some part of him. "Do you have some rich relative you haven't told us about?"

He shook his head and looked back at the moon. Another second passed and he said, "Quinlin's gold."

"That's not funny, Philip." And it wasn't. I hadn't shared everything, but he knew that Glen had given me up for the dream of that gold. It was a nasty thing to say. But then he said something that might've been even worse.

"Could happen."

He quickly reversed himself and gave a cheap smile of apology, reaching out to squeeze my hand. I wasn't sure what he meant by any of it, and now a few hours later, I still can't figure it out. We found our cars soon after, and though it seemed like an awkward way to part, I wanted nothing more at that moment than the comfort of my bed. I said good-bye, got in, and brought the Civic to life. Philip waved and then leaned back against his door and raised his face once more to the moon. He was still there, a dim reflection in my rearview mirror, when I pulled from the curb, leaving him to the night and whatever thoughts had filled his eyes with such sorrow.

They were eyes I'd seen before. I'd seen them on Glen after long nights spent at the Estate, when he'd return home with his fingernails caked with dirt and mortar from digging at the walls. I'd seen them on Wander whenever we talked too long about leaving Lowerton. There was dreaming, we found out, and then there was talking so much that it hurt. Too often our time in my room went past just wishing until I could see her getting almost sick in thinking about how she had to walk home across the courtyard to her trailer.

I admit, too, that I saw them on Meryl Lakewood. It's a hard thing to say, because the woman so often pushed it from her face to yell at me or call Wanda something mean. But she did look that way. Not at first, but definitely in the years that followed. Nothing turned out right for any of us in Little Pines, but Meryl certainly did the least to help her own cause. She'd just sit staring out the window or at a handwritten letter, her eyes vacant and longing. It was the only time I thought we might have something in common.

This all comes back to me now because she left another message on my answering machine while I was away at the meetings. This one stopped me dead in my tracks.

Eve, it's Meryl for about the five-hun ... oh, never mind. This is about Wanda. This Philip guy says you want to find her. I know where

she is. I tracked her down for you, but it's you she belongs to, not him.
Do you want to talk with her? Let me know. I will say this—she's in
a better place.

My first thought was that Wander had died. Isn't *a better*
place the euphemism for that sort of thing? But then I listened
to the message again and realized Meryl had actually offered me
the chance to talk with the girl. I don't think she trucks in the
spirit realm, yet, so I'm assuming Wander is alive somewhere.

My next thought was that she might be in Richmond, Virginia. This thought came because of the same phrase—*a better*
place. Meryl used it more times than I can remember while we
lived together, and it always referred to Richmond, Virginia, the
city she'd left to come to Lowerton. Her home. She told me
about it during the first weeks of her arrival in our trailer; she
told me about it for weeks, months, and years afterward. Richmond may well have been part of the sadness that clouded her
eyes. But all she did was talk. Talk and grumble about how it
was such a better place.

Part of me hopes very much that Wander is there, if just to
rub some salt into Meryl's wounds. The rest of me sees that,
like it or not, I'm now going to have to get in touch with the
woman. There's no getting around it. I doubt our next meeting
will be as congenial as our first.

THE ARRIVAL OF MERYL LAKEWOOD

Before I started primary school and before Meryl showed
up, I spent my afternoons at Mrs. Grayson's trailer on the other
side of the court. An older woman with a great love of tuna fish,
loud German operas, and Chesterfield cigarettes, she'd keep

watch on me until Glen returned home from work in his Nova. Once I saw the car pull into the lot, I'd clean up whatever puzzle I'd been fitting together or put away my blocks, say good-bye and thank-you, and head straight home. That day, the day Meryl arrived, I marched across the lawn and stepped inside the trailer, immediately noticing a stranger's sandals on our welcome mat. Glen didn't think up many rules, but taking our shoes off at the door was one. He wasted too many hours sweeping on the job and wasn't about to lose any more with having to sweep all the time at home. The sandals sitting there that day were a shocking green color, the same green in fact as the tennis balls Cal Kelvin bragged about stealing from Howard's five-and-dime. From the kitchen came a low murmur followed by Glen's voice. "Don't dawdle, Eve. I want you to meet somebody."

I stepped around the coat stand wondering what kind of person would wear such sandals. My answer sat waiting at the kitchen table in a dress that perfectly matched the wild footwear. The woman, seeing me, cocked her head to the side and smiled in a way that reminded me very much of the Davenports' German shepherd when it bared its fangs. "Hey there, Eve. Why, you're nothing but ribs and knees!"

I couldn't say a word.

"Eve," Glen broke in before the silence got too awkward, "this is Meryl Lakewood. She's just moved here from Richmond, Virginia. You know where Virginia is, right?"

I looked at Glen and tried to clear my head. I knew I'd heard the name before and began to remember it from the big blue book he'd pull out when not searching through the big rolls of paper. In my mind I saw it; it was right there beneath Pennsylvania, where we lived now. I could go there someday, Glen told me, I could go anywhere.

"South," I said finally.

Meryl's half smile broadened into a real smile and I gave one back.

My father nodded at me and said, "You're still not crazy about visiting Mrs. Grayson's every afternoon while I'm at work, right?"

I paused. Mrs. Grayson's trailer was always too hot, and she made me take a nap every afternoon, which might not have been so bad had she not put on her records at the same time, all full of bellows and incomprehensible words. Plus the tuna fish was getting tiresome. I gave a nod.

"Thought so," said Glen. "Well, things might be changing. Like I said, Meryl is new here and needs to find work and a place to live. She's not able to pay out a lot for rent, so we thought she might stay here in exchange for watching you while I'm at work. How's that sound?"

"Can I play with my friends?"

"Now?"

"During the day."

"Of course," Meryl said, jumping in. "You and me'll have lots of fun."

I shrugged. It was better than spending my days over at Mrs. Grayson's place.

And so Meryl Lakewood became a permanent resident of our trailer in Little Pines. Mornings found her covered in a cheap blanket or beach towel on the couch, squeezing her eyes tight against the noise of Glen and me readying breakfast. Afternoons offered the promise of *Guiding Light* and also my freedom. Evenings meant a cramped dinner in the kitchen until Meryl got a job as a waitress at one of eight or ten restaurants she'd work at over the years, sometimes returning to ones she'd left before when she found out the ownership had changed hands. This was our new life, and when it remained this way even after I no longer needed someone to look after me, I realized we'd all become, through Glen's doing, some pathetic attempt at a family. And then the troubles began.

Before that, though, Meryl was okay. I remember feeling good about helping the poor woman survive a tormenting bout of homesickness that came on during her first winter away from Richmond.

"Would you look at it out there," she'd say to the window, smoking a cigarette and staring out into an early December blizzard. At the time I couldn't understand why the woman's voice sounded so unhappy. Snow was fun.

Meryl would collapse onto the couch and draw her blanket up around her shoulders. Apparently, just looking at the snow could make her cold. "Where I come from, this sorta thing doesn't happen."

"It doesn't snow?"

"Not this much. And even if it did, the sun would come out the next day and melt everything away." She looked at me and smiled. "Don't you look so disgusted. I know kids around here love their snow, but they're missing out on Richmond. Richmond is the best."

Then, without even being prompted, Meryl would launch into a description of her home. A place where the sun was easy in the summer and helpful in the winter. A town where a light jacket and two pairs of jeans would see a person through January. Flowers bloomed early in the year in Richmond and didn't vanish till almost Thanksgiving. Birds filled the February sky with song because they needn't flee any blight of cold. Life was better. It was a better place.

"I want to go there someday," I remember saying more than once, but often just for Meryl's benefit.

"Glen says you can go anywhere. If I was you, I'd go to Richmond."

SUNDAY, APRIL 11, 1999

See if this sounds familiar.

An extremely wealthy man, obsessed with architectural aspirations and taken by a rocky crag overlooking a dramatic sweep of land, undertakes the design of an unbelievable castle. Inside would be a mosaic dome, three-story stained-glass windows, wall-size murals of the apostles, a thirty-foot candelabra, and a bedroom the size of a palace. Gabriel Quinlin? Nope—this time the plans remained only on paper, and the dreamer wound up bloated and drowned in a nearby lake.

This is the story of Ludwig II, mad king of Bavaria. The pastor used Ludwig's life today as an illustration in his sermon. I'm still a bit unsettled by both.

Ludwig's life troubles me because of the parallels to Gabriel Quinlin. Had Quinlin heard of him? Had he heard of *Falkenstein,* Ludwig's final Gothic vision? He must have known about the castles *Herrenchiemsee, Linderhof,* and *Neuschwanstein*—the last serving as inspiration for Disney's fairyland version, Cinderella's Castle. Is there some deeper connection between the solid, reliable Quinlin and Ludwig, a lonely king tormented by an engagement that was crushed by his latent homosexuality; a young man without teeth who dined alone because he didn't want his servants to see him gum his food; a mad fantasist who emptied royal coffers to build one castle after another?

Worst of all, I am frustrated that I didn't come up with the connection. I've heard of Ludwig before, but his life escaped me in looking at Quinlin. On the surface the two appeared so different that I never thought of the confluence of the buildings they left as their heritage. In a way, this undoes the portrait of Quinlin I was building in my mind. He seems not so much a visionary now as a calculating imitation. Ludwig is the desperate soul whose dreams became nightmares and whose life ended in water, either by accident, suicide, or murder. Quinlin is just the New Haven pragmatist who accounted for every penny, who died reading the financial page of the newspaper, and the Estate now looks less a passion fulfilled and more a shrewd business decision. I need to talk with Ben Sterling about this.

The rest of the pastor's sermon echoed the memories I'd dredged up ever since Meryl called. The title was *Sensucht*, a word he defined as "The feeling there's someplace yet unseen that will satisfy longings we can barely define most of the time, but that drive our actions."

When he said it like that, I thought, *a better place*. But I didn't think of Richmond or wherever it is that Wander is hiding. I thought of Quinlin's Estate. I thought the Estate because to me, it *is* the better place.

It's the reason I stayed at the university, the reason I quit the graduate program, the reason I'm writing to Martin Peterson in New Zealand, the reason I drove to Pittsburgh to interview Embeth in a bagel shop, and the reason I'm going to

swallow my anger to talk with Meryl. It's my love and fascination for the building, its history, and its future. Quinlin's Estate
is that better place because it's the one spot in Lowerton that
didn't have to worry about being in the shadow or out of it, for
it *was* the shadow. It is the shadow.

Then Pastor Monroe dropped the floor out on me.

"If you think there's an answer to this feeling here on earth,
you're wrong. You're headed down the path of Ludwig, building
castles in the sky."

What? I couldn't keep from mouthing the word to myself.

"There's only one place that answers that longing—God's
kingdom of heaven."

Ridiculous as it sounds, the pastor seemed to be looking just
at me now.

"There's one road there—faith in his sacrificed Son, Jesus."

I waited.

"There's only one thing to do if you want an answer to that
longing—call on Him."

Everyone bowed their heads, and the organ began to replay
a hymn from earlier in the service. I couldn't close my eyes.
There was so much else that needed to be said.

I saw the Tower of Quinlin's Estate in my mind, and I
couldn't imagine giving it up. Just as horribly, though, I saw a
vision of it crumbling to the ground amid January's swirling
snow, and I knew the pastor had it right—my longing couldn't
be fulfilled by saving the Estate or anything else on earth.
Despite my best efforts not to, I've been walking the path of
Ludwig and Glen and every other wind chaser who thought he
might grab a handful of breeze and use it to fly, only to grab at
shadows and stardust and come crashing back to earth.

And now this: After I'd finished the above, Martin Peterson
E-mailed me a long response. He answered only a third of the
questions I'd asked a few days ago but promised to get to the
others later. This letter had exhausted him, and he needed some
space from it all. He'd write again with more in a couple of days.

I can only imagine what he'll add.

EVANGELINE AND THE COMMUNE

```
From:      Martin Peterson
Sent:      Monday, April 12, 1999 2:04 PM
To:        Lawson, Eve
Subject:   Evangeline and R2D
```

Ms. Lawson,

It doesn't surprise me that you want to know about
Evangeline Graveston. I'm only surprised that her
name hasn't come up before now. I guess it's proof,
if I needed any, that the people who got loud after
her death really just wanted us gone. They didn't
care about a true reckoning of her life, which is too
bad. Honestly, she deserved one. I guess this will
have to do.

If memory holds, Evangeline Graveston joined our
family during the first week of 1975. She said it was
part of challenging herself for the new year, and
that she was tired of the town's pettiness and
gossiping. Road to Damascus would be a retreat from
that.

I don't want to sound dramatic in this next part, but
I feel that her arrival marked the beginning of the

end for our group. This isn't to place all the blame
on her shoulders, or any even. Rather, her coming
simply forced a wedge into the cracks that we'd
never guessed were developing. It's amazing we hung
together as long as we did. I just know that things
went downhill fast after Eve showed up.

The biggest thing she exposed was the absurdity of
our brother/sister policy. To join R2D, you had to
agree to see the opposite sex as your brother or
sister. If you wanted to date or be married, that was
fine, but you couldn't live at the Estate. Whether
intentionally or not, Eve totally blew that up.

She was beautiful. There's really no other word for
it. Beautiful and unreadable. Except for her name,
nobody knew much about her at all. When we found out
later, after her death, that she was in her upper
thirties, nobody believed it. She had this untouched
quality, and within two months, there was a fistfight
over her. That sparked the jealousy of some of the
other women living in the Estate who decided that
she shouldn't be the only center of attention.
Finally during one of the family meetings, everyone
decided that the no dating policy was silly or
puritanical and revoked it.

What happened then didn't surprise me in the least.
Nobody dated. I could have predicted it, but the
freedom they thought they'd given themselves
introduced so many new, complicated interactions
that most everybody wasn't ready for them. The house
split right down the gender line, and nobody crossed
it because that meant risking rejection, or possibly
worse, acceptance. Honestly, it was like being back

in intermediate school when boys and girls first
notice each other.

Eve was the only person unaffected, not that she
showed any particular interest in dating. She'd flirt
with somebody when it served her purposes, but for
the most part she stayed at arm's length from
everybody, content to wander the Estate by herself.

It was six months after her arrival that we finally
found out what she was doing the whole time. The only
reason we discovered it was that I'd overheard her
having the same discussion with three or four of the
members.

She'd always start a conversation about the Estate
and favorite rooms and then throw in a few prying
questions. "A place like this must have some hidden
rooms; have you found any?" Things like that. One by
one, she talked to every member of R2D. I was last
and of course I had nothing to tell her. Her
persistence worried me so that at the next family
meeting I decided to call her forward to answer a few
questions. Her response stunned me. She told the
truth.

"I came here to find Quinlin's gold."

I remember the whole group of us taking in a breath
and then someone said, "Quinlin's gold?"

Eve's eyes went wide. She couldn't believe we didn't
know. All we knew about Quinlin was what was told us
at the time of purchase, nothing more than a cursory
explanation. When someone asked her to explain, Eve
told us the story about how the Estate was built,
saying that Quinlin died before his wealth, which

he'd converted into gold before the Crash, could be
cashed out into savings. All that gold had been
hidden in the Estate.

Hearing that, our pretenses of living on only what
we needed vanished. For two months the whole group
dedicated themselves to finding that gold. Holes were
dug throughout the grounds. The Maze was searched
over and over. Everyone became thrilled by the
notion of uncovering the treasure.

I asked Keith Wilcox about it and he agreed that
there were stories of the gold that started day one
after the place was built. Everyone knew Quinlin had
a fortune, yet nobody knew where it went. It seemed
reasonable that what was left remained in the Estate
somewhere. But nothing had ever been found, and
after eight weeks of searching we uncovered zilch.

It was now August 1975. On the eighth of the month,
in despair over not finding the gold, Evangeline
Graveston attempted to drown herself. I'm sorry to
say this, but it might have been better had she died.
Instead, we pulled her from the Estate's wishing
well and the real heartache began.

Martin Peterson

Part Four

I waited in Glen's room at Truant Gulch all morning, first for Embeth, who failed to show yet again, and then for Meryl, who arrived right on time. Monday afternoons were her hours for visiting him, and before I'd always been careful to clear out by then. But today I wanted to see her, so I waited. She arrived at just after two and didn't look all that surprised to see me, just stared at me with those absurd green eyes of hers. They've always been the color of soft pine needles.

Even though I knew she would come, I still found myself without words for a long moment. Just seeing her so close ignited that quick-trigger anger. I had to breathe it down before speaking the words I'd been planning out since breakfast. "Meryl . . . I've been hoping to run into you."

She crossed her arms. "Funny way of showing it, not answering your phone ever."

We stared at each other again. She wore a simple navy T-shirt and khakis. Her nails, normally polished and gleaming, looked dull. A small key chain dangled at her waist. I guessed that she'd just gotten off work cleaning at the Furrows, though she didn't look tired at all. She hadn't budged a bit.

"I'm glad you found Wander," I tried.

"I didn't *find* her. I've known where she's been for years now. You've never asked. Nobody has until that Philip called me up."

Things were getting away from us now, each exchange threatening a scene like the first one we'd had two months ago at the nursing home. Dwight had scolded me for that. As we stood there, I recalled his words that perhaps, *just perhaps*, I might be blaming the wrong person. I glanced at Glen and then to Meryl again.

Now or never.

I said, "I never expected to still be so angry. I'm sorry for that. For not being able to get past it. For yelling at you last time and for not calling you. I just never expected it to all feel so close."

Her arms unfolded and, for the first time perhaps, her eyes really searched my face. Growing up it seemed like she'd always had one eye on me, one on the door or the phone or the refrigerator or the television. Here she was looking at me. She took a step into the room, looked down at Glen, and put a hand to the iron foot of the bed, steadying herself.

"It wasn't what you think."

"What?"

"Those years ago. It wasn't me, Eve Marie. Things didn't happen like you remember." She sighed and faced Glen. "But you need to know now. I'll tell you what really happened that night, because it has to do with Wanda too. And that's something else you never knew."

Ten Years Ago, August

Friday, August 12, found Meryl at home rather than work because her hand was still recovering from burns suffered when putting out a grease fire during her late shift at Eat n' Park. She'd finished changing the wrap on her hand, put a video of *Beaches* in the VCR, and was set for a relaxing afternoon when she heard a vehicle squeal to a stop outside and footsteps approach the trailer. Glen burst in moments later, eyes gleaming.

" 'Lo," he said as a greeting and began rooting through the kitchen drawers in search of something. Meryl paused the movie and watched from the couch as he pulled out a gray checkbook. She sat up, interested now. This was the special savings checkbook—"Eve's ticket out of here," he called it—and Glen had never touched it, except for the occasional deposit slip.

"Glen?"

He turned. "Your hand hurt too bad to come with me on a chance of a lifetime?"

"What do you mean?"

"Filch just told me that a manager at the factory got the go-ahead to bargain off all sorts of Gabriel Quinlin's belongings down at Larabie Auctions, including some of the original plans for the Estate." Glen was at the door now. "You coming?"

Meryl looked down at her hand and figured the bandage was good for a few hours. She hadn't been out of the house except to visit the doctor's and could always watch the movie later. Slipping on sandals, she grabbed a clip for her hair and was out the door with Glen in a second.

All the way to the auction Glen hummed and tapped an

insistent rhythm on his old pickup truck's steering wheel. The
stereo got only AM, and so they listened to someone, right wing
or left, shout vitriol the entire ride, arriving at the Larabie lot
in plenty of time to get a seat close to the presentation stage. It
was only as Glen began making tiny pencil marks in the auction
program next to the lots on which he wanted to bid that Meryl
felt her first pang of worry.

The feeling grew as soon as the auction began.

The Quinlin lots appeared first, each starting at over $250.
There were books and papers and business logs and even a
trunk filled with clothes, lot after lot after lot.

Glen bought each one.

Sometimes he was the only bidder, sometimes he was the
highest bidder. Meryl kept a tally for a time, but after Glen's
spending reached $8,000 she gave up counting, closed her eyes,
and prayed for the end. Twelve more lots and an hour passed
before Quinlin's belongings all became the property of Glen
Lawson. Meryl tried not to groan when she overheard a conversation between Glen and Bud Larabie discussing the require-
ment of an immediate transfer of funds for so large a purchase.
Before the auction there'd been about $26,000 in the account.
Now most all of it had been bled dry. He'd almost skipped out
to the car, while she walked through the dust his heels kicked
up. Her hand throbbed. Glen got in and when Meryl settled, he
swung the pickup toward Bellefonte, saying tonight they were
having dinner out.

Meryl would have thought he was drunk, only he was a mel-
ancholy drunk, not a happy one. Tonight he was big smiles and
eager hands that kept grabbing at her thighs as they drove.
Meryl could think up only one question—"Why?"

"Don't you see? Quinlin had to have had it in his head the whole time to hide the gold. It's got to be in his plans or papers somewhere." Glen looked over at her as they crested a hill. "Don't worry about the money. This'll pay back tenfold—a hundredfold! And Eve will never know. We'll find the gold and pay for her college and everything. Then we'll buy a house, maybe a second in Richmond, and things'll be great."

They returned two hours later to find me sitting on the steps to the trailer door, hands balled in fists.

"Did you make the school all pretty for your senior year?" Glen asked as he and Meryl climbed out of the truck. I'd been at the school, cleaning and helping prepare for classes in a few weeks.

"Where is it?" I demanded, standing.

Glen stopped and Meryl felt his hand go clammy in hers.

"Where is what?"

"The money. My college money." My knees trembled now but my eyes stayed hard. "I called the bank when I got home. I call almost every day just to hear the balance read to me. Now there's none left. Where is it?" My voice broke this time as the tears came.

Glen stood in silence.

I waited.

In that moment, Meryl saw what she had to do.

"Your father gave it to me."

My face went white, making my red hair look like flames. The shock was so great even the tears stopped.

"I got behind with some people, and now these hospital bills..." She held up her bandaged hand, which throbbed with the effort.

"Your stupid hand?" I said, almost in a whisper. There was nothing in it that sounded as if I understood.

"I'm going to pay it back," Meryl tried but I was shaking my head. I wanted no part of it.

"That was my college money! He saved it for me. So I could get out of here." I looked at Glen. "All my life you've promised to help me get out of here."

"I'm going to pay it back, Eve."

I whirled on her and gave a mean laugh. "Pay it back? By next year when the first tuition payment is due? You're a waitress, a one-handed waitress!" I waited a beat. "No, I guess you'll have to find some other way. What else are you good at . . . oh, yeah, maybe you can charge for that. Or do you already know how little you're worth to them?"

"Eve!" barked Glen, but I'd thrown up my hands in fury and stormed off the steps and out toward the back grove.

Meryl and Glen stood there frozen, still only two or three feet from the truck.

"Meryl, you didn't—"

"A girl shouldn't hate her own father, Glen," she said and that was it. Meryl then headed inside to watch her movie in silence and try to forget all the things I had said because she knew that's what I really thought of her.

Glen followed and spent his time at the kitchen table. Some time passed with a phone call arranging the storage of Quinlin's belongings, but the majority of the evening he sat at the table and drew circles on the greasy aluminum with one finger. Only after Meryl's movie ended did he suggest they go look for me.

Outside, Glen made a move that angered Meryl more than any he'd made all day—he pointed to Marker Road and said he'd

check there. Meryl knew where I lay hidden and she knew Glen
did as well. Yet this man, this father, this coward, chose to walk
the other way. Meryl simply shook her head and moved to the
grove, to the old fort we kids had fashioned all those summers
ago.

Picking her way through the darkness, she reached the trail
that led back into the arbor. Some steps in she found the old tree
with the rotting blocks of wood nailed to its trunk and stopped
below. She could tell I was lying on the planks above her but
didn't know what to say. For a minute she looked around and
saw that a break in the trees offered a glimpse at the Santa Claus
Glen bragged about impaling on the flagpole. A streetlamp
nearby happened to illuminate it perfectly, and from this distance it wasn't possible to see that Santa's eyes had washed off
after summers of rain or that a decade of children's stones had
dented his round belly and swollen cheeks.

Before she could even say a word, however, I jumped down
off the platform, landed on a thick clump of grass, and was out
of the grove in a blink. Meryl watched me bolt for the trailer,
heard the screen door slam with a weak *chock*, and then heard a
dim buzz of noise as I put on music, loud. Only one door in the
trailer had a lock and it was for my bedroom. Even the bath-
room could be opened at any time. She knew there'd be no talking to me this evening and guessed in truth it'd probably be
much longer than that.

She was about to leave the grove when something behind
her moved. A bush rustled, and not knowing what it could be,
Meryl ducked behind a tree. Some seconds later a pale thin girl
appeared. Her hair glowed silver in the moonlight, and a cigarette burned from her lips. She shuffled down the path as though

she'd lived here all her life. It was the girl's confident walk that caught Meryl by surprise. She knew this girl.

"Wanda?"

The girl flinched, then squinted. Meryl stepped back out into the path so the girl could see her, and Wanda did the most remarkable thing. She smiled—the first smile she'd ever given Meryl.

"I'm not here," Wanda whispered.

Meryl didn't know what to make of that. "But—"

"My mom and I were back in the area. She dropped me off at the Perkins because I said I'd arranged to meet friends. I slipped out and walked over here just to look at the place again."

"Where've you been?"

"Paradise. Is Eve around? Can you tell her to come out here?" She looked toward her old trailer. "I don't want to risk walking through the court."

Meryl hesitated.

"I only have a minute or two," urged Wanda, "it was a longer walk from Perkins than I remember. I need to get back soon for my mom to pick me up again."

Even from the distance, Meryl could still hear the music coming from my room. She knew the door would be locked and that pounding would do nothing. If they screamed for me to turn it down, I'd just put on headphones.

"It's been a horrible night," she told Wanda.

The girl nodded, and Meryl fought back a few sudden tears because of how matter-of-factly Wanda accepted that explanation. Things had always been horrible in Little Pines. Why should it have changed? Why should this night be anything different?

"I gotta go," Wanda said. "Tell her hi for me."

Meryl didn't have a chance to say okay, because the girl had slipped back into the darkness and away from Little Pines and Lowerton once more.

Staring off into the grove, Meryl felt only that she wanted very much to follow Wanda. Instead, she turned and fumbled her way back to the trailer, her hand beginning its throbbing again. Inside, angry music growled from my room while Glen played with the rabbit ears, working to improve the reception on a Pirates game.

"She came back," he said over his shoulder when he heard the door squeak open. For a second Meryl thought he meant Wanda, but then she realized he was referring to me.

"No," she muttered under her breath and rubbed her bandaged hand, wondering when the pain would end.

WEDNESDAY, APRIL 14, 1999

I'm not sure which jolted Philip more, Martin Peterson's E-mail, which I'd printed out for him, or Meryl's story. We'd met for sandwiches downtown at the Lowerton Grille, one of the few non-franchised lunch joints left in town, before our meeting with the mayor to discuss the preliminary response to our proposals. Philip hadn't expected any of the information I dropped on him and made it only halfway through his grilled portabella because of all the questions he'd wanted to ask. Nearly all them matched questions I'd had. But I'd only gotten answers from Meryl; Martin hadn't written again.

"What'd she mean by paradise?" he asked, folding his hands on the Formica booth table and leaning close.

"She meant Paradise. It's a town in Pennsylvania, near Lancaster."

"Huh," said Philip, and I think he was trying to figure out if it all meant something or not. He let it pass and asked what else I'd learned.

"Not much. Meryl got the rest of the story weeks later when she ran into Jessie, Wanda's sister. I guess their mother had moved to Paradise because she had relatives there. Every once in a while, she'd try to get in contact with the girls, but only Wanda would ever listen to her. Jessie felt like she abandoned them. Little by little she convinced Wanda to escape. The father thought about taking the whole thing to court, except he didn't have the money nor the energy at that point. And so Wanda just started living in Paradise."

"Why didn't she ever contact you?"

I shrugged. "Meryl thinks that they didn't know Mr. Maxwell wasn't searching for them. That's why she wouldn't come into the trailer park that night."

Philip seemed to accept that, took a bite of his sandwich, chewed for a bit, and asked the question I knew would come. "So, what about the stuff your father bought?"

I pulled a key out of my purse and held it up. "It's in a storage garage. We're free to go through it whenever we want."

"Wow," he replied, but the smile on his face said something else, and thinking back, I'm not entirely happy about what it was.

After lunch we walked two blocks over to the city hall and met with the mayor. Reading from a response drafted by the city council, he said he had good news, bad news, and no news.

They agreed to the easy one, so September 15 will now offi-

cially be recognized as Gabriel Quinlin Day. It will cost them
nothing but the price of flyers and an hour's work for the dec-
laration at the town square.

They rejected turning *He Saved Lowerton* into a fund-raiser.
It began with free admission and will stay that way. To be honest I'm a tiny bit glad about the decision. This alone says more
about their feelings for the heritage of Quinlin's Estate than
anything.

Finally, they felt unprepared to decide on such a comprehen-
sive partnership with the university. I think there's a little of the
chicken-or-the-egg thinking going on. Why do all the work to
form a partnership when the Estate stands a good chance of
being torn down? But if we partner, we prove to Harrisburg the
interest of the greater community, and the needed funding
might be forthcoming. I need to contact Greg Evans and have
him speak with Mayor Hundley. Perhaps hearing it straight
from the wallet's mouth will be more compelling than hearing
it from three people who've never earned a vote in their combined lives. The days dwindle, and in the meantime Ben and I
will be approaching university contacts—he the dean of architecture and I some history professors—to begin the process on
that end. It will be strange to return to campus.

What else can be said? It's Wednesday evening and I'm
alone in my apartment typing out a journal entry and wondering when the exact moment was that things got so out of control. It's one thing to imagine myself as frustrated and lost, but
quite another to realize the world around me looks exactly the
same way. Good intentions aside, Philip hasn't helped. I thought
he'd be energized by our talk with the mayor, but instead he
seemed sad, almost weary.

"Sometimes things just seem so slow."

I tried to remind him of all the progress we'd made, how we'd found Wander, and how much we'd learned from Martin Peterson about Evangeline, yet none of this appeared to make much difference. The smile he'd had at lunch was gone, and I couldn't figure out what it was that'd driven it away. We walked to our cars in silence, and I was about to get in mine when he spoke.

"Do you ever doubt yourself?" he asked. He stared at the ground and kicked at a pebble with the leather fisherman's sandals he'd been wearing since warmer weather began showing itself.

I said, "Of course."

He took a deep breath, and before I could begin guessing at what he might be doubting, he said, "In the weeks before I went into Astonbury I read a book by John Steinbeck called *The Pearl.* Have you read it?"

I shook my head.

"It's short. So short, in fact, that I read it every single day for a month. Got to know it by heart.

"It's about a poor pearl diver who finds an enormous pearl, perfect in every way, and all he wants is to use this thing to do some good for his family, his little boy. Only everything goes wrong and the thing really only brings his damnation. It's one of the saddest things I've read."

I waited. I expected, *And the moral of the story . . .*

Instead, he said, "Life isn't easy, is it?"

"Are you okay, Philip?"

He clenched his jaw for a second, then said, "I want something good to come from my life."

I tried to give an understanding nod, though I still wasn't sure what'd sparked all this. I looked at him and his eyes eventually found mine. We stared at each other for a few long seconds. Out of the corner of my eye I could see his hands moving. They took mine, gently, and squeezed. He never stopped staring.

"I haven't been thinking about the Estate much at all recently," said Philip, and I knew it was supposed to be a confession. "I just think about you." He squeezed my hands again. It was my turn to respond.

But I didn't. I stood there without saying anything, until the silence went on too long and he dropped my hands with a sad little nod. Then he gave a brittle laugh and kicked the pebble he'd been playing with earlier clear across the road. He moved to his car.

"Philip!" I called after him.

He turned.

"It doesn't mean no."

He raised an eyebrow. "What does it mean, then?"

I hesitated, not sure myself. "It means not right now. Things are too complicated."

He seemed to accept this, got into his car, and with a small, embarrassed wave he drove away.

So just add it to the list.

Meryl's confounded everything I've ever thought about her.

Evangeline Graveston was as obsessed as my father and tried to kill herself over not finding the gold.

Wanda Maxwell lives in Amish country.

Philip von Maarsten likes me.

I, Eve Lawson, am as confused as I've ever been and not the least because I feel there's still something important I'm missing. Only I'm running out of time and places to look. At this point, it'll have to come to me.

In part, it did. Martin Peterson wrote back again tonight with more on Evangeline. There's one more part to go after this, he promised. There needs to be, for this answered nothing for me at all.

ROAD TO DAMASCUS—ACCORDING TO MARTIN PETERSON, PART II

From: Martin Peterson
Sent: Thursday, April 15, 1999 3:31 PM
To: Lawson, Eve
Subject: Part II: Evangeline and R2D

Ms. Lawson,

Again, I'm not surprised that the tale of Evangeline's suicide attempt is new information to you, because we didn't tell anybody what had happened. Such a thing is to our blame, of course, but remember that psychology and counseling were not what they are today. There was little compassion back then for such a person, and sending Evangeline to a clinic would not have been to her benefit.

Or perhaps that's just two decades more of rationalization. We knew our standing in the community, and we knew that if the daughter of a much-loved family was found to have gone insane on our grounds, we'd have been blamed. We purposefully hid the information and tried to counsel Evangeline on our own. You know how the story ends.

The memory of those months from August to October
still baffles me. There were times I felt we were
completely over our heads in dealing with
Evangeline. We had no idea how much older she was
than us, plus if I had to make a guess, I'd say she
would have been diagnosed with either severe bipolar
disorder or even multiple-personality disorder.
Some people read their Bibles and whispered about
possession, which had just gotten its Hollywood
treatment a few years before. I had no answers back
then, and I'm sure things can happen. If that's
really what was at work in Evangeline Graveston,
then we stood very little chance because our own
faith was toppling.

So we were left with our daily lives and wondering
which Evangeline Graveston would appear each
morning. Would she be all smiling or slit-eyed? At
times she'd fill a room with laughter and at others
her weariness infected our family like a virus.
Sometimes she'd head off in the direction of the
basement, and we'd have to send a pair of watchers to
guard the well.

For six or seven weeks this went on. Then in late
September came the change. After a long, intense
phone call (we had someone watching her nearly all
the time at this point) Evangeline stormed from the
Estate saying she was headed for town. We expected
one of two things from her departure. Either she'd
be gone forever or the police would arrive within
minutes to arrest us on some imagined accusation.
Instead, she returned four hours later as normal as
we'd seen her in weeks.

"It's over," she said when somebody asked why she

seemed so happy. She never explained what she was
talking about.

Have to go. I'll write again later.
Martin Peterson

SATURDAY, APRIL 17, 1999

This morning I met with Meryl to see the proof of her story.
I think something in me was hoping against hope that she might
be lying, but the moment we arrived at the squat cement self-
storage garages on Gayle Road that final chance fell away and I
was left facing forty-eight square feet of Gabriel Quinlin's detri-
tus and all those years of revision I'd just started thinking
through.

Meryl Lakewood was not the enemy I had built her up to
be.

My father's obsession with Quinlin's gold undermined his
support of me more than I ever imagined. It's sad and unbelievable to me that over the past weeks the man has plummeted in
my estimation and yet we haven't said a word to each other.
Makes me wonder how far he would've fallen were he not in a
coma.

Everything I know about Gabriel Quinlin could change in
looking through these boxes. Who knows what could be written
in these ledgers? Glen obviously hadn't been able to find the
gold through what is contained here, but that doesn't mean the
belongings might not have some value to our cause. I might be
able to get a hint at why Quinlin passed away or how he

thought up the various rooms in the Estate. Perhaps there's a mention of Ludwig II.

I didn't have time to look through even a single box this morning, because I had to make it over to Truant Gulch. I did manage to avert an awkward moment with Meryl by thanking her for telling me the truth.

"I finally decided there's a difference between defending a man and lying for him," she replied and handed me her own key to the garage. "I want no part of it anymore. Have a ball."

I thanked her and we split for our cars. I probably should've been thinking about what I was about to do at the retirement community, yet my thoughts kept going back to Meryl, and they were as tangled as a knot. For years I'd despised her. For twelve before that, I was ashamed that she lived with us. Now she'd stepped out of my father's shadow and opened a door I hadn't even known existed. I'm not much on forcing people to earn my trust, but I admit that Meryl has taken steps in that direction. Perhaps talking to her about Lydia Furrow and Glen won't be as difficult as I'd thought. By the time I'd convinced myself to call her in the next couple of days, I'd arrived at Truant Gulch. The parking lot, as I suspected, was nearly empty. Saturday mornings were the quietest times here. I was sick of playing by the rules and tired of not being able to talk to Embeth. This seemed the best time to try what I wanted to do.

I went inside and, without hesitating, walked past the receptionist and down a side hallway I knew would take me to the back of the nursing room floor. Nobody said a word to me, and I scolded myself for not trying this sooner. Walk with authority and most people leave you alone. I found a back stairway and climbed to the third floor, crossing a bridge into the assisted

care wing without having to pass through the security doors
because my guess paid off. Rather than deal with the hassle of
sliding a pass card every time they needed to wheel a resident
through, the nurses kept the double doors propped open. In two
minutes I was back down a second stairwell to the second floor,
and soon I found Embeth's room. So long as they didn't have a
guard posted inside, I'd be fine. She answered on my second
knock.

"Eve!"

I put a finger to my mouth and stepped in.

We closed the door and she asked, "How did you get here?"

I gave a quick explanation. Embeth shook her head at how
easy it'd been, then moved to shut off the TV, which had been
tuned to an early morning talk show. She patted a chair cushion
for me to sit and when she'd settled herself asked how I'd been.

"I've learned quite a bit," I said.

"That's wonderful!"

"Some of it is about your daughter."

Embeth deflated. There's no other word for it. She'd been
sitting up tall and pretty and then with that one sentence she
sagged against the back of her seat and her shoulders bowed. I
thought she might be having an episode of some sort but within
a second some light came to her eyes and she regained at least
a portion of her former posture. She asked me what I'd learned.

I started, but stopped almost immediately. It'd been so long
since I'd spoken to Embeth and I'd learned so much about her
daughter since then. Everything from the things Dwight had
told me about her thinking she was a Quinlin to Peterson's suggestion that she'd tried to commit suicide and may have had a

psychiatric disorder. Embeth sat waiting, and I suddenly had no idea how to begin.

"I know it's not going to be pretty, dear," she said into the silence. "I've heard many a rumor about her and they all had a kind of ugliness to them. What I need to hear is the truth."

I nodded and began.

I mentioned Evangeline's conversations with my father and her belief that she was a Quinlin. I talked about her search for the gold during her time living in the Estate and that she attempted suicide when nothing came of it. Embeth's face clouded, and I could see she was struggling to understand. This was all new to her. I finished with Peterson's guess that she might have been bipolar.

"You trust this Martin Peterson?" she asked. I'd expected her voice to be choked or sad, but she sounded fine if just a little tired. The first shock had been the big one. These just seemed to numb her.

"I don't know what he'd gain by lying. He sounds similar to you, just happy to finally be able to tell the truth."

At that she lowered her chin, and when she shut her eyes all the lines of her face spoke both her age and worry. At that moment, I wanted to take back every word I'd said.

"Eve," she said, not looking up. "Everything you've said confirms what I'd known but never let myself believe when Evangeline was in our house. I lost her a long time before she died. Far before. She lived apart from me. From Charles."

"I'm sorry."

She blinked at my condolences. Her eyes finally found mine.

"This is my last chance to know my daughter. I want you to help me, Eve."

"I said I'd try."

"There's one woman who I think knows these answers more than any other. Lydia. She was at the heart of it all. She was the only one who knew."

Before I could ask Embeth to clarify, she did.

"Lydia was the only person in town other than Gabriel Quinlin who knew Charles wasn't Evangeline's father, knew that medically Charles couldn't have been anyone's father. He'd been born that way, which was the reason we never had any more children after we married. Lydia knew it and was at least part of the cause of Evangeline's troubles. I want to know why. I want to know why my daughter died apart from me."

SUNDAY, APRIL 18, 1999

It's amazing to me that it was only a week ago that I listened to that sermon on a better place. Because since then it seems as though I've discovered the world around me is a worse place. Embeth realized for the first time that her sister-in-law might have had some indirect (or direct) hand in Evangeline's death. Philip discovered that his faith, or something, didn't always provide him the comfort and hope he expected. I found out my father let me believe a lie rather than own up to his cowardice. Worst of all, I have to admit now that I took that lie and ran with it, hating Meryl Lakewood wrongfully for a full ten years because of it. Part of that I guess can rest on Glen's shoulders, but most of it has to fall on me. I wronged her and I am sorry.

As for the better place, there are two options in the running now—Richmond and Paradise. Meryl always wanted to flee to the first, and Wander actually made it to hers. I just wonder what name mine has on it.

The pastor at church would think that an idle question. He'd say, *Look, I explained it—if your heart is yearning for someplace better, then what it's wanting isn't on earth, it's heaven you're after.*

Only I have no idea what that means.

What is heaven and where is heaven?

How does a city of clouds, filled with angels plucking harps, satisfy my desire for someplace better? That's crazy. But I guess this isn't what the pastor or other people would say heaven really is.

So what is it? And how do I know when I've found it rather than just Paradise, Pennsylvania?

Those were my thoughts this morning in trying to decide whether to go to church or not. I did and found myself at a praise and worship service that contained no sermon at all, only the singing of very repetitive songs. Not this church's finest moment.

Afterward I sidled up to Philip, who appeared to have recovered from our last meeting. He even gave a sheepish little apology, although I told him he had nothing to feel sorry about and then reminded him again that I hadn't said no. I don't want him to forget, just in case the yes comes sooner than I think.

Rather than our ordinary lunch, we decided to call Ben and have him join us at my apartment for the grand opening of the boxes from the storage garage. Gabriel Quinlin's belongings needed to be sorted at some point and the quicker the better, in case there really was something buried in there that would help us. We only made it through five boxes, but the afternoon ended with two interesting discoveries and a discussion with Ben and Philip on the issue that was bothering me that morning—heaven. In all, quite a day.

The first breakthrough came right away. We'd chosen five boxes from the garage, loaded them into Philip's car, and headed to my apartment. I was gathering drinks when Philip and Ben slit open the first box. Both went quiet at what they saw.

"What is it?"

Ben reached in and lifted out a piece of heavy stock paper on which was drawn a detailed rendering at three-quarter angle of what the Estate could have been. Instead of the Grecian pillars, the front entrance was shown as a fantastical mosque capped by an enormous dome, and in the middle of the building the tower didn't just reach for the clouds but rather cut its way up with a razor's edge. Clock towers replaced the lighthouses. Ben was the first to point out the strange markings on the building's roof in a circle about the tower.

"They almost look like Roman numerals," said Philip.

"They are," Ben said, and I watched his eye thrill over the design. "Do you see it?"

Philip and I looked.

"The sharpness of the tower," he hinted, pointing. "The markings."

It came in a flash and must have to Philip as well. We both nodded.

"They were doing thematic designs at this point," said Ben as he reached into the box to grab another rendering. In this one, towers and spires and rooftops melted into the heads and faces of animals, pair after pair, the templelike entrance resembling some kind of large boat.

A third came out that had the Estate as an Edenic garden.

A fourth was a disturbing portrayal of the Crucifixion, with the central tower standing in for the cross.

The final drawing baffled even Ben for a moment.

"What's with the trumpets?" Philip asked, pointing to a section of the drawing that indeed looked like a phalanx of trumpets raised to the sky.

Ben put a finger to the drawing and traced something I could not recognize. Philip strained to see what was happening. Finally, Ben explained.

"See the lion's body here in this section of roof? Now look at what's tucked in between its paws."

It looked like a goat to me. Perhaps a sheep.

Philip snapped his fingers. "Heaven."

Ben nodded. He then explained the reference by opening the floor for me to ask the obvious question, the one that had nagged at me that very morning. "What do you think heaven's like?"

Philip laughed softly at the question, and I couldn't tell if he was pleased or was patronizing me with the grin one gives a child who's asked something precious. Ben just cocked his eyebrows and gave me a quizzical look. Philip spoke first.

"Roads of gold and jewels," he said and laughed again. "I guess they're images of the beauty and spectacle of the place, but on the other hand I wouldn't be surprised either to see it just as it's described."

I waited for a moment and asked if that was it.

Philip shrugged. "Honestly I haven't given it all that much thought. I know we'll be made whole there. I know our questions will be answered—we'll know in full. Other than that, I'm just not sure. Right now it's the journey there that matters."

Not very helpful, yet I didn't complain. We both turned to Ben, who was still studying the drawing. He spoke without looking up.

"When I was an undergrad at Buffalo I went to a fellowship group. We met once a week, did things occasionally on the weekend, ran some outreach events, and did charity work. One weekend, these upperclassmen I didn't know real well threw what they called a heaven party. To get in you had to bring something that represented heaven to you. Most people brought silly stuff—cotton clouds, cardboard wings covered in tinfoil, that sorta thing. But I remember this one guy, Griffin, brought a guitar, sat on a stool, and started playing a song.

"Nobody even knew the guy played. He just started with a few chords and sang, and it was his voice that did it. He had a real high, trembly voice—sounded like he was from another place. Somewhere far away. And all he sang were these simple words of praise, three lines maybe, repeated over and over again. It stunned the whole place quiet and I just remember thinking, *That's pretty close.*"

"So when you think of heaven, you think of that guy's voice?" I asked.

Ben tilted his head and thought for a second. "Not his voice. Just *him*. I've seen people bow their heads and their knees before, but he bowed his whole . . . being."

I stared at Ben without saying anything, trying to think if I'd ever seen anybody prostrate before God or anything else. The closest thing I could come up with is the memory of my father when he leaned over his blueprints and murmured *somewhere* to himself, as if the incantation alone might light his way.

Devotion, I decided, was a tricky thing.

"What'd you take to the party?" asked Philip.

Ben hesitated, then said, "A broken aspirator."

Neither Philip nor I knew what to say.

"I've had pretty severe asthma for a long time. It hasn't helped in fighting my weight," he said, motioning to himself, "and I'm looking forward to being rid of it."

It didn't seem anything more needed to be said, so I suggested we speed up our search of the five boxes or we'd be here working all night. Philip and Ben agreed, and we were soon moving again through Gabriel Quinlin's stuff.

The first box, besides the architectural plans, contained some early correspondence between Quinlin and a Senator James Wolfenden regarding something called the Nye Report, a congressional special committee investigation of the munitions industry. As much as the letters fascinated me, I knew they weren't what we were looking for, so I marked the box with a tag, put the letters on my list of things to go back over after we'd finished saving the Estate, and moved on.

The second and third boxes consisted of accounting logs—heavy thick books with excruciating columns of figures and tallies. These were the sorts of things over which Charles Graveston must have labored. They reeked of tediousness. I labeled them with the dates the logs covered and shoved them aside.

In the fourth box we found little of interest except for a stained daguerreotype image of a man who had to be Quinlin's father. He looked as stern as a cold north wind.

Ben opened the final box of the evening and whistled. Reaching into the box, he lifted out a dark piece of carved teak or mahogany. Perfectly round, the wood wore symmetric grooves in a winding pattern across its face. Philip leaped to his feet and moved closer to the sculpture, running his fingers over the wood.

"I know this pattern," said Philip, mostly to himself. His eyes fluttered for just a second before widening. "It's the Chartres labyrinth. From a cathedral in France." He pointed to four distinct arms within the pattern. "This is the cross. The path is the journey to the center, where God resides . . . is there something taped here?"

Ben flipped the carving over. Fixed to the back and written in a fine, swirling hand, was a note dated August 18, 1913, and signed by a single name that implied an intimacy never guessed at before.

The story of the Estate continues to be told in these fragments and shards, and sometimes it feels as though I'm rebuilding the thing with my bare hands. I can't imagine having to watch it crumble once more, burying forever these lost voices speaking even from a slip of paper sent across the ocean eighty years ago.

Dear Gabriel

  Our crossing completed, Father and I have enjoyed seeing the last of oceans and channels for the time. Instead we revel in the carriages and steam engines that jostle and rock, but avoid the languorous pitch and roll of being on the water. And though I promised I wouldn't, it proved impossible, during the dark hour of night, to keep one's thoughts from lingering over the happenstance of last year's sinking. I shuddered with the thought of parting the waves over the place of their interment.

  I'm sure you weren't expecting so grim a note, but our parting has put me in a sorrowful mood. Very little of what we've seen has helped either, since most of it causes me to lament your not being with me. These are places, visions, you know in your heart already. We visited them through your books, and it is not fair that I now see them alone. I know you asked that I never speak ill of your father, but I grow angrier and angrier at the thought of him denying your one wish.

I will close only with a glimpse of the future. We'll return here, you and I. Walk the cobbled streets together. Stroll the garden paths on cool spring mornings. Linger hand in hand along the river walks. These things will come to pass. I dream of them nightly.

Yours in joy and devotion,
Marjorie

Postscript: The carving is a gift from Father. He has heard you give the speech about the tangled maze of your faith so many times he felt he had to show you that others have felt the same way. We bought it from a gifted peasant on a lane not far from Chartres itself.

WEDNESDAY, APRIL 21, 1999

Using the same plan as last Saturday, I once again found myself in Embeth's apartment this afternoon. She'd felt bad about being low on treats the last time and so had stocked up since then, offering me a spread of store-bought cookies and my choice of coffee or tea. She fretted about in the kitchen while I settled, more agitated it seemed than I'd ever seen her, once nearly dropping the pastel carafe she'd just filled with coffee.

"Have you heard any more from Mr. Peterson?" she asked after teetering into her living room. There was a slight hitch to her voice as if trying to make the question sound casual when in fact it meant the world to her.

I shook my head and said I didn't know when to expect his next E-mail. I can't be sure but Embeth looked almost relieved by this. When she asked me what I wanted to discuss today, I told her about my father's purchase of Quinlin's belongings and the note Ben, Philip, and I had found taped to the carving.

"Did he ever mention a Marjorie?"

Embeth blinked at me, paused, and said, "You've heard talk of the legend of his passing, that he died of a broken heart?"

I nodded.

"That's who Marjorie was."

"His lost love?"

"And the woman for whom he built the Estate."

I stopped. Embeth stared at me, a small smile on her face.

"I thought he built the Estate to save the town," I said, confused now.

"Who told you that?"

"Well . . . everyone. You, even. I mean, what about *He Saved Lowerton?*"

"He did save Lowerton, dear."

"But—"

"Didn't you ever think that it was a peculiar way of staving off the Depression, hiring a town to build a house in which he'd never live?"

"I thought he loved faraway lands."

"He did. But he loved them because she loved them."

She refilled my cup with coffee and waited for my next question.

The only ones that came to mind were, "How do you know this?" and "Why haven't I heard about it before? Why isn't it mentioned during the Estate tour or at the museum?"

"I know because he told me. The week before he died, Mr. Quinlin, Charles, and I stood gazing up at the Estate—which had just been completed a few months before that. Mr. Quinlin sighed and said, 'She would have loved it.' I asked who and he replied 'Marjorie Hayes.' "

I nodded. It needn't mean he had built the Estate for her, but the woman obviously held some important place in his life. This was, after all, many years after her note and gift had crossed by ship and rail to get to his door. "And why isn't it talked about?"

Embeth didn't answer. She just waited, hands crossed in her lap, until I guessed she wanted me to answer my own question. One answer came quickly, and although it wasn't pretty, it seemed at least truthful.

"We wanted the Estate to be all about us."

She smiled. "Right, we didn't want to be saved as an afterthought. Especially to a woman who'd been dead over twenty years."

"Marjorie was dead?"

"The Estate was Quinlin's memorial to her. As long as it was being built, he had some slim connection with her. When it was finished she vanished forever."

"And so he died."

"So the story goes."

I couldn't help but sigh.

Marjorie Hayes

A supremely patient librarian at Yale University did the legwork on the research questions I put to her. This is what she found:

Marjorie Hayes was the daughter of Colonel Walter Hayes, who was distantly related to Rutherford B. Hayes.

She graduated from Yale in 1913, the same year as Gabriel Quinlin, with a degree in general arts and letters. She'd acted in the drama troupe at New Haven, even taking the lead role in *Electra*, and published one short poem in an undergraduate literary journal.

Her drowning, which occurred while traveling through Europe in the late summer and autumn of 1913, lay steeped in intrigue as her father, Colonel Hayes, also perished in the same river accident. Words of assassination were whispered, but nothing came to light. A year later, following a true assassination, the continent would itself drown in the bloodshed of World War I and the slender life of a young girl would be forgotten in a world choked and blinded by mortar shells raining mustard gas from above.

But Gabriel Quinlin never forgot, and once the world had silenced, he spoke his love for her in a monument of all the places they'd never visit.

SATURDAY, APRIL 24, 1999

Today nothing happened.

I ignored Gabriel Quinlin's boxes. I checked my E-mail only once and found that Martin still hadn't sent his final answer. I talked to neither Philip, nor Ben, nor Meryl, nor Embeth, nor any of the other people I seemed to be tangled up with day to day. I learned nothing at all. And to be honest, I needed the rest.

Instead, I did something I haven't done since last month's visit with Representative Evans—I visited Quinlin's Estate.

Walking the grounds, standing in the cool of the dungeon, scaling the Tower all reminded me again of my real purpose in all this. I'd gotten too far away from it with my focusing on the stories and people. The Estate itself remains a formidable presence, and my hours there today were long overdue.

Oddest of all is how my feelings about the great house have changed in these past months. Before I'd always looked at it only through my own eyes, or perhaps through the greedy eyes of Glen. Now I see Greg Evans's love for the small details of the Estate and Ben Sterling's appreciation of its absurd heights and angles. I can hear Philip's voice in the Maze and can't help but see the ardor of Quinlin's devotion to Marjorie Hayes in every room and twisting staircase. I can picture Evangeline Graveston living out her final days here, see her standing on the bridge over the wishing well and deciding whether to jump or not. I can envision her wandering the hallways, her eyes vacant, haunted. During my climb up the Tower, I thought about how the world must have spun and then gone black when she toppled down this length. Then I pushed through that terrible supposition and listened to the tour guide giving the spiel about the Tower I'd learned by heart during my summers working there.

Three stories above everything else and as cramped as a mausoleum, the Tower at Quinlin's Estate—despite its prevalence in legend and lore—had never been put to much use until Brighton Entertainment began flying their scarlet corporate banner from its tip. In years before, the winding, tricky stairs and narrow uselessness of space proved an inconvenience. For Brighton it became a charming conclusion to their tour that offered paying customers a soaring hawk's view of both Lowerton and the surrounding valley. Guides just had to be sure visitors could navigate the 89.5 steps without congested hearts arresting or reconstructed hips and knees giving out.

Those who made it learned that during the early 1940s, when the banner of the U.S. Army flew from the Tower, a radio receiver was set up that could capture signals from as far south as Richmond, Virginia, and as far north as Toronto, Ontario. Tankers steaming into Baltimore could be tracked as easily as those venturing from Cleveland into Huron. In the Tower cell— the thirty-six-square-foot hexagon with turreted windows in each of its six walls—a rotation of guards kept lookout and monitored shortwave frequencies that, on cool clear nights, crackled in from places as distant as Vladivostok and the island of Tasmania.

When the Estate became the property of Lowerton and served as the town's school following the Fire of '47, the Tower was declared off limits. An iron bar and padlock secured it from the outside, and the cell's six windows were barricaded just in case a student managed to worm his way in. At the bottom level, a forged steel door ordered directly from Quinlin Metal Works was added to keep children off the stairs. The day before students arrived for their first classes, the door clanged shut, and since the orphanage that came later on never bothered to open it, the Tower was hermetically sealed from intrusion for about the next two decades.

Martin Peterson and Road to Damascus, just days after buying the place, swung open the staircase door, pried off the iron bar from the entrance to the upper cell, and removed the barricades from the windows. Three years later Evangeline Graveston toppled down the steps to her death, shocking very few. They'd always expected such a thing. People took Evangeline's death more as a fulfillment of prophecy than the echo of a legend. She was the legendary girl they'd been talking about all this time, the one found broken at the bottom of the stairs.

Oddly enough, even after the death, the doors never again closed on the Tower. Perhaps Lowerton figured that the stairs had claimed their victim and no longer posed a threat, despite the slick granite and corkscrew ascent. Today children race up the stairs, ignoring the protests of weary guides; today couples ditch the group to spend a few lingering moments on top of the world.

Seeing Eye dogs routinely lead their sightless owners upward, while those following behind mutter under their breath about the absurdity of a blind person going someplace to get a better view. They forget that their voices resonate loudly in the stone spiral.

Pranksters have smuggled in everything from fireworks to cantaloupes to live gerbils, anxious to see the punishing effect of gravity.

And of course one person managed to coerce Santa Claus into risking the hazards of flight by wedging him into one of the upper cell windows for a view of the town. The low flagpole of Little Pines must have seemed quite a step down for Saint Nick.

That's the way it is for the rest of us as well, I guess. Every year thousands climb to its high chamber to look out over Lowerton and think, *What a great view. I can see everything from up here. Absolutely everything.* Then they give up their spot to someone else and take the slow walk back down, an old football injury or arthritis dogging each step. They shuffle from the Estate, herded into a tour bus perhaps, and shove off for home where their narrow view of their world is no doubt unimpressive.

I arrived downstairs today convinced somehow of exactly the opposite. I don't want to say all the questions I've faced make sense now or that I know any better how this is all going to end, but there's much less a sense of foreboding than there was before, and I can only attribute it to the realization that we *all* come down from the Tower and live our lives of limited perspective. There's not a one of us who can see farther than the next hill. So if I'm lost, then so is everybody around me. That's a comfort to me today. Tomorrow I might be frustrated by the futility of it all, but tonight I feel what can only be called a kind of connection with the other tourists milling around. We are all down here, mucking about together. For so long I thought I was doing it alone.

Sunday, April 25, 1999

Ben and I went through Quinlin's things today after church. He's been going to First Baptist almost regularly now, and we made the plans in the common room when grabbing coffee after the service. We thought of delaying the task because Philip had an afternoon shift he couldn't get out of. But he said to go ahead without him, that our search was more important than his being in on it. So long as we left him a few boxes to open sometime this week, he'd be okay.

It was the first time I'd been alone with Ben since our trip to Harrisburg. After spending so much time with Philip, who for all of his moods is an excellent conversationalist, it was strange to work with Ben in silence. This is what we found:

Six more accounting logs.

Three antique Mont Blanc fountain pens that, if sold, could fetch a significant chunk of money.

A letter from Pierre S. DuPont, which a museum or collector might be interested in.

A small cache of silver liberty dimes.

A worn leather Bible that smelled of tobacco.

Two empty silver cigarette cases that looked as though they'd never been opened. On each was inscribed, *Sit transit gloria.*

A carved cherry pipe and cracked tobacco pouch.

Yet more accounting logs.

A disintegrating print of Chaplin's 1925 film *The Gold Rush.*

And, finally, an early edition of Dickens' *Hard Times.*

There were no maps or coded clues to the secret of Quinlin's hidden treasure. There was no further correspondence with Marjorie Hayes. It was all just odds and ends and knickknacks that all together may be worth a few thousand dollars to some antiquarian or history buff.

"Glad Philip wasn't here," I said, thinking how disappointed he would've been. At the same time, I wondered about how crushed Glen must have been upon opening these boxes—the magic beans by which he'd squandered my future—and finding nothing. All I know is that Glen and Philip were becoming linked in my head far too often.

"This whole crusade is pretty important to him," said Ben, and it took a second for me to parse out which one of them he was talking about. "Philip's pretty wrapped up in it. I've tried to remind him that things might not pan out for us."

They were the first words of pessimism, or realism I guess,

any of us had spoken aloud, and they hit harder than I expected. "You think we're going to fail?"

Ben shook his head, finished closing up the last box, and took a seat on the cheap butterfly chair opposite my couch, barely fitting. "It is a possibility," he said after a moment. "For me, I need to be prepared for that. I've had to ask myself the question, What if I sink all this time and energy into saving the Estate and it still goes down? All I know is that I'm willing to take the risk." He paused, then added, "I don't think Philip's asked himself that question."

After a second, I said, "I'm not sure I have either."

Ben looked at his shoes and then at me. "Hey, Eve?"

"Yes?"

"What if you sink all this time and energy into saving the Estate and it still goes down?"

I smiled. Ben didn't. He sat there waiting for my honest response. I thought for a moment and said, "I'll be crushed."

Ben moved his head kind of side to side as if he didn't agree.

"You don't think I'll be crushed?"

"For sure, very disappointed," Ben suggested. "But you *will* move on, eventually." There was implication in his words.

"And Philip won't?"

"Philip doesn't. Has he talked to you about his sister?"

I let that pass without answering. I'm not sure how anyone moves on after losing a sibling, especially one lost not to illness or accident but to nothingness. Wanda Maxwell, just a friend, walked out of my life and I've never forgotten her.

Ben got up from the chair and asked if I wanted to open another box. I waved him off, still a bit jittery about the conversation. After all, I remember writing that my greatest fear was that the Estate would fall and that I'd be left with nothing—and in fact less than nothing. Mostly, though, I didn't want to open a box because I wanted to know why Ben thought I'd be able to move on. I asked and it seemed to take him by surprise. He took a deep breath, held it a second too long, and his whole face turned red as he exhaled. I wasn't sure what it meant.

"Can I be honest?" he asked finally.

Nothing good ever came from that request. I nodded anyway.

"I think, and Philip agrees, that some of the things you've uncovered have become more important to you than saving the Estate." He held up a hand. "It's not wrong or bad, Eve. It's just what's happened. And I think you're going to find answers to those questions and they're going to cushion the blow in case the Estate can't be saved. Philip's got nothing. It's not like Karen is coming back."

I startled at that, and Ben apologized for being callous.

We were left without words for a minute. I tried my hardest to point out that I'd been dedicated only to the Estate but saw that in their own way they might be right. Ben grabbed a drink of water as I sat thinking. Only when he'd gathered his backpack and headed for the door did I stir.

"One thing," I asked before he left. "You guys really talk about me?"

Ben swung the pack over his wide shoulders and gave his little noncommittal headshake again. "Philip talks about you," he said. "I answer."

"You're the only one of us with his head screwed on straight, Ben."

He smiled and said, "You're doing better than you think."
I only hope he's right.

Monday, April 26, 1999

I stopped by Truant Gulch today to interrupt Meryl's time
with Glen yet again. It's the one neutral ground between us. I
know I'm not ready to visit her at the trailer park or invite her
to my apartment. In spite of everything I've learned about her,
we still haven't come that far. In fact, today I realized we haven't
made much progress at all, that in some ways we may be worse
off than before. At least then we had some rules of conduct. Now
neither of us knows how to relate to the other. We have almost
two decades' worth of tendencies to overcome, and it isn't easy
to drop a routine that's lasted that long, even if it's something
as unfortunate as wincing at a person's perfume. Our conversation today was halting and irritable. We both said things that
threatened to cast us back to our time in the trailer, back when
we couldn't go two minutes without a sharp word.

Only Glen saved the day, groaning so loudly during one of
our silences that we both jumped from our chairs.

"That was new," Meryl said, staring at my father. She was
closest to the window, just off the side of his bed. She could
reach out to stroke his leg for comfort but didn't. She just stared
at him. "I haven't heard him make that sound before, have you?"

"Sometimes he groans, sometimes he's quiet."

She shook her head. "But that wasn't the usual kind of
groan. That sounded like he might be in pain." Her eyes moved
back to his face, and I felt the slightest twinge. She was here for
Glen. She cared enough to tell the difference between his moan-

ings. She didn't just come here and hold his hand without saying a word, feeling guilty with every glance down to the creeping minute hand of her watch.

"What will you do when he dies?" I asked because it occurred to me that I didn't know what I'd do. Without Glen, there'd be one less reason for me to stay in Lowerton. And if the Estate fell . . .

"I guess that's up to you," Meryl replied.

For a second, for a very weird second, I thought she was inviting me to stay in touch, to forge a friendship. Her eyes, however—those narrow, defiant eyes—hinted at something else. I asked what she meant.

"Glen gave you power of attorney. You're the one who's going to be making all the decisions. If you sell the trailer, I'll leave. Maybe head back home." She laughed but all I could hear was the anger. "How long have I been talking about going back to Richmond?"

"Ever since you got here," I said.

Her eyes flashed and I guess she thought I was taunting her. But then the eyes mellowed and she barked out another of those dark laughs, clogged from her years of smoking. "Guess you're right."

We sat and were quiet for a bit, and it hit me then that all my questions, the information I wanted from Meryl about Wanda and Lydia, would have to wait. I didn't want her to feel as though I were blackmailing her. *Give me the information or I'll make sure things go poorly for you once Glen kicks off.* We'd had bouts of that before in our years together. She'd hold something over my head and I'd lord something over hers. Twenty years was long enough for such as that. I needed her to tell me because she wanted to help and that's it.

In that moment I realized another error I'd made. One committed recently too. So far, all I've been worried about is Meryl earning my trust. I've told myself three times a day that I wouldn't let her take me for a ride. Only now I see that *I* am the one who needs help; *I* am the one with questions that need answers, dark corners that need lights. *I* am the one who needs to earn trust.

I think I made my first step just by sitting with her and Glen in that stale, antiseptic room for an hour or two—the sad family reunited, the prodigal daughter returned to her ... parents? I'm so used to that feeling, I've stopped wishing for something better.

There's that phrase again. It's been popping up everywhere lately.

Something better.

Someplace better.

Somehow better.

Just like Glen sitting at the table and muttering *somewhere, somewhere, somewhere,* I seem to have my own little mantra. Time and time again this one thing has been proven to me: I am my father's daughter.

GLEN

My father became "Glen" to me in the days following that trip to the doctor's when he'd stepped back and allowed the full weight of a huge decision to rest on my crooked shoulders. At first I punched it full of sarcasm, making sure he couldn't miss the impertinence of a sixth-grader referring to her father as an equal. But Glen gave no reaction at all, and so I continued on out of spite until it simply became who he was to me.

I had no mom. There was only Meryl.

Now I had no dad. There was just Glen who, I must say, seemed to enjoy the freedom of not being Dad anymore. I can't attribute this directly to that day, although soon after he spent more time working double shifts at the Estate or passing the dark hours nursing longnecks with Dwight, that is, when his friend was still carousing. He still kept up maintenance on the trailer and drove me to school when I missed the bus and took me to an occasional movie after my doctor's visits, but there were no more half-interested discussions of friends or school. Our only conversation besides those of a practical nature—What did I want for dinner? Did I need money for new clothes?— were his sporadic pronouncements that I'd get out of Lowerton someday. Other than that, we seemed to arrive at the same conclusion: Since I had been the one to decide in the doctor's office if I should grow up straight, I'd also be the one most responsible for it happening. I'd focus on learning and that would get me out of Lowerton. I'd shoulder the burden of becoming a woman strong enough to bear such a load.

For his part, Glen would pay the bills. He'd pay for my brace and visits to the doctor. For my rent and food. I wouldn't have to get a job during the school year. And, he told me one day, as much as was possible he'd pay for whatever education it'd take to help me get out of Lowerton. Then he showed me the savings account he'd opened at the Centre County Savings and Loan, the little gray checkbook where he kept the deposits recorded. We hugged, and I thanked him more sincerely than I ever had in my life. Apparently, with the blush of finding Quinlin's gold, he forgot that day and risked everything he'd promised in exchange for accounting logs and frippery.

In the end he gave me nothing.

Well, that's not quite true.

I have power of attorney, literally the power to step in and end his life.

I have twenty-seven years of memories.

I also have the name he gave me. Eve Marie Lawson. Only now that I think on it, even that he stole.

THURSDAY, APRIL 29, 1999

Today I spent my morning in Lowerton at the *Express*, putting together a story on environmental protests of a mining company's plan to strip one of the Allegheny ridges outside of campus. The environmentalists had been fighting a losing battle (central PA isn't exactly a liberal's paradise) until one of the group pointed out the fact that the scarred, wasted mountain would be visible from the alumni end zone of the university's football stadium, and wouldn't that upset season ticket holders when their sylvan view got reduced to upturned roots and bull-dozed ruts? The plans went into immediate turnaround.

Following that I made some phone calls to Greg Evans in Harrisburg but without luck, checked our post-office box without luck, and headed home to open two more of Quinlin's boxes—those without luck as well.

Tonight I found a stack of personnel records, which included a personnel review of Charles Graveston that called him "honorable" and "a shining example of Christian mercy."

A handwritten copy of the speech given to his board of advisors before the Crash that Embeth Graveston supposedly quoted in *He Saved Lowerton*. Her version reads much like a passage from *Henry V*, whereas his, the real one, an economics dissertation.

Records of insurance benefits received following his father's death.

A single bullet shell.

A half-used pack of cigarette papers.

I packed all of it up, checked my E-mail to find out that Martin Peterson still hadn't written, and switched over to this journal. Yet again, I'm caught up. I am here. I am writing.

SATURDAY, MAY 1, 1999

This morning my little plan to sneak up to Embeth's door failed, and I was caught.

Everything went smoothly up until I reached her hall. As I took three steps down the carpeted floor to apartment 256, a door—Embeth's door—swung open and Lydia Furrow stepped out. She turned to say something to a person inside, and I hoped she might not look my direction and just walk the opposite way, but as the door closed she stood there waiting as though catching her breath. Then, as if she sensed me standing there, her head turned and she caught my eye.

I sucked in a breath, prepared to flee if she made a move toward me. Lydia stared a second longer, shook her head as if troubled by the cross the world had asked her to carry, and stalked off. There's no other word for it. Even at seventy she moved with purpose. All style and effort, she reminded me of a movie star who'd somehow aged wonderfully yet hated it all the same. She disappeared around the corner. I heard the elevator door chime and figured I had only a couple of minutes before security came.

Embeth answered my knock right away. She looked stunned when she saw it was me.

"But Lydia . . ." she tried and let it fall.

"She saw me. Didn't say a word."

Embeth nodded and waved me in. She quickly told me how Lydia had known the entire time that we'd been meeting. Someone on the same floor, a pair of eyes at the peephole, had seen me every time I'd stolen my way into Embeth's apartment.

"But it's all over now," said Embeth, and for the first time she gave a smile. "Lydia confronted me about our visits, and I told her that it was too late, that you knew the whole story already. You knew about Charles and me. You knew about Evangeline. You knew everything."

"What did she say?"

"Stared at me with those black eyes of hers. I swear she reminds me of a raven sometimes with those eyes. Charles had the softest blue eyes. It's hard to see how they're related. Even after so long it's hard to see." She caught herself rambling and continued with her answer. "I thought she would threaten me or yell. She just chewed on her cheek, crossed her hands in her lap, and said, 'You obviously feel some compulsion to go revealing your sins to some stranger. I was just looking after your welfare and the memory of my brother, but you have managed once more to drag that through the mud. Apparently, there is nothing I can do to stop you or that nosy girl. You deserve each other, so I'll just leave you to lick each other's wounds.' And then she left."

"Lick each other's wounds?"

Embeth shrugged. "I never understand half of what that woman says."

I didn't offer my own interpretation.

"But isn't this good news? No more sneaking up here to see me."

I nodded.

"So what do we talk about today? Did you hear from Mr. Peterson?"

She saw from my expression that I hadn't, and a look of worry came into her face.

"You do think he'll write, don't you?"

"I hope," I said and hesitated a moment. "What do you expect to hear from him?"

Embeth didn't say anything for a bit, and I wondered if she'd even heard my question. I was about to repeat it when she said, "I want to hear that things weren't as bad as they seemed toward the end. I heard so many horrible things—I know it might not happen but I want to find out they weren't true." She stood and moved across her small living area to the kitchen. I could hear her sniffling as she went. After spending a few minutes shuffling around, she walked out with a small glass dish of wrapped toffees. Her eyes were dry.

"What do you want to talk about?" she asked.

"Your end of the story," I said. "What happened right before your daughter left for the Estate?"

Embeth sat, waited for me to unwrap my toffee, and began her answer.

The Day Evangeline Walked Out

January 5, 1975, offered itself up as one of those days of
unceasing gray sleet, together with a jagged wind. The streets
in town were treacherous, clogged with slush and mud that hid
long patches of ice still lingering from when road crews took
New Year's Day off. It was the kind of Sunday that had even
elders think about tuning into an AM sermon rather than risk
their cars and ankles for the slim tithe pickings among parish-
ioners who might actually show. It was all this and yet Evangeline Graveston stood in her room packing a suitcase as
though ready to walk out the door any minute.

Embeth watched her from the hall for a few seconds and
tried to translate what she was seeing. "Are you headed somewhere, dear?" she asked, noticing the peculiar intensity on her
daughter's face.

"I'm thirty-six, Mother. This has lasted long enough."

"Where are you going?"

"The Estate," Evangeline replied without looking up. "It's
where I belong."

Her answer took Embeth by surprise. She had no idea her
daughter had any interest in the odd little community living up
on the hill—Road to Damascus she thought it was called. She
and Charles had heard the rumors about the place, had also met
members outside of Lowerton and thought them mostly normal
if not a tad idealistic.

"You've contacted them, then?" she asked. Her daughter
sometimes skipped the practical steps, content to linger on her
own vision of how things would be.

"My room's ready," said Evangeline as she snapped the lid

of her suitcase shut. It was a large tweed carrier they'd bought for her a dozen years ago when she'd talked about going with some other teachers to a conference out west in San Diego. That had fallen through, the way so many things seemed to with Evangeline, and the suitcase had sat untouched in her closet all those years. Now it lay on the bed, packed.

"Should your father and I drive you?" It was all Embeth could think of to say. She knew she should be trying to slow this whole thing down so they could get to the reasons behind Evangeline's choice, but she didn't want to risk grinding things to a halt. Inertia seemed the one thing that marked Evangeline's life, and for the moment Embeth could see no real reason for going against her moving in with Road to Damascus. Her daughter was right—it was time.

Evangeline nodded in response and then said the strangest thing. "Yes, please. Call for Charles."

Embeth paused, decided now wasn't the time to argue such a small thing, and summoned Charles from his tinkering about with his trains in the basement and whispered to him what had happened. He stopped dead in the kitchen. Embeth thought he was going to put an end to it all right there, but instead he just rubbed the back of his neck and closed his eyes. For a few minutes they discussed the situation, and soon Charles arrived at the same conclusion Embeth had. It was now or never.

"We can talk with whoever runs the place today—make sure things are legitimate."

"Agreed," Embeth said. Within minutes they had loaded Evangeline's suitcase and were headed for the Estate.

The drive there, normally a ten-minute ride, took nearly forty. Small upgrades that happened to be covered in ice were impassable, so Charles had to pick his way through streets clear enough to use, sometimes backtracking because he'd run out of options. All the while Evangeline sat silently in the backseat. It was her response to both anger and fear, and Embeth couldn't have guessed which one her daughter was feeling at the moment. Only as the Estate's Tower came into view did Evangeline give a single clue, for she shuddered as their car passed beneath its looming shadow. She was frightened. That more than anything convinced Embeth that her daughter was at least thinking straight. The girl often got lost in daydreams. But if she was nervous about a new change to her life, she'd at least thought it through.

Charles rolled the car to a stop outside the gates. While he unloaded the bag, Embeth and Evangeline crossed the draw-bridge toward the great columns and wide doors of the Estate's entrance. Their knock was answered immediately, and as they stepped through, Charles arrived carrying the suitcase. The doors shut behind them with a familiar *clang* Embeth hadn't heard since volunteering at the orphanage.

A thin man of about thirty smiled at them and asked how he could be of service. "Must be important for you to risk the weather."

"Our daughter would like to ... to move in here?" said Embeth, realizing her statement had turned into a question half-way through. In that moment it hit her for the first time what they were doing and expected the man to laugh at them. This wasn't some roadside motel after all, where one could just show up and hope to get a room.

But that's exactly what happened. The man smiled again and said they had plenty of room.

Evangeline took a step forward and introduced herself. "I'm Evangeline," she said. "This is my mother. And this is Charles."

Before either Embeth or Charles could comment on the strange introduction, the man introduced himself as Martin Peterson and asked if they'd like a tour of the place.

"Eve might," said Charles, "but my wife and I know the Estate quite well. I taught school here and she worked at the orphanage. But we *would* like a moment of your time to ask you a few questions, if you can spare someone else to show Evangeline around?"

Martin nodded and motioned for a redheaded woman to come over, whom he introduced as Melanie. He explained that Evangeline would like a tour, and as the two women left, Evangeline turned to wave and shouted, "Thanks, Mom. Thanks, Dad." It was as honest a happiness as they'd seen from her in a long while.

"So ... you want to know if we grow drugs and sacrifice goats," Martin said once Evangeline and Melanie had disappeared. There was a hint of wariness in his voice, and his hands were shoved deep in his pockets.

"Something like that," Charles replied with a laugh that Martin must have liked, because he joined in as well before waving them over to a set of couches in a small room off the main entryway. There they spent an hour talking about Road to Damascus, each minute reassuring them more than the last. These young people may have been overly idealistic, but it was an optimism built on an understanding and love of God. They felt that this could be a safe place for Evangeline to begin her life outside the Graveston home.

Nine months later that new beginning ended in a fall down the Tower stairs.

SUNDAY, MAY 2, 1999

And now we know it may have been something more than just a fall.

Martin Peterson E-mailed tonight. I logged on after Ben, Philip, and I had opened a third useless box. I called the guys over to read it. Crowded around my tiny notebook computer, we read the words that changed everything.

Philip wanted to get in the car and drive immediately to Quinlin's Estate.

I could barely think.

Ben, bless his soul, played peacemaker and suggested we all take a day to sort out our thoughts. Even Philip couldn't argue with that.

"This changes everything," he said about six times before he left.

I can't disagree, but really, all it makes me want to do is cry. What a sorry waste. All of it.

MARTIN'S E-MAIL

```
From:     Martin Peterson
Sent:     Monday, May 3, 1999 2:11 PM
To:       Lawson, Eve
Subject:  The Rest of It
```

I apologize for the delay in writing. I make no

excuses—this is simply a story I haven't wanted to revisit. Writing the words, I hope, will help put it all behind me for good, but it seems more likely that it'll simply open the wounds again.

This last portion takes place over the final two weeks of Evangeline's life. She'd just come back from a visit to town and was acting strangely normal. We expected anything. Nothing happened.

Then on a Monday, I think it might have been October 6 or 7, Evangeline stood up at a family meeting and announced she was going to take some days to sort things out. She'd been putting together things we said about the Bible with things she'd heard growing up and realized she'd somehow missed something. She said she wanted to study this on her own, that she might even turn it into a short personal retreat like other members did from time to time.

We were taken by surprise, but her words and intent seemed genuine. She asked to have the key to one of the dungeon chambers, and she packed up a blanket, two gallons of water, a dozen or so candles, and a Bible a woman named Patricia had lent her. Her last requests were that we water the fern in her room at least once and that we not disturb her unless it was the most dire of emergencies.

During her first night of seclusion, a brother, Ken Watson, who had a deep love of astronomy, was in the Tower awaiting a predicted meteor shower when he saw a single figure emerge from the shadows of the Estate wall and creep across the lawn. Worried that it might be a prowler, he shouted and threw one of his star maps at the figure. The tactic worked and the

person fled. The next morning he reported what had
happened and included one more fact: "I think it was
a woman. The way she ran away, the scream I heard
when I surprised her."

We all had the same thought. Evangeline. She had
crept out of the Estate for some reason and was
trying to get back in without being noticed when Ken
spied her from the Tower.

We thought about confronting her but then decided we
hadn't the right. She had every freedom to leave the
Estate at any hour. She may have lied about her
intent to remain in the dungeon, yet had we really
expected her to mean it anyway? But we did post a
person downstairs to keep an eye on her just so we
would know for sure.

Night two passed without incident. Ken and another
brother, Stephen, volunteered to split the watch,
and both reported that she'd stayed in the room all
evening. They heard her talking to herself on
occasion, praying perhaps, and heard something else
that Ken claimed sounded like writing, only louder.

It was the afternoon of the third day that we
discovered the evening hadn't passed without
incident after all. Patricia, the woman who'd lent
the Bible, entered Eve's room to water the fern and
found the place turned upside down. Someone had
broken in during the dark hours of night and
ransacked her room searching for something.

This, we decided, constituted an emergency, and so
Ken, Patricia, and I headed downstairs. When we
knocked, Evangeline said she didn't want to open the
door. So we shouted the news of the break-in to her.

She couldn't have cared less.

"Yes, I figured something like that might happen. Is my fern okay?"

I wanted to end the charade right there. She was obviously keeping something from us that might also be endangering others. Ken wavered and Patricia thought we should give Evangeline some more time to work things out. I crumbled, agreeing only on the condition that we watch all the windows and doors that evening. We did and morning came.

Patricia went down the next morning at nine o'clock, found her door open and cell empty, and ran right back to me to report what she'd found. Ken suggested she might have fled, but for some reason that didn't seem right. Something was wrong.

In my last good decision that day I ordered that we split up into pairs and search the Estate for her. The others agreed. Nobody had expected her to disappear.

An hour later we got our first report. Two women searching the Maze had heard Evangeline singing to herself in there.

"The Maze?" Patricia said. "Two people will never find her in there."

And this was when we began making mistakes.

Ken and I agreed with her, and the word was passed for every pair to search the Maze. Surely with over twenty people, someone was bound to stumble across her.

We should never have sent all our people in but

instead should've simply had somebody wait at each
entrance until she came out. I know that now. It
never occurred to us, however, that she wouldn't be
in the Maze. It was only dumb luck that Patricia and
I hadn't yet entered when we saw Evangeline in one of
the long hallways. Honestly it was like seeing a
ghost.

"Marty . . ." Patricia said to me and pointed.

I made a split-second decision—again the wrong one.

"Run to the Maze and yell for everyone to get out of
there. I'll follow Eve."

She should have been the one to follow Evangeline.
She might have stopped and listened. Me she ran
from.

From what you've said, Ms. Lawson, I assume you know
the Estate well. You know that it's a sprawling
place with a lot of weird angles and hallways,
something that can be troublesome when trying to find
a certain room. When you're chasing after someone,
they become a maze unto themselves.

The closest I ever came were more glimpses. For ten
minutes I tried chasing her down, but she always
seemed to round the next corner and slip out of my
view again. Eventually I found myself in the main
meeting hall at the center of the Estate.

As you know, five different corridors empty into that
room, along with four doors to other rooms and
stairs to both the basement, the second floor, and
the Tower. Because the rooms and the Tower were dead
ends, I figured I had six choices, ignoring also the

hall from which I'd just came. But the guessing
never happened.

First, I heard footsteps that sounded a mile away.
Then the scream.

Then, and this still has the ability to tear me from
sleep, the relentless sound of her falling.

It finally ended when her body hit the downstairs
door and she spilled out into the room. I moved to
her instantly and I remember, with thanks, that her
eyes were closed. The bruising had started already,
and a quick check found no pulse.

Everything afterward transpired like a terrible
dream from which I wanted to wake up but couldn't. I
called the ambulance and sat by her feet, waiting
for paramedics to arrive and hoping and not hoping
that one of the other members would emerge from the
Maze. Nobody did. I sat with Evangeline for ten
minutes until I heard sirens coming up the drive. I
just sat there watching as the EMTs rushed in,
gathered her onto a gurney, strapped her in for
transport. There were no police. It was never viewed
as anything but an accident.

As they rolled her out, one of the drivers asked if I
wanted to ride along. It was the last thing I wanted,
but I thought somebody should go and that somebody
should be me. Then, while standing there, a flash of
something moving partway up the stairs caught my
eye, although a quick glance showed nothing had
moved. Instead I had seen something glimmering there
in the dark. A bar of gold.

"You coming or not?" called the paramedic, and I

made my final wrong decision of the day. I shut the
door to the Tower, locked it, and walked out with
him.

Gold was the last thing I needed to be dealing with
at the moment. I figured I would go to the hospital,
find out the news I already knew, and head back to the
Estate to piece everything together.

And my plan worked. I was dismissed as soon as I got
to the hospital for not being a relative. The county
bus showed up a few minutes later, and I paid my
thirty-five cents to cross town so I could walk up the
hill to home. I arrived not thirty minutes after I
had left.

Nobody had yet made it out of the Maze. It takes
hours, as you know. I entered the Estate and walked
straight to the door of the Tower. It was still
locked.

I unlocked it. The gold bar was gone.

About fifteen minutes later a group of twelve of our
members came walking down the hall. Patricia was
leading them. "Where have you been?" they asked. "We
thought we heard sirens. "

I told them what had happened. About Evangeline's
fall.

"How long have you been out?"

"Maybe ten minutes?" one replied and then we all
stood around silent.

One of them, I guessed, had taken the gold.

My opinion since that time has changed. I've talked

with each of those twelve people numerous times since then. They all swear to not having taken the gold, and I believe them.

The only other explanation then is that someone else was in the Estate with us. A person broke in the night before, but who knows if he or she ever left? There are many places to hide in Quinlin's Estate.

So I believe that someone else saw what had happened and waited till I'd gone to unlock the door. Or someone was in the Tower staircase.

Evangeline's scream, as I think back on it, was not in surprise at falling but in terror at something else. Like turning a corner and running into someone hiding there in wait for you. Or opening the upper door only to find someone standing there, expectant, hands outstretched.

The lower door to the Tower locks only from the outside. If you're inside, the handle still turns. And the handle must have turned that day, after I'd left with the paramedics. The handle turned, and someone stepped out carrying a gold bar, the same someone who might very well have pushed Evangeline Graveston down the Tower steps.

But nothing was ever done about it. I admit that I am largely to blame for that. I knew our group was finished in Lowerton, but I at least wanted to leave without subjecting everyone to a police investigation. They were content to call it an accident and so was I.

Only later did I realize how Evangeline's death, even more than her life, had been swept under the

carpet. Somebody wanted it to happen. People
protested her death but only so that it would force
us out. They never cared for Evangeline at all. Her
life required a reckoning and got none. Not even
here. I can offer nothing.

Regretfully,
Martin Peterson

Part Five

MONDAY, MAY 3, 1999

As we'd decided yesterday, Ben, Philip, and I met tonight to discuss the information revealed in Martin's E-mail. I chose a Chili's two towns over just so we wouldn't be overheard. Nothing in that E-mail is fun and games. Not only do we have the possibility that Quinlin's gold exists, but there is the very real chance that Evangeline Graveston's life could have ended under much darker circumstances than we first were led to believe. I'd come in hoping we might agree on plans to deal with both of these revelations. Instead, our little group has pulled in two, with me stuck in the middle.

Philip, of course, wants to find the gold. He said he's known it was real from the moment Dwight told him about Glen's stubborn refusal to be swayed from his search.

"Your father said, 'You don't know what I know,'" said Philip, picking at the appetizer platter we ordered. "That's the same thing Pastor Hopper suggested I say if people doubted me."

Ben gawked.

"I know," Philip said, waving his hand. "I know they're not connected, but the sentiment is the same. It's quiet self-assurance. And besides, other people have believed in the gold. Don't you think if a townful of people nurse a feeling for decades that there might be something behind it? Especially if someone has actually seen what you're looking for?"

I shrugged—and Philip didn't like that at all. He turned to Ben, who just squinted for a second before saying, "Loch Ness."

"Nobody saw the Loch Ness monster, Ben."

"But they thought they did."

Philip nodded as if catching Ben's point. "So you don't believe Peterson?"

"To me, Philip, Peterson's E-mail is mostly irrelevant. The question of Evangeline's death plays a part in Eve's research, but the rest of it is just more fodder for the legend." His face was beginning to flush a bit now. He didn't normally like to argue, and it seemed like each statement seemed to tax him, whereas debate energized Philip, who jumped in with his next point before Ben could take another breath.

"Legend? I'll admit we can't spend all our time looking for it, but what if it's true?" He pushed a drink aside and leaned forward, excited. "Do you know what we could do with that gold?"

"Nothing," said Ben, and it came out in a growl that stopped Philip short.

"What?"

"Whose gold is it anyway? Do you think Brighton is going

to give up its claim just because we found it? It's on their property. They own the corroded plumbing, the outdated wiring, and every crooked stair in the place. You think they won't want the one thing of actual value if it turns out to exist?"

"Maybe—" Philip started but Ben was on a roll.

"Maybe they'll use it to fix up the place if we find it for them? No. They want out. They granted a year reprieve as a favor to the town, but they just want to unload the thing. It'd take a decade to earn back the money poured into fixing it up, and the only organization that's got that much time to wait is the government or a nonprofit."

Philip leaned back in his chair, not saying anything.

Ben looked at me for just an instant and then toyed with his straw. He hadn't eaten a thing since we'd arrived. I wondered if this whole mess turned his stomach as much as it did mine. I was at a loss for what to do, yet I knew they were both waiting for my opinion. I'd been the one to open this Pandora's box. While what I said was the truth, I'm sure it was a disappointment to them.

"I'm not sure what to do."

And I'm not.

I'm not sure what to do. I'm not sure what to think. I'm not sure of anything anymore.

There used to be a few foundations in my life: Meryl Lakewood hated me; Glen's obsession stole him from me; and any small kind of faith, even one in the kindness of Santa, was destined to fail. Now Meryl has unlocked secrets with a single story, my father's obsession may have been real all along, and faith is the thing I can't seem to chase from my thoughts during the dark hours of night.

I'm not sure what to do.

Do I tell Embeth her daughter was probably pushed down the stairs of Quinlin's Estate?

Do I ask Keith Wilcox what he knows about Evangeline's death?

Do I start my own search for gold that we may never get to claim?

Do I risk believing again in something when all it's gotten me before is sorrow?

The only answers we got tonight were that we'll most likely be doing things separately from now on. Ben insisted that he wanted no part of searching for the gold, while Philip maintained it would still be worth it. In the meantime, Philip wanted us to stay quiet about the speculation regarding Evangeline's death, though Ben thought that justice—if it turned out to be foul play—was long overdue. We needed to tell someone.

My road divided. Ben and Philip split the bill, but that was the last thing they'd do together for a while. Were we in the Maze, they'd never see each other again until the end. But we're not and who knows if these separate paths lead to the same answer, or even an answer at all. Do I choose one and follow or do I forge my own? Again, the first steps are the hardest.

FRIDAY, MAY 7, 1999

These past days have been a blur.

Tuesday I met with Ben to discuss further initiatives that might link the Estate with the university. He'd spoken with the director of the graduate student committee who hinted that a good amount of support, and funding, might be found for turning the building into a living humanities research laboratory. So far, though, the only discussions have been with individuals, and no plan has been drawn up.

Wednesday Philip and I spent five hours in the Estate. Searching for the gold. You can guess how that turned out.

Thursday I listened to Embeth leave a message inquiring whether I'd heard anything from Martin Peterson, and Meryl Lakewood ask if I ever wanted to get in touch with Wander. I ignored both—partly because they're issues I'm not anxious to deal with at the moment and partly because I needed to finish two articles for the *Express* next week.

The first was a short follow-up story to the piece I'd written about the mining company being turned aside by the university's alumni association. Apparently they'd made inquiries into more than two dozen towns in the area about obtaining mining rights. The second article was a public opinion piece on what should be done with the now-empty grain and tack store across from city hall. It was a little like writing my own obituary, because if things don't change, I'll be doing a similar article in just a few months for the Estate. Should such a day come, my guess is that public sentiment won't be drastically different from what it is for this empty store. There'll be a brief lament for losing this link to the past and then grand words spilled about new days ahead and bright opportunities awaiting. As if anything could save Lowerton at this point.

Today I E-mailed Martin Peterson a number of questions to tie up loose ends that I felt were left dangling. Then I sat there and tried to guess his answers, which only ended up frustrating me. I thought of calling Philip, then switched to Ben, finally deciding to call the one person I hadn't bothered contacting in a while, the one man who had less invested in this than all of us. Dwight returned my call from work and agreed to meet me after his shift was over.

When I arrived, I could see sleep hadn't come easily to Dwight last night. His eyes were bruised and puffy, similar to the way he looked mornings I used to find him sprawled out in our trailer following a night out with Glen.

"Monique was up half the night talking with her sister again. She woke me up for the other half." He gave a guilty smile. "I shouldn't have said that. I just didn't get my beauty rest. Monique's got the real troubles."

I gave my regrets not knowing what else to say. I watched Dwight and all I could feel was frustration—not at him or Monique, but at myself. For a month I hadn't called them, not once, and now that I needed something I assumed they'd be ready and waiting, as they'd always been. The only other people that act that way are children and fools. In so many ways I feel I am both.

The sad thing is that Dwight still forced me to confess why I'd asked to meet him. He knew I needed something and wouldn't take a wave of my hand as an answer. Sitting outside the graduate commons at a patio table, I told him what I knew about Martin Peterson's confession in a few breaths, and Dwight's face darkened with each sentence. When I'd finished, he looked like a man eager for the escape of sleep.

"Quite a story," he said in a monotone I've never heard before.

"Had you ever heard hints of something like that?"

He shook his head with great thought, then said no. He sighed and then added, "But it doesn't surprise me."

"What doesn't surprise you?"

He looked at me without speaking for a whole ten seconds.

"Dwight. . . ?" I prompted.

"Eve Marie ... you know Evangeline's story. How many folks you think could have done such a thing?"

I blinked. The understanding of what he suggested came on like I was falling—helpless and sickening. He meant Glen. It shocked me both for how much sense it made and that I hadn't yet considered it.

"Was he still talking with her at that point? It was 1975, I guess, right before Meryl showed up."

Dwight didn't answer. I knew he didn't have any more than speculation. I also knew he was right about where the circumstances of the day pointed. There were two people involved in her life, and they were Glen and Lydia Furrow. And I just couldn't see old Lydia pushing Evangeline down a flight of stairs, no matter how nasty she might be.

"That what you wanted to know?" Dwight asked, breaking my reverie.

I shook my head. "I want to know what I should do with the information."

Obviously puzzled, Dwight asked, "You mean tell the police?"

"No. I mean, should I go looking for the gold? Philip believes it's the best way to save the Estate. He found legal precedent that would allow us to keep the gold even if we found it on private property or, at worst, share it with Brighton Entertainment."

"What do you want me to tell you, Eve?" Dwight said after a moment. "I can't tell you not to search for the gold. Your friend may be right. I think, though, that you need to know why you're searching for it. Have you asked yourself that question?"

I nodded.

"You feel comfortable with your answer? Like you could live a hundred years without regrets? Like you could go into a coma and not worry about others thinking badly of you?"

That one stung. I knew he was holding Glen up to me as a mirror. It was one I'd held up myself yesterday for an hour or two, and I wasn't ready to face it again so soon.

"I want to save the Estate," I said.

Dwight narrowed his eyes. "Glen just wanted to help you get out of here."

"So what do I do?"

"Save the Estate," he said. "Any and all ways you can. Gold, meetings with the mayor, bake sale down at the factory—whatever." He smiled now, and I could tell the worst was coming. He'd always hidden the hard lessons in a smile. "The gold's a trap, Eve, you know that. You want to find it and save Glen from what the town's always thought of him, save him from what you're thinking about him right now. Still, in the end, it's a trap. Always has been. Otherwise we wouldn't be here today, would we?"

Looking at Dwight, I was filled with a great appreciation. Dwight wasn't my father, but he was the closest thing I was going to get on this earth, and I realized he wanted me to come to him with problems and worries even when he'd been up half the night hugging his wife and telling her things would be okay. I thought I had something to offer him as well, so before he had the chance to say another thing, I picked up my drink, looked him in the eyes, and asked, "So what's Monique going to do about her sister this time?"

Dwight sighed and slumped in his chair. "It's a mess. I don't want to bother you with it," he said. But then he did anyway. He's a good man.

Dwight's Conversion

Dwight rested for a moment, chin on broom handle and his back to the door of the dungeon cell that still waited to be cleaned. Few visitors to the Estate made it down here, and those that did were looking for something other than an interesting lesson. They were looking for an out-of-the-way corner to light up a cigarette, a quiet spot to finish off the whiskey they'd smuggled in, or a dark place in which to trade spit with someone who insisted on sticking her chewing gum to the wall first. This was the pit of the Estate, and Dwight knew Glen had assigned him to it because of the things he couldn't keep from coming out of his mouth recently.

Things like looking around Gus's Tavern and saying, "Sometimes this all seems pretty worthless, wasting our time in here this way."

Glen would nod and say, "Yeah, why don't we go home instead and watch *Cheers* like the rest of the world. Like there's a difference." He'd say it with a laugh, but Dwight saw the anger in his eyes and so it didn't surprise him when the work order came out on Monday. Nor did it surprise him when the dungeon door clanged shut behind him. Glen was into teaching lessons so they stuck. Sometime, maybe an hour later, the lock would click open and Dwight would be freed. Until then he was to sit and think about what he'd done wrong.

Only that's not what happened.

Dwight took a seat on the cold stone floor, leaned back against the wall, and instead entertained the thoughts that'd been keeping him company during every quiet moment for the last two weeks. He was remembering Monique, their first months of dating and their first year of marriage. When everything was smiles and wry winks.

All of it he remembered with regret, because things had changed so much.

What had happened to their dreams of opening a small greenhouse and nursery? Of buying a small bi-level on the north side of Lowerton, close to the schools so any children they might have could skip riding the bus? Of one day hosting a Thanksgiving dinner so large that they'd use every plate and pot and knife in the house?

Dwight growled to himself. He knew what had happened. *He* had happened.

He'd been the one to start skipping dinners—first once a week, then four or even five times—to chase a burger with two or three beers with the boys after work. Always with the same stupid reason: "I sweated for this money, Nique. I've the right to spend it any way I choose."

And sweated he had.

Dwight held up a single hand before his eyes and stared at it. He was doing this a lot lately, yet he couldn't help himself, for he didn't recognize his own hand. How does such a thing happen? How does a hand become so beaten, so thick that it doesn't register in a man's eyes as being his own? Not to mention the rest of his body when he stepped from the bath in the morning.

Dreams of gardening die easy when one's sucking air after just a few swishes of the rake.

Dwight sighed deeply as he stared at the locked door in front of him.

This is it. This is my life. I made this.

He looked around. To his left he saw the words he'd seen every time he'd been assigned dungeon duty. Only this time he read them.

The engulfing waters threatened me, the deep surrounded me.

He nodded. He'd once overheard somebody saying that the words were carved by those religious kids who lived here back in the '70s, from the story about the man who got eaten by a whale because he ticked off God.

He thought, *That's just about right. That's how it feels.*

Then Dwight felt what he could only describe as a stillness. If there'd been the scraping of footsteps upstairs or the drip of the wishing well down the hall or the groan of the massive dehumidifier, it all stopped. And in that silence, Dwight heard nothing. Yet the stillness, the quiet, was a gift in itself. It didn't seem to be covering over his frustration with how things had turned out, but rather it reassured him in some way that his frustrations were right. He was right in understanding that things had gone wrong. He was right in seeing he'd been the cause of a lot of it. The best was that he was right in thinking there was a way out. The silence was just part of that.

From down the hall he heard footsteps. Dwight stood and waited. They came and came and finally he heard them right next to the door. The lock opened and the handle turned.

Glen stuck his head around the door, a satisfied smile on his face. "Sorry about that, partner. Forgot you were down here."

"No problem," said Dwight. He added then the thing that would get him moving in the right direction. "Glen," he said, "things can't keep on keepin' on. I'll go nuts if they do—I'll lose Monique. I'm giving my notice. Consider this two weeks."

Glen's eyes blazed. He called Dwight a single ugly name and slammed the door shut. Dwight didn't hear his friend's footfalls as he stormed away; he couldn't hear anything at all. Just quiet and silence and the feeling that a corner had been turned.

WEDNESDAY, MAY 12, 1999

Flora Howardson, my editor at the *Express*, likes the job I'm doing, and if I don't watch it I'm going to end up a small-town reporter rather than a small-town historian. In Lowerton, though, that's pretty much saying the same thing. Since I'd written the initial article on the condemned grain and tack store, she's assigned me to cover a town meeting called for next week to discuss the store's future. She hinted that our little article might've shown the city officials something they hadn't been expecting. I convinced her to let me do a piece on the Estate once this story's finished. I only hope the results are the same.

Just before leaving the newspaper office at two, I made a call to the Carters and got the news I wanted. Dwight wasn't home. I asked Monique if I could drop by to talk with her, and she seemed as considerate as Dwight always is. I'm lucky to know this family.

When I arrived, Monique poured lemonade and we chatted for a bit about her sister, about Quinlin's gold, and about a dozen other small things until Vanessa came home and conversation shifted to Lowerton High School and then a phone call pulled the girl away. Left alone again with Monique, I asked the question that'd been on my mind since last Friday: "When Dwight converted, what did you think?"

It was blunt and probably poorly phrased, but I couldn't get it out of my head that the person affected most by such a thing might not be the one changing but rather the one watching the change. Monique seemed to understand what I meant and gave me one of those smiles that must've seized Dwight's heart when they were dating. She looked around as if to check that no one else was watching and leaned forward to whisper.

"Dwight would die of embarrassment if he knew I was telling you this. I haven't mentioned it to anyone, and stories like this should be shared. Eve, when Dwight came home from the Estate that day, I thought he was drunk. He kind of slouched through the door, eyes all bloodshot, and started coming right for me.

"The only reason I didn't turn away like I normally would is that I couldn't smell a thing. I know growing up with Glen that you know the smell of a man who's spent too many hours in a bar. But Dwight didn't have it—not that evening. So he came right for me and grabbed me into this big bear hug. That's when I knew something was going on.

"First off, he was crying. I could feel the wetness on my cheeks. He was crying and whispering how sorry he was. Second, and this was the big one, he was hugging me the right way. Before, Dwight would come through the door and just take. He'd paw at me like I was something other than his wife and there wasn't much use in struggling. I know it's hard to hear; it's hard to say too. But things are different now. Now he hugs me and it's like we're leaning on each other, one as needy and giving as the other. You know what I mean?"

I shook my head.

Monique's eyes softened. "Oh, girl."

I laughed. "Glen patted me on the head a lot. I haven't really found anyone else."

"What about that dapper little fella you're always with?"

"He likes me. I just haven't gotten my head around how I feel for him."

Monique gave a small, sympathetic nod, bit her lip a second as if thinking over something, and said, "My only advice is to not let the dumb part of you trick the smart part into thinking that this is your last chance or something stupid like that." Then she reached out one slender arm and pulled me over to her. She held me there for just a moment, time enough for me to realize how right she was. There's a bit of mutual leaning in any kind of embrace. I guess I'd never thought of myself as helping to hold another person up. Sometimes it seems hard enough to keep myself from falling.

Martin Peterson's response to my final questions arrived this evening. There was nothing all that stunning included, but two points were clarified:

1. Peterson is sure he saw a bar of gold glinting from the darkness, although he has no proof.

2. Evangeline carved the passage from Jonah on the dungeon wall. That had been her room of retreat, and other members of the commune remember hearing a peculiar scraping sound coming from inside. He has no idea what caused her to pick that particular passage other than that its aching loneliness matched the cry of her own heart.

The engulfing waters threatened me, the deep surrounded me.

No wonder she had tried to drown herself. And even then, the well had failed to answer her wish.

THE WELL

A small plywood sign nailed to the railing of the bridge spanning Quinlin's Estate reads, *A wish without faith is the cry of a fool.* It showed up sometime in the '80s, hammered there by a believer apparently disgusted at the proliferation of worthless pleas being spoken to the waters. Caretakers spoke of taking the sign down, but few disagreed with the message and so it was left as a warning to those who yearn in vain.

Below the bridge waits eight-five feet of water.

Quinlin insisted that a source of fresh water be available for the Estate. It took drilling nearly ninety feet to tap into an underground spring. This is sixty feet deeper than any portion of the Estate's foundation, and engineers have studied the effects of the well in its piercing the very heart of the mountain ridge on which the house is built, trying to prove, one way or the other, the validity of the Estate's last great legend—that of its impending fall.

The most simple expression of this can be seen in a children's jump rope rhyme popularized in the '40s:

> *Deep well, deep well, what you gonna do*
> *When someone pulls the plug on you?*
> *Won't you go empty? Won't you go dry?*
> *And won't your house fall from the sky?*

There have been only minor changes to this version of the

legend since its initial creation around the same time the rhyme came out.

One version says that the Tower will remain standing.

A second states that Quinlin's gold will somehow fall down the well shaft and be buried forever under the rubble of the Estate.

Finally, there is a darker legend—inspired no doubt by apocalyptic philosophies that became the rage in the early '70s—that warns of judgment on Lowerton should the Estate collapse. The Estate saved the town so that without it Lowerton will face a kind of disastrous reckoning. Who knows who thinks up such things.

What we know for sure is that the well continues to measure at eighty-five feet deep, that visitors to the Estate continue to toss in their pennies and nickels and, less frequently, dimes and quarters. Children like to drop the coins over the edge and watch them glitter for a second or two before disappearing into the black of the deep water. Their parents look on and some mutter how perfect it is. For don't all dreams flicker for a moment and then soon pass out of view? They are the ones to whom the plywood sign speaks, those without faith who let go their coins and hear only the shallow *plash* rather than the enormous possibility of what it would mean should one simple prayer be answered.

Sunday, May 16, 1999

Today was one of those days when central Pennsylvania became Eden's neighbor. The sky looked like a cathedral dome, the trees pillars, and the sun spilled onto the ground as though filtered through stained glass. It was the kind of day that as a child I would have forgotten my need to eat and become lost in hours of chase and play. I might've done something similar today had Philip not stopped me after church and suggested we skip the Estate, skip Quinlin's boxes, and have ourselves a picnic instead. I agreed. If ever there was a time to give this man a final answer to what was going on between us, today was it.

We met at Stone Valley west of Lowerton and hiked around the lake there until Philip found a wide swath of grass along the shore and spread out his blanket. We ate and threw bits of bread to a pair of mallards and talked and stared at the clouds and turned blades of grass into whistles and watched a father teach his son to fish and tried skipping rocks and laughed at a novice sailboarder who couldn't find his balance and took in the sun as though we needed it to live. It was only toward the end of the day that I began to grow frustrated with myself. I knew the answer now and it would ruin everything.

"Philip, can we talk?" I said, trying to sound upbeat and off-hand, though I think my voice betrayed me because when he turned his eyes looked panicky, like a rabbit's in those seconds of hesitation before it darts away.

"Sure," he said.

I don't know what my face showed, but inside I felt everything sag, all the wind knocked out of me. "It's about this," I started and motioned to the picnic and lake. "What are we doing here?"

"Haven't you had a good time?" Philip asked, and I realized, for real, why I was turning him down. The simple question had been pure Glen, and far too often Philip and Glen came to mind at the same time.

Haven't you had a good time?

Glen could turn a question inside out better than anyone I'd ever met. It always seemed a thing worse than lying. For Glen, the question was always from Meryl, always similar to the one I'd asked Philip—where did they stand? As far as I can remember, she started asking it in the days after she stopped sleeping on the trailer couch, and Glen never answered her.

Don't we have a good time?

Aren't you happy here?

Am I asking too much from you?

And on. And on.

I remember the stab of pleasure I would get from watching Meryl's mouth go slack, her eyes lower to the ground in the wake of Glen's retort. *She got what she deserved,* I'd say to myself, never understanding how wrong I was, that she never got the one thing she deserved most—a truthful, straightforward answer.

"Something wrong?" Philip asked, touching my arm. I tried not to flinch.

I looked at him. His eyes had deepened from blue to gray in the afternoon sun. A stray lock of hair had fallen across his forehead. It was a moment that most couples would have turned into their first kiss, the perfect end to a fine day. I just patted his hand and scrambled to come up with an easy way to do this.

"I thought about what you told me before. I don't think I'm interested right now."

"You're not interested right now?"

It sounded just as ridiculous the second time. I realized I was being as evasive as he'd been moments before, so I decided to spell it out.

"Philip, you're a good guy. I like you. But you don't fill my thoughts. The Estate does and Wander does and Evangeline does. It wouldn't be fair to either of us to do this right now."

"You keep saying *right now*."

I closed my eyes. "You're not the one, Philip. I'm sorry."

I sat there and waited for a response that I couldn't have predicted for all the gold in Quinlin's Estate. It wouldn't have surprised me if he'd moped or if he'd shrugged and said "Fine." To his credit, he took it like a man.

"Well, that's a nice capper to the day."

I nodded. I then waited for him to ask the inevitable question. He'd stopped looking at me, but it still didn't take long.

"What about the Estate?"

"I don't know that this has to change anything in regard to the Estate. Unless you feel differently for some reason?"

At the time, I just asked the question. Now that I write it I hear Glen's voice once again. The question was a trap, forcing Philip either to agree with me or play the bad guy. He chose the former by nodding his head. Then he began packing up the picnic, hands moving without much thought or planning. In a few minutes he'd finished and we both stood. Daylight still had a few hours left, while for us the sun had already gone down. We said nothing on the short hike back to the parking lot where Philip gave only a quick wave good-bye before climbing in his car to leave. I waited for him to pull out of sight before getting in mine and heading home.

Five miles outside Stone Valley, the first tears came. They were as unexpected as a fit of laughter would have been but they stayed with me the whole ride home, following me up the stairs to my apartment and into the bedroom where I collapsed onto my bed.

Even now, a few hours later, I can't quite say for sure why they came. Part of it was for the echo of Glen's voice that still hadn't left me and for the lies we tell other people. And part of it was for the lies we tell ourselves.

I'm not saying I want to be with Philip, yet it's clear for the first time how much I'd like to be with *someone*. Being a couple, being a pair—that's what I think I'm lamenting more than anything else. The dumb part of me, as Monique called it, tried to figure out how Philip and I could fit. Only here I am by myself once more.

It's the thing that still gets to me.

WEDNESDAY, MAY 19, 1999

Monday Ben and I completed our second round of meetings with the graduate faculty, trying to persuade them of the benefits of using the Estate as a research laboratory. Their response was the most encouraging we've had in a while: *If the state agrees to match, we'll discuss funding a portion of the renovation.*

Now we just need final word from the state. And just yesterday I heard from Representative Evans. He would not be back in Lowerton this week as he'd planned but would be stopping by in early June. Would we still be free for a meeting then?

I pretended to check a schedule I already knew was clear and accepted.

The day ended with Letterman and a slow read through Martin Peterson's E-mails again in hopes of picking up an inadvertent clue. There was nothing.

Tuesday I met with Philip at the Estate. He'd been spending his time in the city records office, checking out the same blueprints my father had brought home night after night. He'd found five locations that looked promising for a false floor or hidden door, but after fifteen minutes at the Estate, both of us were convinced he'd found nothing. We parted without mentioning our "talk" and without planning another time to meet. He simply walked away, shaking his head, and I turned on my heel and headed down to the dungeon to find some seclusion in the belly of the whale. Not surprisingly, Evangeline's inscription did nothing to cheer me up.

The engulfing waters threatened me, the deep surrounded me.

It wasn't until later that night I tracked down a Bible and looked up the story. Legend has it fairly right.

Man annoys God. Fish swallows man. Man says he's sorry. Fish spits man out.

What struck me was how Evangeline's line, which seemed so depressing there on the wall, came off differently when read in the text. Spoken from the mouth of Jonah, it's a matter of confession and an acknowledgment that, despite sitting in a fish's stomach, he was sure God would save him. It's an apology and a remembrance—not a bleak image of despair as I'd always thought. It made me think that Evangeline was worse off than we imagined if she'd read this passage and found only despair, trapped in the whale with no way out.

For me, I was stuck on and struck by Jonah's conclusion: "Those who cling to worthless idols forfeit the grace that could be theirs. But I, with a song of thanksgiving, will sacrifice to you. What I have vowed I will make good. Salvation comes from the Lord."

That first sentence conjured images of sandaled men bowing down to golden calves and the strange realization that, had my father been born then, he would surely be one of them. But the kicker was the phrase "forfeit the grace that could be theirs."

So it's back to what I already know, that there's something more.

Something behind the golden calf.

Something behind Quinlin's gold.

And if the passage is to be believed, that thing is salvation. Salvation that comes from the Lord. Salvation gained through sacrifice.

But sitting there, reading it, I couldn't think of a single thing I had to give. I had nothing.

What a surprise.

Today, I've yet to think of a single thing I could offer God that might be worth even the smallest hint of salvation. I suppose I could start dropping my coins in the offering plate on the Sundays I go to church, but really, what would they buy? Isn't this just too much like flipping them off the bridge into the well at Quinlin's Estate in hopes a wish might come true?

Left with little else to do—the few boxes of Quinlin's belongings I've opened have been just more of the same—I drove to Truant Gulch to get my first awkward conversation out of the way. Meryl Lakewood's could come later in the week, maybe after the town meeting tomorrow about the condemned store. Today I had to tell Embeth Graveston what I knew.

But I couldn't. I got there and started my story only to discover partway through that I had no end. Martin Peterson's speculation and Dwight's inferences made sense to me, but they were nothing to hand to a mother wondering why her daughter had died. I remembered how angry Philip got when talking about all the rumors and theories the police told his family in place of the facts surrounding his sister Karen's disappearance. What good would it do to pile that same exasperation on top of the sadness Embeth barely seems able to handle in the first place?

So I didn't lie, but I didn't tell her everything either. She knows the story of how Embeth came to fall down the stairs of Quinlin's Tower, she just doesn't know Glen might've been up there waiting. Even without this knowledge, she wept.

For a few minutes I sat without saying a word, and then when she'd composed herself we changed the topic and began to talk about times past, about the orphanage, the school, Lowerton when the sweeping shadow of the Estate actually seemed to be bringing a measure of blessing. She talked about people long gone as though they might walk through the door any minute. She spoke of Charles the longest and how even when he had palsy he could steady his hand long enough to stroke her cheek. She sighed at the streaks of auburn in my hair and whispered a long-held desire for the color. She talked on, covering my future husband and children as foregone conclusions, advising me to stay away from the "prissy names" all the parents seem to be choosing these days. She became my grandmother and drowned me in iced tea, buried me in butter cookies. And when I walked through the doorway promising to be back next week, the first few steps were taken while repeating a promise made to myself, one made in silence. I'll do whatever I can to help Embeth find the end of her story. In so doing I'll give her the reckoning she and Evangeline deserve.

Thursday, May 20, 1999

The meeting today about the future of the grain and tack store was a meeting only in that a group of people met on the steps of city hall at half past eleven. Where I'd expected an earnest debate about how best to use the space, I found instead a single podium and the mayor hovering over a ceremonial dynamite plunger. It wasn't a meeting about the future of the store; it was a meeting about the future of the *space* where the store once stood. At noon the mayor shoved down the plunger, and carefully arranged charges brought the store down in a rumble of dust.

I'm probably overstating the fact, but I felt like a witness to an execution. The murky day, the crowd that cheered with the greedy anticipation of destruction—it all struck me as gruesome. I'm sure the editors of the *Express* will be thrilled when my article comes back sounding like a postmortem rather than the self-congratulatory fluff in which we seem to excel.

At the center of the pomp and circumstance stood Lydia Furrow and her husband, Lorne. Cochairs of a newly formed group known as the Lowerton Renewal Project—which I'm refusing to call anything but LORP—they were allowed by Mayor Hundley to make a short speech after the ground stopped shaking. Lorne spoke first.

"Sixty-five years ago Gabriel Quinlin saved our town and for that we owe him all the thanks in the world. But for too long now we've lived as though our doors were still locked to the outside world. It's time that ends."

Lydia, looking smart and whippet thin in her gray suit, spoke next.

"Towns across this state long thought dead are seeing the dawn of a bright day called tomorrow. And yet we who've weathered the storms of war, culture, economy, and politics, are now being given our final rites. But there's more life left in these bones than the scoffers can imagine, isn't there?"

The crowd let out a halfhearted cheer.

"Today the Lowerton Renewal Project makes its first stand on behalf of a brighter tomorrow. We are devoted to building a 'Better-town Lowerton' and not a 'Lower-town Lowerton.' Our goals are the same as nearly all of you share—more and better businesses bringing cleaner, more beautiful buildings for a friendlier and gallant town that stands in nobody's shadow!"

The people cheered. I could barely raise my pen to record her last phrase. For the implication couldn't be more clear had she hired a plane to scrawl it across the sky in bloated letters of cloud. Quinlin's Estate was not a better business in a beautiful building bringing chirpy smiles to those who passed through its doors. It was yesterday, and Lowerton's goal was tomorrow.

The clock over city hall chimed one, and the Furrows, together with the mayor, waved to the dispersing crowd and then walked into city hall a tight little pack. We had opposition now, rivals willing to stage this kind of execution as a show of the end that awaited our dreams as well—a tolling bell and the whisper of steel rushing toward cataclysm.

I skipped out on lunch completely and went to Truant Gulch to think. Being there with Glen's pallid husk of a body, even as much as it reminded me of the grain and tack store, presented little distraction. I found the silence necessary to sort through things.

My only solution was that I needed to find out what Lydia

Furrow and her group had planned and try to block it as best I could. Just before I left, my help to do that walked through the door as though she knew I needed her.

Meryl said nothing when she entered, just nodded to me and approached Glen. She had on a simple pair of slacks and a navy T-shirt with her name monogrammed over the pocket, her full name. Before I could wonder why, she said, "Dwight mentioned something about you wanting me to spy on Lydia Furrow for you." She was looking straight at Glen when she said it.

"That's right." No point being coy about it now.

Her hands gave a disdainful little wave to her clothes. "I was just over there. Look at the getup I have to wear to clean her place. Bought me four of these shirts so I won't 'draw unnecessary attention to myself' just in case her townie friends happen to be over." She turned my way now and said, "She always calls people by their full name. Did you know that? 'Meryl Lakewood, have you had opportunity to buff the banister?' Do you know why she does that?"

I said I didn't.

"Because she wants to remind you that you're nobody. She's a Graveston. She's a Furrow. And us? We're a Lakewood or a Lawson, and what use could she have for people like us?"

Her imitation of Lydia had been razor sharp. She could do a mean Glen as well, and I wondered if she'd ever done Eve Lawson when my back was turned or after I'd just left the room. All I know is that I probably deserved it.

"So you'll see what you can find out?"

Meryl crossed her arms and said, "I already know things."

"Like what?"

"I know she's been on the phone to the mayor at least once

every time I've stopped in to clean. I know she and her husband have argued more over these past weeks than I've ever heard them before. And I know that what they're arguing over is you."

I blinked.

Meryl nodded. "Lorne thinks you're not worth the effort. Not worth bothering with and that Lydia's simply holding an old grudge. She insists it's more than that. Their whole reputation's at stake."

"But . . . why?"

"Don't know. That's all I heard."

We sat in silence then. I turned my attention back to Glen. A soft groan escaped his lips like the breath of a person struggling through a nightmare. His hands twitched and fell still. It was all beginning to feel like too much.

"One more thing," Meryl murmured from the other side of Glen's bed, and when I looked up, she was holding out a folded piece of paper.

I took it, unfolded it. Written in green ink were ten digits.

"That's the last phone number I had for them. I'm not sure if it still works."

Wander.

I folded the paper and stuck it in my pocket, though finding Wanda suddenly seemed insignificant, especially with the Estate slipping away from us just when we were getting so close to saving it. Straightening up, I took one large breath, then moved toward the door. Before heading out into the corridor, however, I turned and thanked Meryl. For the number, for her information, for helping listen in on Lydia. For all of it.

"Least I could do," she said, but as I left I realized how wrong she was. It wasn't the least she could do. I knew all about that, could recognize it in a heartbeat because it was what Glen always offered. Standing there in front of his bed, she'd given me more than he ever did. I only wish he could've been awake to see.

SATURDAY, MAY 22, 1999

Ben and I opened six more boxes today. We're left with three still sealed. I don't even know what I'm expecting to find anymore. I guess little. Maybe *nothing*. That seems to be the operative word these days.

I suppose that makes me sound bitter. But really, I'm not. I've just come to recognize how something inside me expected to open up one of these boxes and find, who knows, a map maybe? A blueprint of the Estate with a huge red X marking the spot? I guess as a human I too can develop that great capacity to lie to myself, despite the mounting, unavoidable evidence. Glen did it for twenty-plus years, which is either impressive or pathetic depending on how one looks at it. Devotion and faith of this caliber don't come around very often.

Nor does faith like Ben Sterling's. In fact, the only other people I've seen it in are the Carters. And to both I find myself having the same reaction—part fascination and part frustration. I'm not sure I can explain it other than to say there seems to be an ease to their lives. Not an easiness—because I know some of the things that have troubled Dwight and Monique since their lives got turned around, including this latest battle between Monique's sister and her depression—but a simplicity and grace to how they live. It's like we're birds flying in the same direction, only they've slipped into a steady tail wind while I'm stupidly fighting my way against a gale.

Ben, though I don't know him quite so well, seems very similar. At first I thought it was a casual indifference, with his not caring one way or the other how things turned out. Now I keep getting glimpses and hearing things that make me think otherwise. Rather than being indifferent, Ben is confident—content and assured that all will turn out for the good.

"This project has taught me so much about history," he said today. "It's even gotten me to do more research into architectural history. Read up on people other than the guys we study in class."

This tells me more about Ben Sterling than four hours of him talking about himself ever would. Not that he'd ever talk about himself for four hours. Today he mentioned his undergraduate studies once, his childhood once, and his family twice. Me, on the other hand, I think I babbled on for a half hour about how wrong I'd been about Meryl.

"It's great you two could be reconciled," he said when I'd finished. He smiled so that I knew he really meant it. I nodded in agreement and tore into our final box for the day. More accounting logs.

"Who in the world keeps such good records?" I half shouted this in frustration as I dumped the books back into the box. Ben closed the flaps, then shoved the box back among the rest that we'd opened. I expected him then to begin packing up to head home, but instead he turned around and sat with his back against the boxes he'd just stacked. He looked to be breathing a bit faster than usual, and the bulge of his cheeks was tinged pink. For a moment I wondered if his asthma was acting up. Then I recognized it for something else—nervousness.

"I was wondering," he said, "how your search is going?"

"My search?" I had no idea what he was talking about.

"What you're looking for—something beyond just the Estate. Have you found it?"

I thought of what I'd read the other night, of the Lord's promise of salvation others had found beyond their own estates, and of the sacrifice required to gain it. I remembered the feeling that I'd found an answer and lost it all in the same moment.

"No," I finally replied, and it came out all sadness and loss.

His mouth twitched as though to speak but he said nothing. Just wiped a hand across his forehead and started to stand. I watched him struggle against his weight as he rose and then he gave me one of the friendliest smiles I'd ever seen.

"It's important," he said. "It's just as important as you think. Maybe more."

He didn't have to explain; I knew what he meant.

Ben moved to the door and, before wishing me a good day, turned and said, "I'm around if you ever have questions. It'd be my honor."

With that, he left. I heard the stairs creak under his feet as he descended. In every way, Ben Sterling was a solid man.

BEN STERLING

After four months with Ben Sterling, this is what I've pieced together of his life.

He grew up outside Lake Placid, New York, and his father happened to be at the Olympics for the "Miracle on Ice." Ben inherited his family's love for hockey, but weak lungs kept him from playing anything but goalie, a position he eventually gave up after gaining too much weight during an extended recovery from a badly broken leg.

He credits his father, a structural engineer, for his love of architecture. Saturdays Ben was invited into the office, where roll after roll of blueprints lay spread across every flat surface. Ben's father would point out stress points and talk about buffeting systems and scrawl arcane physics equations on note pads while Ben would pretend to listen. Inside his head, however, those thin blue lines would gain verticality and rise to the very reaches of the sky. Even then Ben knew he wanted to be a part of those lines.

High-school graduation sent him on his way to SUNY Buffalo and their architecture and planning program. It also opened his eyes to the faith in which he'd been sleeping at his hometown church. He saw men and women his own age struggling with things of eternal consequence while he flip-flopped on whether he wanted to be called Ben or Benjamin in his classes. It took two years but eventually he began to sort things by importance as well. In time everything, even his architecture, turned around.

It was no longer about reading and transcribing lines to paper, or just the visions of buildings growing to the heavens. It was about the people who entered those buildings, who spent time in those spaces. Somehow Ben wanted to impart to them a bit of what he was feeling. He wanted to give back to them— even if it was just to help them tilt their heads toward the sky.

During his final year, his passion gained expression with a final project and thesis on community and the role that architecture can play in building community. He studied town squares from around the world, from Moscow's Red Square to Times

288   David Ryan Long

Square in Manhattan. He looked at the abuse of space perpe-
trated by strip malls and sprawling housing projects and
devoted himself to combating these wastelands. But nobody
goes anywhere in architecture without an advanced degree, and
so he turned south and headed for the university here.

Two weeks into his first year, a professor took five students,
Ben included, to Quinlin's Estate. Ben returned every available
weekend for three months.

This was something unto itself, this Estate. And Ben knew
that it wouldn't be long before someone tried to tear it down.

MONDAY, MAY 24, 1999

So today I put a name to the people who would try to make
it fall.

Meryl Lakewood called this afternoon and asked if I could
meet her at the trailer in Little Pines. She had overheard something while cleaning for Lydia and wanted to share it with me
right away. I said yes immediately. Only after hanging up did I
realize how long it'd been since I was at Little Pines Trailer
Park. Five years maybe? The summer after my sophomore year?
Even odder was the fact that Glen hadn't been living there
either since getting laid up from his stroke. This was Meryl's
world now, and I'd just been invited to visit.

The thought made me do something strange. It seemed
right at the time, yet now I look back and wonder.

I went out and bought Meryl Lakewood a gift.

It was nothing elaborate—just a pair of colorful hand-dyed
hemp-and-cork sandals I'd seen a week ago in an artisan's co-op
across from the university. They'd made me think of Meryl

when I first saw them, so before driving into Lowerton I swung by and picked them up.

When I held them out to her after arriving, she looked at me like I'd gone clinical.

"For you," I said. "I thought you might like them."

I don't know what I expected but not much could have prepared me for Meryl's eyes going liquid and teary. She took the sandals from me with the smallest of sniffles, slipped them right on since she wasn't wearing socks, and shifted her weight once or twice, the whole time looking at her feet.

"Comfy," she said and glanced back up at me. Her eyes were still a bit bleary, but she'd caught herself and I know we were both glad. Smiling now, she waved me in, saying, "Been a while since you've been here, hasn't it?"

I would've answered except the sight of what she'd done to the place stopped any words.

The trailer, my former home, was unrecognizable. An immaculate leather sofa and burgundy armchair sat nestled around a carved oak chest. Against the far wall was a bookcase, and next to it hung a landscape of what looked to be the Lowerton valley before settlement. There were plush fabrics on the windows and, perhaps the most unbelievable, somebody had installed faux wood floors and chosen a beautiful area rug to complement the room.

Straight ahead, the kitchen was still just cabinets and linoleum, although each had been replaced in what looked to be the last few years. The wood countertop was the same color as the sofa, and the whole place seemed to be bathed in a warm, chocolate light.

The left half of the trailer was even more changed.

They, she, whoever, had knocked down the walls that'd formed my bedroom and installed a daybed under a large set of windows. The main bedroom still remained sectioned off, but the place had gained an openness, an airiness.

When I could finally speak, the only words I had were, "How in the world?"

Meryl couldn't stop smiling and honestly I couldn't blame her. I'd been in few regular homes that looked as nicely appointed.

"Lydia Furrow," she said and again I had no words to reply. Meryl continued. "She and Lorne redecorate at least one or two rooms every year. One year I heard her talking to some lady friends about getting ripped off at the auction house where she got rid of her old stuff. She was so frustrated that she wanted to teach them a lesson—she'd give the stuff away next time. I said, 'I'll take anything you might have handy,' and I guess she didn't want to lose face in front of her friends because next thing I know I got a couch, a chest, that daybed, everything. Even the window coverings and the painting."

"But the floors? And the new kitchen?"

"I paid for them. I'd saved up some money on the off chance I'd have to get an apartment of my own. But then your dad got sick and Lydia gave me all of this. I couldn't have them sitting on that old carpet, so I used my apartment money and turned the place around."

I shook my head, still not sure of what I was seeing.

"Lydia even dropped by one afternoon after I told her how I'd changed the place. Walked up, stuck her head in, nodded, then looked at me and said, 'Now if we could just work on those clothes.' "

We both laughed as Meryl finally waved me into the living room. I took a seat on the couch, and compared to the consignment store special that sat in my apartment, it felt like riding on a cloud. Meryl plopped into the armchair and couldn't hold in a laugh. The place certainly wasn't Meryl's style. That aside, there was an outrageousness to it that fit as well as the colored sandals I'd given her.

"So, you heard something?" I asked when she'd quieted.

She pulled her knees up into the chair and nodded. "You don't know what it's like to be invisible until you work for that woman. I swear she could walk right through me sometimes. Anyway, I was cleaning this morning and she had her ladies' tea group over. All the talk was about that new group she started."

"LORP?"

Meryl grinned at my inflection. I'd made the word sound as ugly as I could.

"LORP. Yeah, that's it. Anyway, the women were talking about what businesses could move into the vacant lot downtown. Clothing boutiques, a good coffeehouse, a nice restaurant. Lydia smiled and hinted that anything could happen if the right companies were courted.

" 'When's it going to happen, Lydia Furrow?' one of them asked. They all call each other by their full names. Drives me nuts. Anyway, Lydia hedged a bit and said there were still some details to be ironed out, including the sale of the Estate."

Meryl paused for me to respond but I had nothing to say. I was staring across the trailer and trying hard to keep from cursing or crying. *How naïve*, I thought to myself.

"You know Lydia and how she likes to impress everybody," said Meryl, continuing on. "Well, I guess she's learned that nothing impresses people more than influence, because she's always talking to her friends—if you can call them that—about the arms she's twisted or the deals Lorne has worked out. Same thing here. And this one hinges on something only a few people know about the Estate—it can't be purchased by two private owners in a row."

My eyes went to Meryl's. She shrugged.

"I don't know anything about it other than that. Lydia said Gabriel Quinlin set it up so that the Estate would always revert back to some sort of public use after coming into private ownership. He built it for Lowerton and wanted it to stay with Lowerton."

I started doing calculations out loud. "Went to the U.S. Government, then to Lowerton to be a school. After that, the state picked it up and made it an orphanage. Then Road to Damascus. Then the museum. Now Brighton Entertainment." She was right. The Estate had never been owned privately by two consecutive owners. "So Brighton is going to have to sell it back to Lowerton?"

Meryl nodded.

"But how does that affect the development downtown?" The pieces still hadn't fallen in place for me.

Meryl leaned closer to me as if worried about being overheard and said, "They're going to buy it from Brighton. LORP is going to buy it for one dollar."

"But that makes no sense, why—"

"Then they're going to turn around and sell it to someone else. They're just acting as the middleman. They'll make some money for helping with the sale and use that to buy the land downtown. They become developers by leasing the land out to the new businesses wanting to come in."

There was only one question remaining to be answered.

"Who's the buyer? They have to have a buyer lined up or Brighton would never agree to it."

Meryl nodded and said, "You won't like it."

"Tell me."

"The mining company that just started up operations down the valley a bit. They'll tear down the house and tear up the ridge too."

I stood. There was no reason for doing it, but I couldn't help myself. I jumped to my feet like I was ready to take a swing at somebody. Of course there was only Meryl and her words, and soon the fight left me and I sank back down to the couch.

"So it's over?"

"The Estate's still standing, isn't it?"

I nodded.

"Then it's not over yet."

Meryl was trying to help, but her words were little consolation. I rose to my feet once more, this time for good, and walked to the door. Meryl followed, commenting twice how much she liked her new sandals. I did all I could to act pleased, yet my thoughts were elsewhere. In fact, it didn't register right away when I opened the door to step outside and found myself staring at something I don't remember ever seeing before—Mr. Mulligan's flagpole. Bare. No ratty flag. No Santa.

"I guess all hope is gone," I said, mostly to myself. But Meryl had heard me and asked what I meant. I pointed to the flagpole and said that Santa—the one in whom I'd put so much trust, the one who'd failed me when I'd looked to it the night before going to the doctor—was gone.

"He's been gone awhile now," Meryl said. "Nobody told you what happened?"

I shook my head.

"It was weird, I'll say that. You want to hear it?"

I hesitated for just a second or two, then said yes. If nothing else I could call yet another chapter of my life closed. The chapter on faith and how quickly it can disappear when everything that's believed ends in disappointment.

Santa's Farewell

The weeks following Glen's first stroke, Meryl would awaken to the sound of him stumbling through the trailer, talking to himself and sometimes even shouting. They'd been sleeping apart since my room became vacant, and even though Meryl wished she could ignore him, she often found herself putting on her robe and joining him on the couch in the living room. There she'd smooth the hair from his forehead and hold him until whatever demons haunting him had left and he fell asleep against her shoulder.

In the morning he'd startle and glance around, confusion and panic in his eyes as he tried to figure out how he'd gotten to the couch. He never remembered the night before, the words he'd shouted to the empty trailer. Nor did he remember Meryl's soothing hands so that, after collecting himself, he'd grumble to her about allowing him to sleep on the couch. The doctors wanted him in bed.

Rehabilitation, speech therapy, physical therapy at the hospital—this was their new life, week after week. Dinner in a restaurant booth near the clinic or slopped together in a free moment at home. Sleep was often torn apart by Glen's fitful dreams. Meryl put in hours cleaning when she could and spent the rest of the time tending to Glen.

One mid-June evening, Meryl skipped her normal hour for sleep to catch a late showing of *Bringing Up Baby* on one of the cable stations. The wind had been gusting all day, and just as the movie began, the rains came. Their trailer, flat-roofed and metal, amplified the sound until she could hardly hear Katharine Hepburn's giddy one-liners. It didn't matter, however, because the lightning soon followed and ten minutes later the trailer's power went out. Sitting in the darkness, Meryl curled up in her chair and watched the storm as it rumbled down their valley, pulling its way over Lowerton with a trampling assault of thunder. The clatter became so loud at one point that she didn't even hear Glen's door open nor his dragging footfalls as he shuffled down the hall. Lightning flashed, and in that second he was suddenly standing next to her, his face lit blue for an instant, his eyes wild. She startled but he paid no attention. Standing mute before the window, he watched the same storm while one arm, his good side, trembled.

"Coming," he said. "Comingcomingcomingcomingcoming." He said it like a chant and wouldn't stop as lightning forked all around them and thunder split the night sky. Meryl knew the storm was right on top of them now.

And then, without warning, the clouds tore open and both air and land exploded with a shriek of white as painful as the thunder that accompanied it. Glen toppled over, his chatter finally stopped. Meryl swept off the couch to his side.

"Meryl," he said, clutching at her in the darkness, and she saw he was awake.

"I'm here," she said following another clap of thunder. Slipping her arms around him, they both stood. The air in the trailer was charged both with the tang of ozone and something harsher and acrid.

"Look," said Glen, hand pointing to the window.

Meryl ducked to peer through the curtains and glimpsed the licking stabs of flame. Only after some seconds had gone by did she realize it was Santa who was on fire. A lightning bolt had struck Mr. Mulligan's flagpole, and Santa, of course, had gotten the worst of it. He burned like the wick of some tall silver candle, and they watched transfixed as first his hat, then his face, then the swell of his belly glistened and melted and fell away in liquid chunks and spatters to the bare ground below. His belt disappeared next, followed by the red trousers with fur cuffs, and finally the coal black boots. All bubbled and disappeared into flame until *pop!*—nothing remained but the scorched silver ball at the top of the pole.

Meryl and Glen stood side by side next to the window for a quiet moment, their nostrils fighting the chemical burn of the smoke seeping through their doorjamb. It was the silence that helped Meryl to take in how far the storm had blown past already. It had strafed the land with fire and raged on without even a pause.

"That thing never did its job, anyway," Glen said.

Meryl said nothing. She knew what he meant and had no words of comfort for him.

"Come to bed?" he asked, his hand sliding into hers after another moment.

She squeezed his fingers but didn't move.

"All right, then," he said and tottered his way back down the hall.

Meryl stayed staring out the window for a while before retreating to her own bed. In the morning, neither of them talked about what had happened during the night. Later, while Glen napped, Meryl stepped out of the trailer into the thick haze the storm had left in its wake. The afternoon lay grim and heavy on the land. Still the smell of charred plastic hung in the air. Meryl walked over to the flagpole and looked down at the ruins of the Santa, cooled, hardened, and unrecognizable. So what really remained was just the smell and the heaviness. And neither was good.

The storm had blown through but it hadn't erased anything, hadn't destroyed a thing. It'd merely diffused it into what Meryl guessed was its purest essence. In the end, that Santa, that impotent faith Glen claimed he had, was tested by the fire and consumed. Meryl knew about such things. She'd been raised in a church where people swayed and gibbered and talked about flames of refining fire that would reveal all things, even your daily sacrifice of prayers and worship. And how some of the sacrifices would burn pure and pleasing and fragrant while others would go thick and blue and smell like death itself. Meryl had heard them talk that way and had never understood it until this very moment. She realized then that perhaps the one thing worse than no faith at all was faith that would melt away to nothing, faith that was just waiting to be revealed as ash.

Tuesday, May 25, 1999

Ben, Philip, and I met this evening for coffee at a café in Bellefonte so I could tell them what Meryl had overheard. Again, going so far out of the way might not have been necessary, only I'm suddenly more aware of what I say and around whom I say it. Lydia Furrow can talk as much as she wants, but we need every advantage we can get.

Neither Ben nor Philip reacted the way I'd expected when I told them about LORP's wink-wink deal to buy and sell the Estate. Ben balled up his napkin, his jaw tightening with what could only be called anger, while Philip blew out a short breath and leaned back in his chair to stare at the ceiling. I thought their responses would have been switched—Philip angry and Ben resigned—and was even more mystified when Ben spoke first.

"That's pathetic!" he said loudly. "They're sacrificing the Estate *and* the ridge beneath it for the chance to shop at a closer Gap? Like khakis are going to solve that town's problems." He stood and threw his napkin to the table, adding, "At least Faust sold out for something worthwhile," before stalking off to the rest room.

For a moment Philip and I sat in shocked silence, until Philip lifted an eyebrow and said, "Didn't expect that."

I agreed, then said, "I just feel helpless."

Philip nodded, but Ben returned before he could offer anything more. Pink splotches still dotted Ben's neck. It was obvious he'd let off a little steam. An embarrassed smile came to his face when he sat, and I thought he was going to apologize but he said nothing. I was glad, for he had nothing to be sorry for, and we'd need that kind of passion to get anywhere now. I was just about out myself.

"What's left to do?" Ben asked.

That was the question I'd wanted them to answer for me. Thankfully, Philip spoke up.

"Well, it's apparent that we're going to have to offer Brighton more than they'd get from the deal with the mining company. Because of the purchase agreement, we'll need to do it for sure with public funding."

"Which means the state," said Ben.

"Or," Philip added, "we find the gold and set up some kind of trust."

Even I had to nod at that. The situation was getting so desperate that Glen's dream of gold was actually one of our better possibilities.

Ben said nothing for a moment and then also agreed, but with a condition. "I think we should focus on the state first. Representative Evans is coming next week. If we get turned down then, we'll be out of options."

"Sounds good," Philip replied and all at once we had our small group back together.

Four pots of coffee and a few brownies later we had a rough idea of how to attack the next eight days. Looking at it now, it seems a paltry attempt. Nevertheless, it's the best we can manage on such short notice. How things have come down to one week, I'm not sure, but these next seven or eight days are critical. The gold is a last resort, and we can only hope it stays that way.

Broken into a number of smaller segments, the plan includes tasks for each of us to do alone and one final assignment for the group to carry out together. Given Ben's interest in building communities, we assigned him research into "Main Street Revivals." Towns across the country have been working to revitalize their dying main streets. Some have accomplished this through small community businesses, others through luring outside franchises. Our hope is that those with franchised space will find that the majority of money made gets sent out of town rather than staying in the community.

Philip's task is to research the environmental history of the mining company mixed up in this and do some work looking at the impact such a company would have on the region surrounding Lowerton. Besides the obvious blight of stripping the ridge bare, there may be serious ramifications for quality of life that residents should hear about before it's too late.

My job is to examine the Estate's purchase agreement and learn more about the public holdings clause. If Quinlin put such a thing in, he may have written it in a way that disallows obeying it in letter and not in spirit.

Together we're going to compile one more presentation for Representative Evans and also spend some time going through Quinlin's final boxes. Our chances are slim, we know. Still, we have to peek in every corner. Everything's at stake now, and our time is fleeting.

The Clause

Clause is perhaps the wrong word for the thin paragraph slid into every purchase agreement ever signed for Quinlin's Estate. "Gentleman's agreement" is closer to the truth. Or "suggestion."

As Quinlin's Estate was built for Lowerton and by Lowerton, it is taken in good faith that the building will never be separated from public hands for too substantial a time. Private ownership of the Estate is not forbidden; however, the structure and grounds should pass into the hands of town, county, or state officials before returning again to a private buyer, thereby assuring that all transactions are made with Lowerton's best interests in mind.

That's it.

Any hope of using the clause to delay the sale of the Estate would be unfounded. LORP is obeying both the spirit and the letter of the clause. They are doing what they think is best for the town of Lowerton.

The only hope now is that we can raise doubts about that claim.

SATURDAY, MAY 29, 1999

Ben and Philip came to my apartment tonight after four days of research. We have a few more days to fine-tune what they've found before Greg Evans arrives in Lowerton. But most of their arguments are solid to begin with.

Ben's research focused on two small towns: Royersford, Ohio, outside of Dayton and Brackens, Indiana, just east of Indianapolis. The towns are ideal mirrors for Lowerton, being similar in both their size and situation.

Royersford began its "Reclaim Main" initiative in early 1994 following the departure of an independent department store, the closing of two downtown cafés, and the failure of at least three small shops on the main strip. At the forefront of the push, Royersford touted plans for three new E-commerce businesses to take up residence in vacant warehouses on the outskirts of town, each surely bringing not only income but a new sensibility and upscale requirements.

Retailers signed on and by 1996 Main Street Royersford operated at maximum occupancy. Barnes & Noble opened a storefront operation across from Old Navy. Schlotzsky's Deli and Einstein's Bagels moved in for the lunch crowd. Even Gateway opened a store, hoping to cash in on consumer fascination and familiarity with technology.

And for two years the micro-economy worked. Until one E-commerce business relocated to Research Triangle Park in North Carolina and a second business folded, costing Royersford more than three hundred jobs.

Within months, Main Street felt the impact. Gateway, which hadn't caught on with Royersfordians as predicted, left first. Schlotzsky's, pretty much a lunch-only place, lost out to Einstein's ability to serve food all day long and soon had to empty their pickle vats and pull the plug on their meat slicers. Old Navy promised its people it wouldn't leave Royersford, but a relocation to a new strip mall three miles away did take them off Main Street. In the end, Barnes & Noble became the anomaly— the glow from its windows almost the only light on Main Street after eight o'clock.

Royersford went back to where it had started.

Ben's presentation of the town of Brackens sounded quite similar, except instead of E-commerce it was a government-backed research laboratory that began construction. Soon eight hundred new workers would follow as the Brackens Central Square Revitalization Group took to lining up tenants to fill the downtown storefronts.

Two years after completion, budget cuts forced the dismissal of more than half of the laboratory staff. Before too long Central Square grew as empty as Red Square on a cold January night.

"The key," Ben said after finishing, "isn't the stores that come in. It's the businesses that are supposed to be supporting them. If the businesses are reliable and sound, retail works. If not—and I'd argue that the mining company is one of those businesses that's not—then Main Street renewal will be a cosmetic fix that lasts a few years at best."

Philip and I both congratulated Ben for his work. He'd uncovered good research that could make for a compelling case. If Philip did the same, we'd have a leg on which to stand during our meeting. Thankfully he did.

"First off," he began, "any quarrying would require rezoning of the land, which means a township vote. Can't happen without it. So what I don't understand is how Boyd Stone and Lime is getting assurance that the zoning issue will pass."

"It has to be connected to Lydia's group," I said and they agreed.

"I had the same assumption. And that sort of thing can be tried in court as tampering—if we can get proof. The second thing I discovered is that BSL, the quarrying company, got turned down for permission to mine in Spring Township just a couple of years ago. An environmental group opposed it and won. The two main arguments they used were the irreversible ecological impact on the area, and the fact that the company would be quarrying for sandstone, which is found throughout Pennsylvania. There are more than ninety sites already where they mine this stuff. It's not a *must have.*"

Philip shut his notebook and smiled.

"I think we've got a shot."

Ben and I nodded in agreement. Afterward, tearing into the last of Quinlin's boxes, I felt more optimistic than I had in weeks. I even expected to find something important, perhaps a map or a coded letter, hidden among the worthless belongings we seemed to be coming across.

That vision died quickly as we found two more accounting logs, a gray felt top hat, reading spectacles, some economic pamphlets printed at Yale, a half-full pouch of pipe tobacco, an assortment of fountain pens, empty ink bottles, brass nibs, and unlined parchment. It looked like the standard stuff of any office at the time, things left to sit as if the person using them expected to return the next morning and start again on the day's work. Only the day never dawned, and the remnants found the bottom of a box.

From decades past, Gabriel Quinlin could have reached out to us and spoken. But he didn't. His junk—there's no other word for it—stayed as silent and meaningless as it must have been the day he died. He did not speak to my father. He did not speak to me. His Estate will stand or fall without any more intervention on his part.

He built the thing. I guess he thinks he's done enough.

It's our turn now.

Greg Evans awaits.

SUNDAY, MAY 30, 1999

Today I found the slip of paper Meryl handed me some days ago, and I called Wander. Nobody answered. There wasn't even an answering machine to let me know if I had the right number or not.

She's become the wild card in this whole search.

I've dreamed about her three or four times since I quit the history program in January. In my dreams we're children and I'm chasing her through the blind turns of Quinlin's Maze. Like Evangeline Graveston on the night of her death, though, Wander's always one turn ahead of me. I can't ever catch her, and I wake up with my sheets twisted around me or crumpled on the floor.

Of course, I've also had dreams about kissing Ben, about stumbling over a loose cord in Glen's room and killing him, about finding Philip's sister, Karen, about slapping Meryl Lakewood full in the face, and about playing tennis with Albert Einstein, so perhaps I shouldn't go looking too hard for meaning there.

But I want to know why Wander is even a part of all that has happened. I did a word search of what I've written so far and found her name—Wanda or Wander—appears more than 150 times. Yet she barely exists for me!

I'm losing memories of her. I know there were fun times we had, days and hours when we laughed while playing outside, when we thought of things other than leaving Lowerton. I can't remember any of these now. Again and again I come back to the night she walked out of Little Pines, that day she got us lost, and those angry fights between her and Meryl. Will this be what we reminisce about if she does happen to pick up the phone someday? Why does the ghost of this lost little girl refuse to leave me?

Part Six

WEDNESDAY, JUNE 2, 1999

Somebody once said the world ends not with a bang but with a whimper.

Dreams end the same way.

Today, in a small room at the Estate that we'd been given permission to use, Philip, Ben, and I had barely finished our presentation to Greg Evans when he told us he'd already decided to lend support, and possibly a small amount of funding, to the Lowerton Renewal Project. He appreciated our arguments, had made a few of them himself to Lorne and Lydia Furrow. But their answers were quite convincing to him.

"How?" I asked.

"Boyd Stone and Lime will bring in more than two hundred workers for the quarry alone. Plus they've agreed to set up a second administrative office in Lowerton that would mean another two hundred workers, if the plans go through. The quarry itself appears to be a seventy-five-year project. Not three or four. They won't just come and go."

Ben lowered his eyes and looked at the floor.

"What about the environment?" Philip challenged. "You can't just ruin thousands of years—"

"Philip," Evans said, cutting him off. "It hasn't been thousands of years. That's not untouched land. They built the Estate on it, for goodness' sake, which given environmental responsibility back then caused who knows how much damage. If it stands or is torn down, for whatever reason, the Estate affects the ecology of the ridge. Not nearly as much as a quarry, I know, but it's certainly not pristine."

And that was it. No bang, only whimper.

To his credit, Evans appeared less than joyous about his decision. What it came down to was money and jobs and the fact that the town hadn't united in support of the Estate.

"If two thousand people signed a petition . . ." He didn't finish the thought.

"When does this all happen?" asked Ben.

"Six months, a year at most. BSL is still putting together some resources and doing studies on the land before making any final decision about the cost. Brighton's never budged from their December deadline, and all the principal parties want it done by then, if not sooner."

After finishing, Greg stood and I thought he meant to give us his farewell, but instead he slowly looked around the room and shook his head. I suppose it could've been just an act, a display to keep us from disliking him, but I don't want to be that cynical. He'd never been anything other than up-front with us. He'd told us he would always make the decision he felt worked best for his constituency. Two plans came before him and he passed on ours. He didn't do it out of spite or laziness but out of what seems to be genuine concern for the people he represents.

"It'll be strange when the hill is bare," said Evans. All we could do was nod at that. "I remember," he continued, "as a senior in college coming here with my girlfriend. I was getting these thoughts in my head about how I couldn't see leaving school without her, and then when I brought her here, she hated it.

"Couldn't have cared less about the history. Thought the architecture was too gloomy. And she got claustrophobic in the Maze. She wasn't in a mood or trying to be negative, she just got nothing out of it.

"We dated for another week or two after the trip but our conversations kept uncovering more and more things we disagreed about. Pretty soon I suggested we call it quits and she agreed.

"She wasn't a bad person. We could never have gotten married, though. In time I know we would have uncovered those little things, but somehow the Estate brought them to light sooner. For a long while I tried to figure out why, and the best I could come up with is that the Estate's seen so much, been so many things, it's become kind of a perfect mirror."

I don't know why Evans told us this story, but it must have meant something to Ben, because for the first time since he finished talking about Royersford and Brackens, he spoke up.

"I'll always remember my first visit," Ben began. "Some fellas who'd been in the architecture program awhile took a few of us new guys. Basically they made fun of the place, and after ten minutes of that I skipped out on them. Eventually I ended up in the dungeon chambers. To me they're still the most interesting part of this building. They're all about isolation and darkness. Even the damp air. I believe I know what Quinlin was thinking when he designed the dungeon, and he got exactly what he hoped for. Most professional architects can't say the same."

As Ben wound down, Philip cleared his throat, and I could tell he was preparing to speak up next, to tell us his favorite memory of the Estate or what he admired most about it. And then I would follow. But we weren't just talking, we were commemorating the dead. Like a roomful of people sharing stories after a funeral, we were a small band of mourners speaking in memoriam. I thought of this and my fingers went cold. I didn't want these to be the last words shared on the Estate.

Then Philip spoke.

"For me, still, this place is the Maze. I know I told Eve of the first time I entered it and almost freaked out until I came across a guy who *was* freaking out. He was sitting on the ground and crying out for a roamer—and I just didn't want to be him. So I kept going. Just focused on the open path in front of me rather than the walls all around. It was almost two hours later when I made it out.

"The visit I'll always remember—and you can believe me or not about this—is the time I went through the Maze in just fifteen minutes."

Ben and Greg Evans both leaned in.

"No way," I said, and all three looked at me.

"I swear, it's true."

He said it like he meant it. Even so, a half hour wasn't possible.

"I walked as a roamer, Philip. Our routes took forty-five minutes to finish, and we knew all the turns."

Philip raised his hands. "Believe me or don't."

"I don't."

He shrugged and looked to Ben and Greg, who didn't seem at all sure what to say.

"If you don't believe that, then this is going to be even harder to swallow."

We waited.

"I did it with my eyes closed."

Ben and Greg looked at me for an instant and I shook my head. I don't know why Philip felt the need to lie, especially now, but he was.

"I swear," he said again. "I'd been exhausted from work and when I stepped in I took this huge yawn as I took my first few steps. And it felt like my feet were in a groove—like I was being pulled in one direction. Opened my eyes and the feeling disappeared. Closed them and it was still there. So I walked. My left hand couldn't reach anything, so I put my right hand on the wall to steady me and just went. My feet never left that track. Fifteen minutes later I heard the exit doors clang and opened my eyes. Couldn't believe it."

"Odd," said Ben.

"Maybe there's a perfect way through the Maze?" Greg Evans suggested.

Again, both looked at me.

I turned to Philip. "Why haven't you done it again?"

"That's the frustrating thing—I can't. Believe me, I've tried. Just doesn't happen. My feet don't find that groove."

His expression, his words, even the look of sadness and wonder in his eyes convinced me that, in this, he was telling the truth. I still couldn't quite believe he'd made it through that quickly, yet I could see *he* believed it. It wasn't a lie thought up just to have something to say or to impress.

"Must be frustrating," I said.

"You wouldn't believe," he answered, and his eyes went to his shoes.

Ben and Greg kept looking at me. My turn had come and they were waiting.

So I talked. I told them about working here on the first cool night of summer and how the mist would rise off the ground like a specter to sweep across the dungeon floor as though searching for something. I mentioned the occasional night I spent wandering the building when Glen had to work the third shift. I talked about loving my role as Gabriel's angel in *He Saved Lowerton* so much that even when we came up here for the cast party I kept my costume on the whole time.

I finished and the others nodded. We'd completed our commemoration.

Representative Evans shook hands with each of us, apologized that it'd come to this, and bid us farewell. Ben and Philip waited for me to follow as they moved to the door, but I told them I wanted to stay for just a bit. They said they'd be in touch and then were gone.

I was alone.

Alone and wondering why I couldn't put to words the one thing I wanted to say so much about this place. I'd told all those other stories, yet what I really felt I hadn't been able to speak a single sentence.

And so I sat, for twenty minutes and then an hour, thinking through all the reasons this place has never left me. What I've come up with makes me realize I'm not such a different person from the little girl who thought that *somewhere*—the word her daddy whispered to himself over and over—was the most important word in the world.

SOMEWHERE

When I started first grade, Glen said I was too old to waste my evenings out on the street writing words in purple chalk across the pavement. So I came inside, sitting at the kitchen table with him after dinner as he pored over his drawings. I now knew they were called blueprints and that they showed the skeleton of Quinlin's Estate and that when Glen said *somewhere* he really meant gold, or at least the secret corner in which someone had hidden the gold. I sat across from him without anything to do, and before too long I could follow his tracing fingers and picture the exact corridor or room he was examining. I'd then close my eyes and I'd be there.

We visited the Estate every week or two so that soon I'd learned most of the place by memory. Back at the table in the trailer, I'd close my eyes and see the great stone halls and I'd begin to walk them. Glen would be tracing and measuring, while in my head I was turning corners, slipping down passageways, mounting stairs, and ducking around pillars. And then, just before my mind grew tired, I'd find the gold. Always. I'd turn around and Glen would be there, smiling and looking at me. He'd reach a hand to me and say, "Goodness sakes, you found it, Eve! You knew it was someplace and you tracked it down."

Before his hand could touch mine, though, I'd open my eyes. Sometimes Glen would be staring at me and look quickly down to his blueprints. Sometimes he'd be hunched over a legal pad as he punched numbers into a calculator. A couple of times, he'd managed to leave the table without me even noticing. Once he'd even left the trailer and not come back till the next morning.

"Thought I had it," I overheard him say to Meryl that morning.

"You just left her," Meryl whispered back. "I got home at eleven and she was sitting at the table all by herself. You think that's right?"

"It's got to be somewhere, Meryl, and I thought I had it!"

"Some things are more impor—"

Glen closed the bedroom door in her face before Meryl could finish.

After that I stopped sitting at the table with him. I'd watch television or read a book or listen to music, yet I never quit closing my eyes and envisioning the Estate. I only stopped looking for the gold. Instead, I marched the halls and tried to recall every swirl of the banisters, every crystal teardrop in the chandelier. I'd sneak into the ballroom and look at every painting, waltz across the parquet floor, stop and finger a tune on the grand piano in the corner. The great space would fill with the breath of my imagined music.

But I always had to leave, always had to open my eyes. The only thing that made it bearable was knowing that at least, even when open, they'd fall on the outline of the Tower against the sapphire sky. Now that reassurance is about to leave too. I'll open them someday soon and see only a wound in the earth, the gaping emptiness of what used to be. I will truly be lost then.

Part Seven

FRIDAY, JUNE 4, 1999

Glen, it appears, will not even allow me to suffer this in peace. Even this he will steal.

Meryl arrived at the *Express* office today just after I'd finished proofreading my useless editorial on the Estate. The first thing I noticed was that she was wearing the sandals I'd given her. Then I saw her mascara, smearing at the corners of her eyes. She was crying.

Glen, I thought to myself and waited for her to tell me he'd died.

"Your father's taken a turn," she said, words choked and anxious.

I nodded, called to my co-workers that I needed to step out, and walked with her out onto the sidewalk. I told her I'd meet her there and got into my car. Only then did I notice my hands trembling. There is never enough time to prepare for such news.

The ride over was too short to allow any thoughts other than those of the road, so I took a few moments in the parking lot to calm myself and think through what was happening.

Inside, Glen is dying. I said this to myself three or four times, trying to make it seem real. For so long, months on end now, he'd done nothing. He hadn't lived or died. He just *was.* That had changed and I needed to be prepared. *Glen is dying* I repeated a few more times as I headed for the entrance to Truant Gulch.

Inside, nothing had changed. Perhaps some orderly had wheeled in a new machine, but for the most part everything, Glen especially, looked the same. Meryl hadn't shown up yet so I couldn't ask her to explain. I took my usual chair at the side of the bed and reached for Glen's hand.

It was cold.

Glen's hands, typically hot as new ash, were the one thing that'd let me know there was anything left in him, and now that was gone. His hand felt small and weightless, like one of those dead birds children pick up and bring to their parents with vain hopes of a miracle. A machine—the new one—chirped out a slow but steady rhythm, but I knew Meryl was right. Glen had taken a turn.

Meryl entered a minute later, chewing off her lipstick and trying to run her fingers through the snarl she called a hairstyle. For a second, her eyes filled with tears when she saw me holding his hand. But she blinked them away and asked if I'd spoken to anybody yet. I shook my head.

"They called me at eight," she explained. "Said his pulse almost stopped this morning."

"He's cold too."

Meryl nodded. She'd noticed as well.

More silence.

Finally I asked, "What happens now?"

Meryl had no answer so I stayed in the chair, holding Glen's hand and failing entirely to give it any warmth.

That's how the rest of the day passed as well. I didn't sit there the whole time nor did Meryl stand, but we both waited all the same. Nurses came and went, checked numbers and changed IV drips, and around noon a doctor visited for a moment to scribble something on the chart. We asked the unthinkable, and she told us Glen could pass away tonight or last for weeks this way. Meryl pinned her down, and the doctor said a month at the longest. The doctor slipped out but neither Meryl nor I left. We waited. I don't know about her, but I was waiting for him to die.

He didn't.

Finally, at seven, Meryl said, "I've gotta work a shift at Eat n' Park in an hour."

I looked at my watch and realized the time I'd set aside to finish an article for the *Express* had vanished. "I need to get going soon myself."

Neither of us moved.

"I don't want him to die alone," Meryl said.

I sighed. Dying alone—it seemed such a desperate and lonely thought.

"How busy are you?" she asked.

"Not too busy anymore. The Estate is all but coming down."

"Maybe we can split days. Or do every other day. Just so somebody's always here with him."

"I guess that'll work."

We both nodded and then it seemed the right moment to ask a question I'd been wondering for a while.

"Why'd you stick with him, Meryl? He doesn't deserve what you're doing."

"He needed me," she answered. "He never admitted it and you're right, he probably didn't deserve me, but he needed me. And that just always seemed to be more important." She gave a sad laugh. "Pathetic, isn't it?"

I didn't know what to say. For so many years, I'd thought so. I thought of Meryl and Glen, and the exact word that came to mind was *pathetic*. But it wasn't that way anymore. It seemed better, somehow. Like it wasn't a waste after all.

I didn't reply. I just walked to her and put my arm through hers, and together we strolled out of Truant Gulch, arranging along the way the days and hours we'd devote to making sure Glen Lawson didn't die alone.

MONDAY, JUNE 7, 1999

Our days go like this:

Meryl arrives at Truant Gulch at eight in the morning to start her day with Glen. She waits and watches, leaving only for a half hour at noon to grab lunch.

I relieve her at about three o'clock, having just completed my research on a story for the *Express*. She doesn't stay to chat because she has three or four hours of cleaning at the Furrows' to take care of before heading to her evening shift at Eat n' Park.

I sit, wait, watch, leaving only for dinner if I haven't packed something. At ten, I squeeze Glen's hand once and leave for my apartment, both hoping and not hoping he passes during the night. So far there's been no phone call.

After three days of this, I've realized two things.

The first is that, even with our best intentions and efforts, Meryl and I can't ensure that Glen will die with someone nearby. We've been covering a little more than half a day, but I don't know how long even that will last. Meryl's already mentioned that Lydia isn't too thrilled about the cleaning being done so late in the day. Who knows how long we can keep this up?

The second thing is that I'm not going to speak to Glen ever again. He's not coming back, even for a moment. The doctors keep appearing in his room to jot notes on his chart, and each time they look to me and nod, solemn and pitying. Yesterday one explained that Glen's vital signs were showing a slow but steady deterioration between rounds. At this pace he couldn't promise that Glen would make it through the week.

I'm left with the one thing that my years studying history have taught me to abhor—loose ends. Soon Glen will die, and I'll be left without a single clue as to why his life—our lives— turned out the way they did. It's one thing for Dwight Carter to tell me the twisted story of my father's theology, yet quite another to understand *why* the man felt so compelled to give me up. Not give up on me, but give me up to the fates or gods or whatever else he thought was at work. I want more of an answer than something like sloth or nonchalance. I want to know why he didn't care that he became Glen to me and not Dad.

There will be no answers. Glen will pass and Meryl and I will be left to bury him. Who will come to his funeral, I wonder. Dwight and Monique, of course. Meryl. Philip and Ben perhaps, out of kindness to me. Some co-workers. The Gibsons from Little Pines. Maybe even Embeth Graveston. A dozen people at most, and none will be able to offer even the slimmest of answers to the questions I hold. I know because I've already asked Dwight.

He stopped by Sunday evening with an Italian sub and bag of chips, which we shared on the small particleboard table. Meryl had told him of our arrangement. He'd wanted to come pass the time with me.

"It's a good thing you're doing, Eve Marie. There's been a lot of them lately."

I knew he meant fixing things up with Meryl.

"At least she deserved it."

He didn't say anything, just chewed a bite of sub and looked off over my shoulder into what I guessed had to be the gathering shadows of evening. What he saw out there one could only guess. Maybe his friend Glen as a younger man. Maybe his own youth, when such a summer dusk seemed to go on forever.

Or maybe none of those things because when he spoke he said, "Deserve is a funny thing."

"How do you mean?"

"Just that from our own perspective I'd guess we all think we deserve things. If you asked Glen I bet he'd say he deserved what you and Meryl are doing for him."

"That's because Glen—" I stopped before saying too much. The man was in the room after all.

"I guess that's my point, Eve Marie. Get to the heart of it and you realize most of us don't deserve much of what we get. But we get it anyway."

I thought he'd say more, but he left it at that, and it's troubled me for the past three days. There seem to be so many things wrong with the statement, yet I can't help feel that he was right in a way.

I look at Meryl and I don't see pathetic, I see generous. The ways my father used and cheated and failed her could fill an entire chapter in this journal and even a quarter of them would have caused most women to leave. But she chose to stay. Or maybe she's just kidding herself. Maybe she was so afraid to leave, to start over, that she sold herself on a lie of her own compassion.

I don't know.

I do know I deserve certain things, and I can't see how Dwight could say otherwise. I deserve to have my questions answered by Glen, to have him explain why he forsook me for a delusion of gold, to hear him say he was wrong.

And I deserve to put this pale town behind me once and for all.

Only the last can come to pass. A reckoning on the rest will give up the ghost as soon as Glen does. I don't know what's more frustrating—not getting what I deserve or watching someone receive that to which they aren't entitled. If Glen does die and I'm left alone once more, I guess I'll have to put all my energies into leaving this place. The Estate will be gone. Glen will be dead. What's left to keep me in Lowerton?

FRIDAY, JUNE 11, 1999

Today I allowed myself a halfhearted return to the real world by going back to the steps of city hall for another press conference with LORP. Three weeks after their last gathering, the group was ready to announce their triumph. Lorne and Lydia stood flanked by the mayor and representatives from Brighton Entertainment and Boyd Stone and Lime. Their news,

greeted by a smattering of cheers from the twenty or so onlook-
ers, made public a tentative agreement for the sale of Quinlin's
Estate. No figures were mentioned or any specific dates, but the
public relations officer from Brighton confirmed that the transaction would occur before their previously mentioned December
deadline.

"At this point, we feel it's in the best interest of all the parties, including the town of Lowerton, for the sale to move forward with all expediency."

I'd been assigned to cover the story for the *Express*, so I
raised my press badge and asked what steps, if any, were being
taken to preserve the antiques, furnishings, and artwork in the
Estate.

Lydia Furrow stepped forward to answer.

"Excellent question, Ms. Lawson," she said. "It's an issue
very important to our group, and though I have no definitive
answer at this time, we have been in talks with Representative
Greg Evans in regard to state funding of any such purchase.
We'll be in discussions with other interest groups as well and
hope to move as much of the collection to the Lowerton
Historical Society as possible."

She stared at me even after she spoke, and I knew that "other
interest groups" meant Philip, Ben, and me and the measly
funds we'd collected so far. If we couldn't save the Estate, the
least we could do would be to help save what was inside. The
thought chafed, and as the press conference came to a close, it
hit me how thoroughly Lydia Furrow had trounced us. Ambi-
tion and good intentions apparently mean nothing in the face of
well-oiled politics and someone with a plan. I packed up my

notes in frustration and was about to leave when I heard my name spoken.

"Ms. Lawson."

I turned. Lydia stood there, smiling with one hand tucked into the pocket of her blazer. If she pulled a pistol and shot me through the heart, it wouldn't have surprised me. Instead she offered her sympathies for my father's illness and asked if she could schedule a meeting with me to discuss what help my "little group" might be in saving a portion of the Estate.

"I know that wasn't your plan, dear, but I assume that any part you could save would be better than nothing." Her smile never wavered.

"When I'm not working, I'm with my father. If you need to talk to me, you can stop by Truant Gulch any evening."

"I will do so," she answered and turned on her heels.

I aimed myself for the *Express* office, spent two hours writing the article on the press conference, then drove to Truant Gulch to resume my vigil at Glen's bedside. Meryl stood and started packing her things to leave when I walked in. We shared but a few words before I was left once again with Glen and his phalanx of machinery and tubing. In other words, alone.

WEDNESDAY, JUNE 16, 1999

The story I thought I was telling seems to have drawn to an end and no longer needs developing. There's just me and my reflexive need to record the day's activities into this journal. What started as a project I thought might change Lowerton has instead turned out to be a small comfort in my otherwise unraveling life.

The wait for Glen to die (what an ugly thing to write) has become exhausting. Both Meryl and I have agreed that this is our final week. After this weekend we will visit when possible but will no longer mark the time off like watchmen.

Philip stopped by again this evening, still talking about the gold as if there remained some shred of hope for the Estate or our plans. I wish he'd spend his time enjoying the Maze while it still stands. He has yet to acknowledge that we've lost. It's good in a way—"it ain't over till it's over" and all of that—but this can also become tiring, almost troubling. Ben's observation that Philip seemed to be investing a bit too much of himself is beginning to feel important now. What will happen to us when this situation finally comes to a close?

I wonder most if I will still go on writing. Filling silent pages with unspoken words.

THURSDAY, JUNE 17, 1999

Glen is dead.

Glen is dead and I'm writing because I need to put what I saw to paper so that I'll have it there tomorrow when my memory seems untrustworthy and what happened seems impossible.

My evening started with my arrival at Truant Gulch and a few shared minutes with Meryl. She was the one who told me that Glen's vitals had been fluctuating all day and that the instability concerned each of the doctors that entered his room. She could read it on their faces. They'd stare at the charts longer and call nurses in from the hall to make sure what they were seeing was right.

"I asked one of them what was going on, but he didn't say

anything useful. Just that Glen was showing some 'fluctuations.'"

Meryl stayed on a little while longer, unwilling, it seemed, to leave. Something was happening, and she didn't want this to be the last time she walked out of the room, I guess. In the end, time won and she departed, leaving me instructions to call if anything serious should happen. I promised I would, but the thought that such a thing might actually happen never crossed my mind.

But it did. Glen died and died so quickly I never had the chance to give Meryl a call. I wish she would have been with me, though, so that at least one other person had seen what I saw.

And what I saw is Glen awaken, even shudder a bit, when Lydia Furrow walked into his room. Two minutes later he was dead. Lydia never did get to make the request for which she'd journeyed all the way to Truant Gulch. She slipped out amid the crush of nurses and doctors responding to Glen's failing monitors and never cast even the slightest glance in his direction.

He, however—I swear he looked at her.

She startled me when she came in because I'd had my back to the door. When I turned, there she was standing in a trim gray suit as though she were meeting with a loan officer or hosting a brunch. *Crisp* is the word I would use—even the air seemed biting with a cool, clear scent, like ice on an early frozen morning. She didn't give a greeting or offer her hand but instead folded her hands in front of her and said, "I am here, Ms. Lawson, to discuss the matter I mentioned to you on Friday."

"Yes," I answered and was about to say more when a movement caught my eye. It was Glen. He was trembling.

"Ms. Lawson?"

At the sound of Lydia's voice, Glen's eyes fluttered open. His jaw unhinged and I thought he might even speak, though nothing ever came out. The trembling continued, however, and before Lydia or I could say another word, before I could even move, the first of his machines began to chime.

I shot to Glen's bedside, but by the time I reached the railing, his eyes were shut again and the EKG had flat-lined. The first nurse arrived as I picked up his hand; it was startlingly hot. As two other nurses and doctors rushed in, though, the feeling of creeping coolness began to steal into his fingertips. Letting his hand fall to the bed, I stepped back from the rail and saw Lydia slip from the room. It was over. All of it.

Friday, June 18, 1999

I have made it through one full day without a father. Then again, in many ways, I have lived nearly an entire life without one. Yet this seems so much different. Perhaps it's from not going to Truant Gulch at all after two weeks' worth of daily visits. Perhaps it's the narcoleptic reminiscing that seized me like sleep throughout the day. I'd be doing one thing, a simple task like turning over a pancake, and suddenly I'd be watching myself at age six as I struggled through my first cooking lesson, Glen guiding my hands and talking me through each step.

What a sad, predictable realization—in his loss I realize how large a part Glen had in my life. The ache I suffered before is nothing compared to the barrenness of knowing he'll never fill that part again.

It's all words. Words and talk of feeling an absence, as

though such a thing were even possible. Words and memories of a man I cannot seem to help but reinvent, polishing up the rough edges as if I were presenting him for inspection. But for whom? There's nobody here who cares but me, and I've been his toughest judge all along. Faced with having to forge a lasting memory, I'm unable to look Glen Lawson straight in the eye. Rather, I'm playing at parlor games, conning myself with smoke and mirrors. And who is the biggest fool but the illusionist who falls under the spell of her own deception?

Dwight, during his visit earlier this evening, tried to convince me that it's a natural reaction.

"He wasn't all bad, Eve Marie. We've just been talking about the parts that frustrate us for so long that we forgot the rest. That's what you do when someone's alive. Then, when they pass, you remember them for the good."

"I don't want to see him for good or bad, Dwight. I want to see him for who he truly was. I want my memory not to be a lie."

"And what good'll that do?"

The question surprised me and I had no immediate answer.

"You can't tally up a man like you've been doing with the Estate. That reckoning will happen, but we're not a part of it. All we have are the memories we allow ourselves."

"So you want me just to remember the good things?"

Dwight sighed, but I knew it wasn't out of frustration or anything more than his own weariness. I'm sure he'd asked himself the same questions. I wasn't at all certain what his answer would be. We sat quiet a long moment before he finally spoke.

"I think we go about it the wrong way if we *try* and remember anything at all. For good or bad, Glen's touched both of us and we've learned from him. We remember because we can't help to do anything but."

I wasn't sure if I agreed or not but nodded anyway, and that ended our conversation. We chatted on a bit more about funeral arrangements, then Dwight left and I was alone for the night.

The memory came to mind so quickly it was as if it had been teetering there the whole time, just waiting for the moment to present itself.

I was eight and the summer sun burned high above Little Pines. Glen lay snoring on a lawn chair just off the drive, so it must have been a Saturday, his day off. I was playing with the rubber water hose, making rainbows with the mist. A breeze must have caught some of the spray because the next thing I heard was a voice.

"Eve."

Glen, whom I thought had been sleeping, called my name. I cut the water off immediately.

"Yes?"

"Spray me," he said, "it's hotter than the devil's pitchfork out here."

Without a second's pause, I hitched the nozzle his direction and doused him with a shower of water that left dancing prisms brighter yet than any I'd created all day. The moment seemed to last forever, until finally he lifted his hand for me to stop and he said a simple "Thanks."

Why that was the memory that came to me when Dwight left I have no idea. I remember how it shocked me, because usually Glen hated water and didn't even enjoy taking showers much. I can't say what the moment is supposed to have taught me about Glen.

The one thing I've decided this evening is that I don't want that to happen. I don't want to lose the small incidents that filled the years between us. Perhaps Dwight is right—perhaps adding them up won't be a tally of Glen Lawson, but I still need to make the effort. It's what I do after all; it's who I am. Sifting through the past, I try to find answers to questions that may never have been asked. I did so with the Estate, urged on by its impending demolition. I will do it as well with Glen. The only obstruction is my own failing recollection and the fact that he disappears a little more with every moment.

GLEN

There exists a photo of Glen. He's dressed in fatigues, grease paint smeared beneath his eyes and a cigarette drooping from his lips. There's a pistol on his lap, and his eyes are glazed, haunted. He looks for all the world like a sergeant who's heard the air split in two with the screams of the dying.

Only he's seated on the hood of his Nova. The back of the photo reads *Halloween 1975*, and I wonder what in life could teach a man to empty his eyes until all that can be seen is hopelessness and dread.

Up before, or with, sunrise each morning, Glen maintained a fairly strict bedtime of eleven o'clock. Even when out with Dwight, his heavy footsteps could always be heard moving across the gravel no later than ten-fifty. Once, however, when I was about twelve and battling a fever and a sore throat, I woke up past midnight to a dim murmur coming from the other end of the trailer.

Getting up to pour a glass of ice water, I was shocked to find Glen and Meryl sitting on the couch together and watching TV. Meryl looked my way for just an instant, but Glen waved me over and patted the cushion next to him.

"Good movie," he said when I sat. "Just started."

Together we watched the murky but riveting *Les Diaboliques*, and in the put-upon Christina Delassalle I couldn't help but see myself, fighting with all her strength but trapped by both her own frailty and the schemes of others. It didn't help that Meryl was a dead ringer for a cat-eyed Simone Signoret.

After the final chilling scene, Glen kissed me on the top of my head and asked how I was feeling. I assured him I was fine. He sent me to bed then with a squeeze of my shoulder and a quick wink that helped me to sleep when normally I would've been struggling against frightening dreams born from the film I'd just seen.

In the days following Glen's first stroke, he favored his left hand and arm because his right had gone limp. I'd visited him in the hospital and was surprised to see how adept he'd become after such a short time. Training a weak hand in the repetition of daily life takes most people months rather than days, and yet here was Glen writing legible notes, buttoning his shirt, and making do better than I expected.

He was quick to give credit to a broken right arm he'd suffered as a child. I'd never heard the story before and it fascinated me to see the pleasure he got from telling it.

"Two friends and I had just seen an old-time Johnny Weismuller Tarzan film in Bellefonte and decided there was nothing stopping us from swinging through the trees like he did. Got a

length of rope, climbed onto the bough of this old elm out by
Parson's Creek, and tied what we thought was the best knot
ever.

"My friend Walt went first. He dropped from the limb,
swung over the stream, and caught hold of a maple limb with
his right hand. When he'd climbed up, he swung the rope back
to me, and I tried the same thing. Only our knot slipped loose.
I landed right in the stream and snapped my arm in two places
on some rocks we'd put there earlier in the summer to try and
dam up the water.

"After a week off school, I went back and we were just learning penmanship. Teacher wouldn't hear anything about my
right hand being useless, so I learned to write first with my left.
The cast came off, but I never forgot."

One of the notes he penned in his days after the stroke
remains stuck beneath a magnet on the refrigerator in his
trailer. I saw it there the other week when I visited Meryl. It
says *Jonathan Biddle* and then gives a phone number.

Mr. Biddle called me this afternoon. He's a lawyer who drew
up a will for Glen in the weeks following the first stroke. We
are to meet the day after Glen's funeral and read over documents signed by my father's able left hand.

And finally, the memory that will not leave me.

My father's eyelids trembling and briefly raising at the
sound of Lydia Furrow's voice. His whole body shakes and his
mouth opens as if to speak, but by the time I move to his side,
he is gone.

The doctors have assured me that the physical manifesta-
tions of a body struggling against death can result in any

number of previously unseen actions. Comas are broken. The
paralyzed move their hands. Blind can regain their sight. It
means only that the effort to remain alive is so great that it
manages to overcome even the body's failed systems—if just for
a moment.

Rarely, though, is there a triggering mechanism for such an
occurrence. And with that they shook my hand and wished me
condolences, leaving me alone with my thought that Lydia Furrow's presence somehow elicited both the reaction and his subsequent death. A deathbed confession is the stuff of fiction, and
yet that is the intuition I cannot seem to shake.

Lydia Furrow meant something to Glen, something powerful enough to rouse him from the unconscious, and his last effort
was wasted in trying to tell what that something was.

I am alone in this belief.

MONDAY, JUNE 21, 1999

The memories from my previous entry—except my final
vision of Glen—ended up getting added to a few from Meryl
and two anecdotes from Dwight to make the funeral ceremony.
Held at the funeral parlor itself and officiated by one of their
staff, the whole thing went by in a blink. Only the drive to the
cemetery seemed long, what with Meryl's car not having air
conditioning. And so this thing has ended—not with tears or
solemn words tossed to the wind, but the pad of footsteps across
Edgewood Cemetery's manicured lawn, the rattle of Meryl's
engine startling to life.

She and I joined Dwight and Monique afterward for lunch.
We chose Glen's favorite spot in tribute and enjoyed barbecue,

sweet corn, and lemonade with an appetite that belied how we'd all spent the morning. Conversation remained minimal, I suppose because we were all lost in our own thoughts. When we'd finished, both Dwight and Monique wrapped me into great hugs and said they'd see me again real soon. They each shook Meryl's hand and then headed home. Meryl and I followed soon after, driving back to the funeral home so I could pick up my car. In the parking lot, I thanked her for all her help over the past days and weeks and reminded her about our meeting on Monday with Glen's lawyer. She nodded and then she was gone too.

On the drive home I tried to remember each of the fifteen faces who'd appeared to honor my father's memory. Ben came to mind first, followed by neighbors I hadn't seen in years, and Glen's co-workers, who seemed to have attended mostly for the paid time off. Philip made it for the ceremony but had to leave for work as we headed to the gravesite. I need to remember to thank him for making the effort. It's more than my father probably would've done.

Twice in the last paragraph I called him "father" without much thought. For years he'd been known to me only as Glen, and suddenly with his death I find this growing sense of intimacy. I am closer to him now that he's dead than I ever was when he lived. That's just wrong and sad.

What a waste. What a waste, what a waste, what a waste.

That has been on my mind for hours now. It came to me sometime in the middle of one of Dwight's anecdotes about Glen, the point of which was to praise Glen's determination and devotion. And all I could think was, *what a waste*.

Glen's determination produced nothing; his devotion little more.

Quinlin's gold? Not a sniff.

Daughter a successful flight from Lowerton? Nope.

I, as much as anything, am my father's failure. The two seemingly most important things in his life had come to naught. No wonder he didn't respond to my voice from his coma. No wonder he had no interest in reviving.

As I said, *what a waste*. The day ends with Glen gone and his daughter entrenched in a place he'd never wanted her to remain. I can only wonder now how long I'll stay.

The trembling won't stop. I try to slow my breathing yet this seems to have no effect. All I can hear are those words spoken to me by Glen.

"I found it, Eve. I'm almost positive this time."

The phone call had roused me after I'd fallen asleep on the couch following dinner. The caller took a breath and then Glen spoke.

I nearly dropped the receiver.

"Eve? Eve?"

Slowly the inflection changed, and my head cleared.

It was Philip. Philip had spoken in the voice of my father.

"Can you meet me tomorrow? I think I've found it."

"What, Philip?"

"The gold, Eve. I know where it is."

I hung up without answering and unplugged the phone before he could call back. Glen or Philip. Philip or Glen. Either way it didn't matter. When they spoke of Quinlin's gold, to me they were speaking with the voice of the dead.

Part Eight

P hilip left four messages on my machine today, each imploring me to get back to him so we could arrange to visit the Estate together. Home for all four, I never made a move for the receiver. It's all a tangled web that I have no interest in reentering. I did interrupt two other messages today, once to speak with Ben Sterling and another time to speak with Meryl.

Ben called early to see if I wanted to go to lunch and didn't seem to take offense when I told him I'd rather not. He's been a true help in recent days, and while others are treating me like some handblown glass figurine unable to stand the slightest jostle, Ben's simply been caring and concerned—letting me speak, letting me be silent.

Poor Meryl, on the other hand, has crumbled since the funeral. She called today and was crying because she hadn't been by Glen's side for his death. I'm not sure why she's been overtaken by regret in the wake of his passing, and it troubles me some. I know there had to have been unfinished business between them, but I'd hoped that most of it was sorted out before he'd gone unconscious. Now I'm beginning to think that perhaps there was more left unsaid than I ever knew.

Meryl wouldn't admit to it, however.

"No, it's not that," she said. "I'm just feeling him being gone. I'm feeling his absence."

This is the phrase that's stuck with me most since our conversation.

I'm feeling his absence.

If it'd been said by anybody else, I'd have shrugged it off as an overstatement. Meryl's not that kind of person, though. She doesn't make her point through exaggeration but just says pretty much what's on her mind and leaves the rest for the babblers. It's that straightforwardness that makes her statement so unusual to me in its wording.

She's not talking about Glen anymore; she's talking about Glen's absence—like it had weight and a shadow.

She's not talking about the absence of his presence; she's talking about the presence of his absence.

The distinction here, although I can't put my finger on it at the moment, strikes me as important in some way. I've thought it through since she called, and still it eludes me. I want to understand what exactly she means.

WEDNESDAY, JUNE 23, 1999

Jonathan Biddle's law degree came from a school I hadn't heard of, and rather than billing by the hour or based on a percentage of the decision won, he'd written up flat fees for different services rendered. Filing and tendering a will had cost Glen about a hundred dollars up front. Biddle assured us there would be no further costs on his end, that only the government would be waiting for their slice of Glen's pie.

"Glen didn't have a pie," Meryl informed the lawyer and he shrugged.

From his desk he retrieved a rolled piece of paper that was both tied with a satin ribbon and sealed with what looked to be wax. It looked like a diploma or the last will and testament of a character from a Jane Austen novel. Biddle made no comment, just slipped the ribbon off the scroll and split the wax with a brass letter opener. The parchment spun open on his desk, and he pinned the two upper corners down with empty coffee mugs before reading aloud.

" 'I, Glen David Lawson, being of sound mind and body...' "

The legal boilerplate took two minutes to wade through. Glen's actual will took only the length of time it takes to read two sentences.

" 'To Eve Marie Lawson, I leave her mother's belongings and the contents of this envelope.' "

Jonathan Biddle handed me a plain legal envelope. I could see there was something inside, which felt like it might be a key. The lawyer read the second sentence.

" 'To Meryl Lakewood, I leave my remaining material possessions.' "

Biddle read Glen's name, scrawled as it must have been with the man's left hand, and asked if we had any questions.

"That's it?" Meryl asked.

The lawyer scanned the will quickly and, while nodding, produced a modest sheaf of papers for us to sign, agreeing to what had been read. As Meryl stabbed at the paper with an angry pen, I noticed for the first time the fire in her eyes. Something she'd expected hadn't come to pass. I waited until after I'd signed and we left to ask her about it.

"Oh, Eve," she said, "it's just foolishness."

She didn't say any more than that for the time being, as we walked to my car parked in the public lot in back of the town hall. I wasn't sure if the subject of Glen was closed or not until we'd pulled out of Lowerton's main square and headed for Little Pines Trailer Park. Meryl gazed out the window toward the Estate high on the bluff above, and it must have been something in what she saw that made her speak. I didn't say a word the whole time.

"He left us nothing. I don't think I'd ever imagined he could actually do it, but he had one last chance and he did nothing. Do you know what I expected? Stupid me, I thought that lawyer was going to open that will and read that Glen loved me. Or felt bad about never marrying me. We talked about it. In the end he always pushed it off by saying we'd get to it someday. What a sad fool. Instead he leaves me his junk as if that's payment. What a sad fool."

She'd said it twice, and I could no longer tell if she meant Glen or herself. She kept quiet during the rest of our drive, and soon we pulled into Little Pines and up to the trailer. When Meryl opened her door to get out, I caught the brief smell of summer in the trailer court, a combination of mown grass, scorched macadam, and the clinging sourness of the creek bottom now exposed after weeks of hard sun. The calls of children came from the adjacent field. I wondered if they still exhausted the hours playing the same games I'd once played.

Meryl interrupted my thoughts by thanking me for driving. Before stepping away, she remembered something and snapped her fingers.

"Totally forgot," she said. "What was it in the envelope? What'd Glen leave you?"

I pulled the folded envelope from my pocket, tore open an end, and shook its contents into my palm. A key fell out, smaller and simpler than most keys, and I could see a puzzled look on Meryl's face.

"What's it for?"

On one side were five engraved numerals, on the reverse side three initials: LNB. Lowerton National Bank. A safe-deposit box.

"What in the world would Glen put in one of those boxes?" she asked. I didn't answer. Or didn't want to answer, as my only thought held the simplest of solutions.

It would explain my father's lingering obsession with the Estate, despite the years of failure. It would explain the rumors and stories heard throughout the decades. It would bring to a close the dark secret of Evangeline Graveston's death, hinted at by Martin Peterson.

I pictured myself entering the bank and staring at a long gray case pulled from a stack of hundreds. I saw myself slip in the key and push open the lid, holding back my breath so that I wouldn't scream when I looked down and saw the bar of gold that'd been the source of so many terrible things.

With a quick good-bye to Meryl, I spun around my car and took off in the direction that would lead me away from Lowerton National Bank the fastest. That moment, the dread of looking down, was nothing for which I was prepared.

Thursday, June 24, 1999

So I'm left fleeing from Quinlin's gold. After everything that had come before, after all the trouble it's caused in my life, I guess I shouldn't have expected anything less, but still I wasn't ready.

I wasn't ready for Philip to be calling three or four times a day insisting he's found its hiding place.

I wasn't ready for my father to leave me, as my only inheritance, a heavy reminder of the price he was willing to pay in pursuit of what everyone else thought was fantasy.

I wasn't ready for it to begin tainting the Estate itself. The place will fall in a matter of months, and yet I can't bring myself to set foot inside. All I can think of is Evangeline Graveston plummeting down the steps, or my father walking wide-eyed and dazed through the halls seeking any hint of the treasure.

Like I said before, I'm fleeing. Escaping now by burying myself in other diversions and planning for my eventual escape from the town of Lowerton, from the haunted hill where the Estate once stood. I'll stay at least until then, I've decided. I owe it that much. I'll see the Estate come down and then I will go.

Where is without an answer at this point. East Lansing perhaps. Or Madison. Or College Station. I hope to find a place in close proximity to a graduate program just in case I decide to reapply. And the quality of life is a little better in these places. Richmond is even an option. I should tell Meryl to move with me. We could both go to heaven together.

She called to apologize yesterday evening, though for what I'm still not sure. Her bitterness and frustration at Glen's callow final act are completely understandable to me. Would be to anyone. I just hope they don't scar her forever. Glen did his damage. She should be allowed to heal in peace.

Writing that reminds me of what Lydia Furrow once said: "She'd leave us to lick our wounds." That's Meryl and me at this point—licking our wounds. It's sad the damage we do to one another. I wonder what scars I have left behind. Whose blood have I drawn?

The one person who's been nothing but a help is Ben Sterling. Tonight he called not only on my behalf but on Philip's as well. Apparently Ben had received just as many messages over the past few days and hadn't yet responded either.

"What's weird is his insistence that he knows where it is," Ben said. "He's not saying he *thinks* he knows where it is. He basically says he's found it."

"But he hasn't or he'd be knocking on our doors, gold bars in hand."

Ben agreed and asked what I planned to do.

"I don't know. I don't feel like talking about it anymore, but I guess that's not going to happen. So probably in a day or two I'll call him and we'll go to the Estate together and put this thing to rest." I'd have to do the same with my father's safe-deposit box. But I didn't mention that to Ben; I only said, "What is it about gold anyway? Why hidden treasure?"

Ben didn't say anything, although I hadn't asked expecting his response. Besides, I knew the answer. It didn't take a philosopher or psychologist to figure out why Glen had sacrificed his life in its pursuit. Gold promised to solve his problems, every one. It was a cure-all, the ultimate in restorative power. Had he found the gold, his daughter would then love him, the town that'd mocked him for so long would respect him, and he'd justify the long years spent searching. In the end, I think, that was the key more than anything. He searched because he needed to prove to himself that all the effort had been worthwhile. All I can think is that he died a sorrowful man.

I said these things to Ben, and he sighed over the phone as if it was the saddest thing he'd heard in a long time.

"There was a better way," he replied finally.

He didn't need to explain. I knew what he meant.

"What if that's a lie too?" I asked.

"Then we're to be pitied more than all men."

"Super."

"It's not a lie, though. We're not chasing shadows."

"How do you know?"

"I don't."

"Ben."

"You've come a long way, Eve. You wouldn't be asking these questions if it was a lie."

"That's it?"

"I can't make you believe."

"I don't want you to."

"Then what do you want?"

For the first time I paused. It took a long moment to put together the words, and Ben let me have that space. Finally they came.

"I want to know why it hurts so bad."

"It does, doesn't it?"

"Yes. Why?"

"You want the truth?"

"Of course."

"It hurts because you're alone."

I thought that over a second but it didn't seem right. "I'm not talking about losing Glen."

"Neither am I."

"Oh," I said, feeling foolish all of a sudden. We'd returned to the start of the conversation again, only this time I hadn't realized it. And now there was no place more we could go. "Thanks," I said, stuck for anything else.

"You sure?"

"No, but how else do you end these conversations?"

Ben laughed. "Thanks is good enough."

He said his good-byes and hung up, leaving me alone to think over everything he'd said. The phone rang again twenty minutes later but I ignored it, and whoever called didn't leave a message. Most likely it was Philip, growing weary now of trying to reach me. Or Meryl, another unspoken sorrow having surfaced to stab her conscience and bleed her yet again. I let both slip from my mind and puzzled over the one phrase from my conversation with Ben that just wouldn't leave me.

It wasn't him saying that I'd been left.

It was his small remark that I'd come a long way. Just his saying it brought to mind all those thoughts I had weeks ago of the journey I thought I was on. How at first I thought I was alone but then learned that others—Philip, Dwight, Ben— might be with me. I even went back in this journal and looked up the passage. I wrote it in March. Reading those words, seeing myself condemn Meryl Lakewood, makes me think that perhaps Ben might be right. Perhaps I have come a distance. If I have, and because he's only known me since the start of this thing, then I may very well have documented it right here in these words.

So that's what comes next.

Not accompanying Philip to the Estate.

Not prying open my father's last secret.

What comes next is the story of the last six months. Where I've been. And where I'm going.

It all circles back to *somewhere*.

FRIDAY, JUNE 25, 1999

The phone rang just a few minutes ago. I knew it would be Philip, and I answered anyway. He said exactly what I expected.

"I was wrong. I got tired of trying to get you or Ben to go with me and went to the Estate today by myself. The gold wasn't there. I thought it would be, but it wasn't."

I consoled Philip for another moment or two before he said good-night. The word came out as a sigh. I suppose he'd reached that moment where things finally became clear. He'd just realized that Quinlin's gold didn't exist.

Only he is wrong. I'm nearly certain of it.

I went back and reread the journal expecting to play Gretel, expecting to follow a clever path of bread crumbs that trace out the path of my life through these recent months. What I discovered were two things completely different.

First, I found where Gabriel Quinlin hid his gold.

It didn't come with thunderbolts or a choir of angels or any great shouts of "Eureka!" Instead, there was a whisper as I read and suddenly I knew. It had been there all the time, only I'd never looked close enough.

The funny thing (or pathetic thing, or ironic, or hateful) is how little it means to me. Quinlin's gold is a dead-man's bounty at this point. Evangeline Graveston's blood spilled in its pursuit, and my father's wracked body received no comfort from it. There's a kind of wrongness that surrounds Quinlin's treasure, yet riches like this probably don't need a curse. They cloak themselves in the stench of jealousy and greed and desperation. They gleam with the light of one person's covetous eye, which is enough to bring the world down around it.

Perhaps that's too much. I just know that figuring out where the gold is hidden gives me no sense of relief or satisfaction or happiness. For all I can think about is Glen. Glen, who devoted his life to looking for the gold only to be thought a fool. Only with his death is the treasure found, and now he'll be thought worse than a fool. He'll be remembered a bungler, one who wasted his life searching for yet never finding what actually existed.

I'm left with this:

If we find the gold, in spite of what Philip's lawyer friend said, there's no guarantee we'll get to keep it. On the other hand, this is our only hope at this point for saving the Estate. It's the singular option. Without it, the Estate falls. Even with it, the house may still tumble. That's why I have no sense of accomplishment or happiness at all in uncovering where the treasure rests.

The second thing is just as troubling.

Instead of the little comfort that might come from some small progress along that ragged bread-crumb trail, some small indication that my faith is no longer set before a plastic elf, grinning his frozen smile under a mountain of fur even in the warmest days of the year, I found something I expected even less than discovering the hiding place of Quinlin's gold. Rather than knowing which name to speak and knowing that my knees should bow, I found a harsh reflection of my own face, my own life, and I added something new to my frustrations.

I added myself.

WHAT'S WRONG WITH ME

I cringe to think of it. All of it.

How I hated Meryl. Those years of disgust, and all based on nothing.

How I offered Glen none of the grace for which I myself have been searching.

How I considered my leaving Lowerton a natural-born right based on nothing more than my ability to read and pay attention in school.

How I invoked the name of Wanda Maxwell over and over and never once, until just recently, bothered to look for her.

How I ran to Dwight and Ben and Philip every time I had a problem and then gave nothing in return.

How I kept things from Embeth Graveston.

How I pointed out Lowerton's blemishes without once acknowledging that the place has more than a few good points.

How I forgot Gabriel Quinlin's beloved virtues of mercy and provision even as I tried to save the building founded on those principles. If I do save Quinlin's Estate, I need to do it for better reasons. I owe him and the town that much.

I owe.

I don't know that I've written those words in this journal until now. And somehow they seem better in a way than what I'd written before—"I deserve." Better, because I do owe.

I owe Meryl Lakewood apologies and thanks that I'll never have time to offer.

I owe Quinlin's Estate every bit of myself that it has helped me become.

I owe Philip, Ben, and Embeth words of kindness to replace those they've given me.

I owe Evangeline Graveston a reckoning not yet given.

I owe Dwight and Monique the love of a daughter.

I owe Glen—I don't know what I owe him. Perhaps the honesty to look at his life as it was and say I forgive him. I don't know.

And I owe Lowerton a final chance. Gabriel Quinlin reached down years ago and swept the town under his protective wing. I can't do that, but I can help them remember. Remember what it means to be lost. Remember what it means to be found. Remember what it means to be saved.

I suppose this means I've made my decision. In the next days, perhaps with Philip and Ben by my side, I will walk into the Estate, one last trip to uncover Quinlin's gold with the purpose of saving what saved us.

SATURDAY, JUNE 26, 1999

But not yet. Two phone calls of greater importance interrupted any plans I had.

The day started with Meryl calling to say she'd been fired from her waitress job, and ended with my editor calling to alert me to a breaking story coming from down ridge about a possible mining accident. It's from that late night press conference that I just returned, notes and microtape recordings ready for refining tomorrow. Now, though it's near midnight, I can't fall asleep because of the energy built up through a day of worry. I wonder if Meryl is in the same place as I am, given what she plans for tomorrow.

Her phone call this morning forced me to drop what I was doing, which was whisking three eggs for an omelet. The yolks never made it to the stove; I rinsed them down the sink's drain before heading over to Meryl's to talk through what had happened.

"I just stopped going to my shifts," she said when I arrived. She fixed herself a cup of coffee, pausing to see if I wanted any, and when I nodded, she poured a second mug. "What else could they do?"

The surprising thing was how calm she was. Her first words to me on the phone had been blasé, as if she'd called to track down a recipe for a casserole she'd hoped to put together that night.

"Eat n' Park canned me," she said this morning. And now, "What else could they do?"

I said the only thing that made sense. "You wanted to be fired."

She handed me the coffee, took a seat on the leather sofa opposite me, and mulled my interpretation. "You're probably right. I didn't want to quit. Each night I had every intention of going in, but then the time would come to put on that uniform and I just froze."

She was staring off down the trailer, possibly toward her bedroom, where her outfit still hung untouched in her closet, where at least eight different uniforms had hung during the last twenty or so years. Perkins, Bob's Big Boy, Denny's, HoJo's,

Shoney's, and the rest. She'd been working the late shift at some restaurant for as long as I'd known her. It was the first job she'd found when she moved in with Glen and me, and she'd never stopped hauling trays in all that time, BLT after tuna melt after Grand Slam platter after whatever else it was that people order during the darker hours of night.

"He made me keep the job, you know. The hours too. I talked to him one time, after you were older, about switching to the lunch shift, and he just sorta shrugged and said, 'Ain't it true that the best tippers come in at night?' "

"Do they?"

Meryl glared at me, quick and annoyed. It reminded me of looks she'd shoot when I lived at home and asked stupid questions.

"Of course not," she said. "Some of the truckers maybe, but everybody else is just looking for the noise of other people. That was just Glen's way of saying he thought we spent plenty of hours together as it was. So after he died, there was nobody sitting in the kitchen glancing down at his watch every minute as the hand got close to seven."

"Meryl, he hasn't been at home since—"

She waved me off. "I know, Eve, I know. I'm just telling you what I feel."

I nodded. "So what now?"

"Ready for a laugh?"

"Okay."

"Richmond."

I did. I laughed. "You're going home?"

She smiled, as true a smile as I'd ever seen her give. "Why not? I have some family I can get in touch with. Made some calls and found out a few old friends are still in the area. Besides, what's keeping me here? Certainly not Lydia Furrow's dusting and polishing. I told that old barracuda two days ago I wouldn't be back." She smiled again with a satisfied shimmer to her eye as she waited for me to respond. All that came to mind was the sudden realization that I wasn't enough to keep Meryl Lakewood in Lowerton. Which hurt just a little bit.

"What's the matter, Eve?"

I hesitated, but just for a second. We'd spent long years already keeping things from each other, and now she was getting ready to leave. "We were just getting to know each other," I said.

Meryl cocked her head as though she didn't quite understand what I said before reaching out to me with one finger, her polished nail waving back and forth. "No, dear. No, no, no. You can't get rid of me that easy. I'm just taking a vacation ... in fact, that's why I wanted to talk with you. I hoped you might stay here in the trailer while I'm gone. Folks know what's in here, and if they see me packing to leave, the place will be gutted before I get to Lynchburg."

"Well," I said without much purpose, and before I could get much else out I had stood and crossed the room with my arms out. Meryl smiled and stepped into my embrace, the first perhaps that we'd shared. I couldn't remember hugging her before—not even at the funeral—and it felt like the right way to send her off.

"When do you leave?" I asked after we'd dropped our arms and moved to the kitchen.

"Tomorrow. Will you come and see me off? I'll have the keys ready, and you can bring a suitcase to move in."

"Sure. Definitely."

And with that I left, knowing for the second time in two days that I mattered to someone. Meryl wasn't disappearing from Lowerton, wasn't leaving for good the place she'd lived for so many years, and I was part of her reason. I was one of the people for whom she'd return. Just knowing that made the drive back to my apartment all the better and helped smooth out the rest of the day. At least until my editor called with her hint that something had gone wrong with Boyd Lime and Stone.

"Wrong" turned out to be an understatement. At a quarrying site twelve miles down the ridge, workers nearly split the mountain in two when four sets of charges were set off instead of the normal two. Miscommunication between changing shifts was the formal explanation for what had happened. Most everything else that was said began with the words, "We're unable to comment on that at the moment."

Two university mineral science Ph.D.'s had been called in to study the effects of the blast on the remaining hillside, and Walter Boyd himself assured journalists that no further work would commence on the site until the safety and integrity of the quarry had been confirmed.

"Will this speed up plans for the acquisition of the Lowerton ridge?" a reporter I didn't recognize asked.

Boyd started to move his head in what could only be considered a nod, glanced down at a row of dark-suited men in front of him, and saw something that made him stop. "No comment at the moment," he said instead and moved on.

An hour into the press conference, word came from the Centre County Hospital that one of the workers had died while a second had just been upgraded to serious condition. Boyd's face collapsed at the news of the death, and around the room, small groups of men gathered and quietly commiserated over the news. At least I hoped that's what it was they talked about, that rather than strategizing about the best way to rid themselves of liability. The night ended forty-five minutes later with the release of the man's name—William Darling—and a statement by Boyd of condolences to Darling's family and sorrow from every member of the Boyd Lime and Stone Company.

It's a strange thing to end a night mourning the death of a man you do not know. All it did was bring back the unchangeable fact that I too had lost someone recently. As I drove back to my apartment, Glen's face came to me as it had in the first days after his passing. I guess that's what grieving is—nothing but the inescapable memories that slip in over the top of everything else. They push the present away and for a brief moment there's an openness where the past comes to life, if only for a moment. If grief can be described as a sort of haunting, then it's Glen, not Wanda Maxwell, who is to be my ghost.

SUNDAY, JUNE 27, 1999

Meryl just pulled away from Little Pines swearing she'd be back in ten days, even though she'd packed enough clothes to stay a month or more. She left me with only a couple of instructions for keeping care of the trailer and one slip of paper. Except the paper is a check and on it is a large number—fifteen thousand dollars, what she called my "rightful share" of what Glen had left her.

She handed me the check just after she opened the door, saying, "Haven't finished packing. Here's part of Glen's life insurance."

It took a half hour of clothes-searching interruptions to get a full explanation. We then passed a second half hour with me fruitlessly trying to give it back. She would have none of it and played deaf to the majority of my arguments. She was too busy filling a small duffel with what one could only call a generous selection of shoes for so short a vacation.

"Yes, Eve, I do need the money," she said after hearing at least part of what I said. "But no more than you—and certainly not in exclusion of you. I don't know what Glen was up to in dividing things the way he did, but it bothers me and I want to make it right. Now come on, I've only got an hour or so before I want to hit the road. Let's talk about something a little more pleasant than money."

She would've ignored anything else I might have said, so I folded the check and slipped it into my shorts pocket, suddenly aware of how much money I'd just inherited—and from someone who wasn't even dead. Things made little sense these days.

Our last hour together was spent lingering on the front steps, talking about yesterday's tragedy down ridge, going over Meryl's intended itinerary, and simply marveling that one of us was leaving Lowerton for a while.

Finally Meryl glanced at her watch and slapped a hand against her leg. "Look at the time. I need to get out of here." She quickly disappeared inside, grabbed the straps of three stuffed vinyl duffels, and marched back down the steps to her car before I could even offer to help. In what seemed like a second, she was sitting in the driver's seat, the engine growling, the radio turned up.

If it hadn't been real before, it certainly was now.

"You're going to Richmond," I said after she'd rolled down her window for a final good-bye.

"Long time coming."

"It's a hard town to leave."

Meryl laughed. "No harder than any other. Just get in the car and drive away." With that she winked and backed out onto the macadam loop where I'd once written the word *somewhere* with only the vaguest understanding of what it meant. And now Meryl was going to find hers.

It made me think of the only other person I'd known who'd found the place she was searching for all along. I decided to give Wanda Maxwell one more call. This time she answered. But, as it turns out, she wasn't who I was looking for after all.

WANDA

"My goodness, Eve Lawson? Is this really you?"

I assured her it was.

"I can't believe it. How in the world did you track me down?"

"Meryl Lakewood."

"Wow. So wait, what are you doing back in Lowerton? It was always your dream to get out of there."

I told her about Glen blowing my college fund and how I ended up staying to accept a full-ride scholarship at the university. About my plans for graduate school and how the Estate interrupted that. How we had just one final, desperate shot to save it. Then I said, "And it was always both our dreams to get out of Lowerton."

"Nah," she replied, offhanded. "That was you. Don't you remember? I always talked about finding my mother. If she could have stood being in the same county as my dad I never would have left. Say, how's your dad these days?"

I hesitated, then said, "Actually, he just passed away."

"Oh, wow. I mean, sorry."

"He was sick for a while. Do you really mean you never cared about leaving here?"

"I hated Little Pines. I hated living cramped in that trailer. That's it though. I loved Lowerton. The bike trail from the school. Free weekends in the Maze. You always tried to sour me on it, just like you did with Meryl, but it didn't work quite so well. Do you know I hated that woman because of all the things you said about her? She's not half bad."

"She's better than that," I told Wander, and our conversation drifted.

Wanda had eventually graduated from high school in Paradise, taken a year off to travel around the country, then returned home to train as an EMT. She was dating a guy pretty seriously, only he had two kids from a previous marriage, so she wasn't jumping into anything too quickly. Her mother was in a retirement village in Lititz, twenty minutes away, making eyes at the few bachelors in the place and trying to sweet-talk her way into a nicer condo. Life was all right.

"So, Wander—I mean, Wanda—do you ever think about the Estate?" It was the question I'd meant to ask her since I first decided to find her, and even though her answer wouldn't make any difference as to whether the building stood or fell, I still wanted to hear what she had to say.

"You know, I do every once in a while. This area's beautiful, lots of hills and stuff, but there's just nothing very tall around here. Sometimes I think it'd be nice to see that old tower again, way up there on the hill. Man, that thing was high! Or is it? Maybe it just seemed that way 'cause I was a kid. Does it still seem high, Eve?"

"Yes," I answered. "It still does."

MONDAY, JUNE 28, 1999

In this world, I have concluded, we do not often meet our ghosts. Paul Racine, that great nineteenth-century thinker I never did uncover for Dr. Stillman, remains only a name on a single page. Karen von Maarsten, Philip's sister, is still lost in the night. Evangeline Graveston is but a fair-headed girl tumbling forever down a set of winding stairs. Last evening, though, I met one of my ghosts. I found Wander, the real Wander, and she was nothing more than a lonely girl who wanted very much to see her mother.

The other, the Wander I remember who wanted out of Lowerton so badly that she would risk getting lost, was someone quite different, and her name only came clear after last night. She was me. Or who I wanted to be but never could be.

I'm almost certain it all makes sense now. I can see how it *had* to happen this way.

Just like I had to receive that phone call this evening from Philip, who whispered, "Did you hear? Did you hear? The water's gone down. The well at Quinlin's Estate is down three feet!"

It had to be this way, because no matter what I thought at the beginning, no matter what the reason was for starting, this journal has showed me how I've been looking at everything the wrong way. Even at the start I was worrying about finding a path and following it. A silly thought. I have pursued nothing; I have sought nothing.

It has all been done to me.

I've been pursued, found out, and asked to do one simple thing—speak my true name. *Wander. I am Wander.*

Wanda Maxwell, my childhood friend, on the night she stepped across that torn patch of dirt and left the world of here and now forever, became everything I ever hoped. But I wasn't ever brave enough to take that step myself, and so I kept the ghost of her memory alive and called her "Wander." Only it was me. Still wanting to leave, still needing to find my *somewhere.*

Now it's over and there is no more wandering.

Today I spent more hours reading this journal, not caring for once about Quinlin's gold or the harsh things I'd said against people. This time I read it and saw this isn't the story I thought I was writing. This is my story. It has been the whole time. My story and the tale of this very decision right now—I have been pursued and there will be no more wandering. I am God's.

Who can make such a thing sound sane? Who would want to?

It's over. The roaming is through. The wandering is done. I have found. I am found.

Testify

This all begins with Quinlin's Estate and my stubborn inability to forget it looming over my life. Once a person's lived in the shadow of something so immense, she can't help but think of herself as small. She's accustomed to looking up and being reminded there are other things larger than her in the world. Always there was a yearning for all the Estate appeared to represent.

A few months ago this yearning was given a name: *Sehnsucht*, the undeniable longing for something that nothing in this world seems to satisfy. When I became an adult, my dreams of a better place didn't end. There continued to be the *somewhere* of my childhood that I thought existed just beyond the gates, just past the Tower, or around the Maze's next corner.

Somewhere and *someone* as well.

This was the hardest to admit.

For a lifetime I'd always wanted to be someplace else, and to desire a better location was normal to me. Never had I admitted that I was missing out on a person. I couldn't come to terms with this because the one person I truly missed—Glen—had stayed out of my life purposely. What good would it have done to hope for a relationship with a man whose intention was to keep his distance?

But there was something else, a perpetual frustration that made sense now in the wake of my father's death. Meryl put it best—it was the presence of an absence. I was alone but knew the feeling only because I'd been together at one point. And, like I said in my conversation with Ben, this wasn't about Glen.

During those weeks of church I must have listened more than I thought I did. There's been this growing sense that everything might have more meaning than I ever believed possible. There was an answer to be found in the One larger than all, who stepped into the here and now and later stepped out. That moment created both an understanding of all there was to gain and also tore open a wound when the moment ended. The world has suffered and rejoiced since.

God stepped into the world as Jesus, died for our humanness, and departed again. In doing so He left behind a constant reminder of all that's ahead. So what was left for me was to recognize my humanness, and nowhere did it show up more clearly than in every slander, every resentful shot at Lowerton, every disdainful remark I'd made about all those I'd come to despise. There was an ugliness to those words I could never have been convinced existed except for seeing it myself. Worst of all were the years lost in hating Meryl. Yet, rather than getting what's deserved, something of inexpressible beauty is offered, and for that I can only give thanks and testify. Testify here in these pages and then hopefully with my life.

Part Nine

TUESDAY, JUNE 29, 1999

I don't want to press the issue, for most of it is just conjecture, but there seems to be something to the idea that those who truly seek Quinlin's lost fortune are the least likely to find it. Evangeline found it, but only for a three-day retreat when she carved the words of her own lament. I found it as well, but only after seeing a divine pattern to the crooked path I'd been walking. Glen lived out his life seeking nothing but the gold and died holding nothing.

I will speak of what I found—in time. First, though, there is something of greater importance. Philip's claim that the well at Quinlin's Estate was emptying is true. We visited there today, first thing after the drawbridge descended. The ticket-takers and guides all wore anxious expressions on their faces as though they expected the walls to tumble at any minute.

"Seventy-nine feet," one said to me without even being prompted. "Down six feet since Saturday." Depth, apparently, was the only thing on people's minds.

Within twenty minutes of our arrival, journalists and gawkers filled the small wooden bridge spanning the well, and their conversations mounted to a din in the crowded corridors and low stone ceilings. Most everything said was a retelling of the legends they'd heard about the collapse of the Estate.

"Everything but the Tower," said one liver-spotted veteran to his doddering friend.

"Town will go to ruins," suggested a second voice from the back.

"Anyone figure out why this is happening?" I asked a representative of Brighton Entertainment, holding out the press badge I'd brought along just in case I got this very opportunity.

He hedged a bit and said he couldn't comment officially.

"How about off the record?" said Philip. We had our own suspicions, everybody did, and wanted to know if Brighton shared them.

"Off the record," the official said, "we all know that only one thing happened between Saturday and today that could do such a thing."

Everybody stood on the same ground, that this had something to do with the mining accident down ridge.

"Are you investigating?" I asked.

"We're conducting inquiries in a number of different directions."

Between the lines, I heard the words *legal action* loud and clear. This was going to get ugly and soon. If the Estate did end up collapsing, the consequences could be huge. For now, it was just a matter of wait and see, so Philip and I packed up and headed out. But not for good. I had a plan that we needed to carry out quickly or risk losing a chance at all.

On the way home I spelled it out for Philip.

"I'm staying at Meryl's, and she has Glen's master key to the Estate. They never claimed it after he got sick. We can use it to get back in tonight. The security schedules are still the same, so I'm pretty sure we can be in and out without getting caught."

Philip pretended only for a second that he understood. "But why would we go back in?"

"For the gold."

He turned to me so quickly he nearly pulled the car off the road. "You know where it is?"

"Tonight," I answered and let it go at that.

We spent twenty minutes together after arriving at Meryl's, but I'd clearly put Philip's nerves on edge, so he soon excused himself and said he'd be back this evening. When I told him to bring some extra shorts with him, he just gave me a nervous look. I, meanwhile, passed a few hours by making phone calls to Boyd Lime and Stone. Turns out they had little they wanted to share at the moment, and only a quick discussion with a geology professor at the university proved helpful at all.

"That blast was much bigger than they're admitting," he said. "I'd surmise that they compromised the integrity of an underground stream network. It wouldn't surprise me to see some strange things over the next few months. We'll see water in places we've never had it before and no water where we expect it. The environmentalists will go ballistic if they find out."

I agreed they would and hung up. With the halfhearted denials from Brighton Entertainment, the condemning silence from Boyd, and the quote from an expert on geology, I went to work in piecing together the most aggressive and speculative article I'd ever written. Unsure if the *Express* would go for it, I drove to Kinko's and faxed the pages to the office just in case. The paper went to print tomorrow, and if Gloria really wanted to, she could squeeze the piece in somewhere between all the fluff.

That completed, I had nothing left to do but wait for Philip's return while mentally sketching out the night's plan. I wished we could do it without breaking in, yet that wasn't possible anymore, and besides, there was very little time left. This seemed like rationalization then and it still does, but it was the choice I made. We would go in after dark, and if we were caught I would be willing to pay the consequences.

Philip's willingness didn't match mine.

"It doesn't make sense," he said. "Why don't we just go tomorrow and sneak off when nobody's around?"

"You'll see," I replied and he did.

We got into the Estate without incident, having to open only two locks with Glen's key on the way. Cloud cover obscured any moonlight we might've had to avoid, and the security guards were on schedule the whole way through. We came and left without them ever knowing. And the only thing we took was a small slip of paper.

"Where to?" Philip whispered once we were inside.

I pointed to a narrow staircase often overlooked by visitors. Pulling a slim Maglite from my pocket, I twisted on the beam and padded my way across the floor. Philip followed and soon we were downstairs. Safety lights glowed along the corridor and threw enough light on the cracks and rises of the floor to make the flashlight unnecessary. We made our way for a few hundred

feet in silence, passed the dungeon rooms where both Evangeline and Dwight saw God, and finally came to our destination.
Philip shot me a glance but said nothing and followed right
behind me as we stepped onto the wooden bridge where we'd
stood earlier today.

"Here?"

I nodded and leaned over the railing to look down into the
well.

Philip joined me, then whispered the question that had to
have been on his mind this entire time. "How do you know?"

"She didn't try to commit suicide, Philip."

"What?"

"Evangeline. It was in one of Martin Peterson's E-mails,
how she was distraught over not finding the gold so she threw
herself into the well. She wasn't trying to kill herself—she was
still looking for the gold!"

"That's nuts," he said, but there wasn't much conviction
behind it, and he still stared down into the water.

"Think about it. After that incident her personality changed.
Peterson blamed it on her being sick, but I think it was because
she found something and was trying to decide what to do about
it. Also, it's the one place Glen would never have looked. He
hated water. That's why we had to do it tonight. During the day
there'll be too many people here watching the well. And if we
wait any longer, the water level might go down too far."

Philip shrugged. It was the best he could manage, I guess,
because he said nothing more as I took off my shoes and socks,
pulled on a pair of goggles, and climbed the railing, readying
myself for the shock of freezing cold water. "Be ready to pull me
out," I whispered to him and then jumped.

The cold hit harder than I expected. I screamed the second I was underwater to empty myself so I could remain quiet with my head out of the water. Philip's anxious face was the first thing I saw above me when I surfaced. I gave him a thumbs-up to let him know I was okay, then I switched on my Maglite and took three deep breaths, letting each out slowly. On the fourth I dove down.

With the light in one hand and my other hand out in front of me, I tried to go as deep as I could, kicking and pulling at the water to descend until my ears could no longer take the pressure. Everything was dark and frigid, the only color being the fingers of green algae that clung to the rock sides. Soon my lungs started burning, so I turned my head up and began pulling for the surface. Everything around me was a blur of gray and green.

Then black.

And then gray and green again.

My head popped out of the water and I took in air in great gulps, trying to keep my teeth from chattering.

"I saw something!" I said to Philip when I'd regained my breath. "Halfway down."

"Eve," he said, but I left him alone with whatever else he wanted to say and dove once more, finding instantly what I'd passed on my way up.

It was a large hole in the side of the well, a water-filled tunnel leading off under the Estate. I hesitated for a second, but then decided if Evangeline could swim it, I could too. So I pushed myself in. What Philip thought staring down into the water when the glow of my flashlight disappeared, I don't know, but I swam my way forward for seven or eight seconds before the tunnel took a right angle upward. Three seconds later I broke the surface with a gasp and looked around a room that no other person had seen since Evangeline Graveston. My flashlight showed what seemed like a small cavern, maybe ten square feet total and with a ceiling eight feet above. To my left there was a low wall I could pull myself onto. Behind it were stairs. This was everything Glen imagined but never found. I had to tell Philip.

It took me just ten or fifteen seconds to make the swim back to the bridge. Even before I reached the surface I could hear him saying my name—"Eve, Eve, Eve"—over and over.

"Philip," I said with my first breath. With the second, "Shut up."

"What in the world?"

I explained what I'd found, and he couldn't stop shaking his head, amazed. The cold water was now getting to my bones, so I barked at him to pay attention. He immediately stripped off his shirt and then knotted his belt around the bridge railing to use as a grip just in case we didn't find a separate way out of the hidden chambers. Then he was in the water with me and following my lead as we swam back to the passage, climbed out onto the wall, and made our way to the stairs.

We moved forward in silence, shivering from cold and giving only small exclamations to ourselves as we walked. It turned out that the tunnel led exactly to what I thought I'd seen before—a small stone landing that opened to a narrow flight of steps. Up and up we wound, dripping water behind us, until the stairs ended abruptly at a long hall. Made of the same stone as the rest of the Estate, the dimensions of these underlying passages looked to have been built for a single man, and not a tall one either, because Philip had to stoop the entire time.

I won't pretend to know where we were. The halls visitors pay to walk in the Estate are confusing enough. These secreted spaces could've been just about anywhere. We finally ended up at a small empty chamber no larger than the upper room of the Tower. One long, narrow viewing slot had been opened on the far wall, and Philip and I quickly crossed to it, both of us desperate to figure out where we were. I put my eye to it and saw only the Maze.

"Oh!" Philip said.

I agreed. For five or ten minutes (time seemed irrelevant in these lost rooms, and even our wet clothes were forgotten) we stared down at the convoluted twists and turns, when Philip mentioned the thing I'd just seen a moment before.

"There's a path that looks like it twists so much less," he said. "Do you see it?"

"The one that starts left out of that far door?"

"Yeah."

We shared the silence that followed for some seconds, and I realized that perhaps Philip hadn't been lying after all when he said he'd finished the Maze as fast as he did. A person walking that path could cut the time in half, maybe even in a quarter.

I stepped away from the window and was thrown by how much things had changed. That's when one more thing occurred to me.

The room was empty.

"Philip," I said and he turned to me, "there's no gold."

He blinked a few times, stunned. I was still trying to figure out how it hadn't occurred to us. For a long while, neither of us spoke, and eventually Philip went back to the window.

I paced around the room and then knelt to run my finger along the floor, hoping it might glitter with gold dust. It was just the black filth that covered the rest of the Estate these days, the tarnish of too many years. I was about to stand when I caught sight of the piece of paper. Anywhere else it would've been seen as just trash. But here?

I picked the paper up, and penciled in tiny lowercase letters was a short message: *no gold but this, though lydia doesn't believe me. doesn't matter, i know my father, i know her lies, evangeline g.*

Philip walked over to see what I'd found, read it once, and grumbled to himself. Distracted no longer, our cold clothes caught every draft, and despite not finding the gold, we were going to have to leave soon, partly to get back out in the warm night air and partly because the security guards' rounds would take them into the basement in another forty-five minutes.

Following Philip back to the corridor, I almost stuck the note in my pocket to take it with me but then realized the writing might wear off from the water. I was damp from head to toe and couldn't think of any place to store the note. It took me all the way to the narrow stairs to figure out my only option.

"Ready?" Philip asked, stepping down onto the final landing. "It's always colder the second time."

I nodded and, when he'd slipped under the surface, rolled the note into a tight cylinder, took a deep breath, and clamped it between my teeth, doing my best to keep my tongue from touching it. I then dropped down beneath the water and fought my way along the tunnel, nearly swallowing the note at one point. Finally I found the surface and had to tread water for another ten seconds breathing through my nose before I could move to the bridge and grasp Philip's waiting hand.

He pulled me up to the railing. I crawled over, dying now to breathe deeply. Still every place I looked was wet and dripping. I ran off the bridge, found a dry spot, and let the paper fall from my mouth. Philip must have followed because suddenly his hand was on my back and rubbing my shoulders.

"Everything okay?" he asked.

I nodded, inhaling as I did. When I finally got enough wind to speak, I turned to him and shrugged. We hadn't found the answer we'd expected, although we had found one. Perhaps more than one. That was all I wanted in coming here tonight. Resolution. If we managed to gain a bit of reckoning—what Martin Peterson could not provide—for Evangeline at the same time, all the better. For now, there was only the need to escape and the long days ahead in which to fit the remaining pieces together.

MONDAY, JULY 5, 1999

On Friday, Quinlin's well dropped another two feet.

Saturday, three more.

Yesterday it dipped to seventy feet deep, and I expect to hear any minute that today it fell into the sixties. The descent is both gradual and, apparently, inexorable. Attempts to stop the flow down the ridge have proven fruitless, while efforts to refill the well haven't worked either. The whole town was starting to wonder if the legend could be true—that the Estate will stand only as long as there is water in the well. In a few weeks it's possible the well will go totally dry, and the legend will either come true or prove to be as much gossamer and moonbeam as the lore of Quinlin's gold.

Actually, there *was* gold at one point—it just disappeared. Ben made that discovery in helping Dwight and me clean up the storage garage where we were returning the last boxes of Glen's stuff. I'd talked long-distance with Meryl on Friday, and together we somehow came to the conclusion that, rather than renew my apartment lease at the end of August, I should move into the trailer, that is, until I decide what my next move should be. Because her place is already swathed in luxury, it made sense for my feeble belongings to go into storage. And since we still had a few months' rent left on Glen's garage, I decided that made as much sense as anything. Then Ben found the trick accounting logs.

"This is crazy," he said as he sorted the many books into stacks. "There're duplicates of every month here. How could someone keep records like this?" He took one, checked inside, and shook his head. "The numbers don't even match."

I shrugged and then turned to answer a question from Dwight, who wanted to know which of my books I wanted boxed up and which I wanted left out. When I swung back around, Ben was approaching, book open.

"Look," he said and pointed to an inscription. *Public Vol. XXIII.*

"So?"

He handed over a second book. On it was inked, *Vol. XXIII.*

"One set he doctored for the public. Funds were running low—look at how much less capital this lists—and he didn't want to frighten the town. He saw the end of the hard times coming but wasn't sure they'd weather it. It has to be."

Together we made a mad scramble through the other accounting logs until we found the last record, *Vol. XXXIX.* The

final tally was a few thousand dollars. In the public book, the
coffers had more than a million.

"No wonder people thought he still had so much gold," said
Ben.

I nodded and could only guess at the exact worth of one
solid bar of gold back then. Was that bar—the one Martin
Peterson thought he saw, the one that disappeared—the only
thing Evangeline Graveston found in the chamber above the
Maze? Was that the fool's treasure that had lured my father and
spawned so many stories?

He'd spent the better portion of my college savings for an
opportunity to search for an answer among the remainder of a
dead man's belongings. The answer sat there, right in front of
him, but he never saw it. He must have rifled through the junk
as we had at the beginning and tossed it back into the storage
garage with hatred on his tongue and fire in his eyes. I bet his
hand clenched, and he might've even taken a swing at something
had there been anything worth fighting. But there wasn't. The
best he could do would be to swipe a paw at the air and roar
with fury. Everything was ghost and shadow, a trick of the light.
There existed no real enemy but himself. I expect to find this
echoed on Monday when I walk into the Lowerton National
Bank and finally unlock my father's one last secret. Perhaps he'll
surprise me. It'd be nice if he did. Most likely it'll be the same
thing again, another disappointment.

The well will keep draining.

Then run dry.

And we'll see what's real and what's not.

Gossamer and moonbeam, or something else. Something we
could have only guessed at.

WEDNESDAY, JULY 7, 1999

This is what's happening.

The water's going faster now. Down ten feet more since Monday. At this rate it will be empty by August. Brighton Entertainment hired four university professors to research what has caused the drainage so they could sue should anything happen to the Estate. Word is they spend all their time down ridge. The widow of William Darling filed suit against Boyd Lime and Stone and arrived at the courthouse backed by a trio of lawyers from Baltimore. The dollar amount they announced they were seeking boggles the mind. More than it had cost for Quinlin's Estate to be built.

All this while Meryl Lakewood continues to have a wonderful time. She calls every other night to let me know who she's seen and what wonderful foods she's tried. It looks like her ten-day trip may stretch to fifteen or twenty days. The news about the Estate bothers her little, and it's nice to have at least one voice that couldn't care less about what's going on here in desperate little Lowerton. It's the only topic of conversation here. It's strange, but now everybody cares about the Estate.

"Stop the pillage of our ridges!" some protesters chanted down at city hall the other morning. They then switched to "Save the Estate before it's too late!"

I walked by on my way to the bank and tried not to smirk. *Day late and a few million dollars short*, I thought and kept it to myself, saying nothing all the way inside the bank and down the stairs to where the vault was located. One of the attendants took my key and identification, led me to a tiny room where I could wait, and returned moments later with a narrow silver box, the lid closed. He placed it on the table in front of me, pointed to a latch I needed to unhook to open the top, and backed away.

And so . . . I said to myself. I remember that specifically. *And so . . .*, trying my best to be casual and relaxed when really my insides knotted and turned over. I wanted to bolt out of there. Still, there was nothing else to be done, so I unhooked the latch and opened the lid.

Paper. Paper and only paper.

"Buhhh," I think I said, but quickly caught myself lest the attendant think I'd called for him. I reached into the box, lifted the contents, and began placing each item on the table.

There were six all together.

The first was a Polaroid snapshot.

Next, a check, made out to my father.

A typed letter on which I glimpsed my name.

After that was a handwritten note with a map.

A second handwritten note, this one obviously penned by a different hand than the first.

Lastly, a rectangular image that looked like it'd been cut from a magazine.

After I'd finished looking over each, the final pieces fit.

Captured in the photo was a gold bar. Though the resolution was poor, the markings on the bar were still legible. It had been stamped with Gabriel Quinlin's name and the date: February 1934. Little else in the picture proved recognizable except for a woman's slender finger touching the gold as though caressing it. At the knuckle, barely in view, a ring with a high-set diamond. It could only belong to one woman.

That woman's name showed up on the check, printed at the very top—*Lydia Furrow.* Presumably uncashed, the check had been made out for fifty dollars to Glen Lawson on January 8, 1975. The memo line was blank. I couldn't figure out why he'd kept it until I read the second handwritten note. Scribbled in the same furious strokes as the check, it was a note from Lydia to my father.

> *Mr. Lawson,*
>   *Enclosed you will find the last payment for your services. By now I'm sure you've heard that my niece has committed herself to that commune, so you'll no longer be able to provide me with the information I need. We shall keep in touch, I'm sure.*
>
> *Lydia Furrow*

I studied the square of paper I thought had been taken from a magazine. It wasn't. Instead, it'd been purposefully cut out of Glen's high-school yearbook, one of the missing portraits of Evangeline Graveston. I looked closely at the girl's face. Despite the folds and smudges the image had picked up over the years, I could still make out how much of Embeth she had in her, in the almond-shaped eyes, the dagger chin, the tiny dimple in her left cheek when she smiled. Glen had held this photo, for whatever reason, but I'm sure he never saw the resemblance. He must have convinced himself that she had the likeness of Gabriel Quinlin in her, and if that was true, perhaps the old man had left her some word or hint of where the gold was hidden. It might've been a stretch, but Glen grasped at any possibility.

With a sigh I set the photo down and picked up the remaining note—addressed to Lydia Furrow—with the hand-drawn map on it, directions for entering the Estate. The map showed the rear gate and a seldom-used entryway that was blocked by a rock outcropping on the north side of the building. Although the note didn't include a date, I could make my own guess as to when and why it had been written. The final typed letter from my father confirmed my suspicions and made things clear. And they were answers that weren't mine alone.

I signed a form to take possession of the papers, cancelled Glen's use of the safe-deposit box, and headed back outside to my car. Truant Gulch Retirement Community and Embeth Graveston were only a few minutes away, and I decided not to wait a minute longer before giving her the answers to the questions I knew weighed heavily on her mind.

Months ago, when we'd started this quest, she promised me the full story, no sugarcoating, no lies of daisies and sunshine, and she kept her word for as much of the tale as she could. Now it was my turn to finish it, to bring the only closure possible and finish, forever, the story of Quinlin's Estate.

Embeth answered the door at my second knock.

"Eve!" she said, startled.

"It's been Lydia Furrow all along," I said and held up the papers I'd gotten out of the bank vault, even though I knew they'd mean nothing to her until I explained. We both moved into her living room, and she pointed me to the straight-backed chair near the opposite wall.

"Tell me," she said after she'd settled. "What's Lydia done now?"

"Not now, Embeth. In the past."

She waited without speaking.

My words came out in a flurry. Lydia Furrow, according to Glen, was convinced of two things. First, that Gabriel Quinlin's gold remained in the Estate after his death; and second, that

Evangeline, her niece, was actually Quinlin's daughter and would be told of the gold's location when she came of age. Lydia believed the first because her brother, Charles, told her so. And he wasn't lying. The gold, one bar, did remain in the Estate. Lydia was the one who turned it into a treasure. The second was a tale she'd concocted through a quiet inquiry carried out at the factory, a bank teller's gossip that Embeth had cashed a check from Quinlin, her own suppositions, and things Embeth herself had said before she'd fallen in love with Charles. Lydia knew the child couldn't be her brother's, so she convinced herself Evangeline was Quinlin's and thereby wound up poisoning the girl with the lie.

At first she dropped subtle clues, insinuations that she didn't look much like a Graveston. Only later did she say more by persuading the young woman that a legacy awaited her, greater than anything she could dream up. She was a Quinlin, and so the house and all that was in it belonged to her too.

Torn between her love for her parents and vague suspicions that her aunt could be right, Evangeline withdrew and lived out her fantasies behind closed eyes and a locked front door. Rumors of bouts of screaming and strange voices began to circulate, and soon Ms. Evangeline Graveston became a ghost in her own time, staying away even from her aunt.

So Lydia Furrow drafted Glen Lawson to her cause.

When I spoke these words, Embeth moaned. She'd stayed quiet up till now, but this last hope—that someone had actually cared for her daughter—disappeared. Glen had believed only in Quinlin's gold. To him, Lydia's insinuations about Evangeline seemed honest enough if not mean. So he cut out the girl's photo from his yearbook to remind himself of who she was and then went about his task—involving himself in her life to find out what she knew of the gold.

For a long time that proved to be very little. But then Road to Damascus bought the Estate, and she saw an opportunity to get away from Lydia, her parents, and Glen and search for herself. That she did, finding the gold when Peterson accused her of trying to commit suicide.

Glen and Lydia hadn't heard from her in a while, until one day she confronted them both with the news that she'd found the treasure, thus taunting them and daring them to do something drastic. Here's where Glen and Lydia went wrong: they never understood that she'd found only one bar. In Glen's typed confession, the one from which I got most of this story, he stated that Lydia went apoplectic upon hearing the news and admitted that his own greed captured his fancy as well. So together they schemed to break into the Estate and discover for themselves where the gold lay hidden.

"Did one of them hurt Evangeline?" Embeth whispered.

I shrugged.

"Glen claims that neither he nor Lydia pushed her. That she surprised them and startled herself, falling backward by accident and dying in the process."

"For so long . . ." she began, her voice trailing off.

"I wanted you to know. That's what you asked me for."

Embeth turned her eyes to me and nodded, and quickly they teared up. "She stole our daughter from Charles and me."

I quietly took the slip of paper I'd found in the Estate and walked over to her. She took it in her slender fingers and lifted it close to her face to read the words I'd memorized by this point: *no gold but this, though lydia doesn't believe me. doesn't matter, i know my father, i know her lies, evangeline g.*

She read it, then looked at me and asked, "What do you think it means?"

I smiled. Smiled and said, "I think it means what it says." I had to give her that if nothing else.

It was all Embeth seemed to need, and she pressed the paper with her thumbs just once, pushed herself from her seat, and went to a nearby photo of Evangeline and set the note by the girl's face. She turned and said, "I want to talk with Lydia Furrow."

The drive over took only ten minutes. In my wildest dreams I never would have guessed what we found.

Lydia Furrow, gray as death and as haggard as I'd ever seen her, answered her own door while holding a sweating glass of something amber in one hand, her telephone in the other. She waved us in without even a hello or the tiniest hint that she was surprised to see us. The room we entered, a parlor of some sort, lay strewn with books and papers. Meryl Lakewood can be thankful she wasn't around to clean this week.

"Glen must have sent you. Wrote something up in his will, I suppose."

Embeth huddled to my side, not daring to say a thing. I thought she might confront Lydia, but this apparently wasn't what she'd expected. I was a bit confused myself. She was right about the will, though, so I nodded.

"You didn't do what he said, did you?"

I hesitated and Embeth looked up at me.

Lydia gave a dry laugh. "You were supposed to blackmail me with the information for your share of the gold in case I found it, isn't that what he said?"

It was. His confession was on both their parts, and since he knew I'd be seeing it only after he was dead, he ended his letter with a plea for me to hold on to the information until it was expedient to move forward with it.

"I had better reasons for using it now."

Lydia took a swallow of liquor and set the glass down on a set of papers to her left, staring with slow eyes that hinted at a glass or two before the one she'd just finished. Still her tongue was sharp and her hands steady when she pointed at Embeth and said, "You'd waste it on her?"

A thought came to me in a flash. Perhaps Glen had been right after all. . . .

"Yes," I said. "Do you want to hear our deal?"

Lydia's lips parted as if to sneer but lacked the energy and fell into a slack and dazed gape.

"You renounce custodianship of Embeth's care to me, and you can keep this evidence. But that includes no further interference with her at Truant Gulch."

Lydia rocked on her heels for a quick moment, gathering momentum to speak, and finally let out a laugh that sounded like the rattle of bones. I wondered if Lydia Furrow would see another year.

"Best deal I've been offered in months," she said. "Like I need the burden of watching over this crone any longer. She's sung her little song. What more can she do? I'll sign the papers tomorrow. At the moment, I'm busy with more important things." With that she picked up her glass and disappeared through the rear doorway. A door slammed a few seconds later, and it became clear that she wasn't coming back.

"Guess we'll let ourselves out," I said and started moving toward the door.

Embeth followed, murmuring something to herself that I couldn't quite understand. When I asked her to speak up she just shook her head as if it wasn't anything too important. A moment later, right before we got in the car, she looked me in the eyes and said, "I may call you Evangeline from time to time. My memory slips these days."

"That's okay," I replied and said I wouldn't mind at all. She could call me anything she'd like.

THURSDAY, JULY 22, 1999

Three days ago the well ran dry. Brighton Entertainment closed the Estate for fear of what might happen, only nothing did. It was beginning to look like just another myth gone up in smoke. Until this morning, that is. The first crack appeared today. Journalists issued press passes were given a special opportunity to go see the crack, and it was just that. Only it was deep and long. Seven feet long perhaps and already a few inches deep. It's on the back side of the Estate, on the section of wall that resembles a Soviet cathedral. I told Ben about it this evening, and his eyebrows arched in alarm.

"How soon do you think it'll fall?" I asked.

He glanced at his watch as if to indicate any minute, and I sighed. I think we'd all hoped that this last legend might be but a myth, just the result of time and imagination. But obviously there's something to it.

"All that ground water disappearing," he said, "the earth

under the Estate has to be ready to collapse on itself. It compresses with every drop that escapes. The Estate's just adding to the weight forcing the water out."

Which is why Lydia Furrow was drinking the other week, why four days later she and Lorne held a final press conference with LORP, announcing that the deal with Boyd and Brighton, all deals in fact, were off. Well, not all of course. She did sign away her guardianship to me and took all of Glen's evidence off our hands, except the yearbook picture, which I gave to Embeth.

A week later Brighton brought its litigation against Boyd, trying hard all the while to pretend they weren't going to destroy the Estate themselves four months from now. Hog-tied in court and gutted financially, Boyd Lime and Stone left the ridge completely. Their only voice these days has been their acting defense lawyer, a stern man who's never thrilled to give answers to reporters from small weekly newspapers.

It's now just a matter of days. Or weeks. Or months even.

Still the Estate will fall.

In the meanwhile, I'm enjoying my time in the trailer and have agreed to stay in Little Pines another three months. It's too late to apply for graduate school, and I don't want to be in Wisconsin for the winter. So Lowerton will remain my home for a little while longer.

Besides, I've got a surrogate grandmother who counts on me to swing by Truant Gulch to take her to church or to lunch.

I've got Meryl, a mother with a wardrobe that's expanded my vision of the rainbow.

Dwight, a father who refuses to call me anything but beautiful and who's even convinced me once or twice that starting out bent doesn't mean staying that way.

Philip, whose faith seems as tenuous as mine sometimes, but who is someone I can turn to for interesting discussions and quiet remembrances of scaling the hidden places of Quinlin's Estate.

And Ben, who offers me weekly, if not more often, just a little larger vision of what my own faith should come to look like.

Most important of all, I have a God who refuses to leave me alone, refuses to be taken to a high mountain and sell me out for all the kingdoms of the world, refuses to ask anything of me but to come to Him.

Why would I wander elsewhere? Why spend even an instant looking somewhere else? This time, these people, this joy and hope—this is my somewhere.

Epilogue

SATURDAY, DECEMBER 25, 1999

T oo much the child, I roused from sleep during the dark hours of Christmas morning thinking I'd heard something. The years growing up I would have stayed huddled and expectant in my bed, listening for the *clip-clop* of hooves. But last night I crawled from my bed and tried to stay quiet as I tiptoed through the trailer making sure the small tree Meryl and I bought hadn't tipped over or some other miniature catastrophe wouldn't be waiting for us come morning. Everything inside seemed fine, however, and it wasn't until I'd taken two steps back toward my bedroom that I realized how strange it was for me to be able to see everything in the trailer without switching on a single light.

I turned and stared. The entire living room and kitchen lay bathed in a soft silver glow that filtered in from the outside through the curtains. I tried peeking through but couldn't see the source of the light, so I moved to the door and cracked it open. A freezing December gust reminded me that Meryl and I

never did get the storm door installed despite our best intentions, and I folded my arms across my chest to keep warm as I
stepped out onto our front stoop. That's when I saw it.

Not a star twinkling over some lowly crèche, but the
moon—full and high and pale. Talking heads on the news, in
between debates over how the millennium would end, mentioned that the moon would appear unusually bright toward the
end of 1999, and this was what they'd meant. It shone with a
brilliance I'd never seen before, and the dusting of snow we had
the day before reflected the light that spilled over Little Pines.
What are the words? *The moon on the breast of the new-fallen
snow / Gave the lustre of mid-day to objects below.* Whoever wrote
the poem must have seen a sight like this—only tonight neither
Santa nor eight tiny reindeer appeared before my wondering
eyes. Instead, it was Quinlin's Tower that I saw, the only thing
that remained of the Estate after all these months.

The house didn't fall all at once, but in pieces, crumbling and
toppling apart at seams that had never shown before. Gables
collapsed one week, porticoes tumbled a fortnight later. Eventually the domes pitched over and smashed to the earth, snap-
ping straining beams beneath them. Thankfully, Brighton's
evacuation ended long before the walls caved in, and they'd
managed to rescue everything that was inside. But the building
fell—or at least everything but the Tower.

For three weeks I'd taken daily pictures of the destruction as
lead reporter for the *Express* on the story, and in all twenty-one
images the Tower remains true and straight. Now that it's stood
alone on the hill for a few months, I've found myself forgetting
anything else ever surrounded it. Though last night I remembered.

I remembered my first time up on the hill after dark and how the walls seemed to block out the night sky. I remembered those summer days spent in the Maze and how all the time I was walking a long and winding path, never realizing there existed a simpler way to solve the turns ahead. Most of all I remember thinking that in the end, we were all just trying to reach its front gate and hope to be let inside. Something that grand, we just wanted, needed, to be a part of it.

Only now the Estate has come to us. The building that saved Lowerton once may yet do it again. Final plans were approved two weeks ago for a team of architectural and engineering graduate students, led by Ben Sterling, to use the rock and debris from the fallen Estate to construct a permanent town square on the parcel of land LORP wanted to use for Lowerton's economic rebirth. Those plans fell apart with the lawsuits between Brighton and Boyd, and so the town was given a reprieve and left to ponder its situation. Wonder of wonders, they decided with a November referendum that social and civic renewal were more important and that a new memorial should go up in Quinlin's honor. Ben, who'd been working on designs for community gathering places anyway, approached the committee with his idea and won instant praise and eventual approval. I haven't seen his final designs in total, but some aspects he'd been toying with include a stage sunken below the terrace where *He Saved Lowerton* might be performed, the careful tiling of stones so that a maze pathway might come through on the central piazza, and the use of the Atlas sculpture in a new open-air wishing fountain. I'm sure there are other ideas in his schematics, and I can't wait to see them come to life this summer. Best of all, artisans

and laborers from all over volunteered to help build what everyone's calling Quinlin's Square.

"Mr. Quinlin's dream once saved us," someone wrote in an
editorial last week. "The least we can do is to save some fragment of that dream."

So there will be Quinlin's Square. Quinlin's Tower too, so
long as it stands. Brighton made off well from their settlement
with Boyd and also their insurance claim. Afterward they turned
around and sold the entire parcel of land back to Lowerton and
for cheap. The mayor and Greg Evans have convened twice
already to discuss setting aside the land as a state park, but
nothing has come of that. I think they, along with the rest of us,
are wondering how long it will stay. Engineers aren't entirely
sure what's keeping it upright, yet their tests haven't shown any
stresses that might cause it to topple either. For now it remains.

This is why I'm glad, why I pulled out this journal to write
this final entry in the first place—I don't live outside Quinlin's
shadow anymore. Last night, as I stood and stared from our
deck, the moon's bright glow, which before had never cast a
shadow that I could remember, crept behind the Tower, and its
measureless reach swept across the town and did not stop. I
must have been out there for twenty minutes, because I saw the
shadow cross Marker Road and pour into Little Pines with
silence and speed. It moved over the ground and snow—the
pristine snow that still covers the hardness of this place—and
passed over my hands, my face, my body, and this trailer, my
home—like a whisper, a gentle sighing at the ear.

I know it shouldn't be important to me, for it's nothing compared to that murmur I followed months ago, claiming as my
own the promise to end this bent and crooked life. That was of

first importance. This was of reassurance and spoke the words I'm not sure I've ever heard before. *You are blessed. Right here, tonight, and in this place. There's no need for searching, no tall hill to climb. I'll reach down to you. All you need to do is lift your eyes and receive it.*

And I do.

Acknowledgments

My gracious thanks to:

My friends at Bethany House, Luke Hinrichs and David Horton, in particular, for their efforts on behalf of making this a better book.

Peter Glöege and Lookout Design Group for the fine cover.

Maggie Hedde, a good friend and talented photographer whose work sparked this story.

Ryan Bigham for helping me look at architecture a new way.

Some important resources for this book:

White Trash: Race and Class in America, edited by Matt Wray. 1997, Routledge, New York.

Walking a Sacred Path: Rediscovering the Labyrinth as a Sacred Tool by Dr. Lauren Artress. 1996, Riverhead Books, New York.

Communes and Cults by Kathlyn Gay. 1997, Twenty-First Century Books, New York.

DAVID RYAN LONG spent four years in central Pennsylvania while earning an English degree from Penn State University. He is now a full-time writer and lives outside Minneapolis, Minnesota, with his wife and daughter.

Visit www.davidryanlong.com

POWERFUL STORIES
for Literature Lovers!

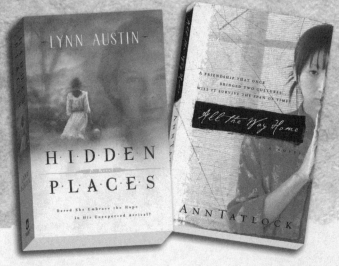

The Long Road of Triumph Over Grief

A young widow trying to keep the family orchard running during the Great Depression, Eliza Wyatt knew only weariness and grief. Slowly, though, her prayers of help gain answers and her barren heart finds love once more.

Hidden Places by Lynn Austin

A Deeply Touching Story of Friendship Lost...and Found

Two young women from different cultures forge a friendship neither time, distance, nor injustice can harm. A tale that spans the decades and the country from northern California to the deep south, *All the Way Home* ultimately is a celebration of the special joy of friendship.

All the Way Home by Ann Tatlock

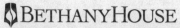